The Hound of Scrying Hollow

Brooke Marley Jones

The HOUND of SCRYING HOLLOW

BROOKE MARLEY JONES

First edition

ISBN: 978-1-7383251-2-2

Cover by Eeva Nikunen

BY BROOKE MARLEY JONES

The Forest Where the Phoenix Sleeps

PART ONE

As my father lay dying,
Bloodied and barely my father at all,
He didn't remind me that he was proud,
Nor that he loved me
The last words to leave my father's lips,
Begged I never follow in his footsteps,
That I swear on my life
I would never,
Enter Scrying Hollow

Lesson One

Keep one eye on the Hollow and one
on the way home.

The scream pierced the cottage like a spray of sharp needles.

Fearing the worst, I tore down the hall. My sister screamed again—unintelligible babble I might have understood had my world not frozen. Caked in dirt and smeared with blood, my brother stumbled across the den. Lottie caught Lysander before he fell, and I rushed to his side. He put one arm around my shoulders but kept the other curled around his abdomen. Lottie let out a garbled choke.

Lysander's hand was the only thing containing his eviscerated midsection.

Like a man possessed, Lysander muttered frantically. His breath brushed my ear, carrying those words I'd never forget.

"The Hound, the Hound, the Hound!"

The front door blew open, and my mother rushed in. Sword unsheathed, she readied to cut down whoever threatened her children. Her furious eyes darted between us, then down, to Lysander's stomach. Her scream was silent—only a sharp exhale, as if she'd received a blow to the gut. Lysander was twice Mother's size, stooping through even the tallest doorways by the age of sixteen, but by the way my mother seized him and brought him to the sofa, you'd think he was a newborn.

"Liliwen!" she barked. "Bandages!"

I obeyed, hurtling down the hall to the room I shared with Lottie. A dress form tumbled over as I crashed inside. With shaking hands, I tossed aside fabrics and half-made garments, looking for something to stop the bleeding. "Where is it?!" An eternity ago, I'd woven a remarkable fabric. I'd known it was special, so I'd stashed it away for an emergency. But now a crisis was upon us, and I couldn't find it! I searched beneath my bed.

Nothing.

"Ugh!" I slammed the floorboards, one of which sunk slightly. Near Lottie's bed, the other end of the board elevated. Scrambling over, I pushed aside Lottie's discarded clothes and weaponry. I yanked up the loose board and found a stash. "Lottie, you brat!" I rifled through a lifetime of items I'd thought were lost. One of my favourite corsets sat in the mess; I snatched it and tossed it under my bed. My fingers tingled as they stumbled over an unassuming white cloth.

"Yes!"

Cloth and sewing kit in hand, I rushed back to Lysander. His head laid in my mother's lap, and Lottie had done her best to clean the wounds. They'd undressed Lysander, though it looked as if he still wore a flayed shirt. The room spun, and I steadied myself on the table. It was no shirt, but my brother's flesh, torn into red ribbons.

"Liliwen," my mother commanded.

Choking back bile, I crouched beside Lysander. Lottie's eyes widened when I handed her the cloth she'd stolen. "Cut this into strips." My pulse raced, but years of practice kept my fingers steady. My vision tunnelled, and I blocked out Lysander's groans. I pretended I was simply mending a leather coat and not my brother. After I put in the last stitch and cut the thread, we wrapped Lysander's wounds.

Seeing her son stable, my mother said, "I'll alert the guard. Lottie, get the physician." Without another word, they slipped away.

And just like that, the cottage was silent.

As Lysander lay resting, I picked bracken from his disheveled, flaxen hair. Ugly scratches ran along his throat. How terrified he must have been, running through the thorns. I hiccupped, and the tears came. Free from my mother's and sister's gazes, I leaned against the sofa and cried. After a particularly noisy sob, Lysander let out a low groan. I blew out a long, wet breath and pulled myself together. Bloodied and barely alive, Lysander looked just like my father had when he'd come home seven years ago. The pain of goodbye still fell heavy on my chest.

My father had been the first to die by the Hound.

Not immediately, like most who encountered the beast, but slowly. His delirious screams continued for two weeks before he finally passed. My mother, broken and lost, left her place teaching and joined the guard that very night. The second Lottie was of age, she joined too.

When we lost our father, we lost our home. The fire, however strong, could not replace his warmth. Our cooking, however delicious, could not satiate our emptiness. The cottage that was once our home became nothing but shelter. I wiped away another tear. The day my father died, I couldn't imagine ever loving someone else so much. Staring at Lysander, I knew heartbreak would come again. I traced Lysander's wounds, and my stomach lurched.

It was bad.

Pushing myself up, I headed to the kitchen. Lysander's discarded satchel caught my boot, and a bundle of bright yellow flowers spilled out. "Hhh!" I snatched the flowers. Last night, while we'd all sat around the fire, Lottie had reminded us of her upcoming birthday.

"I'll be twenty-one," she'd said. Lysander hadn't looked up from the small bit of wood he'd whittled, nor I from the cloak I'd been mending. "I've outgrown my favourite jacket—the yellow one."

"Uh huh," I'd mumbled.

Lottie sighed. "If only *someone* could make me a new one."

I, being someone who could make her a new one, had pointed out that, "The blooms needed to dye the fabric only grow in the Hollow." And perhaps, if she wanted a new garment so badly, she could fetch the materials herself. Lysander chuckled and Lottie pouted. Holding the bundle of flowers, I cursed Lysander's foolishness. Shaking the bundle in his direction, I cried, "If you weren't in such a bad way, I'd whip you!" Storming into the kitchen, I hid the flowers in a cupboard behind some cleaning supplies, where Lottie would never find them. I dabbed my eyes with a towel and turned to wash the blood from my hands. The bubbles lathered as I stared out the window, to the Hollow.

The last home before Scrying Hollow, our cottage sat perilously close to its border. Each morning, when I looked out, I wondered, 'Were the trees always so close to the garden gate?' I poured cool water over my hands, rinsing the bubbles, but my eyes wandered back to the Hollow, like some part of me was afraid to leave it unwatched. As a child, I'd loved seeing rabbits and stoats wander out. I couldn't remember the last time I'd seen any animal dancing among the trees, not even a squirrel. It was barren, like a pond overfished.

Though it was not without occupants.

The front door opened and slammed. Lottie peered into the kitchen; her short tangle of blonde hair was wilder than usual, windswept from the run. "Doc's here," she huffed. Her green eyes were calm and determined—mine might look the same, if they weren't puffy and red. Seeing my tear-smattered face, Lottie cringed and left. I dried my hands and followed her.

In the den, a woman, whose greying hair sat in a tidy bun, knelt over Lysander. She adjusted her spectacles and examined a set of stitches. Lottie pulled up a rickety chair while I leaned on the fireplace mantle. We watched Dr. Phaedra work on the youngest of the Valet children.

"These are quite good, Liliwen." Dr. Phaedra lifted a bandage and examined another set of stitches. "I could use you in town."

Half-smiling, half-grimacing, I said, "I've had lots of practice." Lottie scoffed. She and Mother considered trips to the physician an incredible waste of time. Why would they see a physician when they had a perfectly good seamstress—and occasional surgeon—at home? Even now, Lottie had two stitches above her brow. She told me she'd exterminated a cockatrice...but I had a feeling it was the result of a well-earned punch.

Dr. Phaedra sighed and leaned back. Already, green skin surrounded Lysander's wounds. We'd done our best to clean him up, but I knew it wasn't enough. Dr. Phaedra threw up her hands—the *last* gesture I wanted to see from the physician attending my brother. Dr. Phaedra pushed herself up with a knee. Tilting her head, she rubbed my arm. The same sympathetic gesture she'd offered after the attack on my father. My own knees threatened to buckle, and I clung to the mantle with everything I had.

I was the oldest, and I was ready for the burden.

"Liliwen," Dr. Phaedra whispered, "this is beyond my skill or equipment."

Lottie's chair crashed against the wall. Mortar crumbled and scattered across the tired floorboards. "So, what are we supposed to do?" she blurted.

"We wait." Dr. Phaedra shrugged. "Perhaps, if he is strong, he will defeat the Hound's poison." My father was the strongest person I'd known. If he couldn't fight it, no one could. "Queensfoil," Dr. Phaedra recommended, and I nodded. Though the plant might slow the infection bounding through Lysander, it would *not* cure him.

"That's it?!" Lottie demanded.

"Lottie," I said, rubbing my temple. "Please."

Lottie left, kicking a table as she went. Her voice carried back to us, muttering curses one after the other. "Stupid, ass, bastard!" At the end of the hall, the door slammed. That fire came from our mother. At only twenty, Lottie hadn't had the opportunity to hide it, or at least channel it the way Mother did. Dr. Phaedra gave me one last pitying look and excused herself.

Knock-knock-knock. I rapped on the bedroom door. "Lottie!" I called. "Watch your brother. I'll be back soon."

Silence.

Worry constricted me at the thought of leaving Lysander alone. If I'd been with him, maybe he wouldn't have been attacked in the first place. Blinking quickly, I fought to keep my voice even.

"Don't—don't leave him alone."

Outside, I started down the short path to the road. Passing the gardens, I brushed a chamomile stem. The floating aroma carried a memory of my father, pouring boiling water from the kettle. Whenever we were stressed about food or money, he'd make chamomile tea. 'Drink your daisies,' he'd tease, after I'd remarked how the yellow and white blooms resembled daisies. Deep down, I sought that comfort. Though, my mind was ill-prepared to see my father, knowing what came of him in the end...and what faced Lysander. Feeling worse than before, I hurried down the remaining path and slipped through the small, white gate.

I closed it firmly behind me.

I walked along the road that led into the town of Scrying Hollow, so named after the Hollow that snarled at our cottage's back. It was springtime, and the ditches were filled with purple hyacinths and primroses. All around, wild buttercups covered the rolling hills in a sea of yellow. Out here in the flowers and sunshine, one could almost pretend. *Almost* forget what lay behind me, waiting. I passed the lane leading up to our neighbour's home and a shout startled me.

"Lili!"

A lovely-looking, freckled boy named Ruven waved. We were born a month apart, and owing to proximity, we'd been close growing up. Some of my fondest memories came from Ruven's family's goat farm. Once upon a time, our parents had said we'd marry. Of course, that was before my father died.

After that, I'd no mind to ask for any man's hand.

Ruven jogged down the lane, his copper-hair bouncing the entire way. Arms open wide, Ruven's sweet, sing-song voice carried on the breeze. "And then I saw a pretty girl, walking in the glen. She turned and put a smile on, her lovely name was Liliwen!"

I shielded my eyes against the sun as Ruven approached. The youngest of five boys, Ruven managed to escape the farm life and apprenticed with the blacksmith. The work became him; his shoulders were twice the size as when he'd started. Ruven wore a bright smile. Over the years, I'd learned it was impossible to appreciate his smile without reciprocating. Despite my heartache, I smiled back.

"I wanted to ask you"—Ruven's brows furrowed—"what's wrong?"

I wasn't surprised he knew something was amiss. What *did* surprise me was that he hadn't already heard. News in the village travelled quicker than startled deer. Not trusting myself to look at Ruven, I kicked the dirt and mumbled, "Lysander. He, uh... He was attacked." I begged Ruven wouldn't ask *where* Lysander had been attacked. While I'd promised my father I'd never enter the Hollow again, it was obvious that the fruits of

Lysander's foraging had not come from the safe spots he'd insinuated they had.

"Oh, Lili." Ruven sidled next to me, letting his hand rest on my arm. "I'm so sorry."

Eager to change the subject, I backed away and pointed toward town. "I have to get a few things for Lysander." Ruven nodded, but I halted. "What is it you wanted to ask me?"

"Nah." Ruven rubbed his neck. "It's... It's not the time."

"Well, you must tell me now." I crossed my arms. "I'll be worrying about it all day, and I don't need anything else to worry about." My voice faltered on the last word. I bit my lip and looked away.

In a kind attempt to draw attention away from my inevitable breakdown, Ruven started. "Well, I wanted to ask you a favour. I'm not sure if you heard...about Lauren?" Lauren was the town's blacksmith and Ruven's mentor. "She passed. Last week." Ruven quickly amended, "She had a heart attack."

I had heard. Unfortunately, I'd taken to staying home most days, and the thought of attending another ceremony for death sickened me. I should have gone to see Ruven, or at least sent him a note.

"I'm so sorry, Ruven. I should have come over."

"It's okay," Ruven said, in a way that meant it *was* okay. He rarely said things he didn't mean, and it comforted me to know he held no malice. Ruven continued, "The, uh, the upside of that unfortunate event is that I'll be graduating next week." He beamed and stretched, cat-like and proud. "If all goes well, you're looking at the new blacksmith."

While Ruven's brothers adored the farm, Ruven had never wanted that life. Pride, as if I'd succeeded myself, warmed my cheeks. "That's wonderful! I'm so proud of you." I, too, rarely said things I didn't mean, and Ruven's ears turned pink. It was his turn to kick the dirt and look away.

He cleared his throat and tugged at the sleeve of his dark shirt. "I was wondering if...well, if you could make me a tunic?"

Ruven had barely finished before I shook my head. "Ruven, I—"

"Lili, you used to make the most spectacular garments!"

I did, but that was before. I didn't have it in me anymore. My room was filled with black fabrics, meant for one thing, and one thing only. "I only make uniforms. For the guards." Ruven's shoulders slumped, dragged down by disappointment. Thankfully, he pushed the subject no further.

"I should go," I said.

Ruven glanced around. "Would you like me to walk with you?"

"Thank you, but no." I gestured at the empty road. "I doubt the Hound will snatch me out here in the open."

"We lost three goats this week, in the pasture across the stream. That's nowhere near the Hollow." Ruven shifted and rubbed his jaw. "Nowadays, the Hound cares not." Ruven was right. Though less frequent, it wasn't unheard of for the Hound to attack outside the Hollow's borders.

"I've waited seven years to have a conversation with my father's killer." I patted my father's blade, tied to my belt. "If the Hound comes for me, I have a few things I'd like to say."

Ruven knew I could take care of myself. He also knew that if he questioned my capability, our conversation would sour. Waving me off, he said, "I'll say a word tonight, for your brother. Perhaps there's some magic left in this world." I grimaced but appreciated the kindness. With a wave, I continued on my own. I passed the end of the farm, where a brown goat bleated through the fence.

'Perhaps there's some magic left in this world.'

Magic was gone from this world...mostly. Townsfolk used to say there was a spark of magic in my work, sewed into the fibres of every garment. Old Prunetta once told me she'd been shot with an arrow, only to have it bounce off her jacket and leave her unharmed. I knew the jacket she spoke of, for I'd sold it to her the day prior.

Of course, Old Prunetta was fond of wine and smoke-leaf.

On my left, I passed an apple orchard. White blossoms dappled the branches, swaying in the breeze.

Lottie swore that when I stitched her up, the wounds healed faster. I'd always dismissed it as ingenuine flattery, if only so I'd continue playing doctor for her. Maybe there was something to it?

A wagon passed by; I ducked my head to the driver.

While possessing a touch of magic was indeed a splendid gift, it did come with some...caveats. To protect what little magic remained, those that displayed talents tended to be taken. At least, that's what the queen told the children when they were brought to the castle, to serve her and the kingdom.

When I was six, a distant cousin of mine, Bronwyn, had been taken. I didn't know much of Bronwyn; my mother's side of the family disowned my mother when she wed my father. All I knew of Bronwyn was gathered from gossip. Apparently, she'd had a way with the creatures of the Hollow. At first, the townspeople just thought she was a bit...strange.

That all changed when the lamia came.

The town lost six children, but when the lamia snatched the seventh, Bronwyn intervened. She spoke to the lamia, convinced it to drop the child. The next morning, Bronwyn was taken to the castle to serve. The town held a celebration, but I remember the way Bronwyn's delicate, brown curls bounced against her tear-stained face as the wagon carried her from her home.

Passing the old mill, I offered a lacklustre "Mornin'" to the miller's apprentice, who heaved a sack of flour into a waiting wagon.

Gradually, the farmhouses and fields gave way to town homes. White buildings with dark beams and thatched tops. I veered from the road that led up the hill to the castle gates and headed to the heart of the town. Pausing, I peered in the fabric shop window. Today, a stunning mauve satin hung on display. My imagination spun, creating beautiful dresses and gloves. Reluctantly, I continued on. Pierre's apothecary sat in the cobbled town square, behind a three-story fountain, next to the bakery.

The doorbell tinkled when I entered, and Pierre peeked from the back. He toddled along a wall packed with colourful glass bottles. Pierre adjusted his crescent-shaped spectacles and smiled. I didn't return the gesture. Pierre was a gossipy, middle-aged man, and I didn't much care for him.

"You'll be wanting the Queensfoil then?"

I told you:

News travels fast.

Pursing my lips, I nodded. Of course, Pierre already knew why I was there. How many others had he told of Lysander's condition? Pierre turned away, pulling out a drawer behind the counter. Wasting no time at all, Pierre said, "Do you reckon that blacksmith, Lauren, really died from a heart attack?"

Through gritted teeth, I replied, "Yes."

Pierre withdrew a bundle of leaves. He peered into the drawer, as if there was less remaining than he'd expected. "Well, you never know," he continued. "Lauren was always stumbling home, drunk." When I didn't rise to meet Pierre's gossip, he frowned and adjusted his spectacles. "If you ask me, she was practically asking to be snatched by the Hound."

Stigma followed the families of those that fell to the Hound, a filthiness that clung like mud. Whispers trailed the remaining members, 'Why was your loved one out when they knew they shouldn't be? Why didn't they take precautions? How foolish!' The threat of alienation often led to dishonesty...and very rich coroners, who had no qualm accepting bribes to lie on a family's behalf. Father was the first to die, so we'd escaped the talk, but with Lysander... It didn't matter that he had no choice, that we needed the money from his foraging; when it came down to it, the Hound was a predator, and that was his Hollow.

Lysander should have known better—that's what people would say.

Pierre placed the Queensfoil on the counter. "Oh dear, what am I going to do now that Lysander has gone and fallen to the Hound." He sighed. "Wherever will I get my herbs?" My nails dug into my palms, and I couldn't help but wish Lottie were with me. Unfortunately, she'd been banned after Pierre said an unsavoury word about our father, and she'd gone over the counter. Pierre's eyes darted to my clenched fists. Perhaps also thinking of Lottie, he rubbed his jaw, precisely where Lottie's first blow had landed. Flashing a wide grin, Pierre backtracked. "I'm sorry, my dear! How insensitive of me." He tucked the Queensfoil into my basket, along with a second pile of dried leaves. "Have your brother chew this. It'll help the nausea."

I grumbled, "Thank you," and left.

The cottage den was full when I returned. My mother occupied a chair next to a dozing Lysander, while Lottie sat with her arms behind her head, her feet on the table. A silver-haired man, dressed in the same black outfit as my mother, stood before the fire. Several new pins and distinctions trailed the neck of his cloak; what heroic deeds had the captain done this time?

Captain Marek offered a sullen, "Afternoon, Lili." The fire illuminated half of the captain's face, highlighting his too-straight nose, and casting his sharp, grey beard in darkness. I returned the greeting and took my basket to the kitchen. Not long after my father passed, Marek began calling on us. His visits continued even after he was appointed captain of the guard, a position which didn't leave much spare time. And while Marek visited under the guise of keeping the town secure of the encroaching Hollow, he always found an excuse to linger. 'Just one cup of tea,' he'd say. Or 'It's bitterly cold in the Hollow; would you mind if I warm my fingers by the fire?' I'd always felt that was the captain's way of keeping an eye on us. To make sure that, despite having lost our father, we were okay. I prepared the Queensfoil and returned to the den, where I took my mother's place beside Lysander. I unwound and removed Lysander's soiled bandages.

"You're a tremendous girl, Liliwen," Marek started. "Such a good sister and a wonderful daughter." Marek's voice grew louder at the end, as he watched my mother disappear down the hall. Speaking with such volume, I wondered if the far-off neighbours might hear him, Marek continued, "Your mother should be very proud to have raised such a truly exemplary daughter!"

Whether it was Marek's delivery, or some fault within me, the compliments felt empty.

Marek waited until my mother returned, then spoke up. "Too many of our brothers and sisters have died. Too many farmers put out because of slaughtered livestock. Finally, the queen has heard our plea." Marek withdrew a scroll and unrolled it so Lottie could see.

With furrowed brows, she asked, "What's it say?"

"The queen has offered a reward for the Hound's heart."

Lottie snatched the scroll. "How much?"

Marek snatched the scroll back and rerolled it. "You'd be comfortable for the rest of your life."

Lottie's boots thudded on the floor.

"Where are you going?" Mother hissed.

Lottie gave her an arrogant look, as if *where* she was going was terribly obvious. "To kill the mongrel!"

"You'll do no such thing." Mother pointed at the chair and growled, "Sit."

"You're not a guard," Marek said to Lottie. "You're a trainee. We will devise a plan—a hunt—to capture the beast." Lottie crossed her arms and turned away from the captain. Out of his sight, she rolled her eyes. "I should return to my duties," Marek said, but remained at the mantle. When no one suggested otherwise, he headed for the door. He paused, where my mother stood, and squeezed her shoulder. "My thoughts are with your son." Mother smiled but pulled away. Marek nodded at me and said, "Liliwen," and to Lottie, "trainee," before leaving.

I rewrapped Lysander's wounds, and my mother resumed her spot by the fire. "Did you see the gift Marek brought mum?" Lottie tossed me a book, which I caught and flipped over so I might read the title. *Songs of Love*. I winced. While mother was once fond of reading, it had been many years since she'd talked of love. "How do you bewitch these men so?" Lottie demanded of our mother, with a laugh.

Not conventionally handsome, our mother possessed a severe profile, with black hair pinned on top of her head—a remnant of her teaching days. She waved and said, "I don't know. I certainly don't encourage it." She spoke with a commanding, authoritative presence, acquired through years of instructing. Even now, sitting before the fire, worried for her only son, her posture was one of dignity and power. It was that steadfast assurance that left suitors tripping over themselves to draw her favour.

"Father is gone," Lottie pressed. "You should find happiness elsewhere."

Mother crinkled her nose. "I'm not interested in men, least of all Marek."

"He's not bad," Lottie reasoned. She flexed her arms in mock imitation. "He's strong, and decently handsome. You know, for an old man."

Glaring at Lottie, Mother's dark brows arched. Perhaps, because of Lottie's impertinence…but more likely because Marek was two years our mother's junior.

"If he's *decently* handsome," Mother replied, "why don't you have a go?" Lottie scoffed and made a face that indicated she might consider it. Mother shook her head. "Marek is cold. To be with him would be lonelier than the memory of your father." An ironic comment from my mother, whose stare might freeze the bravest observer.

"Well, if his luck persists as well as the captains before him, he'll be retiring soon enough." Lottie dragged a finger across her throat and stuck her tongue out, feigning death. While grim, it was an unfortunate truth. For a period, the death of those leading the queen's guard was so high, the town began referring to those who were promoted as having the *captain's curse.*

Lysander roused, only to be sick. I gave him the leaves Pierre recommended. Once Lysander was resting, I went out back and sat on a bench nestled amongst the wisteria. I watched the Hollow and my hands tingled—the same way they did when I'd woven an impossible garment.

A vestigial remnant of our ancestral magic.

Lysander's low groan carried through the window, followed by Mother's reassuring whispers.

Perhaps Lottie's plan to kill the Hound wasn't so unfounded. I scoffed, but then considered it more seriously. I'd trapped rabbits, and the occasional bird if we were starving. Surely, the process was the same for the Hound. Lay a trap and deliver the killing blow. Not difficult at all, really.

The sun began its descent below the trees, casting shadows across the garden. They crept up my boots and reached for my hands, nestled in my lap.

I'd be lying if I said I hadn't dreamed of killing the Hound. Since father died, I'd spent many nights fantasizing about taking the beast down, of dragging a blade across its throat until curtains of blood poured forth. An ugly, squirming pleasure rooted in me when I thought of digging the beast's heart from its breast and presenting it to the queen.

In lieu of the reward, I could ask the royal physician to help Lysander. Dr. Phaedra didn't have the skill or equipment to heal my brother, but the queen's healer, that was a different story entirely. If I defeated the Hound, my father would be avenged, and my brother saved. While the plan unfolded in my mind, I continued watching the Hollow.

And the Hollow watched me back.

Lesson Two

You possess five senses. To survive
the Hollow, you must use six.

The net stretched like a spiderweb along the bedroom wall. It was magic—I knew it. Each time I wove a new line, invisible tendrils reached out and kissed my skin. Standing back, I gazed upon the first truly magical thing I'd created in years...and I hated it. Everything I'd ever made, I'd created for good. With every thread, I'd woven love and vitality into the garments that left my possession. But this net, it was a cursed thing, created only for suffering. I hated it, and I hated myself for weaving it. I plucked a thin cord, which bounced back and vibrated with a *twang*.

The net was strong; it would not break.

Lottie leaned on the doorframe. "What's that for?"

"Marek asked me to make it for the hunt." Though I was little practiced in deception, Lottie nodded and turned to leave. "There's a bag by the door," I said. "There's bread and wolf's bane. I'd like you to take it with you."

Despite rumours that wolf's bane might repel the Hound, Lottie performed a dramatic eye roll. "Yes, Mum," she mocked, and left. The front door closed as Lottie headed to training. With my mother already gone, a tugging anxiousness settled over me. What if they didn't come home?

What if they *did* come home, but mangled like Father and Lysander?

Massaging my temples, I pushed the ruminations away. If I didn't quell the panic quickly, I'd be watching the door until dusk, waiting for my mother and sister to walk through.

When the net was finished, I folded it and tucked it into a satchel. I took the satchel out and set it by the door. The bag I'd packed for Lottie remained on the chair. Whether she'd simply forgotten it, or left it on purpose, I wasn't sure. Before heading out, I checked on Lysander. He slept on the sofa, his forehead waxen and sweaty. Though I'd changed the bandages this morning, oozing puss had already stained the fabric a mottled yellow. Leaning on the mantle, I ground my forehead against my palm.

I can't do this again.

I looked out the window, to the Hollow. I loved my family, but sometimes, I couldn't help but wonder...what would it be like? To be *free* of worry.

A fantasy visited me, one I entertained often, of a pretty white cottage. Gardens surrounded the home, and my *only* responsibility was to tend them. Staring through the glass panes, it felt as if the trees themselves had ropes, pulling me to freedom. The urge to run coiled within me. The desperate need to be free of obligation—

Knock-knock-knock.

Guilt tensed me, as if I'd been caught in a crime and not some harmless daydream. I smoothed my trousers and headed to the door. It was no secret that Lysander was well liked in the village. Since his attack, many admirers had stopped by to offer sympathies and gifts. I readied myself to thank the gentleman or lady and cracked the door. Happily, I was met by Ruven's smile. He held up a bag and waved. I swung the door open and invited him in.

"Can't stay long," Ruven said, closing the door behind him.

"Where are you off to?" I asked, only to be polite.

He shrugged. "Business at the castle." Catching sight of Lysander, Ruven then frowned and whispered, "Dad sent these." I accepted the bag and Ruven continued. "Goat's milk and cheeses. Dad swears it'll make you strong, says to give it to Lysander." Ruven's cheek tugged up and he squinted, not believing the words himself.

"Thank you," I said. "Thank your dad for us too."

Ruven drew a hand through his hair. "I uh, I hope you don't mind but, uh..." His cheeks turned red. He opened the door and grabbed a crossbow he'd left outside. "I made you this." Ruven placed the weapon in my arms. It was magnificent...and heavy.

"Ruven!" I chided and tried to return it. Ruven put his palms up and backed through the open door. "I can't afford this!" I cried, following him down the path.

Ruven stumbled and righted himself. Backing away, he said, "It's a gift!"

Just then, the local merchant passed with his horse and wagon. He side-eyed Ruven, and then me, and then the crossbow pointing between us. I dipped my chin, but the merchant clucked at his horse, and they trotted away.

Ruven said, "I thought, maybe, I could show you how to use it?" He paused and rubbed his neck. "Though, your mum or Lottie could probably show you better." Ruven's brows furrowed, as if he'd just discovered a flaw in his plan.

"Thank you." I let the crossbow rest at my side. It was a generous gift, and though Ruven expected nothing in return, my guilt would not allow it. It chipped at the boundary I'd set with Ruven, when I'd refused to make him something to wear. "Why don't you come back tomorrow. You can show me how to use it...and I'll take measurements for your tunic."

Like a soft sunrise, joy blossomed on Ruven's face. "I don't deserve you, Lili!" Without asking, he embraced me. I awkwardly waited for Ruven to let go. "I'll see you tomorrow." Softer, he continued, "In the meantime, my thoughts are with Lysander." He rubbed my shoulder and added, "If you need anything, come to the farm." Ruven jogged down the path, where he paused, then pointed at the crossbow. "Don't forget to name it."

"I—what?"

"So that it trusts you." Ruven's eyes shifted to the trees behind the cottage. "You wouldn't want it to turn against you." I examined the weapon, a gift given to protect me. Only one name came to mind.

"Ev—"

Ruven put a finger to his lips, shushing me. "Never say it out loud. You never know who might use your own weapon to harm you."

Though unchanged, the crossbow felt heavier in my arms.

Ruven waved and, heading down the road, called back, "See you tomorrow!"

"See you tomorrow," I murmured.

Hopefully.

Back in my bedroom, I plaited my hair. I tossed it over my shoulder, where it dangled like a golden rope. Next, I slipped into a forest green cloak. My father and I had made it together; it helped me move through shadows unseen. The golden inscription along the inside hem caught the light. A shimmer travelled across the delicate threads, revealing my father's words from long ago.

The shadows cannot harm what they cannot find.

Be safe, my light.

I headed to the den and tucked my satchel at my side. After careful consideration, I heaved the crossbow over my shoulder. When my mother joined the guard, she often 'borrowed' weapons from the armoury.

She forced us to learn their mechanics and practice before sneaking the weapons back the following morning. I hadn't had the heart to tell Ruven I knew how to operate a crossbow perfectly well.

During my final check on Lysander, I nearly lost my nerve. My instincts begged me not to leave him alone, but logic shoved my feelings aside. It hissed: He will die if you do nothing!

In my heart, I knew that was true.

Quietly, I closed the back door behind me. As I walked down the path, I passed a row of bright green foliage. A long time ago, the foliage was littered with marvelous lavender peonies. They brought my father immense pride; he was the only one in the land who'd managed to turn the petals lavender. I had a suspicion there was some additive from the Hollow, but that secret died with him. As a family, we'd come to neglect the peonies.

They hadn't bloomed in many years.

I slipped through the gate, and the Hollow loomed ahead. The breeze rustled the branches, which rose and fell like the belly of a sleeping animal. I didn't want to enter—didn't want to awaken it—and uneasiness slowed my steps. We used to go in together, my father and I. Just like the crossbow, we weren't allowed to use our names, lest we be drawn away by mimicry or magic. Little Dove, Blueberry, Dewdrop. Those were some of the silly little nicknames my father gave me. The names he chose for himself were far more ludicrous, Lucky Leopold the Lionheart, or Grand Gnome Gnan. They were such terrible tongue twisters that, if I'd had to cry for help, I'd probably have died. Thankfully, I'd never had to use them—or call out for him, even once. In all our adventures in the Hollow, my father kept me safe. Grief crushed my heart. If only he could have done the same for himself. Or maybe, if I had been with him, on the night he was attacked...perhaps I could have kept him safe too.

At the edge of the trees, I paused. A musky, wet smell wafted out.

You promised Father you wouldn't enter Scrying Hollow.

A crow cackled; it's shriek nearly sent me stumbling back to the cottage. Back to the den where Lysander lay, inching closer to death.

I don't have a choice.

One foot after the other, I bade the light farewell and embraced the shadows.

If it's a liar who saves my brother's life, so be it.

"I'm sorry, Father."

"There."

I scraped the last of the leaves over my net. It was invisible beneath the foliage, and the cords were so thin, you couldn't see where they carried up into the trees. When the Hound stepped on it, he'd be swept into the canopy. I plunged a few sticks in the ground, outlining the net. It would be a shame if I fell for my own trap. Now, for the final part of my plan. Bait. What sort of bait, you ask? Well, this also brings me to the stupidest part of my plan.

I'm the bait.

As I strode comfortably through the trees, one might never know I'd abandoned the Hollow. In truth, it was my father's lessons, etched into me from so many childhood visits, that fueled my confidence. Sweet memories of his voice joined me, *'Step lightly, Little Dove. The Hollow listens. And we do not know what sleeps beneath the surface.'*

Deliberately disobeying my father's ghost, I stomped through the brush. With each passing trunk, I moved deeper into Scrying Hollow. Father told me we'd named it after the witches that once gathered here to scry. Though, that was a long time ago. Presently, the Hollow was a place overrun by evil, accessed by only the most desperate. Regret stung me. If I'd continued making custom garments, we might have had enough income, and Lysander wouldn't have been driven into this wretched place... The whispers started.

That's okay, I was expecting them.

'The Hollow whispers, Dewdrop. It's normal, but never listen. And certainly, never follow them.'

In my head, I repeated an old rhyme, focusing on the verses instead of the beckoning voices.

There once was a peckish bone fairy,
Who snatched a child and carried,
Them off to the Hollow for eating.
The girl's father, frantic and fraught,
Caught the bone fairy and fought,
But still, his child was crunched.
Oh, how life is fleeting!

At first, I was reluctant to wander far from my net. The trees inside the Hollow had a way of changing while unobserved. If you hoped to find your way out, you had to find other, reliable methods of navigation. Currently, I walked along a faint path, trod into the wood floor by my father and his father before him. Though the Hollow was nightmarish, these paths were a safe space, and I hesitated to leave them. The Hollow was not so thick here, and the sunlight penetrated the trees. I walked in circles and returned to my trap every so often to orient myself. Hours ticked by, both relief and frustration nestled in my belly.

This isn't working.

Fortunately, my father had taught me a few tricks when it came to maneuvering through the Hollow. Quelling my fear, I strayed from my father's path. I counted my steps and used various woodland ephemera as waypoints. Stones, toadstools, and a particular cream flower, which my father called cream cobbles or cobblestones, so named for their reliable lack of movement.

A branch snapped.

I stilled, becoming a statue in the woodland. The gnarled tree at my side, with a dark hole partway up the trunk, was empty. Up ahead, the underbrush remained motionless. As far as I could tell, nothing moved.

A leaf crunched...behind me.

Be still.

Don't run.

If it were the Hound at my back, I'd be dead already, I was sure of it. Letting my cloak disguise me, I waited for whatever stalked me to wander away. Stay calm. If they cannot find you, they cannot eat you. I held my breath and counted to fifty, like my father taught me.

...forty-eight, forty-nine, fifty.

Slowly, I turned around. Only the Hollow. One foot in front of the other, I resumed walking. Here in the shadows, my father's ghost kept me company.

'The Hollow watches, Blueberry.'

Indeed, I felt it. For some time, an eerie glow, like a lantern cast with green glass, followed me.

'It's a rather peaceful creature who watches, but do not look. Do not turn around. Pretend you don't see its foul grin peering around the trees at the edge of your sight. Once you lay eyes on the Watcher, it will feel threatened. The creatures high shriek is the last thing you'll hear as it eats you.'

You'd think such memories would frighten me, especially here in the Hollow. Despite the terrors lurking in every shadow, this used to be a merry place. Between these trees, my father taught me to forage and survive. Now, his lessons were all I had. They were not intimidating at all; they comforted me. I walked down a small ravine and climbed up the other side. Reaching up, I grabbed the bank.

"Ugh!" I yanked my hand back. It was wet...and red. Shuffling sideways, I hauled myself over the edge.

The lifeless eyes of a red-fanged deer greeted me.

Without a smell or any sign of decomposition, the brown fur still looked soft and perfect—well, except for the fleshy chunk missing from the back of its neck. Red-fanged deer travelled in herds, and they weren't helpless—far from it. They may look like regular deer, but as the name suggests, red-fanged deer concealed quite the surprise. They could unhinge their jaw all the way to their shoulders, exposing a jagged row of fangs.

No, the fangs weren't *naturally* red.

I'll let you conclude why we've named them that, though.

I glanced around and rubbed my fingers together. The blood was still watery.

Fresh.

The corpse was relatively untouched—had I stumbled upon the Hound's dinner? Again, I looked around. Was the beast out there, watching me?

Would it feast twice in one day?

I wiped the blood in the moss and hastened on.

Would I recognize the Hound when I saw it? Like most, I'd only ever heard stories. During father's incoherent rambling, he'd said the beast, 'looked like a wolf, yet not like a wolf.' A guard who'd survived an attack, which unfortunately left another captain dead, said the creature had a tail that was long and thin like a lion's. While the stories each differed, all accounts mentioned the beast's eyes:

Two yellow beacons that shone in the night.

My legs began to tire, and I paused to drink. I walked for another stretch. Apart from the low whispers, and the watchful creature, I didn't find anything. Not a rabbit, or shrew.

"Ugh."

I'd left Lysander too long already, and if I wanted to be home before Lottie and my mother, I needed to turn around. Up ahead, a trickle of light caught my attention.

I'll check that out, then I'll go back.

I passed through a copse of birch trees, the kind with leaves that silvered in Autumn, and stumbled into a large meadow. The sun was just above the treetops, and the last rays shone on a pond, glittering like a mirror in the meadow. I'd heard stories about the pond, Madelena's Pool. When magic was high, people used the pond to travel through space and time. I'd never ventured this far into the Hollow; had Father? Stepping into the sunshine, I batted aside white and pink wildflowers.

I scrutinized the treeline across the meadow and my heart lurched. Shadows darted in and out of the trees. I ducked down, hiding behind the tall grass.

Forest wraiths, seven of them.

They were wisps of a skeleton, with tattered black clothes billowing behind them. I thanked the stars I'd seen them before it was too late—before they sucked the life from me. I waited until long after they were out of sight and stood. The sun was lower in the sky than I'd like, I'd have to hustle back—fear, like a bolt of lightning, froze me where I stood.

Two bright beacons.

Two bright beacons watched me from the wood across the meadow.

At once, I knew the all-consuming terror that floods the goat when preyed upon by a frothing, ravenous wolf. Between the jagged pines, a massive canine, no smaller than a workhorse, sat in the dark. Even seated, the beast's ears disappeared behind the tall branches.

For nearly a decade, my mind spun images of the beast. It was a nightmare, a non-physical thing that consumed me. To actually find and face it...part of me never expected I'd get this far.

Whether I was ready or not, I'd done it.

I'd found it.

The Hound.

Lesson Three

Do what you must to protect those
you love.

The Hound watched me.

It was so still, the only movement a slight nod, tracking my staggered steps when I'd first laid eyes on it. Why wasn't it attacking? All the stories were filled with fury and claws and teeth. But...this beast just sat there, and it *watched* me.

It was unexpected, and certainly unsettling.

Wiping sweaty palms on my cloak, I quickly checked behind myself, making sure I had a clear escape.

"Give me strength, Father."

Flowers parted as I stomped into the bright meadow. "Hey!" I waved. The Hound tilted its head but made no move. Taking a deep breath, I stalked closer. I thumped my chest and shouted, "Come get me!" The Hound yawned. My dagger was a needle compared to the teeth lining the beast's massive jaws.

Why did the Hound not come for me?

"Fine!" I unslung my crossbow. Bracing it with my feet, it took all my strength to load a bolt. I heaved up the bow and nestled the crosshairs amongst the Hound's fur. My finger found the trigger, but I hesitated.

Could I take the beast's life?

Yes, I'd killed rabbits and even helped Father with a deer once—the inability to kill was a luxury not afforded to the poorer folk, but this... This felt different. I wasn't killing for food, and there was a strange intelligence in the way the beast observed me.

Why did this feel like murder?

Doubt cramped my trigger finger. Unafraid, keen eyes stared back at me. It seemed the Hound was calling my bluff. I lowered the crossbow, and I *swore* the beast smiled. It stood on all fours and I tensed, prepared to flee. The Hound did not pursue me; instead, it turned and walked back into the thick pines. Losing sight of the fur, I panicked and raised my crossbow. The Hound hadn't thought twice before it stole my father's life.

I aimed.

Lysander will die if I don't do this. I must return with the Hound's heart!

I pressed the lever, and the bolt left the crossbow in a muted *thwack!* The Hound faltered and slammed into the ground.

I'd hit it!

I lowered the crossbow as the Hound righted itself. Every muscle in its body alive, the Hound rounded on me. The great beast stalked into the meadow. It was bigger in the sunshine, perhaps because it was better illuminated, but more likely because it was coming toward me with great haste.

Tucking the crossbow over my shoulder, I waded through the flowers and ran. Snarling yips chased as I hurtled through the trees, dodging trunks like my life depended on it. From the booming crashes erupting after me, I gathered the Hound was not maneuvering quite so smoothly. I leapt into the ravine—"Hhh!" A thorny bush caught my cheek. Pushing down the pain, I crested the ravine and sprinted. Crunching underbrush followed, so close at my heels. Though my lungs burned, I did not slow. At a cluster of red toadstools, I counted my footsteps.

"One-two-three-four-five!" I cried and veered left.

I hurtled into the clearing with my trap and skirted the stick markers. "Guh!" My cloak tightened on my throat, and I ceased moving. With my cloak firmly in its jaws, the Hound swung me around. Arms cartwheeling, I collided into a nearby tree, gasping out a breathless, "Oof!" I oriented to the spinning woodland. "Ah!" I dodged as the Hound smashed into the trunk, sending the entire tree careening down. Thinking quick, I grabbed a low-hanging branch and climbed. The Hound was after me, chomping at my boots. Its snout hit my heel, almost knocking me from the tree. I regained my grip, then scurried up to safety. My father, a particularly good climber, could climb trees like this from root to tip in just under ten seconds.

I remember his smirk when I'd done it in six.

Out of the Hound's reach, I squatted on a branch. Catching my breath, I panted worse than the repellant beast below. The Hound threw itself at the trunk, but this was no sapling, it was a great ash. Each blow did little more than send a faint tremor through the branches. The Hound ceased its assault and prowled over the thick roots. Its tail whipped, cat-like, behind it.

Perched safely, I puffed my chest like a proud bird.

"Can't get me up here, can you? You stupid mongrel!" Boiling with rage and foolish confidence, I spit on the beast. As if I'd blown on an ember, a new fire erupted in the Hound. It howled and leapt at the canopy. Hot breath blew my hair back, carrying the stink of rotten meat. Claws like kitchen cleavers sunk into the ash below my boots. They raked the trunk, sending up spirals of bark. The Hound hit the ground, its sides heaving.

It sat there, hating me, and I it.

The Hound got up and limped away. The bolt was still embedded in the beast's side, and its rear leg dragged. It must be in agony, dragging itself through the woods like a mutt run over by a wagon. Though I despised the beast, my guts twisted at the thought of *any* animal suffering. My survival instinct grabbed hold of my pity and tossed it aside.

You're running out of time! it screamed. *This isn't the occasion for weakness! Finish the job and get out of here!*

Indeed, long shadows painted the ground, and the whispers that permeated the Hollow were getting louder. *'Stay,'* they beckoned. *'Become one with the soft moss and roots.'*

Covering my ears, I shook the voices out. I could *not* be here when darkness came! I craned, looking for the Hound. After a deep breath, I crawled ungraciously along the branch to an adjoining tree. I did this again, until I sat in a tree behind my net. I surveyed the trunks where I'd seen the Hound exit.

No weakness.

I leapt.

No sooner had my feet touched down when the Hound sprung into the clearing. A flurry of fur and jaws snapped in my face—leaves exploded as the net curled around the Hound like a cocoon. High shrieks battered me as the Hound tore at the net. I knew, in my heart, the threads would not fray. The Hound thrashed, sending blood and foamy drool spraying over me. I wanted to hide from the panic and pain; instead, I unslung my crossbow and aimed. Catching sight of the weapon, the Hound stilled. Its wide, yellowed eyes locked on me. My arm trembled as I drew the bolt back.

The Hound whimpered.

My finger inched toward the trigger.

CRACK!

The splintering of bones filled the Hollow. But...I hadn't pulled the trigger. Another sickening *crack!* rang out as the Hound's rear leg snapped.

By some spell, the beast began shrinking. Limbs twisted and broke, and the Hound's dark hair receded, as if it were slipping from its fur coat.

In a blink, the Hound was gone.

A dirty, naked man hung in my net. With one hand, he gripped the bolt imbedded in his side. The other reached through the woven ropes—to me. A guttural voice rasped, "Please. Kill me quickly." In my arms, the crossbow drooped.

I just wanted to save my brother.

Frozen, we stared at each other. Dribbling blood *pitter-pattered* as the man's chest rose and fell. Was I shocked? Yes. *Shaken to my core* was more accurate. But at the same time, Father had trained me to expect mimicry—that things were not always as they seemed. His wisdom carried from the grave:

'Is it a beast pretending to be a man?'

'Or a man, posing as a beast?'

Through a tangle of coal-black hair, the man's eyes, like two pale sapphires, searched mine. He was young; it was hard to tell through the grime, but he couldn't be older than thirty. I think, if he were a beast mimicking a man, he would look less...foul. He scowled at me through layers of filth and muck. Surely, any monster whose survival depended on tricking a human would appear more...tempting.

I inched closer. The man grabbed for me. I dodged, slipping on loose leaves. Scrambling up, I aimed the crossbow.

"Yes," the man murmured, and relief lulled his eyes.

He welcomed death.

And I... I couldn't do it. Reasons tumbled through my mind, begging me to push the lever, and not push the lever at the same time.

Do it for Father.

I'm not a guard! I am not my mother. Or Lottie, I'm a seamstress! I can't do this!

Do it for Lysander!

I make clothes to protect people, not hurt them!

"Ugh!" I threw the crossbow aside. Even if he was the Hound, I wasn't prepared to *murder* a man. To say this was an unexpected and unwelcome change of plans was a dreadful understatement. Snapping into action, I scaled the tree holding the net. I withdrew my knife and froze.

The threads would not fray.

How could I free him? I jumped down and stared into the canopy. The rope needed to be untied, but with the man's weight pulling it, I'd never manage. Somehow, I had to reduce the pressure. I spotted a rotten log and dragged it over.

"Stand on this."

Whether from pain, or the realization that death would not claim him today, the man groaned. Reluctantly, he shifted and grunted as the bolt pierced deeper. He did his best to stand on the log, but the net wobbled, and he slipped. He cried out, and I watched the log roll away. The low, drawn-out howl of a wolf carried through the Hollow.

"Fuck!" I glanced at the fading sun.

"Go," the man growled. "The wolves are coming."

I searched the clearing until I found a large, flat rock. Using a combination of flipping, and wiggling, I managed to wedge the rock below the man. He stood on it, relieving the pressure of the rope on the branch above. I climbed the tree and fumbled with the knot. The net fell away, and the man collapsed. Darkness seeped through the trees, laying across his bare body like bars. I'd felt wretched before; now, I was positively horrified. Agony twisted the man's spine as he curled around the bolt. The skin around the wound was ripped and jagged, torn this way and that during the Hound's thrashing.

I'd done this.

I was a monster.

This time, a chorus of howls erupted. The wolves were close, and terror somersaulted my stomach. Like a fawn taking their first steps, the man climbed to his feet. He held his side and stumbled away. I reached to help but he braced himself on a tree and snarled, "Go, you fool!" As the distant howling grew close, I grabbed my crossbow and I retreated into the trees. I spared a final glance over my shoulder.

The man shuffled deeper into the Hollow.

Distressed voices reached me before I saw my family gathered behind the cottage.

"What do we do?" Lottie.

"I don't know." My mother.

"I'll call on the men next door. Ruven will come." Lysander.

"Go lie down!" My mother again, presumably shouting at my brother.

"I'm here!" I called, breaching the trees.

Lottie vaulted the short stone fence separating our yard from the Hollow. My mother used the gate but managed to keep pace with my sister.

Lottie shoved me. Hard. "Where were you?!"

My mother pushed Lottie aside. "Are you injured?" She held my chin, wrenching my face side to side, looking for an answer herself. "What happened?"

In a panicked daze, I mumbled, "I, uh... I got lost."

My mother snatched my hands; they were flecked with blood. "What's this?"

"It's not mine," I muttered. My families shocked faces—and Lottie's balled fists—demanded more. "I killed a rabbit." I pushed through them, heading for the cottage.

Lottie's accusatory voice called, "Where is it?"

"Where's what?"

"The rabbit."

I scrabbled absently at my pockets. "Musta got away." Passing Lysander, I said, "You shouldn't be up."

"We were worried about you," Lysander panted. "What were you thinking—" My glare froze Lysander's tongue. His face was shiny with sweat, and he swayed. I reached out, grabbing him before he could fall into the garden. We headed into the cottage, my mother and Lottie not far behind.

"How are you feeling?" I asked.

"I'm okay." Lysander's Adam's apple bobbed, keeping the sick down.

He wasn't.

"Don't worry about me," I said. "Lie down." Lysander did, the sofa groaned and sunk beneath his weight.

Lottie burst in, sending the door crashing into the stone. "I can't believe you!" she snarled. Ignoring her, I started toward my room. Disobeying my mother's hushed threats to keep her voice down, Lottie chased me and barked, "And you're the *smart* one! Think what it would have done to our mother if you didn't come back—"

"Leave me alone!" I screamed. Lottie recoiled, and I covered my mouth. It might have been ten years since I'd lost my temper with her. She and my mother exchanged a look. I fled down the hall and slammed our bedroom door. I sat on the bed, cupping my head. I still saw everything.

The man's frantic eyes, darting around.

His blood-smattered palm, reaching to me.

'Please,' he'd begged—*begged* me to end his suffering!

I shook my head, trying to dispel his face, his pleading. I lay back and tugged my hair. I might not have killed him, but I'd left him to die. I'd treated him worse than an animal. At least with an animal, I would have cut their throat; I wouldn't have left them to suffer.

The Hound killed your father. Even if he is a man, does he not deserve this?

I rolled over.

You left him there, alone, in that place.

I rolled back.

Will he bleed to death, or be eaten alive by wolves?

I sat up, catching sight of myself in the mirror standing in the corner. Blood painted me, and the lines that furrowed my face were deeper than usual. I dragged my hand beneath my nose, stifling a sob.

Did your father raise you to be this cruel?

The morning sun wasn't yet rising over the Hollow when I snuck out my bedroom window.

Lesson Four

Do not trust anything in the Hollow,
least of all the trees.

In my haste to flee the Hollow, I'd left my net. Folding it, I placed it in my satchel. I followed the trail of blood, tracking the man like he was a wild boar I'd shot for supper. I wound through the Hollow, and it wasn't long before I came to the sprawling wildflower meadow I'd discovered yesterday. I brushed a birch trunk, just below a dried, bloody handprint. Hiking up my cloak, I stalked into the meadow, bending the tall grass and wildflowers. Finding a blood trail would be impossible here, but I aimed for the spot where I'd seen the Hound resting yesterday, hoping he'd retreated that way.

Parting the last swell of grass, I paused before entering the pines. Tall and grey, they were a solemn portal. Sunlight failed to penetrate the thick boughs, which grew so close, it was difficult to peer through them. A creature might be only a few paces away, and you wouldn't know it. Pulling my hood over my head, I raised my crossbow. Darkness enveloped me as I pushed through the needled branches. My breath clouded in a plume of white mist, and I tightened the cloak at my throat. Even if the blood trail continued here, I couldn't make it out in the dark. Lowering my crossbow, I glanced back.

I should turn around.

At the cottage, my mother and Lottie would have found me gone. Mother would be worried, and Lottie, most likely already throwing things. As I started to turn, a lump caught my eye. I shoved a branch aside, trying to see better. Was it a boulder? The lump, which was roughly the size of a man...moved.

Glancing around, I approached with caution. Soon, I made out details: dirty hair and skin. I knelt and rolled the lump over. The man groaned. "Leave me." Bits of twigs and leaves fell from his pallid cheeks. Chunks of congealed blood surrounded the bolt I'd put in his side. Looking at the wound, I felt criminal. Shame and a desire to fix my wrongdoing guided my hands as they wrapped around the man.

"We must go."

Carefully, I pulled the man, so he was seated. I helped him stand and wrapped his arm around my neck. "Let's get you somewhere safe—"

A wolf sat on the path.

Not just any wolf, a *thin* wolf.

I'd never seen one, but Father had told me stories. When seated, thin wolves were tall and narrow. If they held perfectly still, you might mistake them for a tree trunk. Even seeing it now, I couldn't believe it. The wolf was so slender, its entire body no wider than it's pointed snout. I craned to meet the impossibly tall creature's eyes. Dragging the man, I stepped back.

The wolf's snout curled into a snarl, which looked remarkably like a grin.

The wolf stalked forward. Movement beside us sent my pulse racing. The tree nearest me spun, revealing another lanky wolf. It's pointed snout parted in a hungry snarl as it, too, prowled toward us. I continued shuffling away. A branch snapped beneath my boot. The nearest wolf lunged. I blocked with the crossbow.

"Agh!" Jaws clamped down on the bow and tore it away. I retreated, faster. All around, the trees shifted and revealed gangly, ravenous wolves. In seconds, an entire pack surrounded us.

But they didn't attack.

Why?

I stepped sideways; a wolf snapped, and I dodged. I felt like one of the goats on Ruven's farm. The wolves behaved just like the family shepherd, snapping and barking at any animal that didn't go where it belonged. I tried moving right. Again, a wolf lunged at me.

Indeed, they were herding me.

But herding me where?

A chill prickled my spine, and I risked a glance over my shoulder. We'd backed into a sort of semi-transparent wall, as if the air itself were covered with frost. Bright light shone through the frosted veil, but dread overwhelmed me at the thought of crossing. One-by-one, the wolves bayed. It was a hunting cry, one I'd often heard from the safety of my bedroom, a hungry chorus that accompanied the shrieks of an animal being torn apart. The sinewy wolves inched closer, snarling and snapping. One managed to catch my sleeve; it swung its head, and my arm flailed helplessly. The wolf let go, and, pulling the man with me, I careened back.

Together, we fell.

As easily as one might fall through the ice coating a frozen lake, we passed through the mysterious veil. My free arm cartwheeled, and we collided against a cobbled path. Sunlight blinded me. I covered my eyes and scrambled up.

"What?" I muttered and squinted from behind my hand.

On this side of the veil, we were not met with trees and darkness. Before us lay a sprawling garden, filled with unkempt hedges and overgrown roses. Farther, between the tangles and brambles, jutted a vast, ruinous castle.

Tall, black windows dotted the grey stonework, like a great many eyes boring upon us. Imposing spires cast the ground in shadows, darkening the area in great strips, looking remarkably like light passing through prison bars.

Stepping closer, I whispered, "Where are we?"

"Don't!" The man clutched my cloak, and frost nipped my nose as he pushed me *back* through the veil. Jaws snapped in my face. I recoiled, yanking myself back to safety.

"Let go of me!" I chopped the man's filthy arm.

The man collapsed and groaned. Struggling to breathe, he muttered, "It's a ca..." A gob of drool hung from the side of his mouth.

Again, I helped the man up and wrapped his arm around my neck. After we'd passed through the veil, the man hadn't shared my surprise in discovering the castle. He seemed both familiar with...and terrified of it.

"Do you live here?" I asked.

The man's face scrunched like he'd smelled putrid meat, and whether he meant to or not, he gave a subtle nod. The movement was enough to send him staggering, nearly yanking me sideways with him. "Alright. Come on." We shuffled along the cobbled path, stepping over blankets of roses and ducking beneath overgrown hedge arches. We passed an untidy topiary, what long ago might have been a dragon. Something caught the hood of my cloak; I yanked it free and looked around. My gaze landed on the topiary dragon, at the bit of green fabric that remained in its curled claw.

Heart pounding, I didn't turn my back on the topiary until we were well out of reach.

Hurrying down the remaining path, we passed a grand fountain. Once, it seemed magnificent swans spewed water down the cascading stonework. Now, only decaying leaves filled the fountain bed. At the base of the castle, two grand staircases split left and right, like the wings of a phoenix. Choosing the left staircase, I tried the first step—the stone crumbled beneath my boot. Scrutinizing every stair, I led us up the precarious steps. We hobbled forward, stopping at a set of monolithic doors. There weren't any doorknockers—or handles.

How do I open them?

Heaving the man up, I dragged my hand along the carving of a stag, its eyes wide and terrified. Ever so slowly, the door swung in, and mildew wafted out. I glanced back to the veil. Like tall trees, several thin wolves sat on the other side. I peered into the dark foyer. The man groaned in protest. He tried to pull away, to stop me from entering, but his wound had weakened him terribly. Dragging him along with me, I stepped inside the castle.

Whoosh!

A gust of air rushed through the foyer and torches flickered to life. The sparse light did little to dispel the gloom. At the far end, flames sputtered in a stone fireplace that was so vast, you could fit two carriages inside. Dust motes floated through the air—

"Achoo!" I sneezed into my elbow. We crept forward onto a luxurious but aged carpet. Fear shot through my boots, and I stumbled off the rug. The threads depicted a scene of a hunt, with hounds tearing frantic foxes apart.

Click.

On the second floor of the foyer, the shadows moved as a door swung open with a gentle creak. The sound was a fist, clenching my already tense stomach. Avoiding the rug, I dragged the man up one of the two imposing staircases. Paintings and tapestries littered the stone wall beside us. Grey in hue, the paintings featured a faceless woman in a white gown. In all depictions, hounds snarled through the frames.

A sudden whisper startled me.

I whipped around, nearly knocking the man over the banister. Though there was no one behind me, I noticed a change in the paintings.

The hounds were gone.

And each depiction of the woman stared after us, as if reminding me that, though faceless, she could still *see* me.

I faltered on the steps, my body beseeching me to drop the stranger and run. Down below, the strip of light along the doors called me to freedom.

In my arms, the man groaned.

I couldn't leave him.

This was my fault. If I fled now, he'd die a slow, excruciating death. For a fractured moment, I saw my father on the sofa—face twisted in agony. Near the end, the only thing that kept him from begging for death was Lottie and Lysander, crouched at his feet, watching.

My grip on the man tightened.

I had to help him. Only then would I flee.

I heaved the man up the remaining steps and veered left. The open door led to a bedroom, with a red velvet four poster bed. At the end of the bed, a fire burned in the crumbling hearth. I hauled the man to the bed and tossed him down. His eyelids fluttered, and he mumbled. I leaned in, trying to hear him.

"It's a cage!" the man bellowed, seizing my shoulders.

Eager to escape the man's rank breath, I pried his fingers off. "Lie down!"

The man obliged, shivering violently. Somewhere in his journey, he'd broken the end of the bolt off. Luckily, there was enough remaining that I could grip it. I put my hand on his chest and braced him. My fingers curled tighter around the bolt, and without warning, I yanked it out.

"Aghhh!" The man arched, bunching the sheets in his fists.

Slipping into surgeon mode, I muttered, "I know, I know!" I pressed the wound while I scrabbled in my satchel for water. Blood poured through my fingers; it didn't phase me.

I'd seen worse.

The man's breath came in heavy bursts, his eyes lulled and closed. When the wound was clean, I examined it. Jagged flesh, a deep incision, a bit of white, which I surmised was a rib. Yes, I'd seen worse—but this was still bad. There weren't many who could sustain an injury like this and survive.

He's no common man, I reminded myself.

Sewing quickly, I ignored the man's groans and acknowledged that I probably wasn't as gentle as I could have been. After the last stitch, I cut the thread and tucked my kit away. I sat back and traced the stitches.

My fingers tingled, and I *knew* he would survive.

The man's breathing evened, and his eyes remained closed. Just as well; he should rest after such a severe injury. My gaze wandered from the man's face, down his throat, where it settled on his left breast.

On his heart.

I could take it.

I *should* take it.

My hand drifted to the knife on my belt. All I had to do was carve it out and give it to the queen; it would save my brother. I imagined it, driving the blade into the man's chest, dragging it through the flesh. I swayed on my knees. I couldn't... I couldn't do that. Maybe my mother or Lottie could, but I wasn't strong enough. I could *not* will my hand to execute a wounded man who lay sleeping.

You might think me weak but, if our places were exchanged, and it was *you* looming over a dying man, the choice, though obvious, may not be so easily executed.

I would have to find another way to save Lysander.

I withdrew a scrap of fabric from my bag and doused it with water. Stringy hair obscured the man's face. I pushed it aside and wiped grime and sweat from his cheeks, one of which bore a light scar. I'll admit, he wasn't a bad looking brute—*Liliwen!* I pulled away and threw the cloth in my bag. He is a monster.

He is *the* Hound.

And he killed my father.

I tossed a blanket over the man's naked body and left. Now that he was taken care of, I was overwhelmed by urgency. An intuitive part of me, the part that carefully noted everything indescribably wrong with this place, screamed, *Get out! Get out immediately!* I jogged from the room and took the stairs three at a time.

The gigantic doors started to close.

Fright nearly choked me. I ran toward the shrinking sunlight, tearing down the remaining stairs and across the sinister carpet. The doors clicked shut and I slammed into them.

"No!"

There weren't any handles on this side either. I pounded the solid wood, but the only outcome was pain, and I shook my hand bitterly.

Creaaaaak.

The sound floated over my shoulder. Below one of the grand staircases, a short door swung open. A breeze floated through the foyer, carrying a voice that whispered, "Liliwen."

An impossible voice.

My father's voice.

Fear spiked my adrenaline. A face, obscured in shadows, was peering around the doorframe. Holding perfectly still, it watched me. Four dark fingers pulled from the stone as the entity disappeared down the hall. The haunting, distorted copy of my father's voice whispered, "Liliwen. Come, look."

Mimicry was a weapon used often in the Hollow, and I was not foolish enough to believe my father was here, in this castle. Tentatively, I crossed the foyer. The question was, who—or *what*—was mimicking him? I peered around the door and down the shadowed hall. Sunshine peeked through the other side. I proceeded with caution, ready to flee at the slightest provocation.

Entering the bright courtyard, I squinted at the tall walls surrounding it. Was this the heart of the castle? Just ahead, the cobblestone gave way to a garden. Sunbeams shone through the parapets and bathed a central tree in buttery, welcoming light. My steps echoed against the cobble as I approached the garden. Large, fat fruits dangled from the branches. The smell was intoxicating, and saliva pooled beneath my tongue. I reached out and picked a ruby-red fruit. It pulsed, wriggling like an egg about to hatch. I dug my thumbs into the flesh and cracked it open. Inside, hundreds of seeds twinkled like tiny gems. The aroma was dizzyingly sweet. I grazed a seed.

My fingers burned.

During one of our foraging trips, my father and I had happened upon a cluster of delightful red and white capped mushrooms. I'd plucked up a mushroom and put it in my basket, but my father put his hand on mine. He withdrew the mushroom and broke the little red cap in two. He brushed the mushroom against his lips, and then did the same to mine. Almost immediately, my lips burned, and I cried. It was a harsh lesson, but to my father's credit, I'd never put a poison mushroom in my basket again. I rubbed my burning fingers together...and tossed the fruit aside. If I was hungry, I had food in my bag. I turned my back on the tree...

Wait.

Was that bird always there?

Beside the hall where I'd entered was a bust, the facial features long worn away. Perched upon the bust was a raven. It looked real, though it remained stiller than the statue below it. I scanned the courtyard. That was the only exit, I couldn't leave without passing by.

Cautiously, I approached.

Was it alive? Surely, it would have flown by now; I was only a few paces away. I covered my nose. The air was suddenly ripe with the stench of rotting flesh. I scrutinized the bird, who stared into my very core. A small, writhing insect fell to the cobblestone.

Maggots.

The bird was rotting. A patchwork of bones and decayed flesh covered its body, where more maggots squirmed beneath dark feathers. I wanted to reach out and touch it, knock it from its perch so I might know if it was real or some trick of the Hollow.

Its beady eyes watched me.

I reached out—*CAW!* In a fluttering of feathers, the bird leapt forward.

"Agh!"

Claws raked my face, and I winced, protecting my eyes. Cackles faded, and I turned to curse the bird. "Lousy—"

The tree had moved.

Shadows enveloped me, as if the entire tree had curved and bent toward me. The bark was different too. It was black and had a sort of sheen to it. The kind blood might get. My eyes travelled all the way down the tree...to the wrought branch almost touching me.

A fruit dangled there, so close I could take it.

Another of my father's warnings floated back to me. *'Keep your eye on the prize is an adage for royalty. My advice to you: always look behind.'* Though there were walls separating me from the Hollow, I must remember I was still inside its borders, and I needed to be more cautious.

Keeping the tree in my sight, I backed away and slipped into the dark passage.

I cast a startled look over my shoulder. Though there was no one behind me, a second set of footfalls followed mine. I ran through the door and slammed it. Exhaling, I turned to—

"Did you eat it?!" the Hound cried.

"Guh!" I clutched my chest and fell against the door.

Stooping, the Hound gripped my shoulders with such strength, I cried out. His irises darted frantically across my face. In the meagre torchlight, his eyes adopted a strange glint—almost a shine—like an animal caught out at night.

"Well?" The Hound shook me. "Did you?!"

"Did I what?!"

"Did you eat the fruit?!"

"No!" The Hound's fingers were iron; I struggled to pry them off. "I didn't eat anything!" The Hound slumped, and he fell against the stone wall. Still naked, the Hound did nothing to hide himself, and I avoided looking down. "Let's go." I took the Hound's arm and guided him up-stairs. The weight of his body leaning on mine seemed less. His health was already returning. Again, I laid him down and tossed a blanket over him. I skirted the bed and peered behind the lengthy, red drapes hanging along the bedroom wall. Magnificent windows displayed a view of the front gardens.

Thud.

My forehead pressed against the glass. There was a balcony out there. I struggled to escape the drapery—an endeavor which was made worse by my false assumption that the fabric had come alive to strangle me—and found the balcony door. Grasping the handle, I held my breath. I turned the knob…and the door opened! I snuck out and stood between two proud gargoyles, who sat upon an intricate stone railing. Down below lay the overgrown gardens and path that brought us in.

"No," I murmured. Just beyond the murky haze of the veil, sat two dozen thin wolves. At least a dozen more than when we came through. Tall and narrow, I knew they were wolves and not trees because of the occasional blink.

The Hound was right.

This was a cage.

"It won't let you leave." The hoarse voice gave me such a panicked start I jumped against the railing, sending bits crumbling down. The Hound loomed in the doorway, his hulking body distorted to peer through the frame. "And if you manage to escape"—he jutted his chin toward the veil—"the wolves will butcher you."

Biting back fear, I cried, "How am I supposed to get home?"

The Hound shrugged.

"You are home."

The drapes shuffled and the Hound disappeared inside.

But not before a brief, fluttering smile curved his cheek.

Cold regret tiptoed through me, freezing my limbs. While I so often heard my father's voice, through memories of his lessons, it was my mother's voice that offered me advice now.

'You should have killed him when you had the chance.'

Lesson Five

A cage, however handsome, is a cage.

The Hound was in bed and asleep before I'd even made it through the balcony door. When I tried to wake him, he growled and pulled the blanket over his head. It reminded me of rousing Lottie for school and summoned old bitterness. I huffed and kicked the bedframe. The Hound did not wake.

'You are home.' The Hound's words haunted me.

"We'll see about that," I muttered and left.

Down in the entrance, the giant doors remained closed. I crossed the second story of the foyer, my steps softened by a crimson rug. I stopped at a door, and an ornate staircase leading to the third floor. Behind the door, I found another four-poster bed, this one fitted with lilac drapes. I brushed the fabric—a soft velvet—and a cobweb floated down. In the corner, a gilded vanity sat against the wall. I dragged a finger along the mirror, it came back grey with dust. Brushes and hairpins inlaid with pearls sat, lost in time. All the trinkets were tarnished, and I had no doubt they were silver. I considered taking them, but the thought was met with sharp indignation. Not for the act of thieving, but the belief that any object in this place was undoubtedly cursed.

I wiped dust on my trousers and wandered out. The stairs to the third floor were best described as untrustworthy, and I chose to explore elsewhere. Down in the foyer, I hustled past the door concealing the courtyard—and the evil tree—and headed for a door tucked beside the massive fireplace. When I cracked it open, I was struck by a bright light so foreign to the rest of the castle, it was almost as if it were an intruder. Sunshine shone through windows that ran the length of the room, their tops curved in intricate, rainbow-coloured designs. Spectrums of light fell on rows of tall shelves, each one packed tightly with books. It was—

"A library!" The word spilled out, breathless with reverie. Clutching my chest, I braced myself against a shelf. In a thousand lifetimes, I never thought I'd see one. The shelves blurred, and I blinked, banishing the tears. I walked through the shelves, touching each leather spine. My mother came from a wealthy family—they'd disowned her over my father, of course—but, unlike Father, Mother could read! And she insisted Lottie, Lysander, and I learn as well. Though we only owned three tattered books, and I was certain Lottie merely memorized them, thinking reading a waste of her time.

I bumped a ladder, and it rolled along the shelf. Chasing after it, I climbed to the ceiling. I pulled a book out and tore it open. My finger traced a sentence. *'I couldn't kill the creature, so I trapped him in a burrow until there was someone who could.'* In a daze, I slid the book back and climbed down. At the end of the library, two highbacked chairs of red velvet sat before a fireplace. I plopped down and crinkled my nose against the puff of dust that billowed out. Brushing the soft velvet, I relaxed into the chair. I could spend a lifetime in here. Lottie might not appreciate the books, but I bet Lysander would...reality settled over me like a sudden sickness.

Lysander is dying.

Each day I spent trapped here, Lysander crept closer to death.

I left the chair and approached the towering windows. The stained glass adorning the window tops was quite miraculous. A phoenix bursting from a mountain, the panes coloured in bright reds and oranges. A figure, cast in shades of blue. In the centre most window, I found a knob, inlaid with a jewelled daisy. I turned it, and to my surprise, the large window swung open. I strode out onto an exquisite veranda, careful not to lean on any of the crumbling railings. As far as I could see, a tall, stone wall surrounded the castle grounds. I sidestepped a pot—the original contents were long dead; only brittle sticks remained—and headed to the grand staircase. Navigating overgrown roses and disintegrating steps, I made my way down.

At the base of the steps, I was greeted by the statue of a woman. Her face was long obscured by ivy, and her hand rested on the head of a stone wolf. Another wolf lay obediently at her feet. Passing the statue, I travelled along a gravel path almost entirely lost to grass, and down the sloping lawn, until I came to a covered well. Inside, it was dark, and I couldn't make out the bottom. I wound the lever, drawing the bucket up. Cool water sloshed over the side as the bucket approached the lip of the well. I scooped a handful and drank. It certainly tasted nicer than anything from our well out back. Beyond the well was a giant pond. I dried my hands on my trousers and wandered to the water's edge. I startled a giant bull frog, which let out a throaty croak and disappeared into the thrushes with a *splash*. An old, wooden bridge arched over the water and landed on a small island in the middle of the pond.

Judging by the state of the castle, I didn't risk the bridge.

Several feet into the water, something disappeared beneath the surface. Waves echoed out in neat rings. Was it a turtle? I approached the edge of the pond, moving aside reeds and grass. As the water lapped back and forth,

I tried to make sense of the shadows. Rocks sat amongst the silt and—a face.

A jolt of shock stilled me.

Black hair surrounded the face like seaweed. Realizing I'd seen it, the creature smiled. Like some underwater serpent or fish, the figure floated from the shore. It put forth a hand, beckoning me. I eyed the creaky bridge, wondering if it might offer a better vantage point. Perhaps sensing my thoughts, the watery figures smile deepened into a grin.

I backed away, quickly.

Hurrying across the unkempt lawn, I skirted messy hedges and abandoned vegetable gardens until I came to the high stone wall. Searching for anything I might climb, I glanced left and right. Though everything was neglected and overgrown, nothing came within ten feet of the structure. I followed it all the way back to the castle, hoping to find a hole or breach, but there wasn't one. The castle might be crumbling, but the wall appeared more secure than ever. Reluctantly, I walked up the veranda and went back inside.

In the foyer, the front doors were open.

I stared at them.

After a scan of the room, I approached. The doors were only open a crack, but I could probably squeeze through if I tried. Again, I surveyed the room. Suddenly, all my childhood trapping lessons seemed incredibly relevant. Examining the doors, cracked just enough that I could *almost* slip through, I felt so much like a squirrel approaching a snare. On the other side was freedom—my nut, if you will. Surely, I was smarter than a rodent... What was that?

A rattling sound carried down the stairs.

Had the Hound awoken?!

More shuffling...from the Hound's room. He was definitely rousing. I needed to go now or risk the beast catching me. I snatched a decorative helm from a side table and tucked it between the doors. Sucking in my chest, I slid between them. A hurried shuffling sounded behind me—I turned back to the foyer. Beneath my feet, an invisible force kicked the helm. It sailed through the air and clanged loudly down the castle steps.

"Wha—"

The doors closed on me.

"Oof!" Pressure crushed the air from my lungs.

Creeeeak.

The door beneath the stairs swung open.

Terror spiked through me, and I tried to slide through. But I couldn't. Like approaching fog, shadows crept across the foyer, carrying with them the sound of footfalls. Not padded steps, but the *click-clack* of claws.

Though I couldn't see it, an entity approached.

I hammered the door, trying to pull myself to freedom. The shadow reached the far side of the rug, and a foul odour, like rotten eggs, assaulted me. Just like a snared squirrel, I struggled frantically, nearly strangling myself. Out of the corner of my eye, the encroaching dark was almost upon me. In my desperation, I clawed the door and cried out when a nail broke against the wood. An iciness settled on my arm, like cold fingers wrapping them. I sucked in my chest and stood tall, making myself as thin as possible—

"Agh!" I pulled myself through and skidded across the rough stones. My breath came laboured and fast as I stared at the cracked door. In a blink, a set of yellowed eyes disappeared into the shadows.

The doors swung open.

Pushing myself up, I bolted down the stairs. I leapt over tangled roses and gave the scattered topiaries a wide berth. When I approached the veil, I slowed. Like a line of saplings, several thin wolves greeted me with devious grins. Trying to catch my breath, I leaned on my knees. It wasn't enough, and I collapsed. Several paces into the Hollow, my crossbow lay in a patch of underbrush. When my heart finally calmed, I addressed the gathered wolves.

"What's worse, being out there with you, or in here with *him*?"

"That depends."

I leapt up and, in my haste to greet the gravelled voice, nearly fell. Standing still as a statue, with hands clasped neatly behind his back, was the Hound. The grime was gone from his face, and his hair lay tied in a tidy ponytail at the nape of his neck.

Backing toward the wolves, I asked, "On what?"

The Hound's smile curved his clean-shaven cheek, dimpled further by the scar that ran along it. As if the very act of carrying a conversation was unfamiliar and foreign, the Hound coughed and cleared his throat.

"How quickly you'd like to die."

The Hound's lips, bearing the stain of his crimes, were too red. His canines—his weapons—were *too* sharp. He strode forward, and his lavish jacket, the colour of bright rubies, gleamed. To wear red was an insult in this land, a threat to our queen and the throne. Did the beast know that? Or did he simply not care? Still, I admired the way the fabric caught the sun, like a faceted jewel.

The Hound stretched a hand to the veil. It rippled, like a pool against his fingers. The thin wolves stood, drawn like moths to a lantern. "Thin wolves are patient beasts. They'll hunt you for days, waiting for the perfect opportunity. When the pack leader reveals itself, the attack comes. Not from ahead, but behind." The Hound's lithe hand caressed his neck. "Their prize is your throat, and once you're on the ground, the rest of the pack sets upon you. While you're alive, they feast. The entire process can be quite...chaotic."

The Hound's eyes narrowed on me. "One good"—he snapped his fingers with a deafening *SNAP*—"from the Hound's jaws could end it all." He smirked. "Just like that."

I didn't dare disagree, didn't point out that my father had died slowly, for fear the Hound might decide to prove his point. I looked at my crossbow across the veil. The Hound followed my gaze and scoffed. "That's maddeningly close, is it not?" I didn't trust myself to answer. To my right, the Hound towered, cunning and proud. To my left, the thin wolves prowled along the veil. Both wore sly, starved grins.

"You look...frightened?"

I yanked up my fists to protect myself.

The Hound stood directly in front of me, so close he might stoop and tear my head off. My hearing was good—better than good if the occasion called for it. Left unwatched, the Hound was completely soundless as he crept nearer to me. His lip curled and he laughed—a bitter, mirthless laugh. "No, I must be mistaken! Not you, who thought you might slay the Hound single-handedly." His tone was mocking and cruel when he asked, "Could it be you're simply cold?" He waved at the castle. "Shall we head back inside?" Without waiting for an answer, he strode away.

Wolves or Hound?

Beside me, drool fell from the drooping jowl of a thin wolf, who's nose touched the veil. Along the path, with his hands still clasped behind him, the Hound walked away, unbothered by my existence. Clean and dressed, he looked every part the gentleman.

Maybe he could be reasoned with?

The thin wolf let out a low snarl, sweeping me in rancid breath. I fought the urge to scream, to let the frustration burst forth. In a retrospectively ludicrous display, I reached through the veil and flicked the thin wolf on the nose. A snapping of teeth and flurry of howls ensued. The thin wolf rose to its full height, towering over me like a seething, sentient tree. I offered it my middle finger. Whether it was the correct decision or not, I abandoned my crossbow and trailed the Hound.

Hearing my footsteps pounding the old cobblestones, the Hound turned. Even striding backward, his gait remained steady. To watch him was mesmerizing, his movement as fluid as the foxes bounding through the Hollow. "Clever choice," he said, while dodging a branch he couldn't see but knew approached. When he ascended the stairs, he walked around the crumbling spots, as if he'd memorized each flaw in the ruined architecture. The great doors opened wide to permit our entry. The Hound paused to look at me, his gaze lingering on my cloak. He muttered, "Where shall I put you?"

"You might send me home."

"The sage room." The Hound headed upstairs, and I trailed him. My heart lurched as he walked toward the third floor. Keeping my back to the wall, I carefully climbed the crumbling staircase after him. Through grim hallways, and up even more stairs, we walked in silence. It wasn't until we entered an entirely separate wing of the castle that the Hound halted at a door. Pulling his coat open, he shuffled inside and withdrew a ring of keys. It wasn't lost on me that, while the Hound could have put me in the bedroom next to his, he chose to put me up here.

Far, far away from him.

The door swung in, and the Hound gestured to enter. This room, it seemed, had escaped the ravages of time. Light streamed in wide windows, highlighting the olive panelling and dancing off the gold trim and tassels. An opulent hearth sat against the wall, decorated with vases and figurines. The elegance of it all slowed my steps, and I turned in a circle, trying to admire everything at once. I never imagined staying somewhere so...so rich. I caught sight of the Hound, standing in the doorway, looking awfully smug.

He was pleased with my wonder.

And that pissed me off.

Sticking my nose up, I scowled. "What an attractive prison."

The Hound frowned. "What's your name, girl?"

"Call me a prisoner," I sneered. "For that is what I am."

"As much as I find your theatrics entertaining, I will not disrespect you so." A muscle twitched in the Hound's jaw when he repeated, "Your name: give it to me."

After a short stand off, I mumbled, "Liliwen."

The Hounds lips mimicked, *'Liliwen,'* tasting it for themselves. Silence pressed in on us. I didn't ask his name; I didn't care. He was the Hound, and that's all that mattered. The Hound entered the room, striding until he loomed above me. I reached for my father's knife.

It was gone! Had I lost it? I checked the empty sheath on my belt.

"It's not lost." Back in the doorway, the Hound brandished the knife.

"Give it back!"

"It will be safe in my care," the Hound replied. He held the knife before him, absently turning it in slow revolutions. He'd better hope I didn't get it back; the moment it was in my grasp, I'd stab him right in the—

"This castle is unlike any other, and you will come to learn it well," the Hound said. "I bid you a word of caution, as I can smell the arrogance on you like night soil."

I started, but the Hound continued talking, much louder. "Do not wander, and certainly do not fall asleep outside *this* room." He reached out, drawing a hand along the doorframe. "The architecture has a way of...sensing your nightmares." His hand dropped from the frame, and his tone was serious when he said, "You might fear the Hollow, but I promise you, its inhabitants are sweet children compared to the monsters that stalk these halls."

"The Hollow is filled with dangerous animals," I agreed. "But there is only one so lacking in humanity—consisting of such irredeemable filth—to be deserving of that word, *monster*." I gestured at the surrounding walls. "The same goes for this castle. One monster, worse than the rest." Looking up and down the Hound, I spit, "I'm confident I've met both."

The Hound traced a canine with his tongue.

And he did *not* disagree.

"If this place is as dangerous as you insinuate it is," I snapped, "a gentleman would leave me with a weapon."

As leisurely as one might sip wine, the Hound tucked my father's blade into his jacket. "You don't trust me," he said, "and I don't trust you, and I certainly don't trust you to heed my warning. You look like the type of person who would try something very stupid, at least once. What I do next—I do for your own safety." The Hound left and closed the door behind him. A *click* echoed through the room as the door locked. I bolted over and tried to pry it open. It didn't budge, and I slammed my fist against the wood.

The Hound's muffled voice called, "I will see you in the morning."

Giving up, I circled the room and stood in front of the large windows. A wide balcony lay on the other side. I climbed out and leaned over the railing. Several stories beneath me were the matching gargoyles that guarded the Hound's room. Off to the side, pale pink roses weaved in and out of a thin trellis that carried up the castle. The roses grew all the way up, and the thick canes curled around the balcony railing.

I dragged my finger along a curved thorn.

The Hound would have to try harder to confine me.

"Ow!" Thorns tore my forearms as I descended the world's most painful ladder. When I reached the Hound's balcony, I held my breath, worried even the slightest huff might bring him forth. Thankfully, the curtains didn't stir. Inching down, I leapt from the rose covered trellis. When I hit the ground, I crouched and listened, half-expecting the Hound to appear on his balcony.

He did not.

Dawn hadn't yet broken, and I kept to the early morning shadows. I padded quietly along the grass beside the cobbled path until I hit the veil. My crossbow was still there, just a few paces into the Hollow.

The wolves were gone.

Glancing left and right, I wiped sweat from my palms. Nothing moved in the Hollow; it was almost welcoming.

If you're going to do it, do it now.

I didn't think, didn't give myself a chance to back out. A cold mist washed over me as I sprinted through the veil. The crossbow loomed closer, but a shuffling noise started after me. My arms pumped as I closed in on the weapon. Snarls erupted, and a heavy weight collided with my back. I flew forward, propelled over the crossbow. A thrashing thin wolf skidded along next to me. Twigs and thorns needled my palms as I righted myself and crawled toward the bow. I reached for it—jaws seized my arm.

"AGH!"

Teeth ribboned my sleeve and skin. The wolf thrashed, trying to tear my arm off. I grabbed a rock and clubbed the wolf's snout. It yipped and fell away, just as another wolf nipped my boot. Flipping over, I kicked the wolf. I scrambled up and grabbed the crossbow. I aimed—a broad shoulder pummelled my stomach, and a gust of air left my lungs in a wheeze. My feet left the ground, and the bow tumbled from my grasp. The trees pitched forward as I was thrown over someone's shoulder. All around, wolves encroached.

The Hound's voice growled, "Get back!"

"Let me go!" My lacerated arm spewed blood as I pummelled the Hound's back. A wolf approached, and I screamed, "Watch out!" My world spun with the Hound. He kicked the skulking wolf and sent it sprawling. The Hound's strength was breathtaking, and the crushing grip on my waist dizzied me as he ran for the veil. Drooling mouths lunged for my throat, I punched snouts and teeth. Relief and frustration coursed through me as we passed through the veil.

"Foolish, stupid girl!" The Hound dragged me forward, into his arms. I threw my head sideways—a move I'd learned from Lottie—and smashed the Hound's nose. His head snapped back, and I hit the ground. I rolled away and righted myself, rubbing my bruised rear. Blood poured from the Hound's nose, which he tried staunching with the back of his hand. It was no use; he gave up and spit. Looking suddenly vampiric, blood trickled over the Hound's mouth and dribbled through the opening of his white, flannel shirt. His chest heaved as he gestured at his side, where a splotch of red seeped through his shirt: the crossbow wound reopened.

"Well, that's just marvelous!" he snapped. My own blood dribbled down my arm and splattered the cobblestones. Seeing my mangled limb, the Hound pointed and cried, "I knew it! I knew you'd try some idiotic escape!" He paused, gasping for breath. "Between you and me, I thought you'd be cleverer than this!" He swept a hand toward the wolves. "I'm astonished you managed to do something *so* intolerably stupid! *So* reckless—"

"You know nothing of me!" I shouted. "I won't stand here while a *beast* questions my intelligence!"

The Hound's nostrils flared. "I'm not questioning it!" he snarled. "I'm denying its existence entirely!" He shoved angry tangles of hair from his face and strode forward.

"What're you—" I took a tentative step back.

The Hound continued advancing, I turned and ran. "Don't—where do you think you're going?!" The Hound overtook me, grabbing my good arm and shoving me toward the castle. "Go!" His voice rattled my eardrums and sent birds flying from the nearby trees. Pointing to the castle, the Hound shouted, "Where I can see you. Right now!"

I wrenched my arm from his grasp. "I didn't need your help!"

Standing in shocked disbelief, the Hound started to speak and stopped. He started again, and then snapped his mouth shut. He looked like a silly fish gasping for air.

"I had the crossbow!" I continued. "I shot you; what makes you think I couldn't have done the same to them!" I waved at him, and then the frothing wolves. "Thanks to your meddling, we'll never know!"

The Hound tilted his head, fixing me with a petrifying, unblinking focus. Clenching his fists, the Hound bellowed, "Walk, or I'll throw you back to the wolves!" There was such conviction in his voice, I obeyed. One foot in front of the other, the prisoner walked back to their cage. The Hound, accompanied by his incensed, obnoxious breathing, followed me all the way to the sage room. When we were safely inside, the Hound snapped his fingers and barked, "Show me your arm!"

"Keep your claws off me!" I wriggled from his grasp. The shock from the attack had worn off, and an excruciating ache throbbed up my arm. I had to work fast, before pain altered my capabilities. I cleaned myself with the water skin from my satchel and then crouched by the fire to examine the lacerations. Though he was probably just observing, the way the Hound loomed over me felt...supervisory, and I struggled to see through the rage that tunnelled my vision. With trembling fingers, I sewed the punctures. The Hound watched in a horrified trance as the needle pierced my flesh. I didn't flinch, not even once. I met the Hound's eyes on the last stitch for emphasis.

He scowled in response.

As I tucked my sewing kit away, I caught sight of the blood marring the Hound's shirt. His proud stature had changed, slightly stooped to his right, as if he was expending a great deal of effort not to curl around the flaring pain. Though I couldn't see the wound, I knew what I'd find if I lifted the fabric. The gash in his side, raw and bleeding. The skin around the stitches stretched, like a deer hide spread and hooked for drying. Disgust turned my stomach. Whether I wanted to admit it or not, he tore those stitches while prying me from the jaws of the wolves.

With slow determination, I withdrew my sewing kit. I hated the Hound, but my fingers could not sit idly while any creature—even a beast—suffered. To heal, to ease the agony of others, it was a *compulsion* I couldn't explain. It was for my own benefit, not the Hound's, that I pointed to a chair by the fire and said, "Sit."

The Hound raised his brows and scoffed.

"Fine." I shrugged. "Bleed to death."

Shaking his head, the Hound did as he was told.

"Shirt," I sniped.

The Hound grimaced and leaned into the chair. Through strands of dark hair, his cunning eyes inspected me. One-by-one, the Hound undid his buttons. He watched me as he pulled his shirt away. The muscles along his chest and stomach were well-defined, though he was thin. Like he'd come out of a plague, starved. Kneeling beside him, I ripped out the first stitch and the Hound flinched.

Through gritted teeth, I asked, "What's your nam—"

"Rook." The word slipped out urgently, like one might call for help. The beast *wanted* me to know his name. Perhaps hoped I'd see the man, and not the monster.

Impossible.

After removing the remaining stitches, I said, "One of our neighbours, Colette, used to have a problem with rooks in her orchard." I sewed in a rough stitch, enjoying the Hound's accompanying wince. "They'd steal all the ripe apples just before the harvest..." My words faded into a thoughtful smile. "I think she poisoned them."

Rook gave an absent, disgusted shake of his head. "*Everard* Rook. I prefer Everard. That's what my companions called me"—his brows pulsed bitterly—"when I had companions."

I put in the last stitch and traced my work. I'd done a good job; it would heal well. Tucking my sewing kit away, I said, "I'm all done here, Rook." I stood while he buttoned his shirt. "So, what happens now? Is it your intention to imprison me, forever?"

Rook raised a finger, silencing me. I eyed the digit, and it wasn't a small part of me that considered biting it off. "Now," Rook said, gesturing to his bloodied face and shirt. "I will clean the evidence of your lunacy from my clothes." His gaze travelled from my face to my feet and back. "I suggest you do the same. You look every part the witless swamp dweller that I'm certain you are."

Fortunately, years of arguing with Lottie had hardened me to petty insults. "For someone who kills so freely, I'd have assumed you were accustomed to sitting in blood." I returned the same condescending look Rook had given me. "Or are you upset it's your own blood, hm? Unaccustomed to victims fighting back and spoiling those *pretty* clothes?" Rook pushed to his feet, and I swore the room darkened as he towered over me.

"You know *nothing* of what I'm accustomed to."

Refusing to be intimidated, I snapped, "Tell me then! What is it you do, if not slaughter and trap innocent people in this castle with you?"

"If it were up to me, my loneliness would remain unbroken!" Rook shouted. "I am not your warden, I am your cellmate! Like it or not, I'm trapped here, just as much as you are."

"Liar!" I spit.

Rook recoiled like I'd thrown hot coals on him. I advanced, yelling, "I found you outside the castle!" I pointed through the window, toward the veil. "You can evade the wolves!" Rook's angry, baffled eyes tracked my movements, as if he were viewing some agitated badger, and not someone who had the audacity to speak to him so. Irritated by Rook's silent stare, I shouted, "Well?!"

"You come here, barking questions at me?" Rook's thin finger jabbed his chest with such force the knuckle cracked, and I was fairly certain it broke. "At *me*?!"

Observing the man before me, my words were true when I screamed, "I'm not afraid of you!"

Rook stooped so that his face was a breadth from mine. "Then your idiocy is depthless!" The copper stench of blood hit me, and I covered my mouth. A muscle in Rook's jaw clenched, and he pulled away. "I will return with water, so you might clean yourself."

"I'll do no such thi—"

"This is a castle, not a pen for unwashed livestock," Rook interrupted. "We're trapped here. Together. I will not spend my life recoiling when you draw near." Rook headed to the door but paused. "I am not your jailer; I will not lock you in. If you decide to run like a frightened rabbit into the mouths of the wolves,"—Rook shrugged—"I care not."

Rook closed the door.

A boiling, childlike rage filled me. I looked for anything I might throw. On the fireplace, delicate objects littered the mantle. I snatched a porcelain figurine and—it was too nice. With an angry huff, I put the figurine back. My foot nudged the stand holding the fire implements. I lifted the heavy iron poker from its hook. After nudging around a few logs, I examined the red-hot tip. Heat radiated from the iron; it was nothing compared to the fury burning in my veins. I nestled the poker back in the fire.

And I waited for Rook to return.

Lesson Six

Never bargain.

An impatient knock came at the door. Rook's muffled voice called, "Are you decent?"

"I'm clothed, if that's what you're asking."

The door pushed open, and Rook entered with a bucket. "This is hot—"A wave of smoke trailed the poker that arced through the air. Throwing up a hand, Rook caught the make-shift weapon before it struck him in the nose. Rook's brows furrowed at the soft sizzling coming from his palm.

Shock parted his lips.

"Guhh!" He tore the poker from me and threw it on the floor. The handle bounced and sent the hot end springing into his trousers. Silvery smoke trickled up as the fabric scorched. "Ugh!" Rook slammed the bucket down and snatched the poker.

Anticipating a fight, I raised my fists.

Rook sidestepped me and went to the balcony. After an unintelligible shout, he threw the poker into the air. Impressively, it cleared the veil and disappeared into the far-off trees. Storming back inside, Rook screamed, "Are you mad?!" He held up his hand, where a bubbling welt spread across his palm.

From behind my fists, I shouted, "Tell me how you bypass the wolves!"

Body trembling, Rook's eyes bulged. His shaking hands reached for me, but they stopped, clenching in mid-air. I stuck my chin out, daring him to strike. Rook's breathing quickened, like the panting of a sick animal.

I was so taken, my fists drooped.

"Ugh!" Rook shook his head and refocused on me. Though he still seemed intent upon strangling someone—well, *me*—his hands fell to his sides. With great effort, he whispered, "Wash yourself."

"You'd like that, wouldn't you?"

"Ha!" Rook laughed with such enthusiasm he may as well have spit on me. "You have *nothing* to tempt me." Rook kicked the water bucket. "Let me know if you need anything else. Soap, perfume—an etiquette tutor." Scowling, Rook bent in an exaggerated bow. "For I am just an obedient servant." Rook shot me a nasty glare while he confiscated the remaining fire implements. He paused at the door, leaning back to snatch a decorative bronze pineapple from a side table. He probably thought it could be used to bludgeon someone. Crossing my arms, I stewed in silence.

Why hadn't I thought to hide the pineapple after I'd practiced swinging it?!

"When you resemble a human again," Rook growled, "join me in the hall." On his way out, he slammed the door with such passion, a splinter of wood chipped and bounced along the floor.

I scoured the room for something else I might use as a weapon. The pillows were reasonably heavy, but unless Rook was asleep in the hall, I didn't think they would do the trick. Tucking that idea away for later, I started cleaning myself. I considered not doing it, if only to offend Rook further, but the blood on my arms was beginning to itch. And so, I wiped the grime from my cheeks, picked bits of bracken from my hair, and replaited it. Then I sat on the bed and took my time removing each speck of dirt from beneath my nails. After the better part of an hour, I met Rook in the hall. Leaning on the railing, Rook was so enraged he wouldn't even look at me.

"In regard to your little stunt earlier"—he breathed deeply, reigning his fury—"if you're going to attack someone, you might be certain to land a killing blow the first time." He side-eyed me. "Lest you be hurt in the aftermath of their survival."

Smoothing my trousers, I replied, "I'll keep that in mind next time." Rook shook his head and resumed glaring at nothing. I enunciated every word when I said, "Tell me how you escape."

Beneath Rook's fingers, bits of stone crumbled from the railing. Through gritted teeth, he ground out a, "Follow me."

Bristling against the order, I asked, "Why?"

"Do you want to know how I escape or not?" Rook headed down the stairs. "By all means, remain here with your ignorance." After a moment of annoyed hesitation, I accompanied him. Rook avoided the cracks in the steps. When I came to the same pitfalls, I caught Rook's eyes in various gilded mirrors, watching that I navigated the steps properly. He probably thought me too stupid to trace his path and avoid careening to my death. I fought the urge to push him down the remaining steps.

Rather than head to the foyer, Rook entered his bed chamber. When Rook was wounded, I had no problem entering the room. Now that he was healthy and of sound mind, I hesitated. Rook caught me looking at the bed.

"I assure you," he said, and scoffed. "*You* have nothing to worry about."

I heard his words.

But I *saw* his eyes. They lingered on me, carrying with them the same far-off look I recognized from my own reflection, when I saw beautiful fabrics in a shop window. I longed to reach out, to touch the threads, and always wondered to myself...

How do they *feel*?

Rook batted aside curtains and headed to the balcony, which offered the best view of the path to the veil...and the wolves perched on the other side. Leaning on the railing, Rook said, "You said you found me outside the castle. That's not true. You found the Hound outside the castle." He fidgeted with a bit of lichen on the railing. "When I change... They're fearful of the Hound, the wolves." It struck me, how Rook referred to the Hound in third person, as if he were as separate from the beast as the rest of us.

Rook couldn't fool me.

Escape was the only thing on my mind when I said, "So, you can get me out?" I crossed my arms. "Change into the Hound and scare them off?"

Rook pointed to his wounded side. "Thanks to you, I won't be changing any time soon. Not until this heals up." Perhaps delighted at the thought of my suffering, Rook's voice was pleasant when he said, "You're stuck here."

Our eyes met.

All at once, I realized I couldn't kill Rook. I needed him. I *needed* the Hound to get me out of here. Fury for my father and Lysander burned fresh in my chest. Rage rose up and warmed my cheeks. The pain, the grief, it threatened to possess my body. I resisted the urge to throw myself at Rook. I wanted to bite and punch and maim—but I didn't. I couldn't let Rook know why I was here. If he knew I sought revenge for my father, or his heart to save Lysander, he'd never trust me. And I needed him to trust me.

So, I buried it. The suffering. The agony. I hid it all beneath a timid smile. My intuition told me I could convince Rook to trust me. While his features were warped by feral hostility, he couldn't keep his eyes from wandering back to me. Even when he believed I wasn't paying attention, I caught him in the mirrors, watching. And although the words he uttered were contemptuous, there was an undeniable eagerness in the way he said, "You're stuck here."

You're stuck here...*with me.*

While Rook assured I had nothing to tempt him, I think that was a lie—concocted to protect himself from loneliness and the ravishes of desire.

Could I exploit those feelings?

Under the guise of affection, I might discover Rook's weaknesses, and in doing so, learn how to kill the Hound for good. Once free of this place, I could come back with Lottie and finish the job. My weakness in sparing Rook the first time would not happen again. I was strong, and I would not fail my family a second time.

Unfortunately, my planning was interrupted, betrayed by none other than my own stomach. I couldn't recall the last time I'd eaten even a scrap, and my stomach growled. Loudly.

Rook frowned. "You're hungry."

Who was Rook to tell me what I felt? Crossing my arms, I replied, "I'm fine."

"You don't sound fine."

"I have food in my bag."

"For how long?"

"What?"

"How long can you survive on what you've brought?"

"I don't know, a day or two?"

"That's no good." Rook pointed back the way we'd come. "Walk."

I wanted to spit on Rook and tell him to burn. I resisted. In my sweetest voice I said, "Show me the way." Rook offered a curt nod and left the balcony. There was a lightness in my step as I followed him. For the time being, I'd play nice. Contain my wrath and tell Rook what he wanted to hear. I'd offer civil conversation and false companionship.

I would be Rook's friend...until I held the Hound's heart.

We moved silently across the castle grounds. Rook seemed unaccustomed to small talk; I was simply disinterested in speaking to him. A dark strand of Rook's hair came loose in the wind, and his slender fingers tucked it behind his ear. His presence was calm. As if this was just a normal day, and we weren't prisoners, and he weren't a monster.

Lying was Lottie's strength, not mine. I must confess, I was worried my fear and hatred for the Hound would leave me in a state of vigilance beside Rook. But, as he strode through the grass in his cream flannel shirt and suspenders, Rook seemed so terribly human. We paused at a stream, where a two-step bridge allowed crossing. With a tilt of his head and a wave, Rook indicated for me to go ahead. I did so, and I realized, to my horror and relief, that pretending Rook was an ordinary man...took no effort at all.

We skirted the large pond, and I scanned the bank, looking for anything lurking in the reeds. Arriving at the edge of the trees that backed the castle grounds, Rook entered a small stone hut and returned carrying several baskets. We walked along the wood edge until we approached a bramble of blackberries. Rook plucked a few berries from the bush, and put them in a basket, showing me how it was done.

"Fill this," he said, and handed me the basket.

"Thank you for the demonstration." I picked a berry and dropped it on the ground instead of in the basket. "Oh!" I slapped my forehead. "I'm such a foolish, stupid girl!" Despite Rook's fierce glare, I offered him the basket. "Can you show me again? I think I'll get it this time."

The muscle along Rook's jaw twitched. "I'd appreciate it"—his throat bobbed—"if you lost the attitude."

Wouldn't have one if you weren't such a fuckhead.

"Of course." I smiled. "Apologies."

Rook muttered, "Stay where I can see you," and headed to a grove of trees farther on. Watching Rook walk away, I wanted to run, to flee somewhere he might never see me again.

As my father used to say, the Hollow is no place for a coward.

So, I picked the berries.

When my basket was full, I ate a handful of blackberries and headed to find Rook. Wandering into an apple orchard, I peered around a tree...

"Look at this one," Rook said, appearing from nowhere, and nearly stopping my heart. A suspender slid off his shoulder, he readjusted it and held up an apple the size of his palm. Rook rubbed the fruit along his shirt until it shone. He devoured it with his eyes and murmured, "You'll enjoy it." Rook placed the apple in a basket, already filled to the brim with both apples and pears. It sat next to a sack packed with hazelnuts.

I waved between the baskets. "Surely, this is enough?"

Rook's brows furrowed; he disagreed.

"How much do you think I eat?"

"I don't know," Rook grumbled. "I could easily eat all this."

"Well, you're going to have to. This is too much for me."

Rook frowned. "I can't eat this."

Without thinking, I asked, "What do you eat?" Rook didn't answer. He turned away, but not before his eyes drifted to my throat. That one, subtle glance reminded me that this was not an ordinary day. And that, despite how he presented himself, Rook was not an ordinary man. Rook loaded the baskets onto a carrying pole and heaved it over his shoulders. He turned and walked back to the castle. Like it was a ripe blackberry, I plucked out every ounce of courage from within.

I was going to need it.

After I ate—a pitiful amount, owing to stress and Rook's unblinking stare—Rook showed me around our prison, starting with a room in the cellars. From the diagrams on the walls and the various bottles and experiments littered about, I gathered it was a physician's office. I examined some fruit decaying beneath glass domes. Each dome had a hastily scribbled date beneath it.

Wait.

The experiment in front of me bore this year's date, but one across the table was dated fifty years ago. The numbers were all scribbled in the same rough penmanship. "Hold on," I said, and pointed to the label. "Did you date these?" After leaning over to look, Rook nodded. "How long have you been trapped here?"

"The day I stumbled into the castle..."—Rook's face scrunched, calculating—"that was seventy-five years ago."

My jaw dropped and I blurted, "You can't die?"

Rook's eyes narrowed.

Don't sound so disappointed, you fool!

"You're immortal?" I asked, with enthusiasm.

Whether he believed my enthusiasm or not, Rook said, "I don't age, on account of my...affliction." Affliction was an interesting word choice. Pneumonia, leprosy—those were afflictions. Turning into a flesh-eating beast? That was an affront to humanity. "Though," Rook continued, "I've had enough brushes with death to know I'm not immortal. I heal quicker than humans, but I will die one day." He wiped a bit of dust from the table and muttered, "Killed, most likely."

Whew.

I inspected an intricate diagram of a hand. "If you're a physician, why'd you let me stitch you up?" I pointed to the sketch. "It looks like you know a lot more than I do."

"Decades have come and gone since I've felt another's touch." A lively spark quirked Rook's cheek. "And you were *quite* forceful." An unwelcome blush came over me, and I looked away. Appalled at my own reaction, I left Rook's words hanging in the air, unacknowledged. Instead, I pretended to examine a rotting melon, fuzzy and white with mold. "Anyway," Rook continued. "These sketches... They're remnants of a time before me. I'm no physician." He gestured to the empty room. "If I can't mend myself, who will?"

I suppose he had point.

Rook said, "I was a woodcutter before...well, *before*." Rook waited for me to tell him what I did; I ignored the expectation, instead examining more rotten fruits. Rook stooped below a table, drawing up a leather bag. Inside were medical instruments of all sorts. Rook withdrew a pair of forceps and clacked them together. "These objects, they're imbued with memories for procedures and recipes." Rook shoved the bag forward. "See for yourself." I rummaged in the bag and found something that looked like a sewing needle with a sort of plunger on the end. The needle tingled, like a heatless flame crackling against my fingers.

"Close your eyes," Rook began, "invite the memory in." He closed his eyes in another unnecessary demonstration, and I considered throwing the needle at him while he wasn't looking. Instead, I took a deep breath, and let the needle speak to me.

Rook fell away, and the room came alive. Women rushed around, passing through me as if I weren't there at all. A fair-haired, freckled woman barked orders while filling the very needle I held. She flicked the needle, and droplets dislodged from the tip.

"Hold him firm," she ordered.

A nurse, a strapping fellow, did as he was told. Everyone descended on a man lying on the table that held Rook's experiments. The woman in charge plunged the needle into a festering wound along the man's neck. He hardly reacted. Sweat poured from his forehead; his eyes lulled.

He wore the same waxen look as Lysander.

I snapped out of the memory and steadied myself against the table. The room, absent of rushing women, suddenly felt empty. "They used these methods to treat the person in that memory." Rook nodded at the needle and ran his hands along the domed fruits. "I used to think I could make something from these—cure my affliction."

I could think of only *one* cure for Rook's affliction.

I kept it to myself.

"But that was a long time ago," Rook muttered. "I keep these going out of habit, rather than a belief they'll benefit me." A fresh gloom set over Rook as he slid the bag beneath the table. "I suppose my efforts are wasted on such trivial pursuits."

For a fleeting moment, Rook reminded me of my own mother. Though my father was long dead, she still lit the back lanterns every night. He'd tripped once, when we were young, twisted his ankle on the back path. Every night after, my mother rushed home to light the lanterns. And every night still. It was a painful reminder that our minds are clever, and they lose hope easily—but our bodies, where our hearts beat strong, do not so readily forget.

We find ourselves lighting lanterns for someone long lost.

"I'll show you the rest of the castle," Rook mumbled. We left the office, but as Rook climbed the stairs, something caught my eye. Off the main hall, a door sat slightly ajar. Curiosity slowed my steps, and I leaned to peer inside. The hurried scuffing of boots startled me. Rook, who'd abandoned stealth, snapped, "Don't go in there!" and yanked the door closed.

"Why not?"

"Because I said so!" He pointed up the stairs. "After you."

The door had no lock. Though I smiled, I made a note to return later.

Upstairs, dread filled my belly as Rook headed to the door beneath the stairs. I had no mind to be in the presence of the great tree again. Thankfully, Rook stopped at the door, his palm raised. He didn't touch it, as if whatever lay beyond might leech through the wood and wound him.

Without so much as a blink, he said, "If any of my warnings stick, let it be this one: Through this door is the most dangerous part of the castle." My gaze drifted to the door. Though it remained closed, I could still see all the way to the courtyard. See the tree poised in the centre.

Did the branches reach for me?

"You believe I'm the worst thing in this castle," Rook said, tapping his chest. "I'm not—it's that *fucking* tree." Pointing at the door, he added, "This prison is poison, and that's the centre of it." Phantom pain flared in my hands, where the fruit had burned my fingers.

What if I'd eaten it?

I saw a vision of myself, lying at the tree's roots, with eyes like glass and a trickle of foam spilling from my mouth. Or worse, decaying while I lived, like the rotting raven, who'd likely feasted on the fruit.

Rook licked his lips, a nervous gesture I sometimes noticed from Lysander. "I know you'll want to, specifically because it was *me* who told you not to, but don't go in here—and don't ever touch that tree." Even if I knew nothing of Rook's character, I knew fear. If the Hound was frightened of what lay behind that door, so was I.

I nodded.

Rook wiped his palm along his shirt and headed for the stairs, completely ignoring the library. Truly, this was the only room I was interested in, and I blurted, "You're not going to show me the library?"

"I don't go in there," Rook said, and scowled at the library with nearly as much disdain as he did the door below the stairs.

"Why not?" I asked, immediately going in there. Despite his distaste, Rook trailed me. I plucked a book from the shelf and opened it. I cradled the spine like it was a newborn.

Rook snatched the book and uttered a shocked, "You can read?!"

"Oh, yes." I grabbed for the book, which Rook raised above his head. "Top of my class. Of course, that was amongst all the other witless swamp dwellers."

"Teach me."

Angry refusal blossomed in my chest. I jumped and snatched the book. Before I could tell Rook to 'get stuffed', my indignation gave way to understanding.

Rook couldn't read.

That's why he didn't come in here.

"Yes," Rook said, confirming my suspicion. "Another item on my vast list of shortcomings, I suppose." If I wasn't trying my best to feign kindness, I might have asked Rook whether he listed illiteracy above or below murder. Walking through the library, Rook glared at the endless tomes. "They sit upon the shelves and, oh, how they mock me!"

When I looked at the towering rows of books, I saw freedom. In books, my mind was quiet, and I could escape, even if only for a short while. To

Rook, they were useless. What torture it must have been to sit amongst so many books for decades, unable to read a single sentence.

Perhaps I could use that to my advantage.

I slid the book back. "I'll teach you to read," I said, catching Rook's attention, "*if* you help me get home."

The request hardly left my mouth before Rook shook his head. "It's too dangerous; the wolves will rip you to shreds."

Heat flared up my neck and I shouted, "I don't care!" Rook straightened, and I continued, more evenly, "If you promise to help me get home, I'll teach you to read."

The outburst betrayed me, and Rook crossed his arms. "What awaits you there?"

I reached out, brushing dust from a shelf. "My brother... He has a sweating sickness," I lied. My eyes stung, and I refused to meet Rook's gaze, refused to show him any further weakness. "He doesn't have much time; I *must* get back to him." When Rook didn't answer, I glanced back. The power of the bargain belonged to him. If I refused to help Rook read, not much would change. But if he refused to help me escape, Lysander would die. Rook stroked his chin, pondering the deal. Fear choked me. Surely, Rook would refuse.

Rook touched the books, mumbling, "I reckon there might be a cure for my affliction amongst these pages, and I'd never know it, trapped here by my own ignorance."

Excruciating seconds ticked by.

Rook nodded to himself.

Slowly, but deliberately, Rook crossed the library. With each step, the anger that distorted his features slipped away. By the time Rook reached me, compassion had softened the hard lines along his face. Offering me a hand, he whispered, "Teach me to read, and I swear, when I can change again, I'll help you escape." I pondered the deal. Was there a loophole I hadn't considered? Should I specify that I must be alive when I got home? Rook stooped, snapping me out of indecision. "You will see your brother again," he whispered. "I promise."

Maybe there was a shred of humanity left in the beast after all?

I reached for Rook's hand like one might pull a kettle from the fire, hesitant and wary of scorching. We shook, and when it came time to part, Rook's grasp remained. I noticed a silver bracelet, wrought and twisted like thorns, wrapping his wrist. In all the stress of saving his life, I hadn't noticed it. It reminded me of the iron-cuffs I'd seen criminals placed in. The cuff was hideous, though his hand was not. It was muscular and lean, bearing all the benefits of having spent many years wielding an axe.

Rook cleared his throat.

Mortified, I snatched my hand away.

"Come," Rook said. "Teach me."

"Ask me nicely."

Rook paused, turning back to me. One eyebrow raised, silently asking, *'Pardon me?'*

"You heard me." I crossed my arms. "Surely, you possessed some manners before you stumbled in here. If you want to be taught, you'll treat me with the same respect as any teacher."

Rook's eye twitched.

Deal's off.

At Rook's side, his fist clenched.

He's going to change and eat you. He'll get blood all over these lovely books. Glancing at the nearest shelf, I stepped away.

Rook inhaled and I cringed.

This is it.

"I would be forever indebted to you," Rook began, "if you might teach me to read."

"That's a statement," I said, pushing my luck. "Not a question."

Rook's lips parted. Whether the look on his face was bewilderment or admiration, I didn't know. "Liliwen," Rook said, his teeth barely opening to let my name out. "Will you *please* teach me to read?"

"Of course. Thank you for asking!"

While some part of me toyed with the idea of having him call me *Master*, like the schoolchildren used to call Mother—Master Liliwen had quite the ring to it—I figured I'd better not push my luck again. I slipped a book from the shelf and motioned for Rook to sit. Rook turned and headed to a small writing desk beside the fireplace. I had to admit, I felt some relief. Rook hadn't faltered, had looked me in the eye and promised I would see Lysander again.

It might be foolish, but I believed him.

I took the seat opposite Rook, setting the book between us. I just had to do this one thing. Teach Rook to read. Gain my freedom. That didn't sound so bad. I mean, how hard could it be to teach someone to read?

Lesson Seven

People will show you who they are;
you need only watch.

Hard.

There was a reason I worked alone. To say I didn't have a teacher's patience would be a terrible understatement. After we staggered through letters, and stumbled through the basics, I couldn't help but think Lysander would be so much better at this. He was so patient, and good-humoured, and it was really my thinking of Lysander that kept me trudging onward, but after Rook made the same mistake four times in a row, I shouted, "It's almost like you don't want to learn!"

"It's almost like you don't want to leave," Rook mocked, sitting back in his chair. "I'll never learn anything with these dreadful teaching methods." He crossed his arms. "Perhaps you do not love your brother?"

I slammed the book shut. "We're done!"

Rook flinched, only slightly. When he spoke next, it was soft. The way one might speak if they were caught behaving poorly. "We'll take a break," he corrected.

My response was an unamused grunt.

Rook leaned forward and drummed his fingers on the desk. He looked around the library, and then at me, as if he were unsure of what to do next.

He rapped again, an annoying, repetitious thrumming that drew all my focus.

When I could take it no longer, I hissed, "Will you sto—"

"Come, I have something to show you."

Rook led me out to the veranda, and we descended the crumbling steps. He walked down a path around the side of the castle, until we came to a gigantic mass of brown hedges. An unkept archway led into the decaying bushes, and I realized immediately what it was.

A hedge maze.

I paused at the entrance, between the tall hedges. Rook coughed and said, "Um. Hold on. If you'll just..." He walked along the hedge and turned a corner. His head reappeared. "Come." I rolled my eyes at the command but did as he wished. Around the corner, a large hole was torn through the outer hedge.

I peered in. To my surprise, holes were torn through all the walls, in a neat line. "Defeats the purpose of a maze, no?"

"Well..." Rook rubbed his neck. "The first time I went in, I got lost and couldn't find the way out and, uh..." He threw up his hands. "Well, I panicked."

A laugh sputtered out of me. As if he'd forgotten the sound of joy, Rook bristled. I bit my lip. Fake laughs were allowed; *real* laughs were not. Rook smiled—it was uneven and crooked, owing to the scar—but a smile nonetheless. Whether Rook enjoyed my laughter or delighted in knowing he was the cause, I wasn't sure.

Seemingly lost in his thoughts, Rook waved to the maze in an *'after you'* gesture.

One-by-one, I crawled through jagged holes. I scanned left and right, terrified of what creatures might call the rotting maze home.

Behind me, Rook murmured, "I'm here."

Knowing exactly where Rook was, I snapped, "Yes, I know," with no small amount of irritability. It was only after my remark that I realized Rook had meant it to be comforting, to ease my wary looks. Somehow, I found that thought even more annoying. I hastened through the hedges, eager to get this over with. Stepping through the final hedge, I was struck with such vibrancy that my irritations simmered.

Within the centre of the dying hedges lay a small park. Patches of green shamrocks kissed my boots while I walked. Three trees with pale lilac buds rose up, a remarkable reminder of life in the centre of the rotting maze. Petals wafted in the breeze, landing at my feet.

What a lovely dye they would make.

With great difficulty, I resisted the urge to scoop up the petals and stuff them in my pockets. Rook would certainly have questions, and I wanted him to know less about me, not more. As I paused beneath the shadow of the trees, enjoying the delicate scent, a trilling *coo* drew my attention upward. Turquoise peacocks sat amongst the branches. I'd only ever read about them, and I hurried forward. I craned, trying to glimpse them better.

Suddenly beside me, Rook said, "Here."

Cupping one hand below mine, he withdrew something from his pocket. Carefully, Rook dropped a fistful of seeds into my palm. More trills echoed above, and in a flurry of iridescent feathers, the peacocks flew down. Their heads bobbed as they gathered around, and I knelt, offering seeds. The bravest peacock pecked me, and I drew away, startled. I mustered my courage and thrust my hand back. In no time at all, five peacocks surrounded me, each taking turns pecking my palm.

Rook knelt, but I paid him no mind. I marvelled at the feathers splayed across the ground, each one tipped with a brilliant emerald eye. I scanned the area, hoping for discarded feathers. Perhaps, when Rook wasn't looking, I could tuck a few beneath my shirt. Rook followed my eyes as they searched the ground but said nothing. He picked a shamrock and fiddled with it. To my disappointment, I didn't see a single feather. I focused on the peacocks, trying to memorize the colours and patterns. Maybe, one day, I could create something half as beautiful as them. A gown with skirts trailing along the ground like their remarkable feathers...

"Why were you hunting the Hound?" Rook asked.

"Hm?" I mumbled, still fixating on the feathers.

"In the Hollow," Rook said, "why were you out there, hunting the Hound?"

Reluctantly, I turned from the peacock. I collected my thoughts, and said, "A friend of mine... You've been massacring his goat herd. I was merely taking care of a pest." A lie, sprinkled with shards of truth.

"I don't eat goats," Rook mumbled and plucked the leaves from his shamrock. "Were they a *close* friend?"

"Hm?"

"Were you *close* with him?" Rook's eyes flicked up, watching me. "The man you nearly killed me for?"

I brushed seeds from my palms. "Why?"

Rook shrugged and muttered, "I'm just making conversation."

I wanted to know why he thought it was any of his business, asking after my friends, close or not. *Be friendly!* My thoughts screamed. *We need him to trust us!*

"He's *just* a friend."

Rook tossed his leafless shamrock aside. "Do you...have family?" he prodded. "Besides your brother?"

I frowned, wondering how truthful I should be. "A mother. And sister."

"Father?"

"He..." My throat seized. With great difficulty, I said, "He died, a few years back."

"I'm sorry."

Sniffling, I glanced away. "I won't lose my brother too."

"Shall we get back to it?" Rook suggested. I nodded and stood. Wearing a pained grimace, Rook did too. Before I could leave, Rook held up a peacock feather. Delicate fronds floated on the wind.

After a long pause, I took the feather.

Rook and his crooked smile disappeared through the hedges.

Through the library windows, the sky was black. Rook and I sat across from one another at the writing desk. In the dim firelight, I squinted at the text. Rook seemed to have no problem reading in the shadows. We'd spent the afternoon trudging through a collection of fairytales. I'd asked Rook to choose his favourite and do his best to re-read it out loud. He'd chosen a dark, but romantic tale, about a girl from a far-off land and her lover. Though no one knew what became of them in the end, they lived on in local folklore.

I hadn't told Rook it was my favourite as well.

Rook read aloud of a magnificent ball, with beautiful gowns and dancing. I didn't tease him when he stumbled over a word several times, just repeated it correctly. Rook glanced at me, to my chin slumped against my palm. After the conversation about Lysander, I hadn't been in the mood for banter.

Rook closed the book. "We should stop for the night."

I yawned and pushed back my chair. As I rounded the desk, I noticed a lacquered box on the mantle. Made of warm cherry wood, it was quite like one owned by my mother, a relic from her well-off childhood. Wondering if this box operated the same way, I walked over and tipped open the lid.

A plunky melody filled me with nostalgic joy. Memories of slipping on my mother's pretty jewelry returned to me. And the pretending! Pretending I was somewhere far from the responsibility and the stress—even then.

Rook cleared his throat.

I turned and found him standing before me. So still, like the tall shelves behind him. With deadly focus, he offered me his hand.

"Dance with me."

Staring at his hand, a voice in my head hissed, *Bite it!* A second, more reasonable voice, whispered, *Take it!*

Forcing a creaky smile, I placed my hand in Rook's. He led me to the centre of the library and slid an arm around my back. Careful not to let our bodies touch, I mirrored his steps while we danced.

"My father could play the vielle, and he insisted I learn to dance," Rook said. "I didn't appreciate it at the time but..." He lowered his voice. "Well, sometimes you don't realize you miss something until it's taken away." My response was a grim nod. Was it really dancing Rook missed so terribly? In my hand, Rook's thumb brushed my finger.

A dance was rarely performed alone.

"Despite my lack of enthusiasm," Rook continued, "I was voted the best dancer in our village."

I snorted. "Were you the *only* dancer?" Rook spun me away, and when he brought me back, I thudded his chest with an indelicate, "Oof!"

"There were three of us, thank you." Rook laughed a deep rumbling laugh that vibrated his chest and tickled my back. "Although, Yannick fell from his horse the day prior and had an awful limp." Rook twirled me to face him. We swayed, and I shied away from Rook's curious eyes, which reflected faintly in the dim light. Even in my periphery, his eyes arrested my thoughts.

The lightest blue, like a cloudless sky against the summer wheat.

"Actually," Rook started. "I remember the night of the festival well. Our neighbour's son had a dog, a real mutt. It was big. Might have been half-wolf. Anyway, that night, the dog wandered into the Hollow. Well, of course, you probably know more than anyone what that meant for the dog. The child was beside himself." Rook sighed. "I figured I'd just have a look, not go too far in, especially at night. I knew it was stupid, but I was young. And the child had lost his mother the winter prior and..."

Frustration scrunched Rook's nose, and he muttered, "I just wanted to see if I could find the dog." Rook swayed, pulling me gently with him while we danced. "And, wouldn't you know, I found it! Poor thing got stuck in a bear trap." Rook shook his head. "I freed it—but it lashed out." Rook winced, as if receiving the bite to his cheek all over again. "Anyway, the dog lived. Though, I feared my mother would discover it maimed me and butcher it herself. I told everyone I'd tripped and fallen on a rake." Rook chuckled. "I was a clumsy child. They believed it."

Rook danced with such elegance, his movement smoother than a stream. If you told me he was clumsy, I'd have called you a liar. We continued dancing; I offered nothing of my childhood. In my silence, my thoughts wandered to Lysander. The pain must have shown—must have yanked the corners of my lips into a frown—because Rook said, "I'm sorry you're trapped here, and I'm sorry about your brother. Truly." Rook's hand traced a soft circle along my back, and my chest brushed his.

Somewhere between steps, we'd drifted closer.

"Thank you," I murmured. We turned in another lazy circle, and I found the courage to look—to see the sympathy softening Rook's eyes. Before I knew what was happening...I smiled.

Rook tripped.

He recovered, but stepped on my toes as he righted himself. Blushing, he put a fist to his mouth and said, "I apologize for my missteps. I haven't done this in a very long time."

I thought about the last time I'd danced. "It's been awhile for me too..." I trailed off as Rook spun me away. I spun back into his arms—*it was my father.*

Twinkling lights sparkled in the rafters above, and people danced all around. The barn was alive with laughter and music. "To the happiest couple!" Ruven's father shouted, hugging his eldest son and his beloved.

Ruven's eldest brother's wedding.

That was the last time I'd danced. My father had laughed and spun me away. He'd smelled of sandalwood and mead. I remember the way his calloused hand felt in mine.

Shaking away the memory, I released Rook and stumbled back. I covered my mouth, and an unstoppable wave of tears burst forth.

An aghast Rook sputtered, "Was I really that terrible?"

I stared at him, at the monster who'd taken my father.

What am I doing?

"I..." I clenched my eyes, humiliated. "I—I have to go," I said and ran from the library. I didn't stop until I was safely in the sage room. Crumpling into an old chair before the fire, I held my head.

Grief is a fickle thing. Most days, it gets easier. But every so often, a smell or some memory drags us back into the arms of our loved one. Time or distance can't protect us; in those memories, we lose them again and again.

And some days, it doesn't get easier.

As I sat with my grief and my guilt, a boot shuffled along the stone steps outside the room. I ignored it—and the gentle knock on the door.

For there was no more space at the fire.

Lesson Eight

Bodies of water are called so for a
reason.

A gentle rapping, like a crow cracking a chestnut, woke me. I blinked awake as another *rap-rap-rap* sounded on my chamber door. Yawning, I slid from the warm sheets. When I opened the door, Rook withdrew his hand, ready to rap again.

"Walk with me," he commanded. Tired of receiving orders, I crossed my arms. Rook's eyes travelled along my arms, wrapped so tightly around my body that nothing might breach them. "I mean..." Rook's throat bobbed. He looked as if someone had just asked him an important question, the answer to which was completely unknown to him, and his only option was to guess. With uncertainty, he said, "*Will you*...walk with me?"

"I'm not in the mood."

Rook produced a basket from behind his back. "Might I tempt you?" I didn't budge. Rook eased the basket forward, gently nudging my arms. My stomach growled, and I sighed.

"Let me get dressed."

Sitting out on the lawn, we watched the sun rising over the pond. Beside me, Rook leaned back on his elbows. As the light skimmed the water, it shone warmly on his cheeks and the swath of chest peeking through his flannel shirt. Cracking a hazelnut, I asked, "When was the last time you ate?"

"A few nights ago." He scrunched an eye against the sun as he looked at me. "Calf."

"How long until you have to eat again?"

"Weeks."

"Really? You don't get hungry for weeks?"

Rook frowned. "I'm always hungry."

"Oh, I see."

"I don't enjoy it."

I nodded and ate quietly.

"Did you sleep okay?" Rook asked.

I shrugged, and an uncomfortable silence passed. I realized it was my turn to speak. "And you?"

"A little trouble falling asleep, but I'll admit, once I'm out, I sleep like the dead." Rook laughed. "My mother always worried if there was a fire, I'd sleep right through it and into the next life."

Rook fell silent.

His confession—freely admitting a weakness I might use against him—sent excitement rushing through me. Though, as Rook's shoulder's slumped, the thrill melted into something I was not expecting.

Guilt.

Rook reminded me of Old Prunetta, who'd lost her partner fifty years ago. So desperate for conversation and connection, Prunetta's words often tumbled freely from her lips. I recalled a time when she'd admitted to possessing a "dreadful lack of bowel control" without a shred of embarrassment or remorse. I'm not implying she should be embarrassed—it is a natural human function—but it's an odd response to "How are you today?" Sometimes, when Rook spoke, he displayed that same eagerness for the opportunity to talk and be listened to. But, while Prunetta was shameless in her sharing, the moment the words left Rook, he wore a downcast look of regret. Almost as if he were cursing himself for divulging information, simply because he might be lonely.

And he was right to curse his tongue, for I couldn't unhear his admission of weakness.

The breeze picked up, blowing our hair and carrying the scent of spring peonies. Memories of happier times encouraged a soft sigh from somewhere deep within me. I twisted, searching for the source. Sure enough, fat, pink blooms dotted the overgrown garden behind us.

Rook's brows furrowed, asking a silent question.

Though I was reluctant to offer him more information than was necessary, brief joy loosened my tongue. "Peonies were my father's favourite. When he was alive, he filled the back garden with them." I frowned. "They aren't useful; you can't eat them or use them for healing. Ours haven't bloomed in many years." Absently, I stroked the golden inscription on my cloak. "I hadn't realized how much I missed them."

A cry rang out from the trees across the pond. Rook and I stilled, staring into the woods. The cry came again, a pained, frantic screech.

"What is it?" I whispered.

"Some poor creature being devoured, I imagine." Rook stood and brushed off his trousers.

"Should we help it?"

"I'm more concerned with what's eating it." Rook pointed to the ground. "Stay here. I'll be right back." Rook walked along the water's edge. I sat back amongst the grass as he disappeared into the trees. I looked back at the pond—a pale creature froze at my feet, its gangly arms flexed from pulling itself up the bank.

The creature and I stared at one another, frozen.

It resembled a person, but waterlogged and fleshy, with dark, unblinking eyes. To my horror, the thing smiled. Tiny, fishlike teeth poked at jagged angles from its mouth. Broken from my spell, I cried out for the only person who might help me.

"ROOO—"

The creature lunged.

I tossed the basket at it, sending nuts and apples bouncing. Unbothered, the creature grabbed my boot. I kicked and it released me with a wet hiss. I crawled away but fingers curled in my hair and yanked me back. "Agh!" I slammed into the ground, and the creature began dragging me toward the lake. "ROOK!" I pried at the fingers wrapped in my hair, but they were granite. I struggled to regain my footing, but my feet slipped as I was heaved down the bank. Up above, the pale sky passed quickly as the water edged closer. I scratched the creature's arms, felt its skin rip and tear beneath my nails—it didn't let go. The inevitable *splash* rang out and I gulped air just as cold water shocked me. Though I fought to rise, the creature kept me submerged. I wrenched my eyes open; the blurry monster wore a wide, menacing smile. I hammered the hand curled around my throat, but my movement was useless, slowed by the water. Fire radiated through my lungs, but I could do nothing.

The edge of my vision darkened.

So many faces appeared as my struggling weakened. My father and mother, together, as they always would be. Lottie, with her tangled hair. Lysander, not sick and dying, but alive and happy.

I failed all of you.

As the last of my strength slipped away, Rook visited me. *What are you doing here?* I thought, surprised to find comfort in his sharp, blue eyes.

Bubbles erupted from the creature's mouth in a choking spray, ripping me back to the present. Crimson water swirled like murky ink and the grip loosened on my neck. Through the cloudy water, I caught sight of a hand protruding through the creature's chest. The hand withdrew, leaving a bloody hole in its place. Strong arms wrapped around me and yanked me up.

I gasped as I broke the surface. Grass cushioned me and Rook's terrified face appeared.

"Are you injured?!"

My response was a sputtering cough that sent water at Rook. He wiped his face and rounded on the pond. Pushing to his feet, Rook loomed at the edge. His chest heaved as he stared at the creature, who'd retreated safely into the pond. Already, the gaping hole in the thing's breast was shrinking.

"Touch her again and I'll rip your *fucking* heart out!"

The creature did not acknowledge Rook's threat, only slid noiselessly beneath the surface. Rook turned a scowling gaze all around, lingering on the far away trees. Only when he was certain nothing approached did he kneel next to me. Blood dribbled down Rook's arm in watery rivulets. My instinct was to lean away, but I remembered the terror as the monster clutched my throat, knowing I would die. And surely, I would have, had Rook not come along and tore me from the creature's claws. I made no protest as Rook rubbed my back. Soaking wet, a chill settled on me, and I shivered.

Rook directed my face to his. After an examination of my trembling lips, he said, "Let's get inside."

"I'm f-f-fine!" I chattered.

"No, you're n-n-not," Rook chattered back. "Up." Rook helped me. I rubbed my arms as we walked back to the castle.

"Would you like me to...?" Rook reached out. His arms looked awfully warm, and I was so terribly cold...

I shook my head and responded with a curt, "No."

When we made it back to the castle, I tried to head up to my room. Blocking my path, Rook pointed below the stairs, to the kitchens. "They have the largest fireplace." Reluctantly, I followed Rook into the belly of the castle. A fire started, and Rook moved a wooden chair before the large hearth. He ordered me to stay put, then wandered off. I scooched closer to the fire, sapping as much heat as I could.

Rook returned, setting dry clothing on the butcher's block. He knelt and asked, "How are you feeling?"

"I'm fine," I mumbled. "Just tired."

Rook glanced at my lips and frowned. "You're blue." He stood, pulling me with him. "Take off your clothes."

Blinking back at him, I slurred, "What?"

"Your wet clothes—remove them." I crinkled my nose, but Rook continued, "Look." He tapped the dry clothes. "Put these on."

I tried to undo the cloak button at my throat, but my hands trembled. "Let me." Rook's quick fingers undid the button, and my cloak fell away. I stripped off my wet shirt and tossed it aside, then my trousers. Standing in only my soaked undergarments, I hesitated.

Rook stared at my chest, at the transparent fabric that clung to every goosebump on my breasts. Slowly, *hungrily*, Rook's gaze fell lower. An unexpected rush of excitement fluttered through me. It made me feel powerful, to have him there, watching me.

Wanting me.

Perhaps guided by my desire to torture him further or some other, unknown compulsion, I stripped off my wet bandeau. It fell to the ground with a wet *plop!* Gazing at my breasts, a muscle twitched along Rook's jaw.

His starved eyes met mine.

It was only when I bent to slide my underwear off that he turned his back to me. He cleared his throat and said, "I'll give you some privacy then."

"Suit yourself. Would you hand me those?"

Rook mumbled a distracted, "Hm?" and peered over his shoulder. "Oh, hm. Yes." He grabbed the clothes and blindly handed them over.

I unfurled the clothes and scowled. "What's this?" I held a slinky olive gown. The quality of the fabric—a soft silk—was stunning. I savoured it between my fingers, but the cut—there was no modesty in it. "You couldn't find trousers?"

"I don't know." Rook turned so I saw the side of his face. "I just grabbed whatever I could from the first room I came to."

His smirk suggested otherwise.

I brought the silk to my cheek. I'd only ever heard stories of the silk farmers from far away and the ladies who wore the most intricate gowns. In a million lifetimes, I never thought I'd *wear* a silk gown.

"Well, it's hideous," I lied.

Rook muttered something about "ungrateful" and crossed his arms. As I admired the way Rook's shoulders looked from behind, I kept coming back to one thought: He'd saved my life. A reasonable part of me knew it was a selfish thing. Rook was lonely, and if I were gone, he would be alone once more. But again, my thoughts circled back to...*he saved my life.*

"It's a good thing you aren't afraid of the water," I said, wiggling the dress over my hips. "Or else I'd be cold and dead by now." The dress clung to me like a second skin, and I felt dreadfully exposed.

"I'm terrified of that pond," Rook admitted.

"You are?"

The back of his head bobbed. "Can't swim to save my life." I slid a pair of slippers on; they were *so* soft. Rook asked, "Are you clothed?"

"Mhm."

Rook turned around. He admired me and I fidgeted, smoothing the dress. Why was I uncomfortable now, when only moments ago I'd been naked and brave? Hoping to divert Rook's attention, I said, "Thank you...for saving me." My diversion didn't work at all. While Rook nodded his welcome, he would not—perhaps *could not*—look away.

Why did my cheeks burn so?

Rook pushed a hand through his hair. Unbound from all the scuffling, it fell in a dark mess around his face. "It's been a long time since I've felt that way."

Wary of his answer, I asked, "What way?"

"Afraid."

Silence settled between us. Though I'd been collecting Rook's weaknesses like fireflies in a tiny jar, this admission struck me. I wished I might unhear it. Certainly, my mind could. But my heart swallowed it whole, devoured the words and their intention. Rook stepped closer. His eyes flitted to my lips, and he murmured, "Your lips are still blue."

Rook's lips were perfect, supple things... The fire popped, and we tensed. Rook laughed anxiously and rubbed my arms. "May I?" He leaned forward, and I didn't resist as he wrapped around me. His hand nestled at the crook of my neck and held me. As if I couldn't stop them, my arms curled around Rook's waist.

Rook's chin settled in my hair.

Tread carefully, my mind warned. *Play your part too well, and he may never let you leave this place.* I ignored the warning, instead listening to

Rook's fluttering heartbeats. I closed my eyes and was reminded of beating wings, of a bird taking flight.

Tread carefully.

In Rook's arms, it didn't take long for me to warm.

"Would you like me to draw you a bath?"

"No." I hiked up my hem and continued up the stairs. "We should get back to reading."

"Are you sure?" Rook's voice floated after me. "I don't want you to push yourself. You've had a challenging day."

"I just got wet!" I cried. "I'm perfectly fine!"

"The Lady of the Lake nearly killed you," Rook mumbled. I ignored him and climbed into the foyer. Rook rushed around, blocking my path. "Would you like to take another walk? We must keep your temperature up; I don't want you to catch a cold." I gave Rook a stare I usually reserved for Lottie. He conceded and stepped aside. Continuing into the library, I wondered:

Why was Rook so intent on delaying our lessons?

At the writing desk, I went to pull my chair back, but Rook was there, already sliding it from beneath the desk. He motioned for me to sit, and after a wary glance, I did. Rook took his place across from me. A book lay between us; I opened it and pushed it toward him.

Pushing it back, Rook said, "Can you read to me?"

"No. I want you to try."

"Please," Rook said. "Read to me." There was something...different about his manner. Though I couldn't put my finger on it, I *felt* it in my stomach. "I like hearing you," he encouraged. "It helps me learn."

"Fine." Raising one finger, I said, "A single page. Then you're taking over." I picked up the book, a historical tale from hundreds of years ago, and cleared my throat. "Long ago, there was a corrupt queen who held dominion over her people, and her daughter." Above the book, I caught sight of Rook. His chin rested in his palm, staring at me. Doing my best to ignore him, I backtracked. "And her d-daughter," I stuttered, unable to focus. I closed the book on my thumb and said, "Can you stop looking at me?"

Rook laughed and waved at the room. "Where else would you have me look?"

"I don't care," I mumbled and reopened the book. As I started reading again, Rook's gaze drifted to the windows. It became very clear that, though Rook's body was present, his mind was elsewhere. "Rook," I started. "Are you listening?"

"Are you hungry?" he deflected.

"No—Rook!" I snapped. "Can you focus?"

Rook's eyes adopted a mischievous squint. He leapt up and said, "I must do laundry."

"You what?!"

"Laundry. Did you see your clothes? We must clean the pond scum. If it sets, you'll never get it out." Rook headed toward the door. I stared after him, jaw slack. "I could use your help," he called.

Just off the pond, a stream trickled through the ancient trees of the castle wood. Beneath the canopy, amongst the bird song and hum of insects, I leaned against a proud oak. Though the stream was shallow, I watched the banks, afraid to be snatched again. A pile of discarded clothing lay next to Rook, where he bent over a washboard at the edge of the stream. Tearing off his own shirt, he tossed it in the water and dragged the white flannel along the board. I tried not to stare; I didn't want to give him the satisfaction, though it was difficult not to track his arms as they drew up and down the washboard.

"You could help," Rook called.

Being the eldest, and a seamstress, I was quite accustomed to washing clothes. Content to observe Rook at the task, I picked a fleck of bark from my dress and replied, "I'd hate to ruin this lovely gown. I'll just watch, thank you."

Rook's eyes flicked from the washboard to me.

"Besides, you're the obedient servant," I said, mocking the phrase he'd used earlier. "And you're doing such a *good* job." Rook scoffed, though he then continued with a renewed vigor, and I laughed when he accidentally tore a sleeve from his shirt. Hearing me, Rook couldn't help but chuckle too.

"How's your wound?" I asked quickly, pointing at the stitches on Rook's side. "Looks like it's healing well."

Rook raised his arm and examined the wound. He frowned and grunted in a disagreeing way.

He was quiet after that.

Once finished, Rook walked to the edge of the trees, where he hung the clothes along a string to dry. When the last stocking was hung, Rook sat and leaned back on his elbows. I joined him in silence, and we watched the sun descending over the pond.

"If I could change what I've become..." Rook said, "If I—if *the Hound* were no longer around...would I be worthy of forgiveness?"

I inhaled and examined the trees, wondering if I might escape this conversation. Finally, I settled on Rook, patiently awaiting an answer. Throwing up my hands, I asked, "Forgiveness from who?"

He shrugged. "The world." Though it was me, not the world, he watched when he asked the question.

My emotions spiked like a fierce snake in my belly. *No! I want you to burn for what you've done to my family! I want you to hurt and suffer and—*

Beside me, Rook twirled a piece of grass between his fingers. Everything about Rook, from the vulnerability of the question, to the anxious way he fidgeted, was so achingly human.

A quiet part of me whispered... *Maybe.*

Sitting with my contradictions, I recalled another important lesson from my father. When Lottie turned six, she was gifted a crystal dagger. Excited, she'd waved it about, pretending to fight invisible monsters, and she'd run my hand through. The pain was brutal, and worse, I could do nothing while it healed. I couldn't play, I couldn't sew with my father. Every day I sat, *despising* Lottie. Whenever she spoke to me, I refused to listen. One day, my father saw Lottie walking dejectedly away, having given up on telling me a story about a baby weasel she'd seen. Taking me aside, my father had said, "I know you're suffering." He'd hugged me tight and knelt, so that we were eye-to-eye. "Your sister loves you, and what she did was a mistake. I can't make you forgive her, but your relationship will fester if you do not. You must decide what's more important: the person or the mistake."

"But what if she does it again?!" I'd cried, holding up my mangled hand.

"She won't," my father had replied. "And if she does...stab her back." He'd winked and continued, "I'm kidding. Don't tell your mother I said that." He'd sighed. "If she does it again, you do what's best for you, my love. But for now..." He'd nodded at Lottie, sitting alone. In the end, I'd gone to her. More than a decade later, we still fought, but I slept easy, knowing Lottie would run through a thousand monsters to protect me.

"I think forgiveness can be earned," I started, my words careful and deliberate, "and granted."

Rook nodded and turned back to the sunset. As he bathed in the vanishing light, a content, almost pleased look crossed his face. Worry plagued me, and, mustering courage, I asked the question I was afraid to ask. "You will help me escape, right?"

Rook's jaw twitched.

My pulse kicked up.

What if Rook didn't help me?

Lysander would succumb to his wounds, and my mother would die of a broken heart not long after.

"I wouldn't condemn anyone to this life," Rook said, interrupting my spiral. "I will keep my word."

Rook tossed the bit of grass aside. "You know, for the first few years I was trapped here, the longing was *unbearable*. I yearned for food, for company, for my home and my friends. That never goes away, but...you become numb. The longing fades over time. It's a defense mechanism, I suppose." Rook quieted; he turned from the sun. "I hadn't realized how much I'd missed the sound of laughter until you brought it back to me. I... I was unprepared for the desires that came with it." Rook didn't look away, almost as if it was his turn to muster courage and ask a question he was afraid to ask.

"What is it?"

"Before you go, I have a wish." Rook cleared his throat. "A request you might grant me."

"Depends on the request," I replied, unwilling to enter another bargain.

Rook's eyes drifted to my lips.

"One kiss."

Adrenaline, carrying excitement, fury, and confusion, flushed up my neck. The emotions warred, each holding their own spears of argument.

No! they cried. *This is forbidden!*

But part of me... Part of me wanted to indulge Rook's request. It was just a kiss. It meant nothing to me, but it would do so much to solidify his trust.

The Hound murdered your father!

It wasn't the Hound here, it was Rook, his skin painted in flames—orange, pink and violet—all the smoky tints of sunset.

It was Rook, asking me to kiss him.

As if bewitched, I nodded. Rook brushed his palm along his trousers and sat up. He glanced around, making sure we were alone and safe. Rook slid a hand beneath my chin and guided my face to his. We'd almost touched when Rook paused, looking over my shoulder. When he was certain nothing crept up behind us, his gaze settled on me.

Softly, his lips pressed mine.

It was a polite kiss, nothing like the exchanges I'd shared with Ruven when we were young, when we were discovering one another and I'd thought he was the one. And yet, there was hunger in Rook's civility, a quiet starvation that held him against me, that refused to let him break the embrace. A sigh echoed in Rook's throat—a murmur of satisfaction that stoked an ember I thought I'd hidden away. Rook barely touched me, but it felt as though his hands were all over my body, awakening it.

In the Hollow, I was taught a simple equation. Vigilance or death. The two concepts were mutually exclusive. While kissing Rook, I let go of both. Sliding my hand up Rook's arm, I gripped his wrist and rose to meet him. The kiss turned from polite to—Rook pulled away. He exhaled a faint breath, as if he'd forgotten to breathe. Perhaps eager to remember the taste, Rook's eyes settled on my lips again. Starving, but satiated.

For now.

Rook's wrist twitched, reminding me how tightly I held it. I let go and scooted away. Rook smiled. Not the quick, fluttering smiles I was accustomed to, but broad and genuine. As it faded, a sharp canine caught his lip, delaying it falling back into place.

A lifetime of scowls had not accustomed him to joy.

Off in the woods, a twig snapped. Tensing, I looked around. Though the trees appeared safe, I realized, with no small amount of anxiety, that I'd let my guard down for several minutes. I hadn't been looking behind, hadn't been glancing over my shoulder to make sure I was safe...

Because *Rook* had been.

Rook leaned into the grass and turned back to the horizon. A gnawing, shameful pit hollowed my chest. I frowned; my attention drifted back to the pink sky.

It was just a kiss, my mind mocked.

The last rays of sun flickered over the pond like hungry flames. Absently, I rubbed my stomach. Never had a I felt a fire quite like that. Lost in our thoughts, Rook and I watched the sun set together.

Lesson Nine

Intuition exists to protect you, when
all else fails, listen to her.

The next morning, I woke and stretched. I noted a remarkable lack of stiffness in my neck and shoulders. For the life of me, I couldn't recall a time when my neck didn't ache. After I'd turned twelve, I'd thought that was just how I was. Climbing from bed, I changed into my clean clothes and enjoyed the memory of Rook knelt over the stream. With it came the same unsolicited heat that had burned my cheeks when he'd kissed me. At the vanity, I ran a brush through my hair. I tucked a lock behind a pearl studded barrette and left the rest tumbling down my back in a golden wave.

It was strange that Rook hadn't come to call on me yet, and I decided to head downstairs. I passed my satchel and paused.

Take it with you.

Though I couldn't fathom any reason why I'd need my bag, I'd learned long ago not to argue with my intuition. I swung the satchel over my head and tucked it at my side. Before reaching the foyer, I peered in the red room. The bed was made. No Rook. I continued down and into the library, but Rook was nowhere to be found. Meaning to check the kitchens, I headed to the castle basement. On my way down, I passed a door and stopped dead.

The door Rook forbid me from entering.

I held still for a most *admirable* moment. I glanced at the door, then down the hallway to the kitchens...and back to the door.

Do it.

Don't do it.

Open it.

Don't open it.

OPEN THE DOOR!

I grabbed the knob and exploded into the room.

A single candle flickered to life. The room was vast and without windows, and the meagre light conveyed a sense of...hopelessness. Immediately, it was obvious why Rook wanted to shield me from this place. Chains attached to metal collars and cuffs lined the walls. All around, wooden tables were littered with what I could only describe as 'tools', and luckily, I didn't know what their purpose was. Certainly, it was a somber room, made all the more grim by the object in its centre.

A guillotine.

A bit rough around the edges, but a guillotine, nonetheless.

I took a step and kicked a metal tool under the table. Stooping, I grabbed for it. I withdrew large pliers. This tool I knew; Ruven used it at the smithy. I set them down—and drew back.

Teeth.

Two sharp teeth sat on the table.

I stared at them, not really seeing them. Instead, I saw Rook sitting before the setting sun. He smiled, and his sharp canine tugged his lip. I leaned against the table, nudging a tooth with my quivering fingers.

When people had toothaches back in town, they often visited Lauren, the old blacksmith. Nasty business, ripping teeth from people's skulls. The wails that carried from the smithy on dental days were enough to haunt even the strongest passerby. I always wondered: How much agony would someone endure before they willingly submitted to such torture?

The enormity of Rook's torment sunk in. I had a feeling Rook removed these for a very different reason. And to no avail.

How long had it taken them to grow back?

I wanted to run, to leave this room and never think of it again but, there's an allure to the macabre. I couldn't look away—I *wanted* to know. Even if it was ugly.

I skirted a pile of wood and made my way to the guillotine. More wood, which had been roughly cut, was strewn about the base. No denying why they were there.

Practice.

A rope hung from the trigger; it carried all the way to the floor, so that whichever wretched soul lay on the chopping block might reach it. And yet, it wasn't the guillotine or the practice blocks that made my stomach turn. No, the most uncomfortable discovery was the sticky red stain coating the blade.

What did I really know of Rook's torment?

There was a surprisingly urgent spring in my step as I left the cellars. "Rook?" I called to the empty castle.

Had he gone for a walk?

I ducked into the library and exited through the veranda. Just then, the sound of chopping floated from the distant trees. The image of the guillotine, hacking through wood—and other things—intruded into my mind. Shaking away the thought, I chased the noise down the lawn and hurried across the stream.

There, I found Rook, axe in hand, felling trees. Seeing him, the tension melted away. White shirt strained through, Rook's skin glistened beneath the morning sun. Letting the axe rest at his side, Rook beamed and dragged a drooping suspender back over his shoulder.

"What are you doing?" I asked.

Rook spun the axe and laughed. "Is that a trick question?"

"I mean, I don't know. Isn't it a bit...early?"

"I couldn't sleep. I just..." Rook pushed a hand through his hair. "I needed to do something with my hands." Indeed, Rook possessed a frantic energy. He reminded me of Lottie on hunting days. Excited but tinged with wildness, which always left me wondering what terribly unhinged thing she might do next. Rook rested the axe at the crook of his neck and moved to the next tree. Sliding his hand down the axe, he raised it above his head and—*CHOP!*

The axe wedged into the thick trunk. Rook wiggled the handle and dislodged the head. He raised the axe and struck again. This time, a loud crack rang out and the tree listed. It tore through the canopy and thudded to the ground with a booming crash. Rook looked on as I approached the stump. It was thicker than a dinner plate. It would have taken Lottie and me a hundred blows to fell a tree like that.

Rook had done it in two.

"Do you ever worry you'll run out of trees?" I asked, staring at the stump.

"Ah!" Rook tapped his nose. "Come with me." Axe on his shoulder, Rook headed into the wood. Soon, we came to a clearing, filled with knee-high saplings. "To plant trees is to believe in tomorrow." Rook smiled. "My mother used to say that." Rook crouched and brushed a leaf. "Oak. She'll be strong."

A piercing cry shattered the serenity in the clearing. It was familiar, the same cry we'd heard the day prior...right before I was snatched by the so-called Lady of the Lake. Rook stood and reached for me. Warm, calloused fingers intertwined with mine. Part of me recoiled at Rook's touch, hissed at me to pull away, and yet...my hand remained.

Rook pointed to the far end of the clearing. He palmed the axe, and said, "It came from the mausoleum."

"Should I wait here?"

"Not this time." Rook shook his head. "Stay with me."

"We should go back," I said, digging my heels in. "I don't care what's over there. Whatever it is, it's dangerous."

Rook threw his head back and laughed. "Worse than me?" He squeezed my hand and dragged me forward.

"No good can come from investigating."

"Regrettably, this is my home. I'd like to know who disturbs my peace." Rook strode toward the cry, each step more confident than the last. "I can handle it."

Something was wrong. *What* exactly, I didn't know. But I did know one thing:

The Hollow rewarded arrogance with a swift death.

As we reached the edge of the clearing and entered the ancient trees, I scrutinized each shadow and trunk. A grouse flew from a bush, nearly stopping my heart and earning a mighty laugh from Rook. We walked carefully, listening to every crack and chirp. The cry came again—farther this time.

Luring us deeper.

Gradually, the trees gave way to headstones; they dotted the grass like pebbles. Amongst all the stones, a mausoleum sat in the centre. It was built to match the castle, with ornate stone arches and iron spires that reached for the sky. A prominent door sat at the mausoleum's front like a great mouth, ready to devour those foolish enough to step inside.

"Rook," I cautioned, "this feels wrong."

But Rook wasn't paying attention to me. His eyes darted between the headstones—and his nostrils flared. The axe slipped from Rook's shoulder; he held it with two hands. The movement sent a shiver through me.

Why did he need a better grip on the weapon?

"I'm going back," I whispered.

"Let us be swift," Rook growled, and then backtracked into the trees where he stopped. I peered around him. A shadow ducked behind a trunk—not just one. Many shadowy figures crept between trees, blocking the way we'd come. "Back away." Rook pushed me toward the mausoleum.

My calf brushed something that moved. "Agh!" I stumbled into Rook.

Crouched behind me, like a spider ready to pounce, was a living corpse. Milky eyes stared out from an emaciated, grey face. My mind cycled through creatures, finally settling on the name of the vile thing crouched at our feet.

Ghoul.

"I've seen them in the shadows," Rook muttered. "They've never approached me."

"They?"

Rook nodded to the sea of graves.

I didn't see them at first; their bodies blended with the stones. Wide-eyed ghouls peeked from behind every headstone in the yard. A few paces away, a ghoul perched like a gargoyle, on a monument of one *Seerinth Martell*. The ghoul's shoulders touched its ears.

Our catching sight of it had interrupted it from pouncing on our unsuspecting backs.

The ghoul I'd bumped bobbed and sniffed the air. It dragged our scents in, tasting us. Ghouls didn't frequent the Hollow, so my father never warned me of them. I didn't know of their weaknesses or how to avoid them. The only thing I knew for certain was that they ate one thing and one thing only.

Flesh.

The ghoul let out a piercing screech, sending strings of spittle from cracked teeth. The graveyard came to life, and one-by-one, the ghouls shrieked. With a snarl, the ghoul nearest me lunged.

"Agh!" Dirty nails dug into my calf. Rook's axe crushed the ghoul and sent black blood into my face.

"Run!" he bellowed.

I fled, and screams erupted as the ghouls gave chase. I leapt over a fallen tree and checked to make sure Rook was with me. Waving frantically, Rook shouted, "Get back to the castle!" A useless command; what else would I do? I dodged a trunk and—I slammed into a wall and fell. Blinking away the confusion, I struggled to focus. Two feet stood before me. I followed them up, where a monstrous ghoul peered down. Unlike the others, this ghoul was gluttonous and rotund. I flipped and crawled toward Rook, who was fending off seven of the creatures at once. My foot snagged and my world flipped upside down.

"Liliwen!" Rook cried.

The ghoul had me by the ankle. Arms waving, I pitched back and forth, grabbing for anything. Headstones passed on my sides. I caught one and tried to hang on. "Ugh!" My fingers slipped from the lichen covered stone. In the distance, Rook's cries grew faint. Ascending the steps, the ghoul jostled me as we entered the mausoleum.

The light dimmed.

My panic spiked and I swung at the ghoul. My fists did little more than bounce off its fleshy back. The ghoul headed down a staircase hidden at the rear of the mausoleum. Step by step, the light faded. Dust and rot stung my eyes. I covered my mouth to escape a stench that was so strong, I could tear it with my teeth. At the bottom, the ghoul tossed me. I landed in a pile of what I *hoped* were just very white sticks. Scrambling, I leapt up and ran for the stairs—for the pinprick of light up above. I skidded to a stop and braced myself on the wall. Like a swarm of ants, ghouls cascaded down the stairs in a wave, climbing over one another and up the walls. Backing away, I turned to find the gluttonous ghoul staring at me.

It held a rock.

Before I could react, the opportunity to examine the rock more closely presented itself, and a force jolted my temple.

In the dark mausoleum, I collapsed.

When I woke, darkness held me like a blanket. Decay hung in the air, and pain splintered my temple, echoed by a burning in my leg. I touched my eyelids; they were indeed open. How far down could I be that not a trickle of light found me? My thoughts came slow and with great effort, the pain in my temple dragging them away when they almost made sense. I remembered the ghouls, snarling and clawing, and Rook, falling under the weight of them. Had he fared worse than me? Would he be able to find me, hidden in the depths of the mausoleum? I squinted, trying to see anything but black. From somewhere not far off, a growl rose.

I had to get out of here, Rook or no.

Once, and only once, I'd found myself caught in the Hollow after nightfall. The darkness had almost destroyed me, and I'd promised I'd never be caught without a light ever again. I felt my chest and found the leather strap of my satchel. Feeling the strap, I pawed blindly at the flap and ties. I withdrew a bit of iron and flint. Next, I removed a small tin. The smoky scent of fire met me when I opened it, a welcome distraction from the aroma of rotting corpses. I struck the flint against the iron and my heart fluttered at the brief illumination. I struck the iron again, sending more sparks into my tin of charred twigs. After several strikes, a warm glow remained. Picking up the tin, I blew, encouraging the ember. I fumbled in my satchel and found a small candle. I set the wick against the glow and waited. A flame sprung up and travelled along the wick. I shut my tin, smothering the fire, and tucked it away.

I'd been put away in a small room. I shielded my candle and peered around the stone doorframe. In both directions, the hall looked empty. I hadn't the faintest idea which way led out, but I swore the left smelled less foul. I stole down the passage. With each step, my chest grew tighter—my body coiled like a spring—ready should my candle illuminate some horror waiting for me along the hall. The wall gave way to a doorway. Brushing aside curtains of cobwebs, I peered inside. Tables littered the room, covered in equipment similar to the physician's room back at the castle. Though one thing was different. This room was fitted with cages and cells. The iron cages had long rusted, absorbing rather than reflecting my candlelight. I approached the closest cage, illuminating the brown smears smattering the floor.

What a strange fixture in a resting place for the dead.

On the wall next to the cage, a diagram caught my eye. A tree. Though it was no common tree. Branches tipped with blood-red fruits sprung out from the dark trunk. One of the fruits was spliced and enlarged, so I might see the gem-like seeds nestled within. After all these years, the red fruit had not faded. I traced the fruit—terror shot through me and I pulled away.

It was an exact rendering of the tree hidden within the castle.

Holding my candle higher, I examined more diagrams. The first portrayed an ordinary woman, with blonde curls and a lean stature. It was impossible not to see the smear of red in her hands, where she held the fruit. The same woman was in the next drawing, red marred her face and stained her lips. Her back was hunched, and her limbs slightly longer than before. In the next, she had all four limbs on the ground, and her jaw was elongated and wide, a terrifying mix of woman and monster. In front of the final diagram, the candlelight quivered along the wall. It was a perfect likeness to the Hound.

Rook was right; the fruit was poison.

And he'd devoured it.

When I entered the castle, I'd come so close to eating the fruit myself. How easily I could have become a monster, a victim to this place.

Wax dripped and burned my wrist. Absently, I brushed the hot wax away and turned to leave—a woman stood between me and the door, her white gown stark against the dark. I couldn't identify her face, for she had no face at all. Where features might have been, there was only perfect, flat skin. The paintings lining the castle foyer crept into my mind. A faceless woman amongst the hounds. The candlelight flickered, and I couldn't help but notice the woman cast no shadow.

She inched forward.

I tensed but didn't run. Like a child observing an animal, wondering if it was a threat or not, I watched the woman approach. The faceless woman's presence, though unnerving, didn't feel malicious...yet. The woman reached out, and her delicate fingers curled around my hand, which gripped the candle so tight.

In a swirling of shadows, the mausoleum vanished, and I fell into a vision.

The faceless woman sat upon a wide throne. Several people knelt at her feet in supplication. Though I couldn't see it, I knew she smiled upon their bowed heads. Somehow, I sensed it was not a kind smile. The faceless woman raised her arm, dragging a finger across her throat. In seconds, those kneeling were set upon by a great hound. The beast ripped the throats from two of the unfortunate souls—the third ran. They made it only five paces when the beast leapt on their back. Horror contorted the face of the man before me, so close I felt his breath against my cheeks. The hound's teeth wrapped his throat, and the man's neck stretched into pink ribbons as his head was ripped from his torso.

The headless figure collapsed.

The final wheezes of those who bled to death ceased, and the hound sat beside the faceless woman. For the beast's servitude, the woman nodded her approval.

The vision rippled, like a pebble dropped on a still lake, and changed. A floor-length mirror of gilded, tangled vines appeared. My reflection, so often characterized by an anxious frown, wore a twisted grin. I held a beating heart, and with each pulse, blood gushed down my arm.

Rook lay dead at my feet.

In his chest, a gaping hole stared up at me, bloodied and empty. I'd used him. Convinced him to trust me, and then I'd taken his life. Without a second thought, I'd harvested his body to save my brother. I stared at Rook's corpse, and a strange sensation prickled my skin. Like someone snuggling into bed beside me on a cold night—but closer, as if they were trying to crawl into my very body.

"You and I are not so different," came a whisper, piercing the vision. "Little Dove."

I shook my head, fighting the intrusion. Little Dove...that was one of my nicknames—what my father used to call me in the Hollow.

The Hollow.

Get out! my body screamed. GET OUT NOW!

With great effort, I tore myself from the faceless woman's grasp. I sprinted down the dark passageways. I had no idea where I was going, but I had to get away. I looked behind.

The faceless woman didn't pursue me.

A faint breeze ruffled my hair, and I chased it. The passage gave way to a large, dark opening. My heart leapt; several yards away, a shred of sunlight fell down the mausoleum stairs. I started toward it, then halted so abruptly I had to catch myself from falling forward. Laying at my feet, a ghoul blended with the stone floor. With a trembling hand, I held my candle high. Between me and the stairs, countless ghouls lay sleeping.

A ghoul snarled and kicked in its slumber.

I gripped my satchel tighter, terrified of any noise. As intricately as one might thread a needle, I stepped between two sleeping ghouls. It was agonizingly slow, but I made my way forward. I neared the halfway point. A ghoul shifted onto my boot.

Stop moving!

I glanced at the entrance, still so far away, and back to the ghoul. My breathing came quick, and I covered my mouth. I had to get out. It didn't matter what happened once I was free, but I had to get out. Now. The smell, the fear—it was suffocating. Run. That's all I wanted to do. Just run!

Stay calm!

Taking a deep breath, I slid my boot from beneath the ghoul's head. It grunted but didn't wake, and I continued. The light at the entrance flickered, as if someone passed it. Again, I stilled.

This is it.

Surely, this is another ghoul, returning to its lair. I'll be discovered and eaten, my bones left to rot down in this horrible place. But, no. A filthy, but alive Rook tiptoed down the stairs. Catching sight of me, his lips parted.

I thrust my finger to my mouth, silencing him.

Rook's eyes reflected my candle, appearing as two stars at dusk. They travelled along the ghouls, all the way to the corners of the mausoleum, where my candlelight couldn't penetrate, and my human eyes couldn't see. How many more monsters lay in the shadows?

From the look on Rook's face, it was probably best I didn't know.

Rook stepped forward. I put up my palm, stopping him. Indignation soured his face. I pointed at his feet.

Stay there!

Rook continued anyway, and I pointed at him.

Don't you dare!

Rook's chest heaved…but he remained at the foot of the stairs. I stepped over a ghoul—it shifted and I paused again. Rook turned away and covered his mouth, like he might be sick.

I was nearly there.

A breeze carried fresh air down the stairs. Glancing around, I looked for where I might step next. Dread threatened me. There was no path ahead. Too many bodies lay sleeping, back-to-back. I chewed my lip, searching for a way around them.

There wasn't one.

I was stuck.

Helplessly, I looked to Rook. He raised a finger, as if to say, *'Hold on!'* Moving quick, Rook leaned his axe against the stairwell. He pointed to the ground behind me, and then opened his arms. I didn't understand. Rook lifted his hand, palm up. With his other hand, he made a running motion. Then, he opened his arms and tapped his chest.

He wanted me to jump.

Shaking my head, I stepped back—my boot crunched a bone. Rook grimaced, looking as if the faintest noise might stop his heart. The ghouls below me shifted but remained sleeping. Rook waved his arms wildly, catching my attention and beckoning me forward with urgency.

I mouthed, *'I can't!'* and shook my head. Rook pushed his hands through his hair and then clasped them at his chest.

Begging me.

He was *begging* me to trust him.

I looked around, evaluating my options. Even the path behind me had vanished. There was no other way out.

Rook mouthed one word.

'Please.'

'Ugh!' I wanted to scream back at him. Instead, I doused my candle and tucked it away. Careful not to step on more bones, I backed up as far as I could, which wasn't very far at all, and then paused to breathe.

There's no monsters. No danger. Just a jump over a stream, that's all...

A stream that'll gnaw your bones while you're alive to feel it.

Shaking my head, I scrunched my nose and exhaled. I took several hurried steps, and when I was about to stomp on a ghoul, I leapt. I cleared the bodies and careened into Rook's arms. He winced when I fell into his side but remained silent.

The ghouls did not wake.

Safely in Rook's grasp, his arms tightened around me. The same way I might hold something I'd lost and didn't want to lose again. Adrenaline pumping, I scrambled away from Rook and up the stairs. Grabbing the axe, Rook wasn't far behind. I sprinted through the mausoleum and into the sunlight. Each time I navigated out of the Hollow, I was met with a sweeping sense of relief.

The euphoria I felt now put all those escapes to shame.

Behind me, Rook offered an encouraging smile that sent my pounding heart racing even faster. I wiped cobwebs and muck off my arms, and a shiver of disgust rattled me. Rook doubled over to catch his breath, freeing my view of the mausoleum behind him.

And the ghoul crouched upon it.

The ghoul screeched and pounced. It bypassed Rook and snatched my wrist. Without hesitating, Rook swung the axe up, snapping the ghoul's arm like a weak branch. Down below, a chorus of shrieks rose from the mausoleum.

"Go!" Rook shouted.

Already running, I dodged headstones and pried the ghoul's disembodied hand from my wrist. Tossing it aside, I risked a glance back. Behind Rook, ghouls poured down the mausoleum steps in a grey, decayed wave. I batted aside branches as we hit the treeline. Rook dodged a trunk and continued running beside me. Ghouls approached at our sides, sprinting through the trees. My arms pumped tirelessly as I tried to outrun them. Almost like a gate closing before penned livestock, the ghouls ran ahead and blocked our path. I skidded to a stop, and Rook dragged me behind him. A ghoul approached; Rook swung the axe in a wide arc. The ghoul crouched and hissed, narrowly avoiding a beheading. Rook kicked the ghoul and sent it into the trees. More and more ghouls crept from the shadows. My mind rapidly running out of options, I inched closer to Rook, careful to avoid the business end of his axe. Rook shoved me back and I bumped into a tree.

Changing tactics, I grabbed a low branch and hauled myself up. I swung my legs over and shouted, "Climb!" Rook punched and frantically swung the axe, but there were too many. The ghouls overtook him; they snarled and tore at his legs. "Change!" I screamed and hammered the trunk. "Become the Hound!"

"I can't! I'm not strong enough!" Rook shouted. "The transformation might kill me, and you'll be left here alone—" A ghoul lunged at Rook's face.

"Climb up!" I cried, reaching for Rook.

A low growl carried from the trees, freezing my hand in mid-air. The gigantic ghoul who'd taken me into the mausoleum slunk from the shadows. The smaller ones shrunk from it. Wasting no time, Rook turned and grabbed a branch; he wedged his foot against the trunk, then started to climb but swiftly lost his footing. Panicked, I wondered, why was Rook suddenly so clumsy?!

"Drop the axe!" I snapped. "Use two hands!"

"I need it!" Rook snarled and tried again. I slapped the trunk, venting my frustration. Why had I assumed Rook knew how to climb a tree properly? The Hound simply ate anything that pursued it.

"Here!" I cried. "Take my hand!"

Rook reached for me. A ghoul snatched his boot. He slipped and tried to catch a branch. The hand holding the axe hit the trunk. The axe bounced and swung...

Directly into Rook's throat.

"NO!" shrieked a voice, so shrill I hardly recognized it as my own. Everything around Rook vanished. I stopped hearing—stopped seeing anything but Rook.

Blood trickled around the axe, wedged into his neck.

Rook tried to speak—his lips formed words that wouldn't come. With great determination, he mouthed, *'I'm sorry,'* and stumbled from the tree. I swung my leg over and leapt down after him. The axe fell, and a wave of blood spilled over Rook's hand at his throat. Still, he oriented himself between the ghouls and me. As if the ghouls had done something they shouldn't have, they retreated. Beetle-like, they scuttled back into the shadows.

Only then did Rook fall.

"No, no, no, no!" I collapsed behind Rook, easing him to the ground.

Rook started, "I—" but the words gargled in his throat and died. Blood poured from the corner of his mouth, and he looked at me, helpless. I crammed my hands against his neck. The wound was deep, it spewed blood like a river.

Rook was going to die.

In doing so, Rook would take with him any chance I might have of escaping this broken place. Fear for my future rose up within me, but there was something else: an unwelcome sensation far deeper than self-preservation. Frantic energy hammered me, begging the light not to leave Rook's eyes.

What could I do?

I peeked at the wound; ruby-red blood oozed out. Rook was so still, his chest barely rising. I was transported back to only a few nights ago. When Lysander had stumbled in, eviscerated and crawling toward death—wait! With one hand pressed against Rook, I rifled through my satchel for the remains of the cloth I'd used on Lysander.

Rook's eyes fluttered and closed.

I knocked him with my knee and shouted, "Rook!" His eyes snapped open wide but immediately lulled. I yanked out the fabric and jammed it against Rook's neck. He gasped and tried to pull away, but I held firm. Scooting behind Rook, I lifted his head into my lap and wound the fabric around his throat.

Eyes closed now, Rook's chest failed to rise at all.

Holding the wound, a tingling began in my fingertips. It travelled up my arms and dizzied my thinking. "Please," I muttered. "No one else." Tears welled along my lashes, and I leaned my forehead against Rook's.

His pulse no longer hammered my palm.

"Please!" Tears fell heavy, and I laid everything on Rook. My tears, my sweat; if I had any magic, I laid that out too. "Let the fabric work," I muttered. "I was quick enough. We kept enough blood from escaping."

To myself, I muttered, "You can do this."

I pulled away.

Rook didn't stir.

With hands limp at his sides, and a look of serenity, one might pretend Rook was sleeping. A sob wracked me, springing tears loose from my chin. How could this happen again? How could I sit beside another dying person and not help them?! Anger burned through me, and I hit the ground. I couldn't save my father; I couldn't save Rook. Lysander might die—I took a deep breath, and I forced myself back, out of the spiral and back to this moment. As my breathing evened, the anger faded.

Sadness remained.

In my lap, I cradled Rook. I didn't want to let him go, even if he was...

Dead.

Rook was dead.

After my father died, it took me so long to feel again. That same sensation tugged at me, begging me to let it in and shove the despair aside. I felt as if I was high in the canopy, seeing both Rook and myself tangled on the ground. It all seemed like make-believe—like none of this was really happening.

But it was real, and I'd never escape this place.

Lysander *would* die. What would become of my mother? Would Marek take care of her? Mother said he was cold, but he'd spoil her, keep her safe at least. Though, with her children missing or dead save for Lottie, I don't know how she'd go on... And what of Lottie? Oh, she could hardly cook a thing!

I stroked Rook's forehead, moving hair from his face. Perhaps... Perhaps if I cut Rook's heart out, I could escape on my own. My own heart shivered, repulsed by the thought of plunging the blade into Rook, of ruining his body. Blood and dirt smeared Rook's cheeks; a compulsion told me to wipe it off. The same way I might tell a loved one they had food or grime on them. I moved to wipe Rook's cheek—

Rook's hand caught mine.

A burst of air left my mouth in a startled hiss. Rook coughed. I shoved his face sideways. No blood seeped through the bandage.

Turning back to me, Rook murmured, "You saved my life."

You saved his life? An enraged voice screamed. *You saved the beast who killed your father?!* I could barely hear it, could only focus on Rook's pulse gently tapping my palm.

"Well..." I started. "If you died, how would I have escaped this place?" Rook glanced at the wet tracks staining my cheeks. He brushed his own face, where my tears had landed and settled.

And Rook smiled.

Lingering in my lap, Rook gazed upon me. Grief squeezed my heart; I'd seen that look before. Every night when my mother came home, and Father listened to her chatter on about the students. Even if she was complaining, he was just so happy to have her there, to know that she was his and it was his good fortune to look at her. Every night I'd wish—*beg*—I'd find someone who looked at me like that.

Rook brought my blood-spattered hand to his mouth and kissed it. In Rook's reluctance to look away, I knew one thing. I'd gained his trust a million times over, and for better or worse...

Rook was mine.

Lesson Ten

If you inspire suffering, you are no
better than the monster you seek to
destroy.

We walked back to the castle, my arm around Rook, supporting him. Entering through the library, I asked, "How are you feeling?" Rook unwound himself from me and stood on his own.

He hadn't needed my help at all.

Rook unfurled the bandage from his throat. The fabric had done a miraculous job; flawless skin remained. Rolling his neck in a wide circle, Rook said, "Decades have come and gone. I have not been so well as I am now." He reached out, brushing my hand. Suddenly, Rook was too real, and all my plans seemed terribly foolish. Stamping down the fluttering his proximity awakened, I fled to the desk.

"We should get back to your lessons." I needed to fulfill this bargain; I had to get away from Rook as fast as I could. I grabbed a book—Rook placed his hand on mine, keeping the book on the desk.

"Look at me," Rook murmured.

I'd been trying so hard *not* to look at him.

Swaths of blood covered his shirt; the white turned a ruddy brown. Rook squeezed my hand and coaxed me from the desk.

"We should wash ourselves."

"Okay," I muttered and let him pull me away.

Down in the kitchens, Rook placed a bucket of water next to the hearth. I bent to wash my arms but stopped when Rook touched my shoulder. "Please, allow me." He dragged a stool over and sat.

"I can do it myself..." The words trailed away as Rook took my hand. So gentle yet firm, I don't know that I could have slipped away if I tried. "Oh, very well." He dipped a cloth in the water. His rough hands moved over mine, tugging blood from beneath my nails.

"Rook," I started, my heart hammering, "how did you become the Hound?"

Engrossed in the therapy of his task, Rook didn't bristle as I'd anticipated he would. "I was hunting in the Hollow with my mother." The memory quirked Rook's lip in a fleeting smile. The joy slipped away, gone as quickly as it came. "Thin wolves attacked, and we were separated. As night fell, I found this place." Rook waved lazily at the castle walls. "I remember thinking how fortunate I was, that I was saved." He laughed bitterly. "I should have given myself to the wolves."

I recalled the madness in Rook's eyes when he'd screamed, *'Did you eat the fruit?!'*

I hadn't, but...

"You ate it," I murmured.

In a distant voice, Rook said, "It called to me, and I devoured it." He dipped the cloth in the bucket, bringing warm water back to me. "From that night forward, I was cursed." Rook sighed, a lengthy breath that carried so many decades of grief. "At first, I was unaware. It began as a hunger that no food might satisfy. That hunger soon turned unbearable and I... I changed for the first time. I tore through the Hollow, devouring anything in my path." Staring at my hand, Rook paused. His voice was so quiet, I had to lean closer when he whispered, "Every night I think about how broken my mother must have been when I never returned."

"You never went back to her?"

Rook looked up at me, dirty and covered in dried blood. "How could I?" He laughed, his canines glinting in the firelight. "Better she believed me dead than see what I'd become." He shook his head. "My mother was an unforgiving woman; she probably would have killed me herself... Rightly so."

"And after all those years—even when you discovered you could evade the wolves and leave this place, you've chosen to remain here?"

"My exile is voluntary...but necessary," Rook muttered. "It would be reckless to leave. If I tried to live amongst people, whose lives I'm eternally craving... I worry the swathes of corpses would be endless." He sighed. "In some ways, it's a cage of my own creation. But a cage nonetheless."

I'd *held* the fruit. How easily that could have been me. I couldn't help but picture my mother and Lottie, staring over the garden gate. Every night, waiting for me to return. Another Valet, fallen to the Hollow. No body to bury next to my father and Lysander.

Seeing Rook, an unrelenting wave of sympathy stung me. Why hadn't he told me before?

Because he trusts you now.

He'd given me a piece of himself.

The fire crackled, and neither of us spoke. I wanted to—wanted to break the silence and stop his eyes from wandering up and landing on mine. I *needed* to disappear from his sight, stop the warmth from filling my cheeks each time he looked my way.

When my hand was cleaner than it had ever been, I nodded my thanks and backed away. Rook stood and yanked his bloodied shirt off. He admired the stained fabric and laughed. "I'll need magic to get that out." He winked, but I barely saw it. Sweat poured down Rook's chest; it glistened along his stomach, all the way down... Rook sat on the table and gestured to the wound on his side. "Care to take a closer look?"

I didn't trust myself any closer to him than I already was. Taking a half-step, I kept as much distance between us as possible. The wound from the crossbow, though only a few days old, looked more like an ancient scar. Had the fabric's magic flowed through Rook's veins and healed him completely? A few stitches remained; I'd need to remove them. I reached out but stopped myself, just before I touched him.

"That..." I gulped, my mouth suddenly dry. "That looks much better." Rook caught my hand.

His eyes—shining like faint mirrors—captured mine. Rook brought my palm to rest on his chest. He was warm, his body so welcoming...I didn't pull away. Rook's tongue traced his lips, and in the slightest move, his chin bobbed. It was subtle; anyone else might have missed it had they not been looking for permission.

At once, Rook reached for me, and I led his face to mine. We met with such urgency, Rook struggled to remain on the table. He heaved me into his lap, and I straddled his waist, our lips never parting. With a grunt, Rook wrapped his arms around me, dragging me closer.

"Liliwen," Rook breathed my name. It sent excitement trilling through me. His hand slid to my throat, wrapping it gently, keeping my face close to him. I kissed Rook harder, savouring the way he rose to meet me. "Say *my* name," Rook whispered.

I parted long enough to mumble, "Rook," back.

"That's not my name." Pain, not pleasure laced Rook's voice.

I... I couldn't say it. I knew the name, *Everard*, but my mouth wouldn't do it. I slid my hands down Rook, hoping to distract him. They fell upon the faint scar and old stitches—my stomach knotted.

Have you forgotten why you're here?

I tried to push the thought away. To focus on the present, on what was right here. Rook's hand abandoned my throat, coming to a rest against my chest. While he kissed me, his palm remained there, savouring my fervent heartbeat.

The vision of myself, holding Rook's beating heart, struck me like a blow.

I pulled away and Rook followed me, as a flower might chase the sun. His body—firm and inviting—begged me to stay. I slid from Rook's lap. Hoping to hide my laboured breathing, I covered my mouth. Lying to Rook was one thing, but this? This was torture.

"What's the matter?" Concern marred Rook's features. "Are you alright?"

"I-I'm fine," I replied, tugging my hands through my hair.

Rook had already promised to aid my escape, and surely when I came back, he would trust me enough to be close to him. This ruse had gone far enough; I would injure Rook no more than I had to. Through heavy breaths, I said, "I'm—I'm glad your wounds are healing well." Looking down, I smoothed my trousers. "The pain won't distract you from reading."

"Liliwen." Rook slid from the table and started toward me.

"I'll meet you in the library," I said, raising my palms.

As I left Rook to dress himself, one question plagued me.

Who reached for the other first?

Curled by the fire with a book, I read and re-read the same sentence. I dreaded and anticipated Rook's footsteps.

Would he be upset?

When I'd stumbled into this place, I hadn't given a damn about Rook's feelings. Now, I couldn't bear the thought of him being angry with me. The faintest footfalls carried through the library. Those unfamiliar with Rook wouldn't have heard them, but I did. I blocked out every noise and listened for his *almost* soundless approach. I fought the urge to turn and look at him, though a loud dragging forced me to. Rook relocated the second chair next to mine, so close the arms ground one another when he sat.

Rook's features were free of judgment when he said, "May I?" and took the book. He positioned it so I might see the words. "Can you start?"

I frowned. "You should be trying to read yourself."

"Please."

I hardened myself against Rook's hopeful smile...but it was me, not Rook, who sighed and submitted. And so, I read aloud while Rook trailed the words. We continued our story, a tale from long ago, when magic was high. Rook's hand drifted to my wrist; he brushed my skin while I read. Focusing became difficult; I longed to touch him, to trail my fingers along the veins snaking up his arm.

"The daughter of the queen was forced to do the queen's bidding," I said. "Suspicions arose that she was under the queen's control. Later, these suspicions would prove correct. Though records are unclear, sources suggest the daughter of the queen was forced to wear some restrictive object which removed her will." The longer I read of the evil, shadow-wielding queen and her terrifying reign, the more Rook's attention drifted from me, until his hand fell away completely. He glanced from the book to the wrought cuff encircling his wrist. Finally, when I caught him staring at the cuff more than the pages, I asked, "Why do you keep doing that?"

"I—it's nothing," Rook said, though his voice was urgent. "Keep going, please."

"Theories were put forth as to the object forced on the daughter of the queen. A necklace, a ring—"

Rook stiffened. He inhaled and his nostrils flared, sniffing the air like a blood hound. Rook's wide eyes darted to me, and two black pools swelled as his pupils dilated. Though no sound came out, Rook mouthed, *'Not now.'*

"R-Rook?"

Knocking the book away, Rook grasped my arm and yanked me up. Carpet bunched beneath my boots as Rook pulled me toward the door.

"What's going on?!"

"Agh!" Rook doubled over, falling against a bookshelf. The shelf shuddered and rocked as Rook pushed himself up. Lunging, Rook grabbed hold of me again. I tried to pry his fingers off, but his grip was unwavering as he dragged me into the foyer and up the stairs.

Latching onto the banister, I cried, "Where are we going?!" Rook opened his mouth to answer, and a heavy wheeze came out. Sweat poured from his brow as he wrenched my fingers loose. "Ow!" I snapped, thinking Rook would have broken my fingers had I not let go. We reached the top of the stairs, and I flailed, trying to grasp anything that might give me a foothold to resist.

Rook scooped me over his shoulder.

"Put me down!" I twisted, trying to break free. Rook took the steps two and three at a time. I hammered Rook's back and kicked my knees into his chest, but Rook continued climbing. We passed the sage room where I'd been staying. "Rook!" I shouted. "Where are you taking me?!"

Rook's response was a pained grunt. I lurched forward as Rook mounted a rickety, spiraling staircase. Stone walls closed around us, passing quickly as Rook hurried up the steps.

To the tower.

While Rook held me firm, his free hand grasped at the stones, trying desperately to keep us righted. I watched the winding steps below, terrified Rook might fall. The sickening up-and-down of climbing ceased as we reached the top, and Rook tossed me forward. Without letting go of me, he tore open an iron-barred cell door.

Twitching, he pointed inside and grunted, "Please!"

"Absolutely not!"

Rook wasn't asking; he shoved me in. Propelled forward, I hurtled into the wall and hissed as my shins struck the ground. Across the tower, a set of keys hung from a hook. Rook ripped them free and rushed the door. Tremors shook him, and the keys ricocheted against the bars. Violent thrashing wracked Rook's body. He dropped the keys and whimpered, like a terrified stray awaiting a beating. Falling to his knees, Rook tried to pick up the keys. His fingers, twisted and misshapen, would not obey. "Agh!" Rook fell against the wall. Through a sweaty mat of hair, Rook met me with a broken stare.

My hands tingled when I looked at the dropped keys.

Was it instinct?

Crawling forward, I picked up the keys, and whispered, "Which one?"

Rook grunted, "Big one." I held up the biggest key. Rook swallowed and managed a nod. Snaking my arm through the bars, I inserted the key in the lock. I exhaled...and then I locked myself in.

Rook launched forward and snatched the keyring. Turning to the small window, he threw them out.

"No!" I screamed.

Submitting to the compulsion, Rook grimaced as his canines grew, overtaking his lips. Two *pops* rang out as Rook's legs bent and grew. He fell to his knees, and I scooted back in the cell. It wasn't far enough, but I could go no farther. Cold stone pressed my spine. Rook's eyes rolled back, leaving milky whites in their stead. Dark hair sprouted along his neck, and his shirt tore. Like a wildfire spreading across low brush, hair overtook Rook's body. In seconds, Rook was gone. In his place sat a quivering beast, its gangly limbs distorted to fit the tower that confined it. Two feral, yellow eyes snapped open.

The Hound had come.

There was nothing of Rook left in those amber beacons. Mouth suddenly dry, I gulped—the Hound leapt at the bars, spattering me with drool. A swinging claw caught my cheek, I barely felt the sting. The stone ground my shoulder blades as I flattened myself. Paws tipped with knives swiped at my feet, I yanked them back and crouched, trying to make myself small. Massive jaws clamped down on the cell door, and the Hound shook its head, spewing frothy saliva as it tried frantically to tear through the bars.

Let them be strong!

When it couldn't get through, the Hound sat back and howled. I slammed my hands over my ears, but a dizziness overcame me. I braced myself, trying not to slip forward even an inch. A breeze rushed through the tower window and the Hound froze. Its snout pulled back, sniffing the air that carried in. The Hound gave another howl and bounded down the stairs. Scrabbling claws echoed up the tower. They grew fainter, until even my straining ears couldn't hear them. Only then did I notice the pain of contorting my body to avoid the Hound. I slumped into a pile but didn't relax. Fear and adrenaline kept my muscles tight and ready. Though the tower was quiet, phantom snarls pounded my eardrums.

I could still see those eyes, bright lanterns in a sea of shadows.

Every encounter with the Hound left me thinking of my father and Lysander. We shared this bond of terror. How many others would suffer if the Hound was permitted to continue his reign, feasting on our community? I had to get out of here, and regardless of anything I felt for Rook, the Hound must be stopped.

Rook might be a victim to this place, but he was *still* a monster.

On my tiptoes, I peered out the barred window. Beneath the moonlight, the Hound galloped down the cobblestone path. It plunged through the veil and was lost in the trees.

Dread consumed me as I wondered:

Who would die tonight?

Lesson Eleven

I told you: never bargain.

Creaaaak.

Blinking awake, I shaded my face from the light pouring through the tower window. Rook stood in the open door; the keys swung in his hand. I sat up and stretched my neck.

Motioning to the keys, I said, "What if you couldn't find those?"

"Be thankful the Hound couldn't find them last night." Rook mumbled. Shame clung to him; he refused to look at me and took extra care to avoid the thick graze along my cheek. I exited the cell, and he followed like a beaten animal. Descending the steps, it was only when I reached the bottom that I noticed Rook limping.

"What happened?"

Who did you kill?

Understanding the real intention of my question, Rook replied, "They were prepared. Only the Hound was injured." That didn't ease my concern as much as I'd thought it would.

"Show me your leg," I ordered, entering the sage room. "Trousers off." The phrase might have excited Rook once, but today it only reinforced his shame. He unbuckled and slipped from his trousers. "Sit." Rook sat by the fire, and I propped his leg on an ottoman. The wound in his calf was deep, and the flesh jagged. When I realized I could see bone peeking out, I bit back bile. "What did this?"

"A sort of ridged pike." Rook made a stabbing motion. I gave a dizzy nod and set to work cleaning the gash.

"So, you can't always control when you change?"

Lowering his gaze, Rook fidgeted with a shirt button. "I cannot." Pulling out my sewing kit, I bunched Rook's skin and started stitching. Rook's nails dug into the chair and his head fell back.

Hoping to distract him, I said, "It seemed like you knew it was coming."

"I can smell it." Rook waved vaguely at his nose. "It starts soft and sweet, like lilac or apple blossom. Then it thickens...and it hurts." He rubbed his stomach. "There's an unending pain—a hunger. It drives me mad; I'm not myself." Rook massaged his temples. "The scent pulls the Hound toward..." He trailed away and sighed. "Well, you know how it ends."

My father. Lysander. Countless other innocents.

When I finished sewing, the wound didn't look bad at all. There would be scarring, but Rook would be perfectly fine. With some difficulty, I removed the stitches from Rook's side, which no longer served their purpose. I sat back on my heels and rubbed my neck, readying for the conversation to come.

"Rook," I began.

Rook went rigid, already alarmed.

"It's time for me to go."

Rook blinked several times, like he hadn't understood what I'd said.

"You can change again," I said. "I have to go home."

Rook reacted as if I'd thrown a bucket of water on him. A flurry of emotions warped his expressions. Furrowing of denial, snarling of anger. Finally managing to find words, Rook spit, "But I must know!"

"Know what?!"

"What happens at the end of the story!" Rook leapt up, only wincing slightly when he put weight on his leg. "How do they defeat the queen?"

"You've learned your letters and the basics of reading," I said. "You can figure the rest out on your own!" Rook steadied himself on the fireplace, his eyes darted while his mind worked.

He's looking for a reason to keep you here.

"You swore!" Rook straightened and jabbed a finger in my direction. "You promised you would teach me to read, and only *then* would I help you escape!"

"My brother is dying!" I cried. "Every day he creeps closer to death! I must go!"

"You gave me your word!" Rook shouted, his face twisting into a hideous scowl. "You will stay until I can read, not just the letters and basics, but until I can read *without you* beside me!" Rook stooped to yank on his trousers. "If you fail to fulfill your end of the bargain, so shall I." Though Rook's voice had calmed, his fingers shook so violently, it took him three tries to buckle his trousers. He shrugged and said, "You can live with the knowledge that your treachery killed your brother." Rook tore the door open, and it was in desperation that I said the words that would wound him the most.

"What if you hurt me?"

Rook paused, his knuckles bone-white on the doorframe.

"Hm?" I approached him, fists clenched. "Last night, what if you'd torn my head off in your rage? What if you returned and found my mutilated body in that cell?"

Rook glanced back... He looked at my scraped cheek. I'd spoken his fear, thrown it out and forced him to confront it. Though Rook wore an angry scowl, his eyes—tinged pink and dewy with grief—betrayed him. For a moment, that same grief rocked me. I pitied Rook, who mourned the life he might have lived. Part of me wanted to reach out, to console Rook and ease that suffering... No.

I would not let my feelings stop me from doing what I must.

"This is your chance to do something right," I said. "Rook, please. Let me go to my brother." In earnest, I continued, "Lysander. His name is Lysander, and he's the youngest in my family, my baby brother. I have to take care of him." Rook simply stared, unspeaking. Laboured breathing heaved his chest, and when I could take his silence no longer, I whispered, "Roo—"

"Agh!" Rook shouted in my face. Last nights events were fresh in my mind, and I curled inward, protecting myself from him. That tiny reaction—cowering—crumbled Rook's features, and he covered his face. He tore from the room, and I swore the entire castle shook with the slammed door. A small carving fell from the mantle and shattered. I rushed the door, trying to tear it open. It wouldn't budge.

"You talk of forgiveness yet do nothing to atone for your misdeeds!" I cried. "Are you a monster, or are you not?"

Rook didn't open the door.

It was my turn to welcome shame.

Stupid girl. He never intended to let you leave. You'll never see Lysander, or Lottie, or your mother again.

I'd wasted all this time, when really, I should have been trying to escape.

What do I do now?

Out on the balcony, the roses I'd climbed down were gone. At the base of the castle, only roots and tiny, hacked away stumps remained.

Was it a trick of the castle?

A memory of Rook swinging the axe, felling ancient trees like they were saplings, danced through my mind.

Back inside, I sat on the bed. Morning faded into afternoon, and my stomach growled. Rook never returned. My thoughts drifted through the castle, down the steps, and into the library. I could almost see Rook, sat at the fire, staring into the flickering flames, unblinking against the heat, a hand resting against his temple. Brooding in his lamentable misery. Did he long for a goblet of wine? Did monsters long for wine? Or was it bloodlust that beset Rook in his torment?

I dragged the chair and jammed it under the doorknob. Like that would do anything to protect me if Rook chose to come—to unleash his rage on me.

I lay down. In the sage room, I was more comfortable than the tower cell, but caged, nonetheless.

"Liliwen."

A whisper.

"Nng." I grunted against the blankets.

"Lili."

Blinking awake, I squinted. The fire had long burned down to ashes. On the bedside table, a three-pronged candelabra flickered to life.

The bedroom door was open.

Again, a whisper beckoned me. "Lysander?" I muttered.

"Lili," Lysander's voice called.

Yawning, I rubbed a knuckle at my eye but couldn't seem to shake the sleepy haze that clung to me. Slipping from bed, I took the candelabra and shuffled to the door. I struggled to think—to remember where I was. I peered around the door and castle walls met me. Oh...right.

"Come," Lysander's voice called. "Downstairs." Had my family come to rescue me? Warmth, like a comforting arm, curled around me and encouraged me forward. I stumbled, feeling quite drunk and unsteady. I hadn't had anything to drink last night, had I? The same presence that wrapped around my shoulders guided me all the way to the foyer, pausing at the door below the stairs.

It was wide open.

I held the candelabra higher, lighting the way. "Lysss?" My voice was slow, slurred.

"I'm here," Lysander's voice floated out. I scuffled down the hall and into the dark courtyard. Soft moonlight illuminated a figure standing at the base of the tree.

"How'd you get here?" I called. "Was it the wolves?"

Lysander turned. Open wounds ran along his chest; they oozed blood, like thick sap. Lysander reached for me. "I'm dying, Lili."

My breath caught and I stumbled forward. "I'll get my needles, Lys, I can fix—"

Lysander grabbed me and a chill sprung up my arms.

"Stitches can't save me, Lili!" He plucked a fruit from a branch. "But this—this can." The fruit shone in his palm. "Eat this. Escape and come back to me." He picked a second fruit. "Bring me one. It'll make me strong; I won't die." Offering me the fruit, Lysander whispered, "Eat it and save us both." Reluctantly, I accepted the fruit. I wanted to throw it away, but my thoughts were slowed, confused. Why didn't I want it near me?

"I'm not supposed to eat this," I slurred. "It's poison."

"It's not poison," Lysander hissed. "He's lying. Eat, and you won't need him!"

I tore the fruit in two. The cloying scent assaulted me, and the seeds reflected the moon like small gems. How tempting it was to pluck one from the cream-coloured membrane that held it captive.

"Just one seed," Lysander murmured. I wiggled a seed free. Lysander's eyes darted between the fruit and my lips, his head bobbing. He brought his hand beneath mine and pushed it toward my mouth. "Yes! Save me, Lili!"

I popped the seed in my mouth—

"WHAT ARE YOU DOING?!" Rook's voice shattered my eardrums. The courtyard teetered as I was shaken like a doll and Rook appeared. He bellowed, "Did you eat it?!" His eyes, wide and terrified, searched my face.

Fingers shaking, I withdrew the seed. Rook slapped my hand and sent the seed bouncing across the cobblestone. "My brother," I whispered. Rook's head darted wildly around the courtyard; he couldn't see Lysander.

But I could.

Lysander's head tilted. His smile stretched and his pupils thinned to reptile slits. Scoffing, he knelt and crouched on all fours. He backed into the darkness and disappeared. Free from the unwelcome enchantment, a shudder racked me. Rook yanked off his night coat and slipped it around me. He guided me back into the castle.

"Come dawn," Rook said, "we're getting you out of here."

When morning came, I found Rook in the chair by the fire at the end of my bed. Wide awake, his brows furrowed at the book he held. I sat up, and Rook set the book aside.

I blurted, "Did you mean what you said last night?"

Rook wrapped his arms around himself. "When you're ready, we will go." I jumped from bed and tugged on my clothes. Without a word, Rook headed to the balcony. Once dressed, I joined him outside. It was a grey, dreary morning, and the humid pressure of an oncoming storm kindled an ache in my temples.

I thought of last night, of waking to the beckoning whispers of the tree. "Why is this place so intent on me eating the fruit?"

"There's an evil that inhabits this place," Rook started. "It creeps, spreads like an infection. Every wretched creature is driven by some evil that *wants* you to be cursed..." Rook's voice trailed away. Cursed...*like me*.

"To be cursed is to serve this place, to carry out its bidding. And if it can't curse you, if it can't make you bend to its will, it'll kill you."

All the close calls flashed through my memory. The Lady of the Lake, the ghouls dragging me down into the mausoleum. "But why?"

"You can't escape and warn others if you're dead." Rook sighed. What he said next, he said so softly I could barely hear him. "You'll never be safe here." Rook looked out, over the far-off treetops. His fingers tapped the railing, reminding me of a woodpecker rapping a tree. "Before we part"—Rook paused and cleared his throat—"I must apologize for how I behaved yesterday. After I change, the experience leaves me...easily enraged for days. Normally, there are no consequences for these fits but..."

I offered a sullen nod, accepting his apology.

Rook's dark hair, unkempt from the night before, fell in lovely tangles around his face. I wanted to brush it aside, so nothing might conceal him from me. I shook the thought away and gazed over the bramble of roses. Rook couldn't possibly have looked this way when I'd first stumbled in here. Another trick of the castle; like Rook said, it cast some spell—bewitched me into believing him handsome, so I might remain here forever. I closed my eyes and tried to ignore the tapping of Rook's fingers. I tried not to picture his hands at all, lest I be taken with the feeling of them trailing along my skin.

It's no spell, silly girl! My mind scolded. *It's hormones! You need to leave this place. If you must think of him, let it be at night, when you're alone and safely in bed...*

A gentle *'tink'* ceased my rambling thoughts. My knife sat on the railing. "It's beautiful," Rook remarked.

I slid the knife into the sheath on my belt. "It belonged to my father." It seemed there was nothing to do but part ways, and I started toward the door.

"This is a terrible thing to say," Rook began, "but I'm happy you tried to kill me. In a forest of cursed things, meeting you was a blessing." He half-smiled, his scar pulling back into a sweet dimple. "If I should live another seventy-five years in this prison, I'll treasure the time we shared."

My mouth suddenly dry, I swallowed. This was a sham, a forbidden friendship. This man *killed* my father and very well might kill my brother too. The shame I felt was depthless when I realized...I was happy to have met Rook too. The feelings were too complex to voice, and when I said nothing, Rook's smile faded. A clap of thunder cracked above. Rook looked to the clouds, and squinted as the first rain drops fell. Fear leapt within me as the drops kissed my skin. Would Rook use this as another excuse to keep me here? Through the pelting rain, we looked at one another. Rook didn't suggest I stay. In his silence, I wondered if he was considering which fate was worse, for me to catch an ailment from the storm, or to remain here, with him.

My answer came quickly. Rook approached me, pausing so close I could see watery rivulets streaming down his neck, around the goosebumps that sprung up against the chill. "Let's get this over with," he muttered, and went inside. Somberly, I entered after him. Rook waved at the vanity. "Take whatever you wish; it's wasted here." He headed for the door. "I'll meet you downstairs when you're ready."

And just like that, I was alone.

I didn't want a reminder of this place, and I certainly didn't want to take anything, lest it curse me. I examined a bud vase on the mantle. Though, it would be a nice way to teach Lottie a lesson for borrowing my things without asking. I checked the room, making sure I hadn't forgotten anything. I slipped my cloak on and opened my satchel to make sure I'd packed everything: bright peacock feathers filled the satchel. I shifted the feathers, and found a velvet pouch filled with petals, the ones I'd known would make a lovely dye. I withdrew a feather, and the emerald eye glinted back at me. I remembered how desperately I'd wanted to take as many as I could, and how Rook had seemingly read my mind and given me one. Loss pitted my chest.

Perhaps it would not be so easy to forget this place.

I met Rook in the foyer. Arms crossed, he wouldn't meet my eyes. At least, I think that was the case. I couldn't really tell...because I wouldn't meet his. I was nearly through the grand doors when they tried to close on me. Rook's arms thrust out, stopping them. A vein chorded his neck, and he shouted, "Knock it off!" I doubled over and ran beneath his arm. Slipping through, Rook turned on the ruined castle. "On my life," he growled, "she will leave this wretched pit of misery!"

In response to Rook's hushed threats, the many black windows of the castle bore down upon us. I hurried down the crumbling stairs, and my foot slipped on the wet stone, and I flailed. Rook caught me.

"Thanks."

He didn't reply.

We walked through the overgrown hedges and the tangled roses. It seemed so long ago since we'd come in together. As we continued along the cobbled path, Rook pulled his sopping shirt over his head and tossed it away.

The veil crept closer.

Rook unbuckled his trousers. My presence didn't hinder him as he slid out of his clothes, uncaring. He trudged along, naked in the pounding rain. Nearing the veil, Rook tossed his trousers aside. Splintering cracks rang out as his body broke and reformed.

The Hound crossed the veil.

The trees themselves cowered and retreated. Only when one whimpered did I realize they were thin wolves. Unafraid, the Hound advanced. The wolves ran—the Hound lashed out and grabbed the slowest. The Hound shook the wolf like a limp rabbit and tossed it aside.

The wolf was dead before it hit the ground.

The Hound leaned back, unleashing an ear-rupturing howl. It sprung up and pursued the fleeing wolves. Just like we'd discussed, I waited until the Hound was out of sight, and I approached the veil. I couldn't deny there was an uncomfortable reluctance to pass through. *It's this place and its trickery!* I assured myself. I took one last look at the towering castle, at the gargoyles guarding Rook's window. I'll feel better...when I'm home.

I hope.

With less vigor than I'd anticipated, I stepped through the veil. A cloud of breath billowed out, and I shivered. I listened to the sounds of the Hollow.

Nothing.

I ran, grabbing my crossbow on the way. It was slippery, and I was extra careful as I heaved it up.

Be swift, Little Dove.

Ancient trees passed me on either side. Up ahead, the meadow peeked through the gloom. Only when I burst into the fresh air did I slow to catch my breath. The rain had softened to a light drizzle, and I waded through the tall grass and wildflowers.

A far-off growl quickened my pace.

I'd nearly made it to the copse of birch trees when a low howl floated across the meadow. Back the way I'd come, a thin wolf stalked from the thick pines. The grass parted as it crept into the meadow. Behind it, a second wolf prowled. I did my best to reign my panic, but the wolf was closing in, almost sliding through the grass like a serpent. I yanked the crossbow forward and loaded a bolt. Crouching, I aimed. Grey fur exploded in front of me. I flinched and pressed the trigger. The wolf yelped and collapsed, trampling the grass and wildflowers. Though it's body still twitched, the bolt protruded from the wolf's eye socket. It was dead. I braced the wolf's head and ripped the bolt out. *There were two!* My panicked mind raced. *Where's the other one?!* I reloaded the crossbow and peered over the meadow. My head whipped wildly, trying to locate the threat.

Delicate flowers danced in the breeze.

I strained to hear anything—panting, footfalls, crushing underbrush—but only the pitter-patter of rain and the rushing of a far-off stream could be heard.

Movement came from my side; a force collided against me and sent me sprawling, the crossbow slipping from my grasp. Both the wolf and I regained our footing and rounded on one another. A gob of drool fell from the wolf's jagged teeth. I drew my knife as the wolf crouched, readying to spring forward and rip my throat out.

Needles and leaves exploded from the trees at the far-side of the meadow. For one horrifying moment, I thought it was more wolves, that I might be torn apart by a frenzied pack. My horror didn't abate even after I recognized the dark figure of the Hound bounding across the meadow. It attacked the wolf with such momentum as to send them both hurtling through the grass. Pained yips rang out as the Hound pulled the wolf apart—I didn't want to see any more. I snatched my crossbow; squeals battered me as I fled. The trees approached, and an intrusive thought, a memory of my father, pushed into my mind.

Father pulled me outside. At the end of the cobbled path, we watched my mother head off to work. I'd asked, "What are we doing?"

"Waving to your mother."

"But we'll see her tonight, won't we?"

"We will, but what if something happens to her while she's gone? We wave so she knows we love her and hope to see her soon." When my mother reached the end of the road, she turned and waved. I returned it and started to head inside, eager to get back to my sewing. I held the door for my father, but he wasn't behind me. He remained on the road.

Only when my mother was lost from my father's sight did he join me.

Reaching the trees, I stopped to take one last look at the Hound. Watching me go, he stood out, a blight in the meadow. I smeared rain from my eyes, and I couldn't stop myself.

I waved.

PART TWO

Lesson Twelve

The Hollow devours the
complacent.

Soaked through and nearly frozen, I wrenched open the back gate and ran to the cottage. Bursting in, I opened my mouth to explain.

A room of people greeted me.

Ruven and three of his copper-haired brothers were gathered around the table, a map unrolled across it. Lottie, sporting an eye patch, sat at the table with a knife pointing at the map. Leaning in the doorway, with deep lines creasing her forehead, was my mother. Since she'd joined the guard, she'd only removed her uniform to sleep. Now, in my father's green night coat, she looked older than ever. The sofa, the last spot I'd seen Lysander, was empty. Was I too late?

Was he gone?

"Where's Lys?" My voice cracked.

Mother shook away her surprise and uttered, "Bedroom." Throughout the den, brows cocked and arms crossed as the tone shifted from relief...to suspicion.

Pointing the blade at me, Lottie said, "Catch another rabbit?"

"No." I raised my hands, as if I were protecting myself from another pack of wolves. "I can explain."

In an escalating tone, my mother said, "Liliwen *Alouette* Valet."

Punishments had *always* fallen under my mother's jurisdiction, and an old fear rocked my belly. "I…" Scrutinized by so many witnesses, my tongue was suddenly dry. "Well, I—"

"Speak quickly!" Mother demanded, sending a tremor through me. "Everyone here was prepared to *die* to find you. You better have a sound excuse—"

"I went to kill the Hound!"

Everyone in the room gasped. Except for Lottie, who's good eye looked at me like I was the dumbest creature in all the Hollow.

Honestly, she might be right.

"There were wolves!" The words spilled out. "A man saved me, but he was injured." The mention of a man perked Ruven's shoulders, and his eyes narrowed. "I stayed with him to see he was healed before I left."

My mother tilted her head.

Lottie twirled the knife, the tip of which dug into my grandfather's table.

"Yes, it was careless!" I cried. "But I thought if I brought back the Hound's heart, we could use the money, or the attention of the queen's physician to help Lysander!"

With the same tone one might use to address a toddler, Lottie sneered, "Why would you go *alone*?"

"Because I can't lose anyone else!" I screamed.

Ruven rubbed his neck as his brothers shifted uncomfortably around him. They exchanged a word. His brothers removed their assortment of weapons—rusty and worn, the weapons of farmers—and excused themselves. Lysander appeared in the hall, no doubt awakened by my shouting. He was a ghost, but he managed a weak smile.

To Lysander, my mother said, "Back to bed. She's home." Mother gave me a warning glare, and ushered Lysander to his room.

That left Ruven, Lottie, and me. Lottie looked at Ruven, who hadn't taken his eyes off me since I'd entered. She gagged as if she meant to be sick, and said, "I'm going to shoot something." She left, knocking me roughly with her shoulder on her way out.

Ruven sheathed his sword, which was much newer and sharper than the tools his brothers had come with. Crossing the room, Ruven took my hands. "Liliwen, I... When you didn't meet me..." He cleared his throat and pinched the bridge of his nose. He embraced me, letting his chin rest in my hair. "I—I thought we'd be bringing back your body, or"—he choked—"what was left of it." Water dripped down my face, and I realized Ruven was crying.

"Hey, it's okay." I pulled away so I could see him.

Ruven leaned down and kissed me.

With two hands, I shoved him. "What are you doing?!" I wiped my cheek, removing *his* tears from my face.

Ruven sputtered, "I'm sorry!" as horror consumed his tear-stained face. "I shouldn't—I wasn't thinking!" He inched closer. "I was just so relieved to have you back!"

The back door opened, and Lottie entered. She grabbed something from the mantle, and said, "Forgot my grips." Catching sight of my hunched shoulders, and Ruven's cherry-red face, Lottie squinted. "What's going on?"

"Nothing," Ruven stuttered. "Just making sure Lili is okay, that's all."

After a good look at me, Lottie crossed her arms. "You've checked on her. Now go."

"Lottie," I said, "it's okay." Lottie scowled at us both and shut the door. Out of the corner of my eye, her head appeared in the rear window.

"Ruven, I can't do this." I wrapped my arms around myself. "My family needs me."

"If not now, when?" Ruven snapped. "How long will you keep me in your pocket?"

My mouth fell open. The words stung; they shocked any response from my mind. "Ruven—"

Knock-knock-knock, came the rapping of knuckles on glass. Lottie glared through the panes. She pointed at Ruven, then the front door. Her lips formed a very clear message, *'Get out!'*

It was no secret that Ruven never liked Lottie. I mean, no one did. Not *really*. Ruven had always tolerated her with a smile, but now, his nostrils flared into a sneer, so unlike anything I'd ever seen on his bright, happy face. In a blink, the rage was hidden. Ruven offered a tight-lipped smile and, without saying goodbye, left. Lottie shook her head and disappeared from the window. I stared at the door Ruven had vanished through. Over the last few days, my intuition had kept me alive. The goosebumps, the little voice, everything homed in on danger, on things that might hurt me. When Ruven glared at Lottie, his fingers tightened on the hilt of his sword, and his knuckles turned whiter than bleached bone. I couldn't help but wonder, what was Ruven doing to my sister in his mind?

In that brief exchange, I felt as unsafe as if I were in the Hollow.

Shaken in more ways than one, I joined Lottie out back. Sitting amongst the wisteria, I watched arrow after arrow pierce the target set against the short stone wall. When Lottie paused to collect arrows, I asked, "How is Lysander, really?"

"Bad," Lottie sniped. "Worse off from all the worrying you've caused us." I knew better than to rise to Lottie's attacks. When I said nothing, Lottie scoffed and resumed shooting. Crunching footfalls alerted us, and we both tensed.

Marek peered around the cottage. He cried, "Liliwen!" and joined us. "The Leroux boys told me you'd returned; I wanted to be sure of it myself!"

I stood and Marek embraced me. Lottie shot me a curious glance; I returned it with equal confusion. Marek pulled away, but his hand remained on my arm. "You know, I've always felt the need to protect you. Ever since your father died, you've felt like a daughter to me." I smiled, though something inside me drew away, as if I'd nearly stepped on a snake coiled in the underbrush.

I stepped away. "Glad to be back."

Marek stroked his silvery beard. "Ruven mentioned someone helped you."

With slight hesitation, I replied, "Yes."

Marek made an encouraging gesture, requesting more information. "Who?" Though appearing relaxed, there was an eagerness in the way Marek watched me. Perhaps the Hollow had skewed my intuition, the unfortunate result of knowing there were monsters around every corner, and that if I didn't keep my wits about me, I'd be eaten. That suspicion was bleeding into my safe spaces—analyzing everyone's tone and motive. First the exchange with Ruven, and now Marek. Not everyone was out to harm us.

Still, Marek's questions left me...wary.

"Just...someone in the woods."

"A wild man, living in the Hollow, helped you?" Marek scoffed.

"Yes."

Marek laughed and glanced at Lottie, as if to say, *'Can you believe this?'* Smirking, Marek asked, "And what did this *wild* man look like? Did he have large feet and hair covering his body?" He chuckled. "Or was he, perhaps, invisible?"

Lottie threw down her bow. "Why are you questioning my sister?"

Marek, unused to questions, balked.

Crossing her arms, Lottie snapped, "Say what you mean to say or leave!" Marek, looking like he'd just received a slap, straightened. Lottie was resolute in her stare down, and Marek reassessed the situation.

In a strange turn of events, it was *Marek* who raised his palms in apology. "I'm sorry. I'm simply trying to locate anyone who might have more information on the Hound. You must admit, the notion that anyone might call the Hollow home is...unlikely."

"What does it matter?" Lottie said, possessing all the arrogance of her age. "We almost had him last time."

"Well..." Marek crossed his arms and stroked his beard. "You nearly died."

"What?" I rounded on Lottie.

Excited mania entered Lottie's un-eyepatched eye. "The Hound took a swing at me." She raised her hand, where a finger was missing.

"Lottie!" I clutched her hand and examined the nub.

Lottie wormed away and wiggled her remaining fingers. "Didn't get the good ones though." She snatched her bow and shot an arrow. It struck the red-ringed centre of the target, for emphasis.

Staring at the arrow, I murmured, "He nearly killed you."

What if I'd come home, only to find Lottie and Lysander dead? Sickness swelled in my throat, at the thought of their mangled bodies, at the thought of burying them and knowing I'd have to return to a house that was, once again, emptier than when I'd left it. I braced myself on the cottage for support.

"Don't worry," Lottie said and smiled wickedly. She pointed her bow at me, stabbing the air. "I slit him good."

Renewed fury burned my cheeks. I'd been careless and weak. I'd allowed Rook and my childish feelings to distract me. Right here, Lottie stood proudly in the yard. Lottie, whom no one really liked, but I *loved*. Behind me, Lysander, who'd always made me laugh when I couldn't even dream of smiling, lay in bed, nearly dead. I *needed* them. Back home amongst my loved ones, my resolve was stronger than ever.

The Hound would not destroy my family.

Marek, perhaps mistaking my anger for worry, said, "We will catch the Hound; there will be justice for your father and your brother." Marek talked of Lysander as if he were already gone. Grief hit me anew, but I was more worried about Lottie's deep breath, readying to say something to Marek—

The back door opened.

"I thought I heard voices," my mother said, and joined us. I was in heaps of trouble, so I avoided her gaze. I noticed Marek anxiously tugging his sleeve.

"Might I..." Marek started. "Might I have a word with your mother?"

Neither Lottie nor I moved, waiting instead to see what our mother wanted. "Both of you go inside," she instructed. "Lottie was about to start dinner anyway."

"Ugh!" Lottie tossed her bow. "I hope you fancy gruel for supper," she muttered, and we headed in. Neither of us went to the kitchen. We crouched beneath the window and listened.

Marek's muffled voice said, "How are you?" He asked the question so casually, one might assume he was inquiring about the weather, and not the well-being of a mother bearing the weight of nursing her dying child.

"Captain, what do you have to say?" My mother's voice quickened. "Do you have news of the Hound?"

"Um, well—no." Marek stumbled on his words. "I can carry this burden no longer."

"Marek..." Mother spoke with cautious authority, as if she were handing out a warning to one of us, and not addressing her direct superior.

Heeding no warning, Marek blundered forward. "I have a question I must ask you." Fabric shuffled on the stones.

"Marek! What are you doing?!" Our mother's horrified voice yanked Lottie and I up to the window.

Marek knelt on one knee. "Evette, please! You are the most beautiful creature! I have loved you from the second I laid eyes on you. You must marry me!"

"This is not the time, nor the place for such nonsense!" My mother hauled Marek to his feet. "Stand up! We've got a beast to slay, and you a town to protect!"

Perhaps harbouring a great deal of guilt, Marek snapped, "I'm doing my best, Evette!" He sighed. "It's like people *want* to be killed." Mother's stare silenced Marek. "I'm—I'm sorry," Marek apologized. He reached for my mother; she backed away. "Are you... Are you certain you won't have me?"

Wrapping my father's night coat tighter, my mother said, "My answer is no. I do *not* want another husband." Marek frowned, his face akin to a pouty toddler. "You're handsome, and a captain. Someone will be overjoyed to be your beloved, but it isn't me."

"But—"

"No," my mother interrupted, appearing so much like a teacher shushing a rambunctious student. "I have my children, Captain. My heart is full."

After a long pause, Marek nodded. From the set of his jaw, I knew he hadn't accepted the refusal. Over my mother's shoulder, Marek caught Lottie and me in the window.

He tilted his head, reminding me so much of the thin wolves that stalked the Hollow.

Beside me, Lottie shivered.

As I lay in bed, one of my father's lessons nagged at me. No matter how I tried to push it away, it wiggled back like an obsession.

One morning, Father had taken Lottie and me into the Hollow. It was Lottie's first, and *last*, gathering trip. As we passed a familiar old oak, one we often picnicked beneath, Father heard a distressed cry farther on. He shooed us off the path and instructed me to, "Remain hidden and watch your sister." I did as I was told, but Lottie, who never listened, wandered off. I remembered the sickening spike of terror I felt when I reached for her and found empty air. At that point, I could only obey one of my father's commands. I chose the one I believed to be most important.

Cautiously, I'd crept from my hiding spot to find Lottie.

While I searched for my sister, a hand rested on my shoulder. The familiar weight quelled my mounting panic. My father pointed back the way we'd come, where Lottie crouched beneath the old oak. When Lottie was looking away, the oak changed. A twisted face grew from the knotted bark. Branches inched closer to Lottie, who poked a bug without a care in the world.

Looking between my father and Lottie, I whispered, "Shouldn't we do something?"

"Patience."

The gnarled branches closed in on Lottie. I feared I would lose a sister, and that fear pushed me from the cover of the bushes. "Lottie!"

The branches halted.

Startled, Lottie shot me an angry glare and caught sight of the tree. Though the tree hadn't gotten her, I thought the terror might kill her. Father approached from behind me, wielding a torch. Only then did the tree fade back into its disguise. Lottie ran to me; she'd clutched my legs and hidden herself beneath my cloak while she wept.

Our unsympathetic father only said, "I told you to stay close."

I held Lottie as we left the Hollow. We both learned a lesson that day, though Lottie certainly learned it harder. Just because something has existed one way for a long time, we must never get complacent. We are a blink in a monster's life. They are patient, and they will strike when you least expect it.

With this memory dancing lazy circles in my mind, I fell into an uneasy sleep.

"Father!"

Lysander's voice carried down the hall like an alarm. Lottie met me in the doorway, her hair, messy from sleep, jutted around her face. Her nightgown billowed behind her like a white cloak as we chased Lysander. He shambled to the front door and fought with the doorknob.

"The Hound is coming, Father!" Lysander bellowed. "Get inside!"

Reaching Lysander first, Lottie took his elbows. "Let's get you back to bed—oof!" Lysander's fist connected with Lottie. She stumbled back, hit the sofa, and her feet flew up over her head. Righting herself, she rubbed her jaw. "The sickness hasn't taken *all* his strength." I pulled Lysander from the door; his skin was fire. Mother ran down the hall, wrenching on Father's night coat.

"Let me go!" Lysander shoved me away. He yanked open the door and shuffled down the front path. Pointing to an empty field across the road, Lysander shrieked, "There he is!"

"Catch him!" Mother leapt over me.

"Father!" Lysander wrenched open the gate. "Come back!" Mother caught the back of Lysander's shirt. Lottie and I snatched his arms and wrestled him toward the cottage. He doubled over and coughed. Warm vomit speckled my ankles. Together, we dragged Lysander back to bed. Once we were certain he didn't mean to escape again, Mother sat down and pressed a cool cloth to his forehead. Standing helplessly in the doorway, Lottie and I watched Lysander crumple against our mother. Breathing deep, Lysander's frail body calmed. Perhaps, like our mother, he was also comforted by the smell of my father's perfume, still clinging to the night coat.

"Return to your beds," Mother commanded. "There is nothing more we can do."

Lottie chirped, "But—"

"Now!"

Lottie and I clambered over each other. Back in our bedroom, we climbed into our respective beds. I lay on my side, staring at Lottie, who glared at the ceiling. Did she even see it? Or was she like me, unable to see anything but our mother, clutching our brother so tight he couldn't possibly leave us? I sniffled. Across the room, Lottie angrily wiped her cheek.

"Lottie," I started, "I have a plan, and I'm going to need you to trust me." Lottie turned her glare on me. "I can kill the Hound," I whispered.

"How?" she hissed. "How can you do what an entire coven of guards cannot?"

He trusts me, and I can do what an entire army cannot. I can get close, while he sleeps.

I wanted to confess, to tell Lottie everything and relieve that burden on myself. But, if she knew what I was about to do, she'd never allow it. Once upon a time, I'd thought bringing her was the best option. Facing the choice now, I couldn't risk her life—and I couldn't risk alerting Rook by bringing her. Lottie had a big mouth and a bad attitude; she'd try to murder Rook the second she saw him.

"You're just going to have to trust me," I said. Lottie shook her head and rolled away. "Tomorrow morning," I continued. "I'm going into the Hollow—alone. When Mother realizes I'm gone, tell her I've gone to the next town over for more Queensfoil." I paused, trying to find the strength to voice the end of my plan. "I'll return the following day with the Hound's heart. The queen will send her messengers with the reward, and we'll beg the physician to help Lysander."

Lottie sat up. "There's nothing any of us can do for Lysander!" she hissed. "Now is a time to be together! To be here for our mother when she buries her son." Lottie choked but continued. "How will you feel when Lysander dies while you're off playing in the woods?" Lottie was always so good at voicing my fears. "And what happens if you don't come back?"

"What happens if I succeed, and Lysander lives?" I whisper-shouted. Lottie only huffed and laid back down. "Lottie, I need you to trust me. I can do this."

Lottie's only response was a drawn-out sigh.

"I will return with the Hound's heart."

Silence.

"Keep Lysander alive, just one more day."

When I was certain Lottie wouldn't respond, I rolled away. Tomorrow, I would *not* falter. My emotions would not control me. I would be strong. I would do it for my father and my mother, for Lysander and Lottie. For each person touched by the beast's evil.

I *would* kill the Hound.

But Rook... I shook my head, choking down the guilt. Rook died when that cursed fruit touched his lips. A phantom walked the halls of that ruined castle. I wasn't killing a man; I was killing a monster.

Across the dark room, Lottie sniffled.

I just hoped she would keep my secret long enough for me to do it.

Lesson Thirteen

To survive the Hollow, you must be
the most treacherous of those who
inhabit it.

The skeletons were picked clean.

In the meadow, the wildflowers swayed against the thin wolves' bones. All manner of creatures had slunk from the Hollow and devoured the unguarded flesh. I tried not to think about them as I made my way through the pines, toward the Hollow's most dangerous inhabitant. The farther I trudged, the more skeletons I found. It seemed the Hound had been exceptionally bloodthirsty during my escape. I hadn't gone far into the thicket when a twig snapped. I raised my crossbow and pointed behind me.

Only trees and brambles.

I lowered the bow, but I couldn't shake the feeling I wasn't alone. Some foreign presence, different from the whispers and the Watcher, joined me. Hypervigilant, I trod onward. As I tiptoed around bracken, I went over my plan one last time. Strapped to my thigh, hidden beneath layers of fabric, was my father's blade. Tonight, when Rook was asleep, I'd plunge the dagger into his chest. I'd carve out his heart and bring it to the queen.

Death would not claim Lysander.

As I pushed aside pine boughs, Rook plagued me. The scar marring his cheek, pulling back into a dimple. His eyes, like ice, darting to my lips, yearning for them—*No!* If anyone had been watching, they might have thought me daft, for how violently I shook the thoughts of Rook away. I will take the Hound's heart in repayment for what's been taken from my family.

I'm not weak; I will not fail again.

Movement rustled the bushes, and I drew my crossbow. From the shadows, a hulking figure prowled forth. Here in the grim Hollow, the Hound and I met again. A beast who refused to devour, and a young woman who refused to pull the trigger. A sane person would have fled, and any witness to our meeting would surely have been puzzled. But I...I struggled to see the beast.

I *saw* Rook.

This time, when I lowered my bow, I did not raise it again. As the crossbow came to rest at my side, I swore—*I swore*—I heard a noise behind me.

Bones snapped and broke as the Hound shrunk and disappeared into the underbrush. The bushes shook, and a naked Rook appeared. Gazing upon me, Rook's chest heaved. He blinked quickly, as if he couldn't believe it—as if I were some trick played by the Hollow.

"It's no trick," I murmured.

Rook's face slipped back into the resting scowl he'd worn when I'd first met him. "You came back?" he asked, in a tone as emotionless as granite.

Figuring my presence was answer enough, I simply shrugged in a way that said, *'Obviously.'* Rook stepped from the shadows. He did nothing to cover his nakedness, and I stared at the canopy above. Rook was motionless, like a sculpture out here in the Hollow.

"How... How are you?" I didn't know what to say; I hadn't expected him to be so...so *cold*. Rook offered a brief shrug, his face betraying nothing of his feelings. This wasn't the person I left. *He's hiding from you*, I thought. *Keeping himself safe. Look what happened last time; you ran from him as fast as your feet might carry you. This is a disguise, to keep you at bay.*

Had I lost my chance to get close to Rook?

I started forward. Rook took a wary step back. I had to act fast, needed to say something to bring back that trust. "I—I came back to..." I floundered, thinking quickly. *Make something up!* My mind screamed. But I couldn't think of anything to say. I shrugged and whispered, "I wanted to see you."

With one slow blink, Rook closed his eyes.

As if he'd dreamed those very words.

"Your brother?" Rook started. "Does he live?"

A knife of grief twisted my guts. "He... He got better."

A lie.

Tension eased from Rook's shoulders, as if he'd received happy news of his own brother. Lowering his voice, Rook wore the shame of confession when he said, "I missed you."

I closed my eyes, and somewhere far away, heard myself say, "I missed you too."

Not a lie.

Rook started toward me; a beam of sunlight struggling through the pines banished his mask of shadows. In the light, I saw his crooked smile.

"I figured we'd finish that book," I said.

Beautiful delight blossomed in Rook, parting his lips in happy surprise. That delight cut deeper than any wound.

Rook reached for me, and I opened up to him. "Ha-ha!" He lifted me and twirled. I clung to his neck and stumbled when he put me down. Rook coughed and quelled his excitement. "Shall we go back?" His face lit with a new emotion, one so foreign in my image of Rook.

Hope.

As we walked, Rook spoke excitedly. "I think I'm on the right track, Lili—I think I can cure it. My affliction." My stomach fluttered when my nickname poured from Rook. He continued, "Using the fruit itself." He clasped a fist. "I just need more time." He side-eyed me.

Making sure I was *really* there.

The veil came into view, and Rook stopped walking. "Uh—hold on." Rook found his discarded clothes and put them back on. He snapped a suspender over his shoulder, and strolled back to me. Rook grasped my hands between his rough, calloused fingers. "Liliwen," he said, with such emphasis, such passion, I knew he was about to admit something of considerable importance. "When you first came to me, I didn't want to be cured, not really. To me, death was the inevitable cure, the only way to stop me—stop the memories and the nightmares." Rook's Adam's apple bobbed against his throat. "Emptiness consumed me. Loneliness that stretched for decades." I couldn't look at him—stared only at Rook's feet. But his confession came, nonetheless.

"You took that away, and you gave me hope." Rook stooped, forcing me to look. "I want to live, Lili," he breathed. "And I will fight for it, because of *you*."

In silence, I begged Rook cease speaking.

Please, I cannot bear it.

It was one of the most difficult things I'd ever done but…I managed a smile. A tear welled along my lashes, and I didn't stop it rolling down my cheek. Cupping my face, Rook smudged the tear away. Then, he gave my hand a squeeze and pulled me through the veil.

But not before I had a chance to check behind.

It might have been a trick of the Hollow, but I was certain a figure disappeared into the shadows.

In the main hall, thick boards covered the door to the courtyard. Rook bound up the stairs, taking them four and five at a time.

"Come to me, Liliwen," Rook's voice called.

"Pardon me?" I halted on the stairs.

Rook turned, wearing a, *'What gives?'* look.

"I'm not a dog," I snapped. "I don't come when I'm called."

Confusion muddled Rook's face. "I didn't say anything."

I opened my mouth to disagree—

"Liliwen," Rook's haunted voice called, despite Rook standing in front of me, mouth closed. The voice floated from below the stairs. It begged me to come to the courtyard, to the fruit.

"Uh...nothing."

I joined Real-Rook upstairs. He maneuvered around piles of finery he'd looted from the rooms. I picked up a golden goblet and examined my reflection in a topaz the size of a walnut.

"Redecorating?"

Rook hesitated over a heap of silverware. "Well, I started thinking I might actually find a cure, and I might leave this place." He rubbed his neck. "You know, I think about them, every night. The people the Hound killed." He picked up a spoon, which had recently been polished. "This won't bring loved ones back, but perhaps, if families lost those who provide for them..."

Seeing himself in the polished spoon, a look came over Rook, like he might be ill.

"It's a stupid idea," he murmured, dropping the spoon. "To try and bribe forgiveness for the lives the Hound took." I looked at the first pile, looming high with golden chalices and fabrics.

The pile meant for my family.

"Do you remember the first person the Hound killed?" I asked.

"It was the hardest... I—*the Hound* couldn't finish the job. The man got away, but his injuries were severe; he couldn't have survived." Rook walked away; I chased him. "Only a handful of people have escaped the Hound. Two, maybe three. They plague my nightmares, that they weren't awarded a swift death. Their suffering must have been immeasurable."

I'd always believed the Hound killed people because it was an evil beast beset by an uncontrollable thirst for blood, a monster with no conscience or regard for human life. But, as much as I hated to admit it, I knew that wasn't Rook. "Why do you—the Hound—why does the Hound kill people?" Rook bristled. "The Hound can subsist on animals, right? The blood of calves, and other livestock? So, why does the beast kill *people*?"

"It just...happens." Rook anxiously spun the cuff at his wrist. "I—I don't..." Rook trailed off. "Can we finish that book, please? I think it'll help me make sense of a few things."

"Uh, sure."

He was already walking toward his room. "Hold on," he called, and I waited. When he returned, Rook handed me a small wooden object. "I thought of you, when I made this."

A raven, carved in light cherry wood.

Rook pointed and said, "For your hair." I turned the raven over, and indeed, there was a hole in the back where a braid might pass through. The crafting was meticulous; each feather was carved with such precision, such care.

"I was only gone one night," I whispered, examining the hair piece. Even Lysander, who'd been whittling since he was five, would be hard-pressed to craft a trinket so fine.

"I thought of you often," Rook replied. "May I?" He took the raven, and I turned so he might slide it in place. When he finished, he grasped my hand. Leading me to the library, he said, "When you left, I felt agony and hope."

Each second I spent with Rook, my stomach clenched tighter. Reluctantly, I asked, "Hope for what?"

"That you might return."

I'm going to be ill.

We walked through the library, and I looked for something I might be sick in. "And now that I'm here, what do you feel?"

"Only the latter." Rook squeezed my hand. "How could anyone look at you and not have hope?" Rook waited for me to sit, then did so himself. A vase of fragrant, fat peonies sat on the mantle. I clutched my belly and, again, scanned for some vessel that might hold my vomit. Rook pulled his chair close, so he might see me directly. "Last night, I couldn't sleep. I lay in bed and, come midnight, heard a rapping on the door. In my haste, I fell down the stairs." He laughed. "I thought you'd gotten lost and found your way back." Rook's face fell to despair. "But there was only darkness. Nothing more."

The fire was too hot. Sweat dampened my spine, and I wiped my palms along my trousers. Rook watched my fingers work as they bunched the fabric along my thighs.

"What's wrong?" Rook rested the back of his hand against my forehead. "Are you ill?"

"I'm sorry. I just... The past few days have been overwhelming, with you—and my brother." I gave Rook a weak smile. "My nerves are getting the better of me."

"Shall I make you tea?"

"Oh no. Don't worry about m—"

But Rook was already leaping over the chair. Meaning to help with the task, I rose. "No, please," Rook called back. "I'll get it for you." Feeling both reluctant and a little confused, I resumed my seat. It seemed wrong, for many reasons, to sit there and relax while Rook made me tea. Though I was uncomfortable, I remained where I was.

For about five seconds.

I got up and paced. Pulling a book off the shelf, I opened it and tried to read. I wiped my brow and moved even farther from the fire. Why can't I stop sweating?! In no time at all, Rook returned, carrying a golden tray. Setting it down, he approached me. He held my back and leaned in, as if to examine me.

He knows something is wrong! I thought frantically. Or, even more distressingly: *He's worried about you.*

"Tea will help." I side-stepped Rook.

I picked up the pot, which Rook promptly took. With a great deal of authority, he said, "Will you sit down?"

"Yes, yes, okay." Rook served me, and then, curiously, poured himself a cup. "Can you drink that?" I asked.

"No, but I favour the smell."

I inhaled; chamomile tickled my nose. *Drink your daisies.* Though Rook couldn't partake, he seemed content that I enjoyed it.

"How was your time with your family? You must have been happy, to see your brother better."

Over my teacup, my eyes started to well.

"Oh dear." Rook set down his cup and took my hand. "Liliwen, please, talk to me."

"I just... I love them."

"It's a wonderful thing, to have a family you love." Rook smiled. "What else do you love?"

Scrunching up my face, I thought. What else did I love about them? "Well, Lysander, he's good at foraging, and he loves whittling. He's good with children. I think he'd like to follow in my mother's footsteps, become a teacher..." I laughed. "Truly, I think he'd like to find a companion with a profitable job. He's quite the flirt; half the village is after him. Vexes our poor mother."

Rook laughed. "I bet it does."

"And my sister—Lottie—well." I tried to think of the best way to describe Lottie, and her respective interests. "She likes fighting." Rook and I both laughed. "She's a pain, but she'd do anything for me." I sipped my tea. "I love her dearly."

"I can tell," Rook said. "Though, while I'm interested in *anything* you hold dear, my question was meant to inquire about *you*. What do you like, what do you desire?"

I stared at Rook. Had I not answered the question?

But part of me had heard Rook, because from the depths of my mind, I saw it. The white cottage off in the woods, and the freedom that came with it... I shook it away and gulped my tea. "I—I don't know. I'm fond of sewing, but mostly, I just want my family to be happy and safe."

"That sounds like an awful lot of responsibility."

Though Rook didn't say it out loud, I could almost hear him whisper:

'A cage of my own creation, but a cage nonetheless.'

Silence settled in the library. Rook cleared his throat and said, "Are you up for a joke? Well, more like a riddle. A fellow woodcutter told me it, back in the day."

I wasn't in the mood, but I supposed that was Rook's point. He was overjoyed by my return and wanted to share that mirth.

"Go ahead," I said.

"What hangs at a man's thigh and wants to prod the hole that its often prod before?"

"Um..." I shifted uncomfortably. "Is it..." I stared at the crotch of Rook's trousers.

"Liliwen," Rook remarked, feigning dismay. He withdrew a keyring from his jacket. "A key!"

I groaned.

"I didn't say it was a *good* joke!" Rook defended and laughed. Waving at the castle, he said, "Unfortunately, the court jester died quite some time ago; I checked the graveyard."

"How'd he die?"

"Well," A cringe wiped Rook's smile. "He was eaten."

I sipped my tea, and said, "Do you think he tasted funny?" Rook's somber frown leapt into a satisfied smile. That was the funniest thing of all, and I howled.

I realized with a great deal of sadness...I was going to miss this. We continued talking of nothing. I thought it a wonder, how he didn't tire of hearing me speak of the small things, and before long, the fire was providing the only light in the library.

A yawn snuck up on me.

"We should rest," Rook said. Panic woke me quicker than if I'd been doused with water. We couldn't sleep. If Rook fell asleep...

I'm not ready!

"But, you said you needed answers!" I jumped up and grabbed the book we'd been reading. "We're so close to the end!" Returning to my seat, I opened the book and hid behind the cover.

Rook laughed as I stifled another yawn. "I've waited this long; what's one more night?"

"But—"

"The answer will be there in the morning." Rook tapped my arm. "You've had a long day." Standing, he went to put out the fire.

"Wait!" Rook stopped, poker in hand. Desperate for inspiration, I looked around the library... The music box! I pointed and blurted, "Dance!" I almost knocked Rook into the flames as I sprung up and wrenched open the music box. A soft melody filled the library. "Dance with me!"

Setting the poker down, Rook smiled and said, "Very well." He beckoned me forward, and I went to him. Sliding his arm around my back, Rook pulled me close. I molded to him. As we swayed, I recalled our first dance, how rigid it was. Tonight, there was no space between us. Once, I'd avoided Rook's face, but now, I couldn't stop looking. I wanted to memorize the lines—the scar that ran along his cheek.

Did he hate that scar?

I thought it the most beautiful, interesting thing about him. I'd never told him, wouldn't get a chance.

"This will seem forward," Rook began. "While you were gone, I thought of nothing else." He cleared his throat. "Liliwen, my life is an everlasting road of regret. But, watching you flee across the meadow—I've never known such anguish." Rook cast his eyes down. "It's evil of me, but in that moment, I wished I'd kept you here. Stolen you away from whatever life you lived before me. That regret so swiftly turned to torment. Over and over, I scolded myself. If only I'd told you how I felt, maybe you would have stayed."

"My brother needed me—"

"I know, I know, it's foolish." Rook chuckled. "You always would have left. But the doubtful mind sees mistakes, not reason."

"You were simply lonely," I muttered. "You would say these things to anyone who walked in here."

"No. No, I wouldn't," Rook corrected. "You witnessed my unkindness when you found this cursed place. You could have let me suffer and die. You didn't. You helped me—a beast. Even if I knew *nothing* else of your character, that would be enough." I glanced down. Rook brought my face back to his, refusing to let me hide.

"Only you."

Rook continued, "I promised myself, if I ever met you again, I would tell you how I felt. Once you knew, then you might decide what to do with it, and I would be content. I could rest knowing I'd given you this piece of me to hold or destroy." Rook leaned forward, and I thought he might kiss me. Instead, Rook rested his forehead against mine and closed his eyes.

"I want to spend every moment, every breath, with *you*."

The music seemed to vanish; the crackling fire dimmed. There was just Rook and me, and his forehead pressed against mine. Rook pulled away, and I almost wished he had kissed me. Our lips pressed together would be less intimate than his whispered confessions. Concerned, Rook wiped a tear from my face. "You are dreadfully silent." Beneath furrowed brows, he asked, "Have I been deceived; do you not feel these things too?"

Those were two separate questions. The first was easy, but the second was not so readily answered, and I struggled to reconcile that.

"I see the way you look at me," Rook said. "Before you left, you kissed me with such fervor. Surely, that was not false." Rook chuckled, a nervous thing. "You came *back* to me." When, still, I could say nothing, Rook licked his lip and said, "Please." Dropping my hands, he backed away. "Tell me if I'm mistaken, and I will leave you be."

Seeing Rook leave, I panicked and shouted, "No!" It startled Rook, and I composed myself. "No," I whispered. "You are not mistaken."

"No," Rook breathed, sweeping back to me. "No, I knew I could not be." Rook's hand found the back of my neck, and he pulled me into his chest. Nestled in Rook's arms, I wasn't the oldest daughter. I wasn't on an impossible journey to slay a monster, to avenge my father and save my brother's life.

I was just a girl.

A quiet sob escaped my throat. "What's wrong?" Rook asked. "You look as though someone has sentenced you to death, not confessed themselves so freely!" Rook turned downcast. "Granted, I suppose, coming from me, it is not so much a blessing as a curse."

In Rook, I saw warmth, kindness, compassion, undying devotion—anything I could ever want. It was right there; all I had to do was take it.

"No, nothing is wrong. I just... I'm...happy."

"I would spend my lifetime ensuring you never felt anything less," Rook whispered. "I swear it." The melody picked up, and Rook spun me away. This time, when he brought me back into his arms, I landed softly, a key fitting a lock.

This time, I wanted to be there.

Behind me, Rook wrapped his arms around my waist. They were unbreaking—they were chainmail around my shoulders.

Inside his embrace, I was protected.

Rook breathed deep, grazing my hair, longing to be lost in it. His hand slid up, between my breasts, and along my throat. He guided my face, so I might look over my shoulder at him.

"Do you trust me?"

"I do," I whispered.

Rook dipped me low, so low I might fall. My back went rigid. "I have you," Rook reassured. "Trust me." My tension eased. I relaxed into Rook's arms, until it was only his strength keeping me from crashing down. Closing my eyes, I let my head fall back. Rook's soft breath brushed my throat as he drew me up, back to him.

Rook's restraint was frustrating, so much greater than mine. I longed for his touch—for his lips. And it wasn't a question of whether he wanted me. We were so close, I felt every part of him against me. Every part of him *wanting* me as much as I wanted him. Where was Rook's urgency? Why didn't he fall upon me like he had before? When he'd kissed me and held my throat so I might not escape his starved desires? I searched Rook's face for answers.

He was calm.

Before, there was uncertainty. That I would leave, that our time together was limited, but now... Rook believed we had all the time in the world. Because he'd chosen me.

Me, to spend the rest of his life with.

Without thinking, I brushed a strand of hair behind his ear. Somewhere far away, the music slowed and died. Rook's gaze dropped to my lips, and then back to my eyes. A muscle twitched in his jaw and his brow furrowed, as if he were fighting a battle in his mind. Should I?

Shouldn't I?

I stood on my toes and kissed him.

No!

Stop!

What are you doing?!

A surprised gust of air blew through Rook's nose and tickled my eyelashes. I don't know how long we held that kiss, though it wasn't enough. When we parted, I looked away. I couldn't look at him. I rested against his chest, and I heard it, like the drums of war, building. My goal: the reason I'd come here.

Rook's heart.

No! The Hound's heart! For they were one and the same. I'd stolen one; now, I needed the other.

"I'm not ready to sleep yet," I murmured. "Just one more chapter."

"Of course." The words rumbled through Rook's chest. "Anything."

We untangled ourselves, and I sat back down with our book. "Did you read at all while I was gone?"

"Some. I struggled to concentrate."

I sat down and read. Rook stared into the fire, only half-listening. I didn't stop, even when Rook's eyes lulled. "The queen beckoned her daughter from the room, leaving her beloved to bleed to death." When I turned to the next page, my fingers betrayed me. I fumbled with the book and dropped it.

Rook jolted awake and mumbled, "Bedtime?"

"I'm nearly finished."

Rook rested his head on his hand. Gradually, his lids closed. Still, I read aloud. "To free herself from the queen's power, the queen's daughter cut the ring from her hand, finger and all." Rook shifted, leaning back in the chair. The rise and fall of his chest slowed as he fought sleep. Rook lost the battle; his head fell back, exposing his throat. A sign of trust.

This is it.

I closed the book and set it aside. As I looked at Rook, at the skin peeking from his shirt, my thoughts fought inside me.

I can't do it.

You must!

I can't!

I massaged my temples and sat for a long time with my head in my hands. Part of me wanted Rook to wake up, to stop me before I could complete my task. The other part knew what I had to do for my family.

What will I lose if I fail to return with Rook's heart?

I saw the future—saw Lysander growing up, having his own family, should he choose that path. My mother becoming a grandmother and spoiling any grandchildren that came along. Lottie, teaching them to shoot and how best to annoy their father.

And if I didn't slay Rook, what could I possibly gain?

A life, bonded to a sad, immortal beast? Would I really bring him home and introduce my family to the monster who slayed half our family? That wasn't a life.

There was no happy ending there.

It was not a time for selfishness, regardless of how I felt for *the Hound*. I withdrew the dagger and traced the engraved whorls along the hilt. I had hoped simply holding it would give me courage. It did the opposite. The weight of the blade was impossibly heavy.

Do it for your father.

And Lysander.

And all the people he hasn't yet taken.

Moving as silently as I might in the Hollow, I loomed over Rook. His face, tortured and grim during waking hours, was at peace. How hard would I have to stab? The largest animals I'd finished off were deer—cutting their throats after Father had shot or trapped them.

Rook's advice carried back to me, *'If you're going to attack someone, you might be certain to land a killing blow the first time. Lest you be hurt in the aftermath of their survival.'* A slew of other confessions accompanied his words.

'I want to live.'

'I want to spend every moment, every breath, with you.'

Revenge tightened my grip, and loyalty raised the knife. Justice would plunge it down, into Rook—*into the Hound!* I stared at my target, at his chest. His chest, that rose so softly in my presence. Trusting me not to harm him.

Do it! My thoughts screamed. *Kill the Hound!*

But Rook—*the Hound! The beast who killed your father! Who will kill again if you don't stop him! Do it and get back to your family!*

In his sleep, a sweet smile tugged his cheek.

'Every breath, with you.'

Rook.

I can't.

I can't do it.

My vision blurred. From the start, this was a terrible plan. As soon as the Hound became a person, I should have told Lottie. Or my mother. I should have let them take over. They were ruthless, and they knew what had to be done. I wasn't the strong daughter my father raised.

I was weak.

A sob shuddered through me, and Rook stirred. His lazy gaze readjusted and landed on me. Confusion knitted Rook's brows as he saw the blade. He leapt up with such force the chair fell. Keeping the chair between us, Rook choked out, "Liliwen?"

I dragged my wrist along my face, wiping tears away. "Rook."

Focusing on the blade, Rook muttered, "Pretend." He licked his lips. "This was a scheme." Wanting the weapon in my possession no longer, I tossed the dagger aside. It clattered across the floor, sending up sharp *tings* as it went. "Pretending," Rook mumbled, not really looking at me—seeing his thoughts and nothing else. "So you could... So you could *kill* me while I slept."

"Rook, listen to me." I raised my palms—desperately showing I meant him no harm.

But Rook wasn't listening. He shuffled away. "It wasn't real... It wasn't real." Running his hands through his hair, he muttered, "No, no, no." He repeated it, over and over. Backing into a bookshelf, Rook stood there, grinding his palms against his face and whispering, "Not you—not you!" He slid, curling into himself against the shelf.

Rounding the chair, I said, "I'll explain everything."

A whimper left Rook.

The sound of it nearly brought me to my knees. I reached out, but Rook smacked my hand away. Tears sprung into his wide, furious eyes. "I should have known!" There was a sickened, jaundiced look to his stare. "Who sent you?" The words sounded different, almost hissed, as if there were suddenly much sharper teeth between them and me.

You could really use a knife, couldn't you? Foolish girl.

Glancing after my blade, I stuttered, "I—What do you mean?"

"Someone sent you to kill me!" Rook snarled, suddenly so close, his breath brushed my neck. "Tell me!"

Startled by the brutality, I cried, "No. No one sent me!"

"Liar!" Great gobs of spit flew from Rook's mouth.

"Rook. Please. I couldn't do it!"

"If I hadn't caught you, that blade would be hilt deep in my chest!" Rook was impossibly tall, and his icy blue eyes were gone, replaced by yellow, feral things. "Speak again, and it will be the last thing you say!" I started to speak again, but Rook covered my mouth and shoved me against a bookshelf. Books rained down, crashing all around. I wrenched myself free and tried to run. Rook caught the front of my shirt. The fabric ripped as he slammed me back into the shelf. Rook's hand slid to my throat, forcing me to look at him. Inches from my face, Rook's yellowed eyes bore into me. They were inhuman.

Sick.

Rook's brows pulsed once, *daring* me to speak. *You're in danger!* My intuition screamed. The Hound was clawing its way out of Rook. Nails dug into my throat, five points keeping me submissive. Sharp teeth bared, Rook drifted, so close to my face. His breathing, frenzied and feral, stoked the fear rampaging through me. One misstep, one wrong word, and...

Death.

Rook dragged his face along my collarbone, inhaling deeply. Could he smell the terror that threatened to buckle me? Rook tilted his head, those yellowed beacons widening. Against my mouth, he growled, "You're not nearly frightened enough." Rook's trembling hands fell away. Pointing to the door he bellowed, "Move!"

I tensed against the shout. Crossing my arms, I kept my torn shirt in place and hurried through the library. Walking through the foyer, I stared at the great doors. If I could distract Rook and break free, could I make it through the Hollow at night?

Rook's hand curled around my arm, dashing my plans. "Take a left, Liliwen." He did not wait; his nails dug into me as he swung me to the stairs. I didn't start up them, and Rook leaned forward, his words tickling my ear. "I recommend you walk," he hissed, "while you're able."

If I wanted to live to see tomorrow, I had to be clever.

Slowly, I ascended. I didn't even try to go to the sage room, I headed for the tower's winding staircase. Rook moved stealthily in the dark halls behind me. I tried to keep an eye on him, catching our reflections in the mirrors that scattered the walls. Though I must admit, *seeing* Rook was deeply unsettling. He stalked me with unnerving focus. I hated the way his shoulders raised—coiled—like a serpent ready to snatch its prey. I scurried up the tower steps.

Rook muttered to himself, "I let myself become foolish in my loneliness. Again."

Again?

"Desperate," Rook growled. "Pathetic!"

At the top of the tower, Rook opened the cell. "I tried to save you from this fate, from becoming a monster like me." He shoved me in and said, "You might not change into a beast, but if someone sent you here to kill me and you agreed—"

"No one sent me!"

Calmer now, Rook seemed to have the Hound under control, and I spoke frantically, trying to say as many things as I could before Rook locked me in. "I came here on my own!" I cried. "Yes, I shot you. Yes, I wanted to kill you, but that was before!"

"You came back today with a blade on you. Were you or were you not intending to kill me when you crossed the veil."

"Well..."

Rook scowled.

"But I couldn't do it!"

"You couldn't because I stopped you!" Rook slammed the cell door. "If no one sent you, if these actions are your own, you're more of a monster than I ever could be. You condemn me, but I would never willingly take a life!" Rook shouted. "And neither would the Hound—if it wasn't puppeted by someone with only the cruelest of intentions. I have no *choice* but to serve. Unlike you, I have no say, no control whether I kill, or *who* I kill." Rook turned his back on me.

Confusion and panic sent me hurtling into the bars. "What do you mean?" I cried. "You don't choose who you kill?"

But Rook was gone.

"Rook, please! I didn't have a choice!"

Rook didn't reappear.

Lesson Fourteen

At least until you're on the outside of
the cage...be kind to your jailer.

The fogginess of sleep ebbed, and the horrible memories of the previous night flooded back. I blinked at the floor and caught sight of two black boots through the cell door. Following them up, I found Rook leaning against the bars, arms splayed above him. How long had he been there, glaring down upon me with such contempt? My body ached and I cracked my neck as I sat up.

"You said you didn't have a choice," Rook spat. "What did you mean?"

"I—"

"What were you planning on doing after you killed me, hm?" I smoothed my trousers and waited. Rook huffed and crossed his arms. Seemingly against his will, his eyes drifted down my chest, where the torn fabric was nearly indecent. Even in his rage, Rook wanted me.

And he couldn't *stand* it.

His jaw flexed, and he looked at the ground. Through gritted teeth, he said, "Proceed."

"Our queen. She offered a reward for the Hound's heart."

"Ah!" Rook spit, his eyes bulging. "You'd have killed me for wealth?" He slammed the bars. "How much am I worth? Hm? You could have taken any number of things from this castle, and I would have allowed it, but alas, your greed knows no bounds!"

"The Hound killed my father."

Rook's jaw slackened; his arms fell limp at his sides.

"Why didn't you tell me you couldn't control who you killed?" I asked, though it sounded an awful lot like an accusation.

"You're asking me why I wasn't honest?" Rook's fingers curled around the bars, his face reddening behind them. "You were going to carve out my *fucking heart*, Liliwen!"

Well, I suppose I had that coming.

"When you said you couldn't control who you killed," I whispered. "What did *you* mean?"

Rook re-crossed his arms, and he stayed that way for a long time. His face scrunched here and there, as if he were calculating, trying to solve some complex problem. And it certainly *was* a complex problem.

Deciding whether to trust me or not.

"The Hound really killed your father?" he asked.

I looked Rook dead in the eye.

"Yes."

Rook let his arms rest on the bars. Closing his eyes, he leaned his head against the cell too. "I was here for sixty-eight years, and the Hound never killed anyone." Rook sighed. "One day, someone breached the veil. Ushered in by the wolves, or so I thought at the time." Rook rubbed his throat. "I hadn't spoken to anyone in so long, I was desperate. I welcomed them and spoke freely." He ground his forehead against the bars. "When I woke the next morning, they were gone." Rook raised his arm and spun the cuff around his wrist. "This was left in their stead." Rook's hand dropped. "The Hound attacked the first person that night."

"My father." I nodded. "He was the first."

Rook ran a hand across his face, hiding his eyes. "I'm so sorry."

Sorry wasn't enough; we both knew that.

What else could he do but say it?

"Believe it or not, vengeance isn't why I'm here either. My brother, Lysander, the Hound attacked him also." What little colour remained in Rook's complexion slipped away. "Like Father, Lysander escaped, but the damage to his body... It's only a matter of time before death claims him. In lieu of a reward, I was going to ask the queen—or rather, her physician, to help my brother." I rested my head against my arms. "After losing my father, I just... I can't lose Lysander."

Locked in this cell, I was no closer to helping my brother. The hopelessness struck, and a sob shuddered through me. I couldn't fight it anymore, I let everything out. Ugly, heaving wails shook my entire body. Years of concealing tears from my mother and Lottie screamed, *"Get a grip girl!"* I didn't care! I didn't care that Rook saw the weakness. Let him see! I was done hiding. I was done trying my best only to fail time and time again...

Creak.

The cell door was open.

On his knees, Rook knelt beside me.

There was a flighty urgency about him when he said, "Take me to him."

Wiping snot from my nose, I asked, "What?"

Rook was already picking me up. "I might be able to help your brother." Gently, he pushed me from the cell. "Take me to him."

"What do you mean?"

"Come with me."

Rook's eyes were alight with opportunity. Saying sorry wasn't enough but, if he could help my brother...

It was a start.

In the physician's room, Rook showed me the needle with the small plunger. "Do you remember this?"

"I do." Crossing my arms, I leaned on a table.

"Embrace it again."

"I said I remembered."

"Lili," Rook said. "Please."

Though weary, I took the needle and let the memory in. *Exactly as I remembered, the man lay on a table amongst a crowd of rushing women. As the fair-haired and freckled woman plunged the needle into his neck, I remembered how I thought he had the same waxen look as Lysander.* Ripping myself from the memory I pointed the needle at Rook, who raised his arms in defense.

"We can use this to help my brother?"

Rook walked along the lines of melons and various experiments. "And these. These objects hold memories, recipes, for a sort of...cure. I've been working again, trying to understand it all better, in the hopes of finding something for myself." Rook led me to a table, where a cloth shrouded a large object. Rook withdrew the cloth—the snarling jaws of a thin wolf greeted me. I recoiled so violently, I sent several beakers spilling from a nearby shelf.

"Sorry," Rook apologized, and dragged me back.

The wolf was dead.

A deep laceration trailed down the wolf's neck. I recognized the wounds; the same cuts ran down Lysander's body.

"The Hound bit this wolf and it lived," Rook said. "I brought it back here and cured the sickness that grew from the wounds."

"Okay, but this wolf is dead."

"Well, yes, of course it's dead," Rook agreed. "I think it died of shock. The whole endeavor was too much for the creature's heart..." Rook trailed away. "But! I'm fairly certain I cured the sickness *before* it perished."

My hopes died on the table with the wolf.

"Rook, I don't know." What if I allowed Rook to inject my brother, only for him to die faster—or more painfully. Suddenly, it was Lysander lying on the table, dead. I set the needle down, far away from me. "I just... I don't know."

"Please," Rook begged. "You must allow me to fix this, if I can." I met Rook's pleading eyes. What other choice did I have?

"Fine," I muttered, though barely any sound came out.

Rook wasted no time. He grabbed a bag and tossed items in. After a stack of vials, he stopped. "Lili, this might be difficult to hear, but I don't control who I kill. Do you understand what that means?"

Of course. I hadn't stopped thinking about the implications of that statement. How could I not? But the thought was so appalling, so utterly impossible, that I didn't dare voice it, as if that might lend the insanity some merit.

"Whether you want to admit it or not," Rook said, "someone wants your family dead." How could that be true? I buried my head in my hands. Rook continued, gently. "Do you have any idea as to whom that might be?"

Hugging myself, I whispered, "I don't."

"You can't think of anyone with motive? Anyone who might have something to gain? An inheritance, perhaps?"

I shrugged. "Mother and Lottie are guards, Lysander a gatherer, and I a seamstress. We have little money and even less land. The cottage is falling apart, no one could possibly want it. As far as I know, we haven't mortally offended anyone."

"Who was the last person the Hound attacked?"

After a deep breath, I said, "My sister." Rook stopped packing; his head tilted in mortified sympathy. I chewed my lip and looked at the floor.

"Who would want to harm her?"

I choked on a laugh. "I'm sure half the town has considered throttling Lottie at some point, me included." Rook looked taken aback. "Trust me, you'll see."

"Well," Rook said. "Personality aside, who would have a serious reason to harm your sister?"

"I don't know!" I threw up my hands. "Like I said, everyone kind of wants to hurt Lottie; she's not a good measure. The real question is, who would want to harm her *as well as* my father and Lysander?" I massaged my temples. "And why hasn't the Hound come for me yet?"

"Don't!" Rook threw a bundle of gauze at me. I dodged and he said, "Don't put that question into the world!"

I rubbed my neck. "The person who came to you—what did they look like?"

"I have no idea."

"How?!"

"Do you think it's not frustrating for me also?" Rook growled back. "We drank together; they must have slipped some concoction in my drink. I possess the memory of them, though their face is gone."

"Hair colour? Clothing?"

"No!" Rook uttered. "It could have been a young man; it could have been a grey-haired old woman." He gestured to the dead animal on the table. "It could have been a wolf dressed in a black cloak for all I know."

I dragged a hand down my face. "Alright. Well, one problem at a time."

Rook was quiet as we trudged through the Hollow. Though I tried small talk, his only responses were curt nods and fleeting smiles. When Rook finally spoke, it was grim.

"If this doesn't work, I want you to continue with the original plan."

I tripped on a fallen log and snapped, "What?"

"If your brother doesn't respond to the cure," Rook said, "you should deliver the Hound's heart to the queen."

"I'm not going to do that."

Rook stopped. "Lili, please."

I shook my head. "You said it yourself; you've nearly found a way to cure your sickness. You have a chance at a normal life."

"If this works, and your brother lives, yes. But if he dies... I'd rather die trying to save him than live knowing I killed him."

"Rook, no—"

Rook took my hands, silencing me. "Lili, I can barely breathe when I look at you. Knowing the pain I've caused." In desperation, he said, "I cannot live, having stolen your brother." I tried to pull away, an impossible task in Rook's grip. "I owe you this. Please." Rook's eyes searched mine, pleading. Anxious fingers tapped against me, and his voice cracked when he said, "I'm not a beast."

I held fast. "No." I resisted Rook's grip, and reluctantly, he let go. As we walked back to the cottage, back to Lysander, the dread that I thought could go no further, deepened.

Lesson Fifteen

Love who you love.

It was not yet noon when I approached the back gate with Rook in tow. I pulled the gate open, but he hesitated.

"Is your mother in there?"

Guessing she probably remained home from work to care for Lysander, I replied, "I would imagine so."

"And your sister?"

"Unfortunately."

Rook fidgeted with his bag. "What if they despise me?" The question was so raw, so vulnerable, I didn't know what to say. *What's it matter if they don't like you?* The response died on my tongue. Because he *wanted* them to like him.

Because they mattered to me.

I held Rook's hand. Together, we walked down the path. Just as I meant to push open the back door, Rook stalled again.

"Load your bow."

"What?"

"I'm suddenly feeling quite foolish." Rook swallowed. "We're entering a small space, filled with people whom someone might command I murder at any moment." He backtracked. "In my haste to help, I fear I've put your entire family in danger."

"No—Rook." I grabbed his arm and stopped his retreating.

Rook dug his heels in. Through gritted teeth, he repeated, "Load. Your. Bow."

"Fine, fine!" I unslung the crossbow and did as Rook said. "Happy?"

"If I start acting strange, if you see anything out of character"—Rook tapped his chest—"through the heart." I stared at Rook's chest; he squeezed my shoulder. "You have my permission; I hold no malice for you. Protect your family."

After a deep breath, I entered the cottage. Rook stooped below the frame after me. At the kitchen table, Lottie slept with her head on her arms, clutching an empty ale mug. I crossed the room, and Lottie shot awake with a disgruntled, "Humph." Still wearing an eye-patch, her good eye focused on Rook. Her mouth fell open, revealing a front tooth was missing.

Descending on Lottie, I cried, "What happened?" Lottie didn't respond, instead, she leapt from the table and backed away. Glaring at Rook, she reached for the bow on her back. "Lottie?" I whispered. Lottie was fearless to a fault; why was she alarmed so?

My mother came down the hall, stopping when she saw the stranger in our home. I put myself in front of Rook. "This is Rook. He protected me from the wolves."

"Oh?" Mother said. "This is who you've been running off to meet in the Hollow?" She motioned to Rook. "Leaving us to wonder whether you're alive or dead?"

Rook shifted and mumbled, "It's Everard, actually."

Ignoring Rook, I started, "I... We think he can help Lysander." My mother's stony expression was beyond comprehension. She examined him, and the scar. Surely, she wouldn't turn him away. "Please," I begged, bringing my mother's attention back to me. "I trust him." It was hard to ignore the sharp intake of breath behind me, from directly where Rook stood.

My mother studied me good and hard.

"Please," I repeated.

My mother pinched the bridge of her nose...and she stepped aside.

"Mother!" Lottie yelled.

My mother shot Lottie a silencing glare. "If he saved my daughter," she snarled, "perhaps he can save my son."

I hurried through the den with Rook. The pungent, acidity of sickness met us in the hall. The stench didn't hinder me, but coming into Lysander's room, his frail body was staggering. He'd always been so proud—so tall. But now...he already looked like a corpse. Rook grasped the doorframe for support. My mother joined us, watching Rook closely. I stepped aside, allowing Rook by. He knelt beside Lysander, who didn't stir.

"Only sleeping," Mother murmured, quelling my fear. She never left Rook unwatched, and her hand never left the hilt of her sword.

Rook flipped open his satchel and withdrew the needle. "We may need to hold him." Rounding Rook, I stood near the headboard, and my mother settled on the end of the bed. Rook peeled the bandages from Lysander's chest. Rook gagged.

"Here. Let me." I reached for the needle. Rook glanced up, his brows furrowed, considering my request. With a *'hand it to me'* gesture, I said, "You hold him, and I'll do it."

Rook's jaw twitched and he turned back to Lysander. He dragged a hand down his face, took a deep breath...and plunged the needle into one of Lysander's wounds.

"Aghhh!" Lysander jarred awake. I thrust his shoulders into the bed. Lysander thrashed, and my mother threw all her weight on his legs, holding him firm. Lysander leaned sideways; he was ill down my trouser leg.

"Lottie!" my mother shouted. Lottie didn't come. Figures. When there was work to do, Lottie always disappeared. We managed on our own anyway. I think, when my mother called for help, she was remembering Lysander as he used to be. It hurt my heart, how little effort it took to keep my once strong brother immobile. Rook withdrew the needle. He refilled it and plunged it into another gash in Lysander's chest. Gradually, Lysander stopped thrashing and relaxed into the bed.

"Who's this?"

Ruven stood in the doorway.

Beside me, Rook examined Ruven as one might inspect a curious insect. He remained entirely undisturbed by the newcomer's presence. But Ruven... He looked as if he might burn down the entire cottage, regardless of who was left inside it. Looking between Ruven and Rook, I thought, *please, don't do anything*. Not with Lysander and my mother in the room. Deciding this was not something to leave to fate, I rose and pushed Ruven into the hall. He craned to the side, so he might still watch Rook. There was such intimidation in Ruven's posture, as if he were observing a rival or some monster he must slay. It reminded me of how he'd looked at Lottie, and the way he'd gripped his sword so tight...

Hold on.

Someone had sent the Hound for Lottie.

Rook's voice floated back to me. *'Who would want to harm her?'*

I scrutinized Ruven.

Ruven, who was promoted because the blacksmith had died. He had motive to kill Lauren but, why my family? Was he angry I hadn't given in to his advances? My stomach turned... Could Ruven really want to destroy us? From birth, Ruven had always been there. He was a pillar in my memories. My friend.

"Ruven," I whispered, "why are you here?"

Ruven's features were set in a scowl of furious surprise. He pointed at Rook, and snapped, "Who is *he*?"

"A friend."

Was Ruven shocked because he didn't recognize this new man in my home? Or because he *did* recognize the man and knew exactly what he was. "Why are you here?" I repeated and stepped in front of Ruven, obscuring his view of Rook. Ruven's attention fell on me, and the malice melted away. He offered a sad smile, and I saw him. The boy who snuck across the goat fields and watched the stars with me. Who napped on the job, so he might stay awake with me on those nights so filled with terrors, sleep might never come.

I saw my *friend*.

"I wanted to apologize," Ruven said. "I didn't treat you the way I should have treated a friend, especially not one I hold so dear, and I'm sorry." He brushed my arm when he said, "You owe me nothing."

Something shifted in Lysander's room.

Both Rook and my mother stared after us. I'm not sure who wore a worse glower as they beheld Ruven. Rook's cool indifference was gone, replaced by a nose curling scowl that one might expect to see if someone had just smelled rotted garbage. Ruven cleared his throat and retreated farther down the hall.

"I wanted to let you know: I've been *offered* a position at the castle. I'm heading there tomorrow and"—he paused, unsure how to finish the sentence—"and, uh, I'll be staying." Offered was a generous word used by those in the castle. I doubted Ruven had a choice in the matter. Ruven loved his family terribly; he wouldn't leave them willingly. I knew Ruven occasionally worked at the castle; he *was* a talented blacksmith. Too talented for his own good, it would seem. Temporary suspicions forgotten, my heart ached for Ruven.

"I'm so sorry."

"Hey—hey, it's okay. It's... It's an opportunity," Ruven said, trying to dispel my upset. "Anyway, I should go. I just wanted you to hear it from me, that I won't be around anymore." Though I knew he didn't want to, he smiled in that familiar way, the way that tugged my own cheeks up. I looked at Ruven and I knew.

I knew.

It wasn't him who'd sent the Hound for my family. Shame consumed me over the idea that I'd even suspected Ruven in the first place. Ruven and I stood awkwardly, unsure how we might part. In perhaps the most awkward of all possibilities, Ruven offered a hand, and I shook it. Ruven gave Rook a final parting glance. Though he seemed genuine, the jealousy in his voice was unmistakable.

"I hope *he* can help your brother."

I hope so too.

With that, Ruven left. I resumed my spot at the head of the bed. Rook glanced at me, asking a silent question. I shook my head. *'Not him.'* I'm not sure whether Rook's furrowed expression was one of frustration or relief.

When finished, Rook got up and backed away. I took his spot, slipping to my knees. Mother switched to the head of the bed, where she moved sweat-soaked hair from Lysander's brow. I ran my hands along the wounds, and my heart fluttered. I could always tell how a wound would heal. When I dressed Lysander's chest so many nights ago, I felt loss...

"It's going to work," I sputtered.

My mother's throat bobbed. "Are you certain?"

I felt Lysander's chest, and I was met with the springing sensation of possibility—of a future. A noise between a laugh and a sob sputtered out of me. Though my mother didn't cry, her arm snaked around Lysander's shoulders, and she buried her head in his hair.

Lysander would live!

"Lottie!" I cried and wiped my nose. "Come look!" No movement came from the cottage. Standing in the doorway, Rook glanced over his shoulder. He shook his head and shrugged. I turned to my mother and sniffled. "Where is she?"

"Outside, practicing?" Mother lowered her voice. "She didn't seem to like your visitor."

"No." I pushed myself up. "I noticed that."

"I should go," Rook said, backing down the hall.

Mother stood. "Stay for tea."

Rook backed away faster. "Really, I must go."

"You *will* stay for tea," my mother commanded and joined us. Passing Rook, she added, "I'd like to know more of the man who saved my children." She headed to the kitchen, leaving us alone. Rook looked at me, helpless.

I mouthed, *'Good luck,'* and then said, "I need to change."

Standing at my wardrobe, I couldn't decide what to wear. I dragged garments along their hangers, finding fault with every single one. Finally, I came to the last hanger. It held a beautiful dress I'd only worn once, shortly after I'd made it many years ago. It was olive and cream, with pink threads. A little cream dove carried stitches along the hem. Father possessed a remarkable attention to detail; he'd squealed with delight when he'd seen that dove. This was a happy dress—a happy memory. I pulled it out.

I changed and met Rook in the hall. He'd remained exactly where I'd left him, almost as if he were too frightened to leave and risk meeting my mother. The dress fit me well, but it was a touch tight in the chest. Rook's gaze dropped to my breasts. His eyes snapped shut, and he looked away, appalled he couldn't control his wandering gaze.

Pushing a hand through his hair, Rook pointed to the crossbow I'd leaned against the wall. "Keep it handy." We walked to the den, and he said, "You're sure it wasn't the red-headed lad?"

"I'm certain. I trust Ruven."

Rook's brows pulsed once, conveying a slight irritation at the idea. "He cares about you."

Had it been the way Ruven looked at me? The way he'd longed to reach out and embrace before he left? I asked, "What gave it away?"

"The way he looked at me."

Back in the den, I felt shame. To see Rook sitting in the crumbling cottage, in the old, worn armchair, I couldn't bear it. I started tidying, kicking a bit of crumbled stone behind the sofa. I moved to pick up a pillow, but Rook caught my hand.

"I feel more at home here than any castle. I beg of you, please, sit."

I set the crossbow on the arm of the sofa and sat. Leaning back, I glanced at my mother in the kitchen and lowered my voice. "This hasn't felt like a home in a long time." I fluffed a tattered pillow. "I think we're ready to move on, but we're scared to go somewhere my father never existed." I gulped and fluffed the pillow again. "It would be difficult."

"I understand." Rook smiled. Though it was *not* an encouraging smile. Shame weighted his shoulders, and he focused on the table between us.

"Even if we wanted to leave"—I looked at the crumbling walls—"we haven't the means."

"I could build you a home," Rook said, with an eagerness that startled us both. "I mean, I could, if you wanted." He cleared his throat and resumed staring at the table. "My mother was a builder. My lumber deliveries often ended in exploited labour, on her part." Rook continued, "I considered building myself a cottage, inside the castle walls. Something of my own, away from the drafty cage." He frowned and gestured vaguely. "But what was the point of it, if it was just me?" Rook fluffed his own pillow. "But for you..." Rook watched me closely when he said, "If you wanted it."

Somehow, Rook had peered inside me and unburied the dream I'd kept hidden for so long. Gazing upon the fire, I let myself picture it. A bright new cottage in the woods. I took my time, seeing all the details that were blurry in previous imaginings. The walls a soft cream, letting light through airy lavender curtains. I'd heard you could dye fabrics lavender using cherry roots, but I'd never had a chance to try. I could try now. In the morning, I'd wander outside and tend my own peonies. I'd bring in vegetables for supper. And in my fantasy, at the end of the day, when I sat by the fire with a cup of tea and my sewing kit...

Rook sat next to me.

"I think—"

Mother joined us and set down a tray of biscuits. She placed a kettle in the fire and settled on the sofa with me. Her brows furrowed at the crossbow, but she didn't ask. She wasted no time in setting on Rook.

"Where are you from, Everard?"

Rook blanched. "L'orée du bois." The town across the Hollow.

"Parents?"

"My mother was a crafter. She built homes, and my father was an artist."

Mother waited.

"They're dead," Rook said.

"Sisters? Brothers?"

"None."

"Beloved?" Red crept into Rook's cheeks. I took a biscuit. Mother's gaze shifted to me, lingering on my dress. "What is your profession?" she asked Rook. "Are you a physician?"

"I am not," Rook replied.

"How is it you came to possess a cure for my son?"

Rook tilted his head and his eyes darted to me. They narrowed, crying, *'Help me!'* I shoved the remaining biscuit in my mouth, so I didn't have to speak. Mother cleared her throat, reminding Rook she'd asked a question, and it was only polite for him to answer. Rook's bulging eyes moved back to my mother.

"I suffer a...similar affliction, and I'm seeking a cure myself."

"You are?" Mother said, glancing down Rook. "I'll admit, you're thin for a crafter's boy, who I presume can afford food. But truly, you don't *seem* ill."

"I assure you." Rook gulped, wiping sweat from his brow. "I am."

Mother nodded, but rather than continue with the topic, she waved at the table. "Eat."

"Uhhh..." Rook rubbed his throat, and this time, I did jump in to save him.

"We ate already."

"You did?" Mother turned to me. "Where?"

"Rook's home."

"In L'orée du bois?"

"Yes." I nodded.

"It's quite a long walk from L'orée du bois, is it not?" Mother asked. "When did you depart?"

"Oh, very early this morning," I assured—too quickly. Rook gave a subtle but violent shake of his head, as if I'd misspoken.

"By my measure, you would have had to have left yesterday evening," my mother said. "I'm surprised you aren't still walking!"

"Oh! Uh, well..."

"If you only left this morning, and arrived here just before noon, I'd have assumed you were coming from somewhere *much* closer. Surely, the only place you might depart to arrive here in that time would have been the very centre of the Hollow." She laughed and smiled at Rook. "But of course, no *person* would live in the middle of the Hollow. How ridiculous!"

Rook and I exchanged an awkward chuckle. When neither of us replied, Mother pursed her lips. My mother was not stupid—in fact, I don't know anyone who hadn't told my mother her cleverness was wasted as a guard. If there was deception to be found, she would find it. I wasn't the best of liars, and seeing Rook skirting my mother's questions, I was fairly confident he was worse. At any given comment, he might crumble beneath my mother's interrogation.

"Stay for dinner," Mother said. "Liliwen seems quite taken with you."

"Mother!"

Doing little to conceal his blush, Rook stood. "I thank you for your kindness, but I must bid you farewell."

My mother nodded, accepting the refusal. "Thank you for saving my son." Her tone dropped to a whisper. "I wish his father were here to thank you too." Rook hesitated, and my mother continued, "Lili's father was murdered—slaughtered—did she tell you that?"

Rook gulped.

"One of my greatest fears is that Liliwen might follow in her father's footsteps." She patted my knee. "Anytime she leaves my sight, part of me worries she'll fall victim to his killer. Share her father's same *brutal* end."

The fire crackled in the hearth, and no one said anything.

Mother sipped her tea.

"Anyhow," she said, smiling broadly. "I won't keep you!"

Rook nearly ripped the door from its hinges in his haste to depart.

"I'm going to see him out." I headed after him.

"Liliwen," my mother cautioned, her tone stilling me in the doorway. "You *will* be back for dinner."

"Yes," I muttered. "I will be. I swear it." Though her lips were a tight line, my mother waved.

I met Rook outside, waiting on the short path. As we headed to the back gate, I said, "Thank you. For saving my brother."

Rook opened the gate and slipped out. "He wouldn't have needed my saving if I hadn't attacked him in the first place." My heart leapt as Rook shut the gate behind himself, before I might slip through.

"It wasn't your fault," I whispered. "I know that now."

We stood with our homes at our backs, and the pretty white gate between us.

Rook pushed a hand through his hair. "You have a beautiful family." He laughed, a sweet, longing thing. "I'd caution you never to take it for granted, but I know you better than that."

I glanced back at my home, at the stones that housed all those I cared for. Well, almost everyone.

I eased the gate open. "I'll walk with you, just for a little while—"

"I have been selfish," Rook interrupted, and slammed the gate closed. "I don't want you to come with me." Ignoring Rook, I stepped back and searched for a break in the garden where I might jump over the fence. Stupid me, putting on a dress because I thought it looked nice. "Liliwen," Rook snapped. "Are you listening to me?" I crossed my arms, a gesture that earned a concerned grimace from Rook. Softening, he said, "You have a chance at a wonderful life here."

He was right. I wanted to argue, but he was right.

"I see many copper-haired children in your future," Rook teased with a wink.

I scoffed, refusing to acknowledge the comment. Fear rocked me as Rook backed toward the Hollow. "But there's still someone out for my family! What if you change before you find a cure and come for us?"

Rook was already shaking his head. "I'm not going to let that happen."

"But—"

"Liliwen, I'm not going to let it happen. I will not be the weapon that destroys your family." He swallowed and looked down. "We are going to say goodbye, and I'm going to do something I should have done a long time ago."

His words hung between us.

A cure would take time. I had a feeling Rook was thinking of a much quicker and more efficient solution.

Rook smiled, though his eyes were dewy—filled with pain—and I knew it was a smile for me. Though Rook was right in front of me, I saw through him, all the way through the Hollow and into the castle. Into the room with the guillotine.

And the sticky blood coating the blade.

I'd had a moment of relief with Lysander. But, seeing Rook back toward the Hollow, the hand that seemed to squeeze my guts until they ached returned. *No no no no no!* my mind shouted, but nothing came out. I just stood there, shaking my head like a fool. I wasn't prepared for another fixture in my life to depart, especially not so...permanently. My hand settled on the garden gate.

"I'll just... I'll walk a little way with you."

Rook wouldn't even look at me as he retreated, shaking his head.

"Everard."

Rook's head snapped up; his eyes met mine with startling intensity.

I mouthed, *'Please.'*

A muscle clenched along Rook's jaw, and he glanced back at the Hollow. *He's going to refuse me*, I thought. He'll flee into the trees, and I'll never learn how his story ends. Despair tugged at the edges of my lips. I wanted to say goodbye, but my mouth was stuck in a trembling frown. I looked away, hiding the oncoming tears. The warmth of Rook's hand found mine, resting on the garden gate.

"Just a little way," he whispered.

Birdsong accompanied our steps, and Rook strode wordlessly beside me. I stepped over toadstools, admiring their little red caps, and brushed aside moss dangling from a tree. Had the Hollow always been so beautiful, and I'd never noticed? It's a shame I'd never come in here again; the Hollow had taken so many things from me. My father...and Rook. In less time than I'd hoped, Rook halted beneath an aged ash. He reached out, brushing a set of claw marks in the bark. I glanced up, into the canopy. It seemed a lifetime ago that I'd climbed that tree and spit on the Hound.

"Liliwen." Rook's voice was softer than the birdsong above. He looked back the way we'd come.

Disregarding Rook's hint, I recalled a tale from our childhood. "Sometimes, when we were young, Lysander and I would come out and forage with our father, just so we might get away from Lottie." I stooped and picked a nettle. I waved it absently at Rook, not really looking at him. Not wanting to see him telling me it was time to go home. "One time, Lysander had an entire basket of nettle, and a blight badger leapt out. Scared him half to death."

I dodged another of Rook's glances.

"Anyway, we decided to head back. Lysander was so jumpy"—I laughed—"I tread on a branch, and I swear, he sent the entire basket of nettle into the canopy. We got the basket, but all our hard work remained in the branches." I was quiet. "We had to have cabbage soup for dinner. Lottie was furious." Rook caught my arm. Still, I refused to meet his eyes. Rook brought his hand to rest beneath my chin. With one finger, he turned my face.

"Liliwen," Rook repeated, "you should turn back." A quivering rage shot through me, and I swatted Rook's hand away. I wanted to shove him, to cry and shout in his face. *I'm a grown woman! You will not tell me what to do!* But, seeing Rook's weary eyes, my animosity slipped away, melting into the mossy earth beneath our boots.

Guided by desire, I reached out and brushed a dark tress from Rook's face. He smiled, and his scar dimpled in that crooked, uneven way. Standing on my toes, I tugged the front of Rook's shirt. He bent so easily toward me, as if the entire time he'd been fighting the very urge to do so. Once again, our lips met in a polite kiss. My grip on Rook's collar tightened; I had no intention of being courteous. I traced his lips, begged he open them for me. Rook groaned and slipped his arms around me. He held me so tight, I felt each finger clutching my ribs. Time and consequence vanished. I did my best to memorize the way our arms felt, curled around one another. If I might have anything in this world, let it be this. Forever.

"I should leave," Rook breathed against my lips. "Run as fast as I can away from you." I gripped his shirt tighter. "Tell me to go," he whispered. "It will be easier."

"I don't want you to go."

"I know," Rook said. "And I cannot bear it."

This was *not* our ending.

I wouldn't allow it.

Rook didn't resist as I encouraged him to sit by the ash. He leaned against the trunk, pulling me with him. Lifting my dress, I settled in Rook's lap, my knees resting in the soft moss. I cupped his face, kissing him again. My thumb traced lazy circles along the scar. Rook brought his hand to rest at the nape of my neck, keeping me close. I couldn't ignore how firm Rook was beneath his trousers. In fact, I savoured it. I wiggled against him and delighted in the low moan that rose in his throat.

A branch snapped, somewhere deep in the Hollow.

In Rook's lap, I stilled.

"Whatever it is, it wouldn't interfere with me," Rook mumbled. His hand slid down, between my legs and under the hem of my dress. He paused at the sheath wrapping my thigh, my knife tucked safely inside. "You're not waiting until I'm in a compromising position to pull that on me, are you?"

"It was one time," I mumbled through a kiss. "Get over it."

Rook teased aside my undergarments, sending my stomach somersaulting. I wanted Rook terribly, and his fingers slipped effortlessly inside me. He groaned, longing to join them. I moved up and down on Rook's fingers, releasing soft moans against his ear. There was a freedom, being in the arms of the beast that governed the Hollow. For the first time, I was blissfully unaware of the horrors. Leaning my head back, Rook placed delicate kisses along my throat. Teasing my sleeve down my shoulder, he carried kisses along my chest and twirled his tongue around the nipple that spilled out.

Out of the corner of my eye, I noticed something lurking behind a far-off trunk—a figure that stood out. I fought the hazy bliss and focused, trying to make sense of the shape against the trees. A faint, green glow kissed the surrounding trunks. My blood chilled as I locked on the mysterious creature, peering around the trunk. Realizing I'd seen it, the creature's eyes widened. I sucked in a panicked breath.

Watcher!

"Roo—"

A high-pitched wail buried my warning. The Watcher moved lightning fast; I was torn from Rook and thrown back. Tearing the knife from my thigh, I leapt up.

Two Rooks stood before me.

One used his body to shield me, his arms spread, ready to catch anything that might come for me. The other was a few paces away. Sort of hunched, the Rook that wasn't Rook wore a vile grin. It shifted on its feet, head swivelling to track me each time I hid behind Rook's outstretched arms.

"Mimicry," Rook muttered. "Don't let it grab you." I saw Rook's arms, spread in front of me, and I doubted anything might breach them.

"Don't let it grab you," the Watcher-turned-Rook mocked. It chilled me, how closely it resembled Rook's voice. Fleeing sideways, the Watcher looked so much like a spider as it climbed a tree and disappeared into the canopy.

Leaves and twigs reigned down. Rook hissed, "Run!"

Too late.

The Watcher landed in front of us, kicking up a cloud of leaves and twigs. Smelling of rotting compost, it was a caricature of Rook. As if an artist had molded Rook in clay, giving him evil, exaggerated features. Shoving me aside, Rook lunged at the beast. It feinted and ducked, snatching my ankle as it went.

"Oof!" I hit the ground and the Watcher dragged me. Shrubs and bracken shredded my arms as the Watcher sprinted through the Hollow. With great difficulty, I curled up and slashed the Watcher's hand. A squeal rang out—like the screams that carried from Ruven's farm on slaughtering day.

I cut again, this time severing multiple fingers. The Watcher let go and rounded on me—the imitation of Rook's face exploded into an enormous mouth. I couldn't count the layers of teeth, endless rows carrying deep into the belly of the creature. I raised my blade, ready to plunge it into the Watcher's throat.

I didn't get the chance.

A howl thundered through the trunks, and like the billowing of swift storm clouds, the Hound burst from the shadows. The Watcher threw up a hand, and a snarling snout bit it clean off. The Hound struck again, sinking its teeth into the Watcher's neck. Blood sprayed, and I clambered back, avoiding the splattering viscera. The Watcher was a ragdoll in the Hound's jaws, offering no resistance as the Hound threw it into the dirt. Pitched wails battered me as the Watcher disappeared behind the Hound's hulking body.

Flipping over, I pushed myself up and fled. More shrieks pierced the Hollow, followed by a pained gasp that sounded an awful lot like Rook. I ducked behind a trunk and held my chest, recovering my breath. Though the Hollow was silent, that cry haunted me. It was probably the Watcher, still imitating Rook. But...what if the creature had slipped from Rook's grasp and injured him? What if the Watcher possessed some trick, some weapon we didn't know about?

I have to go back!

But what if I find the Watcher, victorious over the Hound's corpse? Rows of teeth floated through my mind, and I hesitated.

Rook might be hurt!

It was the image of Rook gasping for air that hardened my resolve. Palming my blade, I readied to go after him...

A hand slammed against the tree above me, sending splinters raining down. Rook crept around the trunk, keeping so close I *tasted* copper on his breath. He was naked, and his eyes, frenzied with bloodlust, were only inches from mine.

"R-Rook?" I stuttered and backed against the tree. Seemingly unaware I'd spoken at all, Rook stared at my neck. His nostrils flared, and he drifted forward. "Rook," I warned, raising the knife. With a grunt, Rook knocked the knife clear out of my hand. His palm skirted my cheek, and his fingers tangled in my hair, yanking my head back.

Then, Rook went for my throat.

"Agh—"

Rook's hand muffled my cry. Warm breath ebbed up my neck as he moved, so close his lips brushed my skin. "Sh sh sh sh," he growled. He dragged his fingers down my lips, along my throat, and held my breast. Rook grazed my ear, and sounding so much like the wind whispering through the leaves, he murmured:

"I *will* have you."

A tremble of longing shook me, and I pressed into Rook's hand. A satisfied groan rumbled through his chest. I leaned to kiss Rook—but he pulled away. He knelt, catching the hem of my dress as he went. Bunching the skirt, Rook said, "Hold this."

I did as I was told.

In one quick movement, Rook ripped my undergarments. He tossed them aside, and buried his face between my legs.

This time, I stifled my own cry.

I squirmed against Rook's tongue—so wet and hot and *hungry*. Rook gripped my hips; every ounce of his strength forbid me from escaping his mouth. "Rook!" I begged, feeling the pleasure spilling down my legs. But Rook didn't stop; he devoured me as if he were starved, as only someone who'd suffered an enduring hunger might. Only when the pleasure was nearly cresting, and I thought that bliss would wash through my body, did Rook pull away.

On his knees, Rook dragged a forearm across his lips. It was Rook at my feet, I knew that. But, there was something about the tilt of his head, something not entirely human, that made me wonder: Is it only Rook? Or is that glint in his eye the beast, begging to join us?

Rook's fingers curled tighter around my hips.

And he smiled.

Leaping to his feet, Rook spun me around roughly. I braced against the tree and Rook slipped a hand around my throat, as if some part of him expected me to flee.

A pack of wolves wouldn't frighten me away.

Spreading my legs, I met Rook's gaze over my shoulder. I pressed against him, and he groaned. A casual observer might have mistaken the look in Rook's eyes for anger—a furious rage. But I saw it for what it was.

Lust.

After so much restraint, Rook unleashed a lifetime of desire as he slammed into me. The force sent me forward, but Rook's grip on my throat kept me against him, preventing my escape. Warm satisfaction swelled within me. Rook's free hand snaked down, settling between my legs as he thrust into me again.

"Say my name," Rook ordered.

His lips were so close, commanding me to submit. At my front, Rook's fingers moved between my legs, rubbing me relentlessly. Behind me, Rook thrust again. My legs buckled, and it was only his strength keeping me from falling.

"Rook," I cried, fighting the irresistible pressure building within.

"That's not my name," Rook snapped, pushing into me so forceful-ly, I gasped. With each stroke, the inevitable crept closer. Rook's fingers strummed me, teased me, begged me to release into them. To let that wave of bliss wash over me—

"Don't you dare!" Rook growled, stopping me—stopping the pleasure from taking me. "My name," he demanded. "Say it!" The hand at my throat slid up, forcing my head sideways. Through a tangle of dark hair, Rook's fervent eyes captured mine. "Look at me," Rook growled. "Do you want me?"

"Yes," I moaned. More than *anything*.

"You want me, you will take *all* of me." Rook plunged into me, sending sweet satisfaction rippling through my body. "Now," he commanded, punctuating his words with rough thrusts, "Say—my—name!" He buried himself inside me—giving me *everything* I needed.

The euphoria started and I slipped into a well of pleasure so deep, it curled my toes. Distantly, I was aware of myself, moaning one word.

"Everard."

His name barely left my lips when a cry left his. Trembling, Rook kissed my neck, he breathed, "Liliwen." I savoured the ways his arms—like granite—wrapped around me. Tremors wracked his body as waves of ecstasy rushed through him too.

Even as he regained control of his spasming body, Rook refused to let go, wanted to remain in the glow of unity for as long as we might.

Finally, Rook fell, dragging me into his lap as he went. Through heavy breathing, he planted soft kisses on my forehead.

"Come back," I murmured. "Have dinner with us."

Rook's eyes flitted down, meeting mine. "If my life depended on it," Rook panted, "I would not leave you." I felt a tear well along my lash and fall down my cheek. Rook smiled and used a thumb to brush it away.

Leaning his forehead against mine, he whispered, "I am *your* obedient servant."

Lesson Sixteen

Betrayal comes from those you trust;
that's why it burns so.

Mother was surprised when we both returned to the cottage. "Oh?" she began. "But Everard was *so* stern in his refusal." She plucked a leaf from my hair. "I wonder, how did you persuade him to dine with us?"

Seeing me squirm, Rook leapt in. "Is there anything I might do to help?"

"No." My mother pursed her lips. "Liliwen and I can handle it. Please, sit."

"Are you sure? I don't mind."

"Sit," my mother ordered. "Liliwen, help me with dinner."

Tucked in the kitchen, Mother stood over the butcher's block. She chopped potatoes while I gathered dishes. "You went into the Hollow to find the Hound," she said, her voice hushed. "This might seem like a silly question, but did you ever find him?"

Startled by my mother's words, I dropped the cutlery set I'd retrieved. You see, if she were indeed referring to the beast that stalked the Hollow, she likely would have used the word *it*. But she did not. She used the word *him*.

Him, as simply as one might refer to a guest sitting in their own den.

"Liliwen," my mother cautioned, setting the knife down, "I was young once, and I know nothing encourages a foolish decision quite like infatuation. My family disowned me for choosing your father—" She choked, and her throat bobbed as she cleared it. "*Your father.* My husband, whom I cherished..." My mother's stoic face cracked. For the first time since my father passed, I was going to see my mother cry.

The front door opened and closed with a slam.

Abandoning my mother, I peered out. Lottie was in the den, glaring at Rook. Mother approached from behind me, her veneer of stoicism returned. She set glasses and a bottle of wine on the table.

"Where were you?" Mother asked.

Lottie scowled at the wine. "What are you doing?"

"Celebrating," Mother replied evenly. "Liliwen's...*friend*, Everard, has cured your brother."

Lottie straightened. "He what?"

"Mhm." Mother nodded. "Will you sit now?"

Lottie tore down the hall to Lysander's room. Silence settled on the cottage. When she returned, Lottie looked rather ill.

"Lil," Lottie said, "I must tell you something."

A knock came at the door.

Every year, Lottie grew more arrogant, more unshakeable. And yet, this was the second time today she'd looked at me, panic in her eyes.

"I didn't know, Lil," she whispered. "I'm so sorry."

Resisting the urge to shake her, I muttered, "What did you do, Lottie?"

Mother answered the door, and asked, "What's wrong?"

Pushing my mother aside, three cloaked guards entered. Horrified, I turned to Rook—but he wasn't on the sofa. Rook stood in the corner, wearing such a pleasant expression, one might think he was greeting old friends. There was little conviction in the guard's voice when they said, "We've come to take you, beast." Grinning, Rook tilted his head. My worry shifted from Rook to the guards. They spread out, surrounding him. Rook watched them as a cat might observe a stray mouse.

The guards fell on Rook.

Grabbing the sleeve of the first, Rook yanked them forward. They collided with the stone fireplace as Rook's fist connected with the second guard's jaw—which was only a moment before Rook snatched the final guard's collar and slammed his forehead into their nose. In seconds, all three were on the floor, two seemingly unconscious, and a geyser of blood spewing from the third guard's nostrils.

I grabbed Lottie's collar and snapped, "How many more are coming?"

As if in a trance, Lottie wiped a drop of blood from her cheek. Examining the blood, she murmured, "All of them."

Leaping over the dazed and unconscious guards, I shoved Rook toward the door. "Go!" Rook left, and I grabbed my crossbow. Heading out back, I bumped into Rook and peered around him.

Four more guards blocked the path to the Hollow.

An indifferent Rook strode forward. I started after him, but my mother yanked me back. She and Lottie held me, pulling me toward the cottage. I raised my crossbow, though I dared not fire it, lest I strike Rook in the chaos. Though Rook didn't need my help. He disarmed the guards as if they were children and not the queen's most skilled. Rather than use the mace he'd just taken from a guard, Rook tossed it over the fence. Despite the attempts to harm Rook, he was trying *not* to kill anyone. He headed for the back gate, but the tallest of the guards fell on him, holding him back. While Rook wrestled with the woman, I wondered, why doesn't he change and flee? Rook tossed the guard over the fence, but two more grabbed him. As he fought them off, I noticed Rook kept glancing my way. He did it again. No—not me. My mother. He didn't want her to see.

He didn't want her to know the beast who'd slayed her beloved.

A guard recovered their sword and swung for Rook, who dodged and planted a boot on their chest. The force sent the guard shuffling back, the sword swinging wild. I leapt away but was too slow.

"Agh!"

The blade slit the front of my dress, stinging my belly as it sliced. I grabbed my stomach, where blood oozed through the fabric.

Rook's nostrils flared.

My mother dropped to examine the wound while Lottie grabbed my arms, pulling me from danger. "It's fine," I hissed, batting them away. "Only a scratch." I shoved them aside, keeping Rook in my sight.

For the most part, Rook *looked* human. But every so often, there were glimpses—cracks. Rook climbed on the guard, straddling them so they might not escape. Almost tenderly, Rook's hands wrapped their throat. Rook grimaced, and his canines, sharp knives behind his lips, were on full display. Leaning forward, Rook whispered, "Scream for help." The guard choked, unable to speak. Rook squeezed harder. Beneath him, foam pooled at the corners of the guard's mouth.

Rook's cheek pulled into a crooked smile.

A stark reminder that Rook was a monster wearing human skin.

To Rook, the world seemed to disappear. He focused only on his victim, suffocating below him...

Clank! A collar snapped around Rook's throat. Confusion muddled his face, and his hand darted to the collar. Shuffling and grunts filled the yard. Iron cuffs were slipped around Rook's wrists, and his arms wrenched behind his back.

I watched in stunned horror as Rook was subdued.

Standing behind Rook, the tall guard produced a cloth. She shoved sweat-streaked hair from her face and muttered, "The captain told us to gag the mutt."

"Careful! The beast bites," joked a second, burlier guard, who gripped Rook's arms. The first took the joke as a warning. Curling her fingers in Rook's hair, she wrenched his head back and shoved a gag in his mouth. Rook grunted as she tied it roughly at the back of his head. Only when Rook was gagged, bound, and surrounded by guards, did the back door open.

Marek's dark frame stood in the doorway.

He joined us, pausing to caress my mother's elbow. He noted my crossbow, pointed at Rook. Tapping his nose, Marek said, "Good girl." Chest puffed, Marek looked remarkably like a proud rooster as he paraded toward Rook.

Rook's nose scrunched, as if he'd caught a familiar but revolting stench.

Above the gag, Rook's eyes widened. "Nnng!" His scream muffled against the fabric. He tore himself free, but the tall guard kicked his knees. Rook smashed into the dirt, where he was kept on his knees. Rook's terrified, pleading eyes locked on mine.

They darted toward Marek.

Marek, who was made captain after the previous was slaughtered by the Hound. Marek, who had always loved my mother, and was rejected by her time after time because she already had a family.

'I have my children; my heart is full.' That's what my mother said the last time Marek propositioned her. When it wasn't enough that he'd ordered my father killed, Marek came after us, one-by-one. The attack on Lysander, on Lottie. Marek wanted us gone, so he might have my mother all to himself.

How long until Marek commanded the Hound to come for me?

Marek lifted Rook's shackled hands, examining the silver bracelet. "This is remarkable. Stolen from a victim, I imagine?" Rook's eyes yellowed, and he snarled against the gag. Bones snapped as he began to change. "Ah ah ah," Marek said, backing away and slipping an arm around me. "Wouldn't want to risk anyone here getting hurt, would you?" Rook's eyes righted themselves. After a powerless groan, he slumped in the shackles. Marek beamed, and I considered pulling the crossbow trigger, the crosshairs of which were pointed directly at Marek's boot.

Unfortunately, I didn't maim him. Instead, I considered the dreadful scenario facing us. I possessed only one bolt. Even if I shot one of the guards holding Rook, another would replace them. And what then? Risk my family being slain right here in the back garden for conspiring with the Hound? Lysander would come running when he heard our screams. Finally healed, only to be cut down with the rest of us. His last moments spent watching the blood of his mother and sisters watering his father's beloved peonies. When I woke this morning, I couldn't possibly have anticipated standing here, calculating how many lives I might lose if I made the wrong decision. If it were just Rook and me, this would be different, but here, surrounded by my family, the risk was far too great.

Though it destroyed me, I remained silent.

"Let's bring the beast inside, shall we?" Marek opened the door. "I have some exciting introductions to make!" Marek ushered in the guards holding Rook, then my mother, Lottie, and me. The den was extra crowded, with two more visitors waiting there. I recognized the first, for she was my very own cousin, Bronwyn, who was taken to serve the queen so many years ago. Her curls were wrangled into tight braids that pulled back into a sweeping ponytail. Bronwyn smiled when she saw me, and I struggled to return the gesture. Beside her was someone I didn't recognize from memory but from rumours. Wearing a black cloth over their face—a provision of anonymity—was the queen's advisor. Whom we only called advisor because we weren't allowed to use the true word.

Executioner.

But why were they here? Shouldn't they be with…

In a dim corner of the cottage, the shadows shifted. Like a rippling waterfall, the darkness fell away. The shadows pooled along the floor, creeping out like a wave of smoke. An individual hidden beneath an amethyst cloak remained in their wake. When they drew back their hood, a great length of raven hair tumbled out. My breath caught, and everyone in the room bowed.

Bringer of storms and wielder of shadows.

Queen Aenor.

Focusing entirely on me, Queen Aenor jerked her chin. Marek pulled me forward. Nerves got the better of me, and I stared at the queen's boots peeking from beneath her cloak. Behind me, my mother cleared her throat. Lottie reached out and tapped my arm.

Reminding me they were there.

"I'm told it was you who captured the Hound," Queen Aenor said. I was so stunned by the softness in her voice that I didn't immediately respond.

Marek squeezed me. "Yes!" he cried. "Our dear Liliwen discovered the beast's identity and transfiguration abilities! It was her cunning bravery that brought the Hound to our doorstep!" Resisting the urge to shoot Marek through the neck, I leaned away.

Queen Aenor watched the strange exchange but left it unacknowledged. She waved and said, "As promised." The advisor approached; they held a bag of purple velvet. Rather than hand over the bag, the advisor turned their clothed face on Marek. It wasn't until Marek stepped away that the advisor handed over the pouch.

It was the heaviest thing I'd ever held.

The advisor returned to their spot behind the queen, who said, "I've been informed your brother is ill?"

"Uh—" I floundered. No, Lysander was no longer ill, because *Rook* helped him. But...I couldn't admit that, couldn't put my family in danger for working with the Hound. My thoughts came quick; how could I explain Lysander's sudden recovery?!

"Yes!" Marek interjected, the first time his interrupting me might have been a boon. Returning his arm to my shoulders, Marek cried, "The boy was attacked"—he swept his arm toward Rook—"by the beast!"

Giving little attention to Marek's theatrics, the queen said, "To reward your courage, I will grant him the supervision of *my* physician."

When I'd set out so many mornings ago, this was all I ever wanted. The Hound captured, and my brother cared for. Now, I couldn't help but look at Rook. The gag cut into his cheeks like wire. Manacles and chains clanked as he swayed.

I'd never felt so wicked.

My eyes stung. It would look terrible if I'd been handed a bag of gold, and told my brother would be attended to, only for me to weep. I tried to muster a smile.

I could not.

Queen Aenor frowned.

"She's grateful, my queen!" Marek blurted. "Just in shock, I think." Marek squeezed me and snarled, "Liliwen, thank the queen."

"Uh..." I swallowed. "Thank—" The queen crossed the space between us, silencing me. I found myself looking down again. She brought her hand to rest beneath my chin, commanding me back to her. Lavender eyes, passed down over many generations, arrested me. Tiny ice crystals kissed my skin where her fingers met it, and a peculiar sensation prodded my temples. As if she were sifting my very thoughts.

"Strange"—Queen Aenor stared at Marek—"that while the entire guard was hunting the Hound, it was a single girl who managed to capture it."

"Well..." Marek paled. "She's quite a *unique* girl."

Still addressing Marek, Queen Aenor turned back to me. "She is the one you've told me about?"

Eager to direct attention away, Marek shoved me forward. "She is!"

Queen Aenor remained motionless, assessing me. "I've heard rumours of you. Your garments, in particular."

"Oh, no!" I backed away. "There's nothing exceptional about—"

"Nonsense!" Marek dragged me back. "Our Liliwen is so modest!" He laughed. "With my own eyes, I've seen an arrow bounce from a coat of her weaving."

Circling me like a vulture, Queen Aenor murmured, "Is this true?" As she prowled, the shadows in the cottage crept closer, constricting me.

"Well..." I looked at my family, at Rook. So many helpless faces. The shadows drew closer, and I found difficulty drawing breath. "Yes," I gasped. "Yes, it's true." The queen merely offered an absent nod. She turned to leave, and the command I'd always dreaded came to be.

"You will come reside in the castle."

The order didn't shock me, but Lottie blurted a distraught, "What?!"

The queen's glare silenced her. "Magic is nearly lost. Those who present with the gift must be protected." Queen Aenor looked at me when she added, "And those with magic *must* serve the kingdom."

"It's an incredible opportunity!" Marek beamed. When I showed no enthusiasm, he shook me and continued as if I hadn't heard. "Your queen has invited you to stay at the palace." The word *invited* was generous. If I refused, I would be taken, or killed, so I might not aid an enemy.

In my moment of distress, I couldn't help but glance at Rook. I sought comfort, some sign it would be okay.

In his stooped shoulders, I found only despair.

Queen Aenor pointed to the back of the cottage. "Collect a bag." The advisor pried Marek's fingers off me and started marching me to the back, toward my room.

"But—but my family is here," I cried. Down the hall, Lysander peered around the doorframe.

My mother started, "Surely, she can stay here and travel to the castle as the guards do!"

"Stand down," Marek spat at my mother. He tore me from the advisor, who hissed and raised his fist to strike Marek. Bronwyn coughed. The advisor froze, their arm suspended in mid-air. Slowly, they lowered their hand. Marek clicked his tongue and ducked his chin at Bronwyn, shooing the advisor away. In my ear, Marek whispered, "You will go." The grip on my arm ached, and cold severity twisted Marek's features. He wanted me gone. Out of this cottage and away from my mother. Without me, Lottie and Lysander would be unprotected.

Lysander stood in our way. Though he swayed on unsteady feet, he would not let Marek pass. "Step aside," Marek ordered. Lysander needn't respond; he simply loomed above Marek.

"Captain," Queen Aenor's voice floated behind us.

She looked upon Lysander with a slight, sympathetic tilt of her head. To me, she said, "You may spend the night here." Marek huffed, but his grip didn't loosen. "In the morning, I will send an escort to collect you. My physician will accompany them." She turned to my mother. "On behalf of myself and the kingdom, I thank you for your loyalty. Without your sacrifices, we would be nothing."

My mother bowed but failed to respond. In her silence, I often feared her most. That was as true now as it ever was. The vein that trailed along her temple and disappeared into her hair looked like it might burst.

Queen Aenor's lavender eyes set on me. "You *will* be ready at dawn." She exited the cottage, and Bronwyn and the advisor trailed her. Chains clanked as the guards shoved Rook out the door. I struggled after Rook, but Marek held me back.

Shaking me, he snarled, "What has that beast told you?"

"He didn't tell me anything!" I shoved Marek.

My mother stepped between us. "You may be the captain of this wicked kingdom, but this is my home." She pointed a steadfast finger at the door. "Leave it!"

Putting up his palms, Marek soothed, "Calm down."

My mother's hand slipped to the hilt of her sword. Marek weaved around her and embraced me. I considered ripping the sword from my mother's side and running him through. "I'm just glad you're okay," Marek said, loud enough for everyone inside—and outside—to hear. Lowering his voice, he continued, "I know the Hound might not look dangerous presently, and I imagine a young woman might be swayed by its appearance but..."

I wanted Marek dead. I wanted to string him up and shoot him right in the—

"You of all people know what it's capable of," Marek finished.

How *dare* he allude to my father, to Lysander, to all the harm he'd brought us? I ripped my arm free. Seething, I asked, "What's going to happen to R—the Hound?"

"The beast will be executed. Publicly. The queen wants this dealt with immediately; I imagine the creature will be dead within the week." Marek clapped my shoulder. "Brilliant work, Liliwen." Marek turned a hopeful smile on my mother.

She swept her hand toward the door, like one might shoo a rat.

The door closed behind Marek, and I rushed to the window. At the end of the path, Rook resisted the wagon. He struggled, and the advisor punched him in the jaw. Unable to balance, Rook fell back. I ran, yanking the door open.

Lottie caught me and growled, "Do you want to lose your head for conspiring?" Lysander and my mother joined us, ready to grab me should I do anything foolish. The advisor climbed on Rook, landing another blow. Rook couldn't do anything but let his head smash against the stony path. The advisor struck again.

And again.

And again.

There was such rage in those blows. I fought Lottie's grasp. In agony, my heart leapt, wishing it might leave my body and block the strikes from driving Rook's temple into the rock.

Bronwyn tapped the advisor and muttered, "That's enough."

The advisor rounded on Bronwyn, ready to attack her next. Bronwyn wagged a finger, as if to say, *'No.'* Trembling, the advisor dismounted Rook's beaten body. Marek strode down the path; he grabbed the front of Rook's shirt and righted him. Rook's face, purple and bloodied, was hardly recognizable. Though one eye was swollen completely shut, his other caught mine. He looked as if he wanted to apologize, as if even the beating were his fault.

Is this it?

Will I ever see him again?

If this was the last time we saw one another, it wouldn't be like this. Though I wanted to fall to my knees, I forced a smile. If I could give Rook anything, let it be that. The last thing I might give him was the thought that our eyes meeting brought me joy. That seeing him was my happiness, even like this.

Perhaps it might comfort him during what was to come.

Against the gag, Rook's bloodied cheeks returned the smile. It turned into a grimace as Marek shoved him into the wagon. With a snapping of whips and grinding of wheels, they took off. Lottie loosened her grip; I shoved her and tore down the path. I stopped at the road, and as the wagon crested the hill...I waved. Those in the wagon thought it was for Marek. Indeed, he returned my gesture.

But I knew. And Rook knew.

Below the shackles adorning his wrists, Rook's fingers reached for me. I'd let myself picture a home with Rook, a life filled with slow mornings and evenings by the fire. I remained on the road, watching the wagon until it disappeared, stealing that life—*my dream*—with it.

Lottie met me on the road. "I... I'm sorry," she said. "But he killed our father!"

Pushing Lottie, I screamed, "Marek killed our father!" Fat, furious tears rolled down my cheeks as I advanced on Lottie. Mother hurried down the path, stepping between us.

To me, my mother whispered, "What did you say?"

My breathing chugged as I sobbed. I dodged my mother and punched Lottie. She fell back and I screamed, "You couldn't listen to me—couldn't do *one* thing I asked, could you?!" Mother grabbed my arm and twisted it behind my back. "Agh!" Pain splintered through my elbow. She kicked my knees and I hit the ground.

Crouched over me, my mother hissed, "Did you say Marek killed Jean?"

At once, I stopped fighting. When was the last time my mother had said his name? Through sniffles, I hiccupped, "Yes."

My mother processed that word.

Slowly, she helped me up. Lottie remained several feet away, tracking my movements. Eerie calm settled on my mother, though a muscle twitched, just below her eye. Guiding me back to the cottage, she said, "Tell me."

I did. I told them everything. Of my hunt for the Hound, of Rook, the curse, and Marek. It was no coincidence the previous captain fell to the Hound. It was a title desired by Marek, so he simply got rid of anyone who came between him and the position. Marek took the same approach with our father. He believed that, with Father out of the way, Mother would need a new husband—and a *captain* too! Though Marek underestimated the bond between my parents. Even with Father dead, Mother showed no interest in Marek. He hoped then, with her children gone, my mother, left with nothing, might seek solace in his arms.

When I finished, Mother stared vacantly at the wall. Surprisingly, it was Lottie who reached out and urged her to say something. "Mum?" My mother rose and threw a cloak on.

"Where are you going?" I asked.

"I'm going to cut his throat," Mother replied, as simply as if she were popping out for milk.

I leapt up. "No, you—"

"We'll go together," Lottie interrupted, and grabbed her cloak too.

"You'll do no such thing," Mother snapped. "You'll stay here and care for your brother!"

"I'm coming with you," Lysander said, shambling from his room, where I'd assumed he'd been sleeping off the excitement.

"You're ill!" Mother pointed down the hall. "Back to bed!"

"I feel better!" Indeed, colour crept back into Lysander's cheeks. "The sickness won't rob me of passing justice on that weasel!"

"And I'll not let Marek rob you of your futures!" Mother cried. "This is my battle." She opened the door, which Lottie promptly slammed. Lottie was the only person in the world who could receive the glare my mother gave her, and live.

"Let's think about this," I said, backing toward the table.

"I'll not be talked out of it!" Mother shouted, reaching for her weapon.

"No one is talking you out of it." I slid a chair back, encouraging my mother to sit. "You're the cleverest person in town. Surely, *you* can think of a better way to pass justice on Marek. Preferably, one that doesn't involve walking out and slitting his throat in front of an entire town of witnesses."

Mother stared at the chair.

Finally, she said, "You're right." Removing her cloak, Mother sat down. Lysander set a goblet and bottle of wine in front of her. Despite our mother's years of abstinence, she poured herself a large glass and drank. Mother coughed and choked out, "I want him to suffer."

"That's good," I soothed. "That's a good start." Lottie and Lysander sat with us.

Together, we came up with a plan.

Lesson Seventeen

Sometimes, in our willingness to rely
on others, we find strength.

Crickets serenaded us as the bright moon sailed through the clouds above. Lottie and I sat around an old hunting pit we'd dug out, our legs dangled like children at the riverside. A few steps away, Lysander slumped against a tree. Though he might feel better, he wore the exhaustion of battling a terrible illness. Clearing his throat, he broke the strained silence.

"Do you remember when that griffin showed up in the field up the road?"

Lottie groaned and buried her head in her hands.

I chuckled. "What did Lottie say when she saw it?"

Mimicking Lottie, Lysander said, "Daddy, how come it has five legs? Don't griffins have four legs?" Lysander laughed. "And then she counted"—Lysander laughed so hard he wheezed—"one-two-three-four-*five*!"

I snorted and looked down, suppressing my giggles.

My father's face was quite pink as he explained to Lottie, in front of everyone, that it was a *boy* griffin.

Lottie's voice muffled through her hands. "It's no wonder I only ever courted women." Both Lysander and I burst out laughing. Before long, Lottie joined in too. Lysander wiped a tear away as our laughter faded to chuckles.

The silence returned.

Lottie whispered, "I'm sorry." I knew Lottie was sorry. I knew by the way she wouldn't look at me. It gave me some comfort, because I also knew Lottie would do anything she could to repair the damage.

Carrying voices slithered out to meet us.

Lottie and I rose and helped Lysander stand. Together, we disappeared into the trees.

"Where are we going?" Marek's voice asked.

"It's just up here," Mother's voice answered.

"The Hollow is a dangerous place, even more so at night," Marek said. "We should continue no farther. Whatever you wish to show me can wait until dawn." I peered around the tree. Mother wore a lovely spring dress, one that inspired pride and homesickness.

Father made that dress.

The pale-yellow fabric swished as my mother hiked up her hem, trouncing through the brush. With her hair sweeping her collarbones, it was as if the wrinkles vanished. She wore youth like perfume, and she shone in the pale moonlight. Her smile was pretend, but I wondered, is that what she looked like before life changed her?

Is that the girl my father loved?

Marek eyed the hem of my mother's dress, lingering on her bare ankles, but he made no move to follow. Mother giggled and gave Marek's hand a playful tug. "Don't be a coward."

Marek's jaw dropped.

"Come," my mother beckoned him. Marek shook his head but pursued my mother, who approached the edge of the pit. "Look. Down there."

Marek came to the pit, doubling over to peer in. "I don't see anything." Swooping forward, Mother shoved Marek. His arms cartwheeled as he careened over the edge. "Aghhh—"

Whump!

Lottie and I ran from the trees. Lysander lumbered after us.

Black hair unbound and catching the breeze, my mother peered into the hole. I was reminded of paintings I'd seen in books, of vengeful sirens, readying to devour their helpless victims.

I did not envy Marek.

We reached our mother, and Lysander placed an encouraging hand on her back. Marek rubbed his leg and groaned. "I think—I think my leg is broken!" Dirt rained on Marek, and he covered his face. "Wh—What are you doing?!"

Shovel in hand, my mother said, "Giving you the same treatment I gave my husband, as you envied him so." She stooped and tossed another scoop onto Marek's face.

"Evette, please!"

"Don't call me that!" My mother shouted, shovelling in more dirt. "Confess, or I bury you alive!"

"My only crime is loving you! I never did anything—Ugh!" Marek coughed as a smattering of soil choked him.

Mother abandoned the shovel. Using her arms, she pushed heaps of dirt into the pit. Hysteria pitched her voice as she screamed, "Help me!" shocking Lottie and me into action. We too, pushed in piles of dirt. Beside me, Lysander used his foot to drag loose soil over the edge.

"Did you have my husband killed?" my mother cried.

"I—Evette let's talk about this!"

Voice rising an octave, my mother shrieked, "Did you have my husband killed?!"

"Yes!"

My mother stilled.

"Yes, I did!" Marek pushed dirt aside, his lower half already buried. "But I did it *because* I love you!" Mother fell back, kneeling at the edge.

Far off in the Hollow, a wolf howled.

Marek was so small down there. So tiny compared to the terrifying beast we'd created, the only thing strong enough to kill my father. What a terrible waste, my father's entire life taken because of this man's poisonous jealousy.

Another wolf call.

Closer.

I rubbed my mother's back. "We should consider leaving." Mother rose. Without a word, she walked away.

Lottie drew her bow and pointed it at Marek. "Shall I finish him?"

"Leave him," Mother called. "Let him endure the same fate as your father."

"No, please!" Marek shouted. "You mustn't leave me here!"

Lottie pouted and put her bow away. We took one last look at the man who killed our father. "Please!" Marek begged. "Help me before the wolves come!" As a group, we turned from Marek and pursued our mother. Another low howl pierced the night as we caught up with her.

"Let his evil not consume another moment of my story," Mother whispered, shoving aside branches.

Marek's shouting continued. Right about now, the first wolf was probably slinking from the trees. More would follow, snaking their way to the pit. I imagined the moonlight, glinting off so many teeth, smiling down on Marek.

Both hunter and hunted knew a feast approached.

How terrified Marek must be, knowing the food was his flesh.

As if in answer, Marek's shrieks reached a high, terrified pitch. Did he have a weapon? My mother must have been thinking the same thing, for she withdrew a long dagger—bearing the captain's markers—from the deep pocket of her dress. Even Lottie grimaced, her good eye meeting mine.

'Yikes.'

Was it difficult for my mother to sneak the captain's blade away?

Absently, Mother tossed the weapon aside.

Marek's hysterical screams accompanied our procession. The farther we walked, the more the cries faded—until they choked and died, as if Marek's vocal chords were no longer tucked safely in his throat. A frenzy of yips and snarls started, as the wolves fought over who would consume which piece of meat. Chin held high, my mother continued walking.

Would Rook feel Marek die? Like a leash pulling taught and snapping, the bond that held them forever broken. I hope he felt it, wherever he was.

Far behind us, baying howls called to the moon.

The wolves were fed.

And it was done.

My mother, whom I'd only ever seen cry once, collapsed. The day my father died, my mother hadn't said goodbye. Every morning, she woke, loving him still. Sometimes, when I left my bed at night, wandering for a cup of water, I'd hear her whispering to him...

'It was a tough day, beloved.'

'You should see our children grow.'

'Lottie was in trouble again, fighting with that girl.'

'I miss you.'

Marek had no capacity to understand my mother's devotion. And yet, that wasn't his greatest error. No, Marek's true failing was his arrogant assumption that he might single out my father. It's true, Mother and Father were strong together. But Marek underestimated how strong my mother was...on her *own*.

That mistake cost him his pathetic life.

None of us rushed our mother while she sobbed. As I waited, watching her weep, I considered two unequivocal truths.

Firstly, over the years, Mother had developed an *obsession* with justice. We believed it to be the result of escaping strict parents and exercising her agency to choose right from wrong. It was a wonderful thing...until our father was killed. Every day, Mother woke, carrying the grief of not being able to pass justice on his killer. When someone is slaughtered by a wild animal, there isn't justice. Even if you kill the animal, it doesn't *feel* just. The animal can't comprehend what it did; it's only an animal.

But Marek knew exactly what he did. And this spoke to my mother; *this* was her language of justice.

A second truth: Mother was not soft—was not one for touching or affection. She tended to lean away and growl, 'Not here!' when my father kissed her in public. No, my mother's love was in her actions, providing safety and comfortable spaces.

Or, in this case, feeding Marek to the wolves. Though gruesome, *this* was her way of showing our father she loved him, even now. While she cried herself empty for her lost love, part of me believed that a few of those tears were crafted with pride.

Pride in *herself*.

Gradually, Mother's crying subsided. "Come. Help me up," she murmured. "Let us never look back on him again." As we walked out of the Hollow, I let everything sink in.

The man responsible for our father's death was dead.

This was a momentous occasion in all our lives. Justice had been served for my father, Lysander was alive, this was all I ever wanted. I should sit with it, appreciate all we've accomplished, but...a new desire burned within me.

And I would chase it with everything I had.

"I won't let Rook die."

Back at the cottage, my mother and I sat at the table drinking. Lysander lay on the sofa, and Lottie stood by the fire. Maybe it was the drink, or the fire flickering against the old beams overhead, but the cottage seemed warm again. It reminded me of holidays, autumn harvests and the midwinter celebrations. All of us together, drinking around the fire. How it used to be. How it *should* be. This is what I wanted for the rest of my life. There was just one thing missing.

"I have to free him," I said. "I *have* to."

"Our family is safe." Lottie pinched the bridge of her nose. "We need to quit while we're still breathing."

"Oh, yes," I started. "I'll be very safe up in the castle, all alone. Tell me: How will you rearrange our bedroom once I've gone?" No one responds well when reminded of mistakes, but the way Lottie scowled at me, you'd think she was considering substituting the next bit of kindling with my bones.

"At least *I* didn't bring a monster home to meet our mother!" she shouted and balled her fists. "Tell me: Are your prospects so pitiful? Hm? I mean, come on, Lil! Ruven was right there! Sure, he's dumber than a stump and looks like a top-heavy carrot, but at least he doesn't eat the neighbours!" Lottie looked to Lysander and Mother for support. None came. Her eyes widened, baffled they didn't agree with her. "I mean, there's a one-eyed dog up the road that would make a better partner. Monsieur Moustache. I'll introduce you!"

I crossed my arms, doing my best not to rise to Lottie's attacks. "Rook saved me in the Hollow." I pointed at Lysander. "He healed our brother."

"Lysander wouldn't have needed fixing if your stupid-ass *friend* hadn't tried to eat him in the first place!" Lottie roared back.

"He's not stupid!" I snapped, rising to Lottie's attack. "And he had no control over hurting Lysander! It was Marek—" My mother touched my hand. We all knew it wasn't Rook's fault, including Lottie. We'd reached the inevitable point where Lottie was arguing just to argue.

"And what do you propose we do?" Lottie shouted. "You haven't been in the castle; I have. It's an impossible task!"

Lysander chimed up. "I'm in."

"Ugh!" Lottie kicked the sofa.

"He saved my children," Mother said between sips.

"What happens when we get caught? Hm?" Lottie paced around the den. "They'll execute us, one-by-one after him."

"If you're too frightened," Mother said, "you might remain here." Lottie crossed her arms. She adored violence—why the sudden caution? Her eyes darted to Lysander, and she chewed her lip.

It seemed there was one thing Lottie cared for more than bloodlust.

"What do you propose we do?" she continued.

"I have a plan," I started. "Though, it isn't without risk." I gulped down another drink. "Well, a great deal of risk, actually."

My mother, already quite drunk, smiled over her glass. "Sounds like something Jean would approve of."

I chuckled. Actually, it did.

"Our family has given enough!" Mother threw her glass down, startling us all. "We will free Lili's boy, and then we will flee this despicable place!"

Lili's boy.

The words twisted my gut. I bit my lip, not trusting myself to speak. My mother hiccupped and said, "We *will* free him." Around the room, all eyes set on me.

We will free him.

Together.

"I can't believe it." A gnarled old physician sat beside Lysander. He lay in bed, arms tucked proudly behind his head. She inspected his wounds, which had shrunk by half since Rook's injection. The physician's eyes were suspicious slits. "I've never seen anyone fight the Hound's poison on their own." Lysander and I exchanged a glance.

"Ah!" Lysander grinned and tapped his nose. "You've never examined *me*." He raised an arm and flexed. The muscle was not nearly as prominent as it used to be, but I admired him for trying. "The Hound's lucky he's locked in a cell where I can't get to him." Lysander mimed punching and beamed. The physician laughed.

She did not ask any more questions.

"Not that you need my help, but..." The physician trailed her fingers along the wounds, slowing over Lysander's stomach. The dark lines that ran under Lysander's skin pulled back and shrunk. She patted Lysander's chest, more than once, and said, "You're a lucky boy. You'll be just fine." The physician stood and picked up a leather bag twice her size.

"Only fine?" Lysander buttoned his shirt.

I trailed the physician as she waddled down the hall, her gait bouncier than when she'd come in. Three guards sat at the table, waiting. All of them rose and stared at Lysander behind me.

"Here. Allow me." Lysander grabbed the bag I'd leaned against the table leg. He winked at the guards on his way up, one of which, a skinny lad with black hair, blushed. Outside, we found eight more guards on horseback. Had they come to protect the physician?

Or prevent my escape?

The driver offered to help the physician into the wagon. She *tsk*'d their outstretched hand and gave them her bag. Lysander threw my bag into the wagon and backed away. "Ahem," the physician coughed. Lysander offered a hand; she took it, and he helped her into the wagon. She sat, her smile broad as I climbed in after her.

Lysander clapped my knee. "Don't do anything I wouldn't do."

Stay safe.

The wagon started, and when we were almost out of sight, Lysander waved. If everything went as planned, I would see him soon.

PART THREE

Lesson Eighteen

The finest garment is the blood of
those who have forsaken you.

The castle was alive.

People bustled to-and-fro like bees, bumping me and talking over one another. Such a stark contrast to the cursed castle in the Hollow. A man with a powdered face caught sight of me. He smirked and whispered to his companion; they both laughed.

Concerning castles, I preferred the company of the latter.

I walked the halls, passing gilded paintings and expensive furniture. I thought it interesting that castles represent luxury, and any *reasonable* person would want to reside here. And yet, I hadn't once entered a castle that didn't feel oppressive.

The guard accompanying me said, "On your right."

I started up a set of stairs. With each step, I regretted every criticism I'd ever thrown at the tired walls of our cottage. What I wouldn't give to be back at the hearth with my family. I was brought to the sewing room, located in a drafty tower where the light was best. The only occupant was a woman, maybe ten years my senior, who spoke a language I was unfamiliar with. A wrought, spiral staircase jutted from the middle of the room.

My boots kicked up metallic *thunks* as I climbed the steps, exploring my newest prison. Each level stocked different fabrics and accessories. Shimmering satins and silks, golden tassels, bright ribbons. I stopped on a floor filled entirely with colourful threads. So many beautiful things, right here at my fingertips.

Behind me, the stairs vibrated. Bronwyn's brown braids appeared as she climbed the steps and joined me. "It's incredible, isn't it?" Bronwyn touched a spool of emerald thread. "Growing up, my mother had one pair of trousers." She chuckled and raised a finger. "Just *one*. Every night, when she came home, my father would bring out the needle and resew the crotch she'd ripped while working at the mill." Bronwyn frowned. "And then you come here and see this." She shook her head. "Silk from across the sea, half of it woven with gold."

I stopped hearing Bronwyn. An iridescent cream thread caught my eye, and I couldn't help but think it would have worked perfectly for Lottie's birthday coat. My mind wandered to my family, to Rook—

"Well?" Bronwyn said.

"Sorry," I backtracked. "What did you say?"

Bronwyn rubbed my arm. "You'll miss them less, as time passes." Her words offered little comfort.

"What happened to the Hound?"

"Dungeon."

Though I didn't mean to, I frowned.

"Don't worry," Bronwyn continued. "You're safe. Even if he manages to escape, he won't make it far." I rubbed my throat, feeling ill. "Hey, it's okay," Bronwyn soothed. "The Hound has caused so much suffering, the queen won't delay his punishment." I gulped and headed down the staircase. Bronwyn said, "You'll start your stay with an execution. How exciting!" The tower spun, and I gripped the railing for support. I made it to the bottom, and the sight of a familiar face snapped my swirling world into focus.

"You could have used this time to make me something nice," Lottie said, examining her fingernails, several of which were missing entirely.

"You'd only ruin it," I breathed, leaning on a table with my head between my arms.

"Lottie," Bronwyn said, dipping her chin. Lottie smiled and ran her tongue along the giant gap where her front tooth used to be. "I'll leave you be," Bronwyn muttered. She squeezed around Lottie, who made no move to let her by, and left the tower.

"Did you bring it?" I whispered.

Lottie shot the other seamstress a look, then nodded to the tower stairs. We headed down a level, where Lottie paused and snuck a small pouch from her cloak. Inside, I found all the items I'd asked for. The sweet stink of rot and alcohol burned my nose as I rooted around, locating the flint and iron.

"Know your way around yet?" Lottie asked. I blew out a stream of air and my eyes bugged. Crossing her arms, Lottie leaned against the stone. "Told you. It's big."

"Is anyone asking of Marek?"

Lottie craned her neck, making sure no one else occupied the stairwell. "I have it on good authority that he was last seen entering the Hollow at dusk." Lottie shook her head. "There are few who could survive a night out there, and Marek was no exception." After an exaggerated, uncaring sigh, Lottie said, "Anyway, his remains were brought to the castle coroner this morning."

"Was there much left?"

Lottie raised her hand in a *so-so* gesture. "Head and torso were gone. Some gooey buried bits were recovered. Legs and ass, I think."

"Shame," I muttered. "Who was promoted in his stead?"

Lottie scoffed. "You'll never believe it."

"Who?" I glanced down the stairs, where another familiar face approached. One word left my lips in disbelieving exhale. "No!"

Above several new pins and distinctions on her cloak, my mother's grim face met mine. Even before the Hound started slaughtering captains, the role turnover was high. To see those pins on my mother's breast was akin to seeing her grave. My mother's face was best described as disappointed but not surprised. This town had failed her many times.

She hadn't given up yet.

Pausing on the landing, my mother addressed us. "As the mother of the maiden who snared the Hound, they wanted to bestow me this"—her eyes darted to the ceiling, as she chose her next word carefully—"honour."

They wanted to keep my mother close, keep an eye on her.

"They would not have my refusal," Mother continued. "And, to celebrate the Hound's capture, the queen is throwing a ball—in your honour."

"Wha—no!" I snapped.

"In three days time," Mother said, ignoring me. "In a continuation of her gratitude, Queen Aenor has granted you permission to create a gown from the castle's finest materials."

"I'm not goin—"

"You don't make decisions here," Mother interrupted. "You obey orders." The height of her eyebrows asked, *Do you understand?* I crossed my arms. Finished with me, Mother turned to Lottie. "What responsibilities are you neglecting in being here?"

Lottie balked and rubbed her neck. "Weeell…"

"Can… Could one of you check on Rook?" I asked.

Lottie opened her mouth to answer, but my mother replied, "No." Glaring at Lottie, she repeated, "No!" Lottie began a dramatic eye roll;

Mother yanked her down the steps. She pointed up the tower and said, "Go. Make yourself a dress."

Lottie winked. "Shock 'em."

"Don't!" Mother pointed at me. "A *normal* dress!" She looked at Lottie, who closed her eyes and whole-heartedly nodded her agreement. But as our mother left us, Lottie mouthed, *'Fuck 'em up.'*

In the sewing room, I wandered through fabrics. So many stunning shades of periwinkle, olive, chartreuse. There was no vermillion, no scarlet, or berry-coloured hues. To wear red was to offer insult. It was a threat, a condemnation of the throne. I examined a light, cream fabric.

The perfect fabric for dyeing.

My fellow seamstress watched curiously as I left the tower. On the way down, I passed a girl and boy. The girl started, "We're meant to help with your gown!"

"Wait for me upstairs," I replied. "I'm going to gather supplies."

"But everything you need is here," the boy cried. "Where are you going?"

"To the coroner."

The three days leading to the ball passed slowly *and* swiftly. Whenever I thought of Rook, agony seemed to stall time. Sluggish moments passed as I wondered if he was safe—if he was in pain. But while I worked on my gown, the daylight sped away, and before I knew it, I was sewing by candlelight. I'd dismissed the children sent to help me—told them I was skilled enough without them, only to disguise the true reason. While there were times I didn't think I'd manage the task, I'd done it. Only an hour ago,

I'd slipped into my gown and hidden it snugly beneath my cloak. Now, the time had come. I headed to the ball.

Clutching my cloak, I walked along the second story path surrounding the great hall. Though there were no windows, the room was brighter than noon on a summer day. Torches adorned the rows of stone arches, flickering like tiny hearths as far as I could see. I paused, leaning on the railing. If I had to choose between wandering into the Hollow and fighting a thousand monsters, or what was about to come...I would choose the former. Down below, musicians dressed in green hues—juniper, pine, and moss—played harps and flutes. Along the wall, an array of acrobats climbed over one another.

I picked a pink petal from the garland adorning the rail. Greenery and flowers had been brought in, turning the sterile stone castle into a magical woodland. The pillars below were wrapped in boughs and trailing ivy. Everywhere I looked, bright displays of flowers mimicked a spring garden. How many living things had died to make this room hospitable? How much work had it taken so everyone here might pretend they were somewhere else for just one night?

I dropped the petal and watched it float all the way down.

A familiar, sing-song voice carried behind me. "And then I saw a pretty girl, walking once again. Why if it isn't our triumphant maiden, the ever lovely Liliwen!" My troubadour leaned on the rail, and I followed the black sleeves up to a mess of copper hair.

"Nice to see a familiar face," I said.

Ruven bumped me. "I heard your brother is well."

"He is."

"I'm so pleased." Ruven smiled. "And you're here now; that's wonderful!"

Shying from the enthusiasm, I turned back to the tumbling acrobats. I was faintly aware of a drumbeat, playing quickly. Though I searched the great hall for a drummer, I couldn't see one. The only music floated from the harp and gathered flautists.

"Where are you staying?" Ruven asked.

"The tower, in the sewing rooms."

"Ah, makes sense. They've got me downstairs, practically in the dungeon." I grumbled a lacklustre response, the way I always did when I was nervous and my mind was elsewhere. "Have courage," Ruven said. "It's only a ball." That did little to calm my nerves. "Shall we go in together?"

"Ruven." I backed from the rail. "You don't want that."

"Nonsense!" Ruven tucked my arm around his and patted it. "I want nothing more." We walked along the path, down the stairs, and headed to the magnificent double doors of the great hall. A woman dressed in black offered to take my cloak. After a brief pause in which I considered fleeing, I gave it to her. The woman paused with the cloak, her eyes widening. She left to tuck it away, casting a wary glance over her shoulder. Ruven looked at me as if I were a ghost. We prepared to enter the great hall, but Ruven did *not* offer me his hand. That's fine; I didn't need it. I walked through the doors anyway.

Pausing on the landing with me, Ruven hissed, "It's no small thing, to insult the queen."

"Have courage," I whispered. "It's only a ball."

From my neck to my fingertips flowed a deep crimson gown. A silk skirt pooled around my ankles, as if a river of blood poured from me. Under the gaze of everyone, I took my first steps. Strings of rubies fell down my bare back, cooling my skin where they touched. I'd spent my life creating garments meant to heal, to protect. Not this one—this was a gown of trickling blood. Into every seam, I wove sickness and poison—every evil, cruel emotion I could muster. When they looked upon me, I wanted those who governed this castle filled with stolen children to choke. I descended the last step and strode into the sea of bodies. As if tied to my anxieties and fears, that far off drum grew louder, until it was a great chorus I struggled to ignore.

People parted for me as if I were armed with a sword and not just a young woman in a pretty dress.

Next to me, someone covered their mouth. Another doubled over and held their belly. I paid them no mind and walked along the long banquet table. Heaps of cheese lay around a tower of delicate pastries. Farther down, an entire deer was cooked and laid out, as if it were only sleeping. I passed the doe and stopped before what I had *incorrectly* assumed was a turkey. Delicate blue and emerald feathers lay around a plucked and roasted peacock, it's flesh golden and crisp. I bit back nausea and turned, searching for Ruven in the crowd. With a heavy heart, I watched my friend leave the ball.

Though the room bustled with music and discussion, I'd never felt more alone.

Sticking to the edges of the room, I lurked in the shadows. It was there, hidden behind a pillar, that a hand curled around my arm. I came face-to-face with the dark mask of the advisor. Ripping my arm away, I cried, "Don't touch me!" The advisor didn't heed my warning. They dragged me, as if I were a child, toward the great doors.

Bronwyn intercepted us. "Let her go!" The advisor gripped my arm so tight, their forearm trembled. Bronwyn's lip curled as she hissed, "Drop her." Those around us stared, and I wished I might disappear into the floor. One finger at a time, the advisor released me.

"What an enchanting gown."

I stilled at the voice—the one I'd feared most when I'd first slipped into the gown. The music, the chatter, even the chorus of drums faded as I cast my head down and turned to face the queen. Queen Aenor greeted me as an amethyst might greet a hunter of gems in the darkest mine. How many hours had gone into the creation of her gown, which drew all eyes in the room? How many layers of fabric to create the skirt that kept people from getting too near? Tassels and golden strings shimmered as the queen approached.

"In capturing the Hound"—the queen's eyes roamed down my crimson dress—"you have demonstrated much courage." In an unlikely turn, she smiled. "As the person of honour, you will sit next to me." She beckoned me forward. Her skirts swished as she turned and headed to the lengthy dining table. Smoothing my dress, I reminded myself to breathe and accompanied the queen. "You might think I'm offended by your appearance," Queen Aenor said, rounding the table. "On the contrary, I find your dress quite...enchanting." She sat in a tall chair. "It brings me pleasure to imagine the daring gowns you'll create for me, while you're up in that tower for many, *many* years to come."

With drooping shoulders, I took my place beside the queen.

Still eying my gown, the queen said, "Did you hear? The captain of my guard seems to have died—well, been eaten." She plucked up a grape and ate it. "I didn't particularly care for the man, but I must admit he possessed a healthy respect for the Hollow. It seems odd he would wander in and allow himself to be eaten, does it not?"

Gulping, I anxiously adjusted a vase of daffodils. "I heard they found him in a hole. Perhaps he tripped?"

"Oh, indeed!" The queen laughed. "The freshly dug hole. Do you think he dug it first, and then, falling victim to his own hubris, tripped?"

"Anything is possible," I whispered, dusting a pile of pollen from the tablecloth.

Queen Aenor pursed her lips. "Captain Marek was quite fond of your family, was he not? Your mother, in particular, I've heard." She laughed. "That is, if you subscribe to silly barrack rumours."

I fidgeted with a spoon. "I never noticed."

"Mhm," the queen muttered.

Throughout the meal, I ate nothing. Food nauseated me, and thoughts of Rook preoccupied my mind. What was it like in the dungeon? Was he being tortured? During my worrying, Bronwyn took a seat beside the queen. I hoped she might divulge news of Rook, but the Hound was not mentioned once.

I couldn't help but notice the way Bronwyn's pinky stroked Queen Aenor's beneath the table before she left.

A familiar face entered the great hall, and a shred of comfort eased my worry. Lottie relieved one of the guards, just inside the doors. She caught sight of me and grinned, eyepatch, missing tooth, and all. Her eye widened as she took in my dress beneath the table. She chuckled and gave me a subtle thumbs up below her waist. Suddenly, Lottie's eye darted to my left, and the smile died. She adjusted her cloak and straightened. I glanced sideways and met Queen Aenor's gaze.

"You and your sister are young, and you are reckless." A bold statement; there were fewer than ten years between Queen Aenor and me. "Despite what you might believe, I am not your enemy." There was a steady pause. "Whether you like it or not, you will obey me, and you will serve the kingdom." I looked away, instead focusing on the napkin I'd mangled in my lap.

We'll see about that.

My skin tingled as the queen beheld me. I'd read of a queen who had the ability to catch another's thoughts, like passing shouts on the wind. Though I had no way of knowing if Queen Aenor possessed such a gift, I repeated a rhyme in my head, like I often did in the Hollow.

There once was a peckish bone fairy...

The queen clapped, sending a jolt of shock through me. The merry hall quieted. "Now," Queen Aenor began, "the reason you've all come." The great doors opened, and a thin shadow sliced through the murmuring crowd, splitting it in two.

Shackled and beaten, Rook stood in the doorway.

The advisor appeared like a shadow behind him. They gripped Rook's filthy shirt and tossed him forward. Crashing down the stairs, Rook's head hit the stone with a sickening *slap!* The advisor hurried after Rook and dragged him up by a metal collar. Fresh blood poured from a slit across Rook's forehead. Trailed by Bronwyn, the advisor and Rook shuffled toward the table. When they neared, the advisor kicked Rook's knees, and he fell. With the back of their hand, the advisor struck Rook. I winced against the beating, as if I'd received the blow. Through my grimace, I caught sight of the queen. She wasn't watching Rook.

No.

As Rook was beaten, Queen Aenor watched *my* reaction. I schooled my face into complacency. Still, the queen smirked. The advisor yanked Rook up by his hair and readied to strike again.

"Enough!" the queen shouted. With great restraint, the advisor backed off. Rook's breathing was ragged as he crawled to his knees. He spit a gob of blood. Looking upon the queen, Rook smiled. Ruby-red blood filled the cracks in his teeth.

The defiance sent my pulse racing.

"You have plagued our land, killing wantonly, for far too long," Queen Aenor said, eliciting a wave of boos. "You will terrorize us no longer. Come dawn, we will see you executed." A chorus of applause boomed. The woman beside me clapped, and then curled her hand around her mouth to echo a cheer. "We must all thank your captor!" The queen waved at me. "Our triumphant maiden, Liliwen Valet!"

The applause deafened me.

"For without Liliwen, you would be free." Queen Aenor stood, leaning over the table toward Rook. "Without Liliwen, you would not *die*." The queen raised her hand, and against my will, I got up. Queen Aenor flourished her fingers, and a blade of ice formed in my palm. She waved to Rook, on his knees. In an even voice, she commanded me to, "Draw blood." Her smile said everything her words did not.

'Blood for blood. I can offer an insult of my own.'

Unable to control my body, my feet carried me around the table. They stopped me in front of Rook. I begged my fingers to release the blade, hurl it across the room and be done with it. They would not obey, instead I brought the blade to Rook's cheek. Though fresh blood cut down his face in a red river, I was relieved to see most of the swelling from his previous beating had subsided. In a subtle movement, Rook leaned into my hand, brushing my skin. He smiled. It was more for me than him. He gave the slightest of nods.

'I forgive you.'

With a quick slice, I nicked the flesh. Rook barely winced as a line of blood dribbled down his cheek. Hoots and cheers carried all around us.

"Marvelous!" the queen cheered. "Take him away, before we lose our appetites."

The advisor yanked Rook up. As he was dragged from the hall, Rook raised his shackles. He gave the queen a playful wave and blew a kiss.

The crowd gasped and Rook laughed. He remained laughing until he was dragged through the great doors. But in that last moment, Rook's eyes found mine.

And the laughter vanished.

"Now that the mongrel is gone, we shall celebrate until dawn!" the queen cried. "And then, we'll watch his head roll." Music took over, and everyone lapsed into excited chatter. I didn't return to my spot at the table; I found an ivy-drenched pillar and leaned on it.

An older woman pursed her lips, obviously sickened by my dress. Her own gown had tension problems, and a terrible seam allowance, with bunching in the back she'd tried to conceal with a shawl. The woman whispered something to a friend. They looked at me and laughed.

I gritted my teeth. "Do you like my dress?"

The woman looked at my back and stuck her nose up. "We were wondering if you ran out of fabric." The comment earned another laugh from her friend.

"You didn't have your gown made in town," I said. "Did you?"

The woman straightened and tugged anxiously on her sleeve. "Well, no. I made it myself." Her companion seemed surprised by the admission.

I leaned forward and said, "I can tell."

Before the woman could decide whether I'd meant it as an insult or a compliment, Lottie appeared beside me and said, very loudly, "Yeah, you look like a big bag of *shit*." Horror dropped the woman's jaw, and she fled. Lottie waved and leaned on the pillar. Pointing at my dress, she asked, "How'd you do that?"

"Chimera root powder. Keeps the blood red longer."

Lottie's response was to cringe and lean away. "And are those...ivory?" She reached out and touched one of my earrings.

"No. Have you seen Ruven?"

Crossing her arms, Lottie said, "Nah."

"He was here earlier; I'm not sure where he went."

"He doesn't seem to enjoy this crowd," Lottie said. "From what I've heard, he sulks around the castle, not really trying to fit in."

That didn't sound like the bright-eyed, happy boy I knew. "I'm sure he misses the farm. I would…"

Bronwyn and the advisor rejoined the ball.

"I've never seen such cruelty from the advisor," Lottie whispered. "I mean, they're an executioner, usually they're professional, but this business with the Hound… They're savouring it; this is torture." Lottie shook her head. "And you know, I'm all for torture, but…"

"Do you think the Hound killed someone they loved?" I asked. Lottie shrugged in agreement. "Do you have any idea who it could be, beneath the mask?"

Lottie exhaled and pulsed her brows. "Whoever she is, I wouldn't want to run into her in a dark passage."

"You think it's a woman under there?" I glanced back at the advisor.

"Don't you?" Lottie scrunched her face. "She's so foreboding. No man could ever be so frightful." Lottie paused. "You know, I once saw the advisor grab a beating heart from someone's chest, and then punch them in the face with it." I turned an alarmed eye on Lottie. "Yeah." She mimed punching an invisible foe. "Their own heart. Their own face." Lottie shivered. "It was great."

"My word, Lottie."

"Don't get me wrong. It was terrifying." Lottie nodded rapidly. Her voice faded to an awed whisper. "But great."

Sometimes, of all the terrors I'd faced in my life, Lottie scared me the most.

Lottie looked at the banquet table. "You eat?"

"Yes."

"Good. Do you have everything you need?"

"Mhm." The bag holding my flint was tied to my thigh. At midnight, when the ball attendees were content and drunk, I'd slip away. I'd stashed several alcohol-soaked rags throughout the castle. With the flint and iron, I'd bolt through the castle, lighting as many fires as I could. While the fires grew, Lottie would sneak into the dungeon and free Rook. We'd have to be swift, for fire would not slow Queen Aenor for long.

Across the hall, the advisor turned their dark hood upon us.

"Why are they staring?" Lottie glared back, puffing her shoulders in defiance.

"They know we're up to something," I whispered.

"No, they don't." Lottie sniped. "How could they know?"

"I have no idea. But they do." As if summoned by our whispers, the advisor started in our direction.

"Gotta go!" Lottie pushed from the pillar.

My heart leapt. Lottie waved. I returned the gesture with a shaking fist and a tight-lipped smile that said, *'Don't you dare leave me!'* I looked for an escape—too late.

The advisor was upon me.

They bowed low. Refusing to return the respect, I only bowed my head. The advisor offered me a gloved hand. All around, people gawked. Surely, this wasn't allowed. An executioner, showing favour at a ball? I stared at the hand that had nearly beaten Rook to death. At the hand that would likely land the killing blow if we failed in rescuing Rook. I caught sight of Queen Aenor's smug face.

She laughed as if to say, *'Not so brave now, are you child?'*

Raising my chin, I took the advisor's hand. It was light and nimble, like a bluebird on a branch. They led me to the middle of the hall and placed a palm respectfully on my back. People gave us a wide berth and stared. I barely saw the shocked faces. Conjured images of the advisor, chopping Rook's head from his shoulders, blinded me. Injustice boiled beneath my skin. Rook, shackled so he might not fight back, beaten in an unfair fight. Shoved to his knees and laughed at. All because of an innocent mistake, made so long ago. We danced in silence, and though there was something comforting about the way their hand fit in mine, my hatred for them grew, step-by-step.

When I could contain my fury no longer, I said, "That man, the Hound—he's not who everyone thinks he is." The advisor's clothed face swivelled to me. "He's a good man." The advisor spun me and brought me back. I glared at the spot I knew their eyes would be. "If you hurt him, I will saw off your *head*." The advisor responded with an exhale of air that might have been a laugh. The song came to an end, and the advisor bowed low and departed. Watching their back, I suddenly felt very foolish. Why had I threatened them?!

'Because you're young, and you are reckless,' the queen's voice mocked.

Which was more infuriating? My own impulsivity or proving the queen correct? Sweat dampened my palms as I watched the advisor leave. Surely, they'd go straight to Queen Aenor, and I'd be taken into custody. But the advisor didn't go to the queen. They climbed the steps into the great hall and stood alongside Bronwyn.

Why?

I retreated to a corner. If the advisor's allegiances did not lie with the queen, where did they? In my shadowy corner, I passed hours watching people. Dancing, feasting, and laughing. When I couldn't stomach the joyful faces, I focused on the musicians. It was almost soothing, to watch their fingers plucking the harp strings. Gradually, the tall candles adorning the tables burned to short nubs, and the light dimmed.

Excusing myself to no one, I took my leave.

I headed toward the tower, and when I was sure there was no one around, I ducked into a side hall. Walking quickly, I entered an infrequently used privy. Here, I'd hidden my first tinder bundle, a combination of dry twigs and alcohol-soaked rags. I hiked up my skirt and withdrew my flint and iron from the pouch on my thigh. After a few tries, the flame caught, and I set the bundle down. Crackling and popping, the fire ran up a beam and spread along the wood ceiling.

No going back now.

With the first fire burning, I had to hurry. There were four more bundles throughout the castle, and if I made haste, I could light them all before anyone noticed. By the time someone discovered something was wrong, an inferno would come. I exited the privy and took off. Four more to go, and I could flee this miserable castle.

That didn't seem so many.

I ran toward a guest bedroom down the hall. Slipping inside, I pulled back a magnificent tapestry and found my second bundle. I knelt, striking my flint and iron, until a flame sputtered to life. I stood just as the bedroom door opened.

"Lili?!"

My heart hammered; I hadn't heard anyone stalking after me. With fire in hand, I turned to greet whoever had caught me.

Stuffing something in his pocket, Ruven cried, "What are you doing?" My eyes darted between Ruven and the flaming bundle. Ruven backed away. "You're going to try to save the beast, aren't you?"

"Ruven, he's not what they say he is."

"He killed people!"

"It wasn't his fault!" I cried. "You must trust me." Ruven grabbed the door, ready to slip out. "Ruven, please!" I ran forward, slamming the door and preventing his escape. "If you *ever* cared for me, you will leave, and you won't tell anyone what you saw."

"He's fed you lies, Lili!" Ruven shook his head. "And you've devoured them!"

"Ruven, you don't know who he is."

"I know *what* he is!"

"And what? These people who steal children from their families are any better?" Ruven remained quiet. "I just want to go back to my family," I begged. "Please. You feel the same—you can't deny it!" Ruven's irises danced along my face. "You need to make a choice," I said. "Please, make the right one."

Chapter Nineteen

Rook

The dungeon was equipped with eight cells, built in a neat line. Through the bars, two more prisoners sat in their respective cells. One might think the ability to see fellow prisoners was reassuring. This is a false thought, I'm afraid, as witnessing what was done to them offered little comfort. An array of metal tools hung along the adjacent wall. I was curious about one device in particular, only because I'd never seen it. Comprised of criss-crossing iron, it was covered in a fair amount of its previous victim's entrails. I wondered which of the tools, if any, I might have the pleasure of experiencing. Though none of the instruments could be more damaging than the *smell* coming from my fellow prisoners. I rested with my hand over my nose, and any time I nodded off, I'd wake up gagging on the taste of sour milk and excrement.

I dragged my foot along the stone, resting it against the cell door. If I could muster the strength to transform, could I break out? I reached forward, gripping the bars.

Solid.

Even the Hound could not tear through iron.

Beaten and weak, I doubted I could change anyway. Just as well; death was welcome. I leaned against the damp stone. When death came, I would greet her as an old friend.

The hurried *pitter-patter* of paws rang out. A remarkably well-fed rat crept from the dark. I considered snatching the rodent and devouring it. Standing on two feet, the rat sniffed the air. Why take a life to sustain myself when my own would end so soon? The rat scurried back to a crack in the wall.

In my pocket, I stroked the gnarled cuff that held me captive for so long. A few nights ago, it had grown hot. So hot, I'd woken with a scream and torn it off. An act I hadn't managed since my visit with Marek, so many years ago. Sitting in the castle dungeon, my newfound freedom from Marek was bittersweet.

My thoughts wandered the same path they always did when it was quiet. They chased a memory of a woman crouched at my bedside and landed on the face that brought me comfort in my isolation.

Liliwen.

Did she think of me?

Did her thoughts of me consume her?

Closing my eyes, I met Lili again. Wearing the red dress that stood out like a wildfire in the night. The garment stunk of rusted metal—of blood—which only excited me further. An...unfortunate byproduct of what I'd become. How I envied everyone that might look upon her when I was dragged away. That I was forbidden to perceive the one person who might bring me solace in my final hours. I begged she kept her silence, to protect herself and her family. That she would be strong—strong enough to let me die.

Would she be at the execution?

At the end of it all, a selfish part of me wanted her near. It was pathetic, but, even if she had set out to kill me all those nights ago, I wanted her with me now that the end was near. The scene from Lili's cottage ran laps in my mind. Her sister had betrayed us both. I could see Lili's horrified face as she turned to her sister and cried, *'What did you do—'*

"Lottie?" The guard at the end of the cell block said, surprised. Lottie traipsed through the stone archway. Her eye wandered down the row of cells, widening when it caught mine. Summoning every shred of charm scattered about herself, Lottie spoke to the guard.

"How are ya...Celia?"

"Um, it's Celine, and not very good, actually. Dad passed last week."

"That's great, Celise." Lottie said, patting Celine on the arm. "I'm here to relieve you."

"But, my watch just began."

"I'm sorry." Lottie rounded on Celine. "You think I'm wrong?"

"Uh." Celine cowered. "No—no, of course not. I was probably mistaken."

"That's what I thought," Lottie said. Celine's footfalls echoed down the stairs as she hurried up and away. Lottie strolled down the dank cellblock. I noted the bow at her back. Perhaps, to save her sister the pain of watching me die, she would kill me here. Rather than draw her bow, Lottie leaned on the bars.

"Well, well, well...how the king of mongrels has fallen."

Too weary to respond to the insult, I muttered, "You turned me in."

"I did."

"And you stabbed me with a pike, if I remember correctly?"

Lottie grinned, showing gaps that teeth used to call home. "And I'll do it again, if you don't shut the fuck up and listen." I exchanged glances with the prisoner in the cell beside me. Lottie's youthful arrogance was astonishing. I wrinkled my nose; she smelled so strange. Lottie raised two fingers and a nub. "Three questions." My distasteful scowl did nothing to dissuade her. "My sister, what colour are her eyes?"

"What?"

Lottie kicked the bars where my foot rested. I yanked it back and shouted, "Green?!"

"That sounded an awful lot like a guess—"

"They're green," I interrupted with confidence. A beautiful, mottled green, like the moss that grew at the base of the statues near the pond.

"What's her favourite flower?"

"I—I have no idea."

"Better think. Time's running out before what's-her-face realizes I lied and comes back with friends."

I sifted through memories. When we sat next to the lake, Lili talked of flowers. They were pink...or maybe white? With so many petals, like the rows and rows of a skirt. They were her father's favourite; could they be hers too? I'd even brought them in the castle, if only to be reminded of her. But what were they called?! Roses? Daffodils? Artichoke? No, no, that was a vegetable—

"I'm surprised my sister showed affection to someone so unobservant," Lottie remarked.

"Do I look like a gardener?" I snarled. Using the bars, I pulled myself up. "Can *you* name a single flower?"

Lottie examined a nail-less finger and said, "I'm not trying to court anyone's sister."

I dragged my hands down my face and thought of every flower I'd ever heard of. I tried to remember Lili, the cadence of her voice when she'd said the word. Roses? Primroses? P. It started with p—"Peony!"

Both Lottie and I glanced anxiously down the cell block. "Fair enough," Lottie said. "I'd've assumed lilies." Lottie looked me up and down. "Do you love her?"

My mouth fell open, and…I didn't know what to say. I slouched against the wall. So often, I remembered Lili with a book in her lap, lips bathed in firelight, forming words as if they were sweet melodies. How I'd longed to reach out and touch her—to satisfy all my wonders and curiosities. Is her skin as soft as it looks?

Does she crave me the way I crave her?

Still, I could not answer Lottie.

My shackles clinked as I rubbed my chest, trying to ease the ache that settled there. I remembered when Lili and I first kissed beneath the sunset. My world changed, and I could hardly breathe—

The cell door creaked open.

"Let's go." Lottie unshackled me. My bonds fell away, and she muttered, "Marek's dead."

"He is?"

"Yup," Lottie said. "Sisterly advice—stay on Mum's good side."

We climbed out of the dank dungeon, and the mildew gave way to fresher air, laden with melting wax and candle smoke. At the top of the stairs, Lili's mother greeted us. Her gaze travelled up and down me, assessing. A few days ago, I was the one who'd saved her children. Tonight, I was just the beast who'd acted out the death command on her beloved. Shame almost sent me back to the cell. Lili's mother half-smiled, and hope stalled the spreading shame.

"You may call me Evette," she said. "For now."

"*For now* is all we'll have if we don't hurry," Lottie mumbled. "Let's get out of here."

"I can't leave without Lili," I said.

"My first-born is capable." Evette dragged me on. "She will meet us once we've escaped."

"Let's go," Lottie hissed.

Reluctantly, I chased after them. I heeded every sound and scent as we snuck through the halls. All my focus should have been devoted to avoiding the guards, but I couldn't help trying to find *her*. I inhaled, searching for the smell of Lili's soap, of the lemon salve she used on her lips. It terrified me that I smelled nothing of her at all. What if she'd been hurt? Rage tunnelled my vision. If anyone touched Lili...

Terror and thrill filled me as I thought of ripping their throats out, of the hot blood drenching my lips and coating my throat. I shook my head, doing my best to clear the lust. I made sure Evette was close. No more of Lili's family would die—not while I breathed.

Ahead, Lottie rounded a corner. She reappeared, jogging in our direction. "We're gonna go that way, uh, quickly." She pointed behind us. A shout rang out from the way she'd come, and two guards rounded the corner. Lottie cried, "Run!"

I waited for Lottie to pass, then trailed her and Evette. "I don't want to alarm you," I said, "but I smell smoke."

Without slowing, Lottie shouted, "Oh, good!"

"They'll have evacuated the great hall," Evette said.

"Where's our back-up exit?" Lottie asked.

Breathing heavily, Evette replied, "We'll go past the great hall and exit through the kitchens." As we ran, I thought I caught sight of Lili through a door. I stumbled, but by the time I'd backtracked, she was gone. "Everard!" Evette called from the end of the hall. "Move!"

I hastened, but then a guard came from a room, separating me from Evette and Lottie. "You!" the guard shouted, raising a crossbow. I fell back and leapt into a side room. Slamming the door behind me, I dove over tables and around furniture. I reached a door on the other side and skidded into the hall. A smoky haze floated through the castle, and I coughed. I hunched, trying to sink below the smoke and covered my mouth. Without any idea of where to go, I jogged down the hall. Passing an open door, I—

A force slammed into my side and sent me sprawling against the wall. The guard raised a blade and stabbed. I thrust my head sideways, dodging the attack. Her blade bounced off the stone, but she raised it again. *Thwack!* Warm droplets spattered me, and the guard ceased fighting.

An arrow stuck through her throat.

Blood gurgled in the guard's mouth, it poured around the arrow and down her neck. She groaned and fell aside.

At the end of the hall, Lottie lowered her bow.

The guard's blood broke against my boots, sending a quiver of ravenous mania through me. Delicious, life-giving blood. I knelt, wanting so much to drink, to eat—

"Rook!" Lottie waved me forward. "Don't be weird!"

With great effort and a pained shout, I shook away the desire. Wiping blood and smoke from my eyes, I ran toward Lottie and coughed out, "Your mother?"

"Ahead, scouting the exit." Lottie wrapped a cloth over her nose and took off. I started after her, but a hand tangled in my hair. The castle spun as I was turned roughly to face my attacker. At once, I noticed two things: a swath of red hair and a cold blade at my throat.

"You're uglier than I remember," Ruven snarled.

"If not my looks"—I choked against the blade—"I wonder how else I might have tempted our mutual friend?" I cast my eyes down. Ruven shoved me against a door, sending up a loud *bang!* The sword dug into my neck, suffocating me.

The sound of a rope growing taut snapped as Lottie drew her bow and pressed the arrow against Ruven's temple. "Don't make me do this," she said.

"Why am I not surprised you'd align with him?" Ruven replied, never taking his eyes off me. A chorus of boots scuffed down the hall.

The guards were coming.

Urgency sprung within me. I struggled against the sword and sputtered, "Run!" to Lottie.

"I'm not leaving without you, you twat." To Ruven she said, "I will put this arrow in your head, I swear it."

Shouting carried through the castle as the guards approached. Could I disarm Ruven? I might be able to get away, but I'd likely be maimed in the process. I'd never escape, and I'd only slow Lottie down. Individual voices stood out from the rising shouts.

"Kill him the moment you see him!"

"Kill them all on sight!"

"Not the new girl—keep her alive."

Hearing those final words, Ruven's eyelids fluttered. Though rage shook him, he lowered his sword. My relief was short, as Ruven leaned over and opened the door supporting me. He put a hand on my chest and pushed me. I backpedaled and fell into a table.

"Oy!" Lottie cried. "What the—" Ruven managed to get Lottie's bow, and she too was thrown into the room. The door banged shut. It didn't take long to discover there were no other doors in the parlour.

Our escape had failed.

Lottie snatched a decanter from a side table.

"What are you doing?" I asked.

Holding the neck of the decanter, Lottie covered her good eye and smashed the bottle against the stone. Running back to the door, she brandished the jagged bottle at me. "I can take at least six of them. More if I *have* to," she said in a hushed voice. "What about you?" Lottie didn't wait for my response; she pressed her ear against the door. In the hall, the crashing footfalls ceased, and voices picked up.

"Any sign of the beast?" someone asked.

After a considerable silence, Ruven replied, "Not yet."

A disappointed voice said, "You need to evacuate."

Ruven's response was a soft, "Aye."

Ear pressed to the door, Lottie mouthed, *'They're leaving.'* Lottie hurried back as the door swung in.

Ruven stepped aside and indicated for us to exit. "I'd suggest haste." He handed Lottie her bow.

"Thank you," she whispered with more gratitude than one might expect from a returned weapon. Ruven only offered a grim nod. "Goodbye Ruven." Lottie didn't wait to see the lacklustre wave Ruven parted with. She took off down the hall. I started after her—

"You're a selfish bastard."

I halted and stared at Ruven. He turned and walked away. Watching his back, I was met with the vision of Liliwen, safe in a farmhouse somewhere, with a happy, red-headed baby in her lap. As I turned to join Lottie, I couldn't seem to shake the guilt that settled in my weary bones.

Hustling through a doorway, Lottie's head whipped frantically as we approached the great hall. The massive doors were hardly visible through the smoke. Evette appeared from a servant's door farther down, running toward us.

"They've blocked the kitchen," she panted. "They're coming."

"What do we do?" Lottie snarled.

"Secret exit." Evette dragged us toward the great hall. "Through here and out the back." She leaned on the doors, trying to push them open. Lottie joined her, throwing all her weight into it. I bent over them, pushing with everything I had.

The doors creaked open.

Evette peered over her shoulder. She grabbed my shirt and yanked me down. I choked, "Wha—" as an arrow struck the wooden door. Guards spilled into the hall, all coming quickly toward us. Lottie squeezed through the opening, and I ushered Evette through. Sucking in my chest, I slid in after them. A grey wall met me, the smoke thick and heavy. I heaved myself against the great doors, closing them as guards slammed into the other side.

"Come on!" Lottie cried, disappearing into the grey expanse.

"Go!" I shouted, halting Lottie. The image of the guard, with an arrow through the throat, flashed through my mind. If the queen hadn't planned on executing Lottie for jailbreaking, she certainly would now.

Now, she was a murderer.

I knew, in my heart, Lili would want me to do anything in my power to protect Lottie. Waving, I cried, "Get out!" The doors behind me jostled open. I turned, slamming them closed.

"Rook!"

The sound of *her* voice.

"Lili?" Through the haze, I barely made out Lili, running to Lottie and Evette. Soot smeared her face, like the girls returning from the mines in the evenings. Her hair, so often tied back, was strewn about, singed and smoking in some places.

She was breathtaking.

Lili pulled Evette and Lottie, encouraging them to head down the great hall, toward the hidden passage. Speaking quickly, Lili said, "She knew—Queen Aenor suspected something; we have to get out." Starting toward me, Lili beckoned. "Rook, let's go!"

Don't do it.

If I let go of the door, guards would pour in and overtake us. "I can't!" I strained against the weight. Shouts rose on the other side, something about 'the second story entrance.' Our time was running out.

"The way is clear; we can all make it!" Lili cried. "Come on!"

Against my better judgement, I abandoned my spot. As I sprinted away, the door blew open, and shouts filled the hall. I ignored them; crossing the distance between us, I ran to Lili's outstretched hand. Smoke swirled as a blur whizzed by.

Lili stilled.

Brows furrowed in a pained grimace. Lili's hand dropped to her stomach...and curled around the arrow stuck there. Everything around me, which had been moving with frightful speed, halted. Hundreds of footfalls hammered the cobblestones as guards poured in. Someone knocked my legs, and I slammed into the floor. Hands came from all directions, holding me in place. More guards surged by; they parted around Lili like water parting around rocks in a stream.

She was a threat no more.

Evette and Lottie were overtaken and forced to their knees.

Lili stared at me, lost and confused. I thought I'd known agony—I was a fool. No amount of despair could have readied me for this.

The first person I'd cared for in decades collapsed.

Someone tried to gag me. I threw my head forward and shattered their nose. "Please!" I begged. "I'll do anything you want! I'll return to my cell. Just help her!" Ignoring my pleas, more guards piled on, crushing me. Lying forgotten on the floor, Lili struggled to breathe. Seeing that arrow, phantom pain flared in my side, where the bolt had struck me. I wanted to do anything—*anything*—to take that pain away from her.

And destroy who dared strike her down.

"Agh!" I tore from my captors. A guard clung to my arm. I punched them, snapping their head back. When I was halfway to Lili, a guard caught my leg, and I tripped. I fell but managed to free myself. Crawling the last few feet, I slipped my arm beneath Lili and drew her to me. Lili's eyes lulled, barely seeing me. "Liliwen," I whimpered. "I've got you." Drips of water fell down Lili's chest, and I was aware, distantly, that I was crying. "I'm so sorry!"

I wish I'd never come into your life!

"It's okay," Lili murmured, caressing my cheek.

"You deserve so much better than this." I wept, resting my forehead against hers. I held tight, so that no one, not even death, might rip her away. "Please," I begged. "Please stay with me." Breathing deep, I tried to be one with her for as long as I could. Muskiness crinkled my nose. Lili no longer smelled of lavender and lemon, but the same, strange odour that accompanied Lottie. Realization struck me like lightning.

Liliwen smiled.

CRACK!

The fingers holding my face snapped and broke.

The arrow Lili clutched fell away. It hadn't pierced her. Marek's voice ruptured my frantic thoughts. *'I once saw an arrow bounce off a garment she wove.'* My pulse raced, spurred by the sparkle blossoming in Lili's eyes.

Lili twisted and cried, "Aghhhh!" Light fur grew along her skin, tearing her dress. I fell away as growing limbs flailed against the stone. An entire hall of guards watched in terrified awe. In seconds, a massive, snarling hound stood in the great hall.

When I was cursed, I'd lost everything. Lili knew of my suffering; I'd admitted the loneliness, the pain, and the unending hunger. I'd done everything in my power to assure she didn't share my fate. It seemed my effort was wasted.

In the end, she'd eaten the fruit anyway.

"Shoot it!" a guard shrieked, while another aimed. They pulled the trigger, but a gloved fist knocked the crossbow down. The bolt went wild, striking a guard through the calf. A hysteric, high-pitched scream left her throat as she cradled her leg. Like splintering wood, a chorus of loud cracks drew all eyes to the far end of the hall.

Evette and Lottie were gone.

The room stopped, as if everyone inside were bewitched. Could it be? Had their eyes deceived them?

Indeed, it was no trick.

The great hall held three monstrous hounds.

To their detriment, a guard reached for their sword. A hound, possessing only one eye, snatched them. The guard's body broke. It sent out a sickening *crunch*, like the bite of a crisp apple. Smattered in a bib of blood, the hound reared and released an ear-splitting howl. Stillness broken, arrows flew as the hounds unleashed themselves on the small army. I wanted to change, even tried, but collapsed, half-fainting from the strain. Through the smoky haze, I could barely make out the carnage. While the dark hound with a grey streak—Evette—and Lili seemed keen on merely taunting the guards, the hound with one eye was particularly vicious. She played with the guards, toying with them before leaping forward and nipping their heads clean off. Respect, and no small amount of fear, graced me as I beheld Lottie in hound form. In mere seconds, she'd torn limbs from no less than six guards. She was a natural; it was hard to believe she hadn't been born this way.

Regaining my footing, I stumbled toward Lili as the doors to the great hall exploded open. They crashed against the stone, and a gust of frigid air threw splinters across the hall. The force knocked the breath from me, and I squinted against the brutal wind. A figure stood in the entrance, hair blowing in the gale.

Queen Aenor.

The room went dark.

Shrieks and snarls battered me. A hand slid inside mine, yanking me up. Its owner was a mystery to me; even *I* couldn't see in these manufactured shadows. The stranger didn't immediately stab me, so I allowed them to drag me away. *Click.* The gentle sound of a door opening. My mystery saviour shoved me into a tiny passage, barely illuminated by torches. Tucking an ill-fitting shirt into her trousers, Evette grimaced. A wet shimmer caught the light, blood covered her collar.

"Are you injured?" I asked.

"It's not my blood." Evette pulled a cloak on and pushed passed me. "Move."

Digging in my heels, I cried, "Not without Lili!"

"Trust my girls!" Evette yanked me onward. "They will come!" Ignoring her, I retreated. Evette snatched my shirt. "You are the weakest thing in this castle!" Her eyes were fire, her canines sharp points as she roared, "You will not crawl back in there to be captured, only for my daughters to risk their lives freeing you a second time!"

Every fibre of my being disagreed. "I won't leave her!"

With brute strength, Evette tossed me down the passage, I clutched the wall for support. "This is not a discussion!" She drew her sword and nodded on. "My daughters do not need you saving them!" With great effort, I straightened. Evette's sword dug into my spine, encouraging me.

Lili had always claimed I was the deadliest beast in the Hollow. In truth, I'd lost count of how many times she might have slain me. How often had she loomed above me, prepared to do it, stopped only by her kind heart?

I begged that same heart led her back to me, even if she had to betray her very nature to do so.

Reluctantly, I began down the cramped path. Soon, it widened, allowing me to stand straight. I rounded a corner and moonlight appeared at the end. Freedom. Yet it was dread, not relief, that rocked me. Lili was back there, fighting for her life. How could I get back to her without harming Evette? She was strong now, stronger than me for certain.

A shadow crossed the moonlight.

"Hold it," said a woman, the one so often at the advisor's side.

"Bronwyn," Evette slipped around me and raised her sword. "Step aside." I wondered if I might flee, back to Lili—but rising concern for Evette kept me rooted.

"Captain!" Bronwyn cried. "The Hound killed your husband!"

Evette's sword wavered, but she didn't back down. "The Hound might have landed the blow, but it was not this man's fault." To hear those words, it was like I was freed from Marek's control all over again. "Please, Bronwyn." Evette softened. "I *just* want to be with my children. Liliwen, Lottie, and Lysander." She said their names, carefully and deliberately. "Surely, you can understand."

Bronwyn didn't move.

Realizing it wasn't working, Evette lowered her sword and undid her cloak. The fracturing of bones echoed against the stones as she shifted. I side-stepped the sprawling limbs. Gobs of drool fell from the hound's mouth. Its head craned against the ceiling, looming over Bronwyn.

Strangely...Bronwyn smiled at the snarling beast. She raised her hand, and a milky haze swirled in the hound's eyes. The beast swayed, as if in a trance.

No!

This woman, Bronwyn—could she control beasts?

"You will remain here," Bronwyn ordered.

I elbowed Evette—hard. "Change back!" But Evette was lost. She sat, like an oversized sheepdog. I snatched Evette's dropped sword. The weight of the weapon was familiar, not so unlike my axe. Lunging at Bronwyn, I sliced.

The blade was sharp, the cut clean.

Bronwyn's hand fell from her arm as easily as a leaf might be shaken from a tree. A geyser of blood spurted from Bronwyn's wrist and her shrieks filled the passage. Evette shook her head, coming out of her trance. As she shrunk back to herself, horror distorted her features. Bronwyn clutched the bloodied stump, wailing in agony. I snatched the cloak and wrapped it around Evette's shoulders.

"Run!"

Together, we thundered into the night.

"This way!" Evette skirted rocks and hurtled down the mountainside. Sprinting, we didn't slow until we reached a less-trodden path by the creek that serviced the castle. In a waiting wagon, Lysander smiled. Though his eyes grew solemn as they trailed the path behind us, toward the castle.

Where his sisters did not follow.

Evette collapsed against the wagon. With barely breath to utter it, she said, "They will come." She climbed up next to Lysander. "We have a meeting place; we will go."

"I—I can't." Every instinct commanded me back to Lili.

Evette and Lysander exchanged a look. Evette nodded, only slightly. Lysander frowned and gave me a sympathetic shrug. "Sorry, mate." There was no time to ask why. Lysander's fist connected with my jaw and my head snapped back so far, I saw the twinkling stars above.

Then darkness took me.

Lesson Twenty

Your eyes are your soul; if someone
seeks to control you, look away.

In times of extreme peril, the castle evacuates. You might think, the first person to be evacuated is the queen.

This is not the case.

A queen is not born a queen. A queen is chosen because she is the most powerful, the most frightening, and the one *most* willing to do what needs to be done to protect the kingdom. So, when the castle evacuates, every terrified individual departs, except the queen.

She remains until the threat is eradicated.

This thought plagued me as I tiptoed the abandoned halls. When the great hall had fallen to ice and shadows, two things happened at once. My mother grabbed Rook and dragged him away. Lottie, drunk with bloodlust and power, went after the queen. I'd chased her and lost them.

As anticipated, it didn't take long for Queen Aenor to douse the fires. The castle bore the chill that accompanied a calm winter morning. The walls themselves were coated in ice, and my breath floated out in a misty cloud. With the castle empty, I no longer heard the drums—the beating hearts of all those humans. Quietly, I searched for Lottie in my human body. As a hound, sensations were overwhelming. The smell, the lust for blood—it was too much. Even in human form, my perceptions were altered considerably. In the shadows, I could see farther. I could hear the rats scurrying around the castle and smell the metallic blood wafting from all the corpses strewn about. Even as a human, it was dizzying, how much I craved the blood. The willpower it took not to fall to my knees and drink was astonishing. Following my nose, I rounded a corner, where a headless guard lay on the floor.

An unfortunate sign Lottie had come this way.

I looted the guard's clothing to ease my shivering. As I tucked the shirt into my trousers, a haunting melody floated through the halls. Almost like a harpsichord, but more...rickety. I was struck with the horrifying image that, instead of ivory keys, the instrument had been threaded with human bones. I tracked the noise tentatively, like a deer stepping out into an open field. The creeping melody brought back memories of a toy I'd once owned. A colourful box with a protruding handle, which played music when you cranked it. When the song came to an end, a jester sprung out, startling the user.

That same apprehension stiffened my movements. Tiptoeing through the castle, I scanned every nook and shadow, taking the paths where the melody strengthened. The strange music beckoned me outside, into the moonlit courtyard. Surrounded by high walls and parapets, this courtyard served as the main entry to the castle. On the far side, the iron portcullis was down, preventing easy escape.

The portcullis was the least of my worries.

On her knees, Lottie was restrained in a wooden device. Like the stocks, her head and hands were immobile, but the device was not fastened down. High in the air above her neck, a blade of ice reflected the moonlight. Queen Aenor stood beside Lottie, absently stroking the strings of an ice instrument. Beneath the moon, still dressed in her amethyst gown, the queen was a sight to behold. I was happy to have found trousers, because they made it easier to maneuver. I'll admit it was less than comforting to see the queen had remained in her beautiful dress.

Which undoubtedly made it *impossible* to flee.

Gait steady, I stalked forward. The queen flourished her wrist, and the instrument vanished. A bone in my hand broke as I started to change.

"Ah ah ah!" Queen Aenor warned. The icy blade dropped several feet, stopping above Lottie's neck. "We're going to have a *civilized* chat."

"Take the blade from my sister's neck!"

"You have access to innumerable weapons if you choose to change. The blade stays." Queen Aenor's skirts swished as she strode forward, stopping a few paces away. "You risked your life, and your family, to free a beast—a beast who *murdered* countless people. The first of which was your own blood." She scoffed, looking at me as if I were mad. "Did you not love your father?"

The compulsion to change blurred my vision. Fury threatened to distort my bones, to grant me the power to rip this woman apart for hurling such a hideous accusation. Behind the queen, the blade of ice inched closer to Lottie. I closed my eyes and breathed. Catching the scent of horse manure, I clung to it, anything to bring me back to the present. "The man you took prisoner," I said, with great difficulty. "His name is Rook—er, Everard."

"Everard?" Queen Aenor interrupted. We stared at each other in silence, woman assessing woman. Finally, the queen looked at me piteously. "Do you *really* believe he returns your affection?"

Indignance readied me to argue, but the question struck a nerve, trapping me in silence.

"Liliwen," the queen started. The tilt of her head, and the accompanying tone, reminded me of my father—of his manner of speaking when he told me something he knew I didn't want to hear, but did so anyway, because he cared for me. A wound of vulnerability opened, and I swayed, suddenly unsteady. Easing closer, Queen Aenor murmured, "Do you think he won't leave you as soon as he's free?"

"I—"

I'd traded my life, and the lives of my family, to break Rook from this castle. Was I so certain of his character?

'The doubtful mind sees mistakes, not reason.'

Smiles, kisses, and pretty words ran through my mind. All from a lonely man in a grand prison. Rook was so rude when we first met; when did that change? Absently, my hand drifted to my stomach.

When he learned I could read.

Rook's demeanor changed as soon as he realized I had something to offer. When I was an opportunity for freedom. When he'd saved me from that Lady of the Lake, was he saving his chance at escaping? The same way I'd saved him after the axe lodged in his throat? For the better part of my friendship with Rook, I'd lied to him, manipulated his feelings, so I might use *him* to my advantage...

Had it been the other way around?

And when Rook did find a cure, when he no longer transformed into a terrifying beast and could leave the hidden castle, would he choose me?

When a world of opportunity was available to him, would he choose me?

Had I been a fool to risk my life, and the lives of my family, for him? Queen Aenor watched me; the longer I delayed answering, the more her smile shifted from concern to satisfaction.

"Don't listen to her," Lottie panted.

The queen whirled on Lottie. "I am *not* speaking to you."

Lottie craned, so she could see me. "He saved Lys. He didn't have to do that, Lil. He did that for you." Queen Aenor advanced, waving her hand. An invisible force struck Lottie's cheek, crashing her skull against the wooden trap. Lottie shook her head, reorienting herself and called, almost drunkenly, "I don't know much, Lil, but he loves you."

Rook kneeling at Lysander's bed.

Rook, leaning against the ash tree, passion heaving his chest—looking at me like I was the bright stars above.

'Your obedient servant.'

No one would come between us, not when we were so close to freedom. My voice was strong when I said, "Rook might be cursed to change into a beast, but none of the slayings were his fault. He didn't choose to kill anyone. That choice was made for him." To *my* surprise, Queen Aenor wasn't shocked. Instead, she crossed her arms and nodded. Part of me forgot I was speaking with the queen when I cried, "You knew it was Marek?!"

Queen Aenor bobbed her head. "That night in your hovel, I discovered it, the same as you."

I threw my arms out. "Then why arrest Rook?"

"He is a beast!" Queen Aenor snapped, her façade of calm slipping.

Lottie mumbled, "Nobody's perfect."

Queen Aenor ignored her and continued. "Despite what Everard might have told you, there is *no* cure! If he cannot be controlled, he must be put down. Even without Marek guiding his steps, the beast will kill again!" Shaking her head, she cried, "Your love cannot change him!"

"Maybe I don't want to change him!" I snarled back.

Maybe I want to be right there with him, tearing into all of you!

"And what of us?" I pointed to Lottie, and then tapped my chest. "Do you think we should all be put down?"

The queen scoffed and made a face that said, *'Don't ask questions you don't want the answer to.'*

"So, you mean to execute us?"

"Your sister, and your mother, yes." Queen Aenor frowned. "But not you, Liliwen. You have a gift." The queen let out a low, melodic whistle. It reminded me of Ruven's father, calling the herding dogs. "While I disagree with Marek doing it behind my back, he had the right idea. Your condition requires a heavy hand." I glanced behind me and saw Bronwyn and the advisor exit the castle. Bronwyn cradled a bloodied stump where her hand was no more.

The queen's lips parted in horrified surprise.

Bronwyn stared at the cobbles, unable to look upon the queen. "The captain and the Hound escaped."

Relief flooded me—extinguished as Lottie laughed. The icy blade fell closer to Lottie's neck, but Queen Aenor appeared unbothered. Joining Bronwyn, the queen brought a hand to rest beneath her chin. "We have her children, and the beast's lover," Queen Aenor reassured. "They will return. They can't help themselves." Lottie and I exchanged a glance and a shared thought. The queen thought she could exploit our love for one another... Perhaps we might do the same?

Queen Aenor nodded toward the advisor.

With her good hand, Bronwyn waved in the advisor's direction and said, "Change."

That word nearly stopped my heart.

No. It can't be!

The advisor shook their head, refusing the command, though it was hard to ignore the tremble of the advisor's fists clenched at their sides. Bronwyn advanced and screamed, "Change now!" The advisor shoved Bronwyn.

Wasting no time, the queen strode to Lottie. Slamming her foot on the device, she said, "Change, or I cut the younger one's head off." Though their entire body quivered, the advisor shook their head in stark refusal. "Fine," Queen Aenor snapped. "Have it your way." The ice blade dropped with a dull *thud*, prompting a pained shriek from Lottie. The advisor and I lurched forward. The queen thrust out a hand, stopping the blade from cutting Lottie further.

The advisor collapsed, taking a knee on the cobblestones. Grasping their head, a sharp exhale pierced the cloth. The quivering of resistance gave way to severe tremors, and ripping fabric filled the air.

All this time, there was another hound among us.

It stood in the courtyard, looking so different than Rook when he changed. Rook was the night, but this beast was fairer than the moon above.

Unbothered by the transformation, the queen said, "Before our kingdom existed, there was another town and another castle, deep within Scrying Hollow. But of course, you know this." She smiled. "You've visited the castle, haven't you, Liliwen?" I barely heard her; my attention was locked on the hound, readying to leap in front of Lottie should it move. The queen continued, "A wrathful woman governed that castle, Countess Alifaire, who was fascinated by the magic of transfiguration." Queen Aenor waved at the fair hound. "Human to beast, in particular.

"The townsfolk tired of their family members disappearing, and rumours spread of the countess's experiments. Whispers of loved ones turned into beasts or fed to the countess's pets. The people rallied and came for Alifaire, but it was her own children who turned against her. Together, they slayed their mother's beasts. Countess Alifaire was cursed to live out the end of her days, trapped in the castle. Her evil seeped into every tree and stone inside that forlorn place, eventually bleeding into the hollow that grew up around it.

"The countess's son fled to the east, founding L'orée du bois. Her daughter settled here," the Queen said, waving at the castle walls. "Alifaire's descendants lost power and favour, and their line faded. The world forgot about the countess and her castle in the Hollow. But, here and there, a child would pop up with their great-great-great-great grandmother's ability to control beasts—"

I gasped and looked at Bronwyn.

"Yes," Queen Aenor said. "Although the countess's practices were barbaric, I admit it's rather useful to govern a beast."

Bronwyn commanded the advisor-turned-hound forward. It did as it was told.

"You have a choice," the queen began. "I admit, it's not an easy one, but it's a *choice*. You may join me, and your sister will be executed efficiently. Unfortunately, your mother and your new friend must also die. But again, it will be efficient and quick. Refuse me, and I will kill those you care for. It will be slow, and their pain, unending. And when they are tortured and dead, and you are begging for death, I will *not* permit you to die."

Stark silence filled the courtyard.

"You will serve me either way," the queen murmured. "The manner in which you choose to do so is up to you." Over the Queen's shoulder, I met Bronwyn's eyes. When Bronwyn looked at me, a compulsion to change swelled. I fought it, afraid if I gave in, Bronwyn would have complete control of my body. Like a crocodile floating along the river, the hound inched closer.

Lottie snapped me from my trance. "Too weak to protect your own castle?" she hissed. "Must keep a dog?"

"Seems *both* Liliwen and I have a pet," the queen replied, unbothered. "I'm just better at controlling mine."

In my time of need, my father had not abandoned me. His most important lesson thundered in my ears, like a trumpeting alarm.

When all else fails, flee.

That's exactly what I did.

If I could get away, there was a chance for us all.

"Retrieve her!" the queen called.

"Bring her back!" Bronwyn shouted.

Arms pumping, I entered the castle once more.

Chapter Twenty-One

Rook

We waited below the crest of a grassy knoll on the border of the Hollow, beneath a tree chosen by Evette. High above, a bit of fabric hung from a branch. "I proposed to Jean here," she said. "I wanted to carve our names in the bark, but Jean wouldn't have me damaging a yew. He climbed the branches and tied my scarf up there." She pointed. "He was quite the climber. He said no one would be mad enough to remove it. I disagreed. That's colossal araneae silk—cost my father five cows. I figured it would be gone the next morning." She waved at the scarf. "I was wrong."

And so, we waited beneath Evette's happy memory.

Lysander paced, rubbing his neck and staring anxiously up the hill. Evette sat, leaning against the yew. She didn't move; I'm not even certain she blinked as she stared at the hill, waiting for her children. Finally, when Lysander had trod a fine path through the grass, Evette said, "Did I ever tell you how I met your father?"

Lysander scrunched his face in recollection. "No."

"Come. Sit next to me."

Each time Evette mentioned her husband, the love I'd stolen, my guts knotted. This time, when I buried my head in my hands, Evette snapped, "Stop that," and patted the ground beside her, the spot Lysander hadn't taken. "This is a happy story." When I made no move, Evette repeated, "*Sit*," with such authority I obeyed.

As I sat beside Evette, I noted the musky smell I'd come to associate with those who shared my curse, but Lysander...smelled only of human sweat. This discovery didn't carry sadness with it; it warmed me.

Lysander's family loved him.

His future was unwritten, and he might choose his own path forward. Whether Lysander decided to become a hound, to find a human and settle down, or some other desire unknown to the rest of us, he might rest easy knowing:

He would *always* be loved.

"Lysander," Evette said, "you'll be familiar with this part, but I'll recount it for Everard's sake." After a deep breath, Evette began. "My parents were wealthy—*very* wealthy. My mother owned a large estate across town. Jean's father was one of the groundskeepers, and, eventually, Jean was hired too. Like Liliwen, he had a gift; he made the most incredible garments." Evette fidgeted, spinning a ring. "This is probably going to be new for Lys, but I... I wasn't a kind person, especially not to your father." Not once had I questioned Evette's kindness. Sure, she was uncomfortably frightening at times, and her manner of speaking was rather commanding, but not unkind.

"One day," Evette continued. "I cornered Jean and asked how he could make such beautiful pieces. He replied, so proudly, that he gathered items in the Hollow. The Hollow was dangerous, even then. In my mind, it took a special sort of foolishness to enter, and I made sure he knew as much. I told him all the effort in creating him must have gone to his fingers, and none to his head. Only an idiotic halfwit would visit the Hollow." While Evette wasn't entirely wrong, both Lysander and I winced. "I know," she murmured, cringing herself.

"Anyway, as you can imagine, he avoided speaking to me. Which I was fine with…at first." Evette's brows furrowed. "Jean was effortlessly beautiful, and kind, and oh, how he vexed me! When he passed me in the halls, I swore I'd forget to breathe." Evette paused, perhaps seeing him in her memory. "Jean had no education, no money, and yet, all I wanted was for him to look at me, and I *hated* him for it. How dare he preoccupy my thoughts so?"

I knew that feeling well. When Liliwen came to me, I'd treated her miserably. I insulted her intelligence at every turn, underestimated her skill, and yet…she consumed my thoughts, knocking out every single thing I conjured to distract myself. Lying in bed, I knew there was a beautiful woman, just upstairs, within my grasp. The desire to take her was incredible—to take her and love her and never let her escape. I'd been so furious, for being able to think of *nothing* but her.

"Well," Evette continued, "one day, when I was in town, I caught sight of Jean leaving the apothecary. He didn't head back to our estate. Instead, he walked into the Hollow." Evette pulsed her brows. "I followed him." She laughed. "I thought, I must have overestimated the danger. If this dullard could survive out there, how hard could it be? Well!" Evette's eyes bugged. "I suppose you know how wrong I was."

Lysander chuckled. "Something got you?"

"Fae," Evette said with a laugh. "Immediately!"

Fae were plentiful back then; the Hollow was full of them. Wrinkling my nose, I examined the branches above, and I did not mention how I knew the fae were delicious.

"I didn't stand a chance. Disguised as a fox, the fae snapped my leg like it was a chicken bone. As the fae was about to eat me, Jean appeared."

"How'd you escape?" Lysander asked.

"He tricked it, offered it milk laced with some concoction of herbs. While the creature choked, Jean carried me from the Hollow. I realized then how cunning and clever your father really was. He taught himself how to survive in that place. No book ever taught me that. I think… I think I loved him before that day, but that day, I realized how brave he was, and I knew I could be brave too. Despite my parents' wishes, I pursued Jean. My parents *hated* him, and they hated me. How could I do this to them? Falling in love with one of the hired boys? They disowned me without a second thought. I remember my mother's words, 'I will mourn your loss.'" Evette chuckled. "It seemed like such a silly thing to say to a living child. I didn't understand it then, and I thought maybe it would make more sense when I had my own children. But…now I'm a mother, and I understand it even less." She patted Lysander's leg and sighed. "It was hard at first, but it got easier. And I had Jean. When his father passed, we moved out to the cottage."

Lapsing into silence, Evette stared at the stars.

"I had seventeen wonderful years with Jean," she whispered. "That's more than many people get." Out of the corner of my eye, I caught sight of tears slipping down Evette's face. Lysander held her knee, comforting her. Evette patted him and covered her mouth, stifling a sob. "I'm so grateful for those years," she cried. Biting back tears, I rubbed Evette's back. I hadn't thought it possible to need Lili to crest that hill any more than I did a few minutes ago.

I was wrong.

Lysander sniffled. He brought a hand to his face, shielding his eyes. Evette leaned over and bumped him. "Your father loved us; he never would have left us if given the choice," she said, with such beautiful confidence. "He would have done anything to survive, and it's *his* blood that runs wild in your sisters' veins." Tears gone, a stony resolve settled over Evette.

"They will do anything to come back to us."

Slowly, we turned to watch the hill.

Lesson Twenty-Two

I will always love you, Little Dove.

I bolted through the castle. Bounding footfalls pounded after me. I didn't make it far—the fair hound leapt at my back. "Agh!" I cried out, knees and elbows crashing against the stone. The writhing hound tumbled over me, dragging the rug as it skidded down the hall. Regaining my footing, I ran into an adjoining chamber and slammed the door. What could I do against a beast ten times my size? Running across the room, I yanked open a heavy door and tore down the hallway. I slipped into a small parlour as a howl pierced the thick walls.

The hound wasn't far behind.

I ducked into a cloak cabinet and covered my mouth, staunching my haggard breathing. What now? I could change and run for it. Two problems: I couldn't leave Lottie to torment and death. Secondly, if I changed and Bronwyn caught me, everything was over. No, I was going to have to solve this as a woman.

But, how?

My thoughts wandered to the Hollow, to my lessons that had kept me alive for all these years. Once, out gathering, Father and I had been set upon by a grim bear, a mangy, ferocious creature. To protect me, Father had hidden me beneath a spray of roots and drawn the bear away. He'd looped the creature in a circle and then ducked behind a trunk. I remember it so well because...it was the first time I'd seen my father afraid—truly afraid. Pressure had tightened his jaw; the responsibility of his child's life had rested in his hands, in the action he took next. If he failed, he would die. He'd looked at me, huddled beneath the roots.

If he failed, his baby would *die*.

My father's chest had ebbed until serenity washed over him. The bear had prowled closer, and its paw settled beside the trunk, concealing my father.

Father then struck.

Aiming for the heart, Father had driven his blade deep into the bear's underarm. The bear howled and collapsed. Clinging to life, it gasped. Father always refused to let any creature suffer; he'd quickly cut the bear's throat.

From within the castle, the hound howled once more.

I couldn't stay trembling in this cabinet forever.

I knew what I had to do.

Sliding from the cabinet, I pressed it closed behind me. This was a modest parlour—well, for a castle. An elegant fireplace sat beyond the gilded chairs and sofa. Keeping to the carpet to silence my footfalls, I dodged a side table and ran to the fireplace. I reached above the mantle and removed the decorative spear adorning the wall. It came loose with a gentle shifting of metal, and I paused, listening for the hound.

Nothing.

I crept to the door and peered out. No hound. How had it lost me? Surely, the beast knew my scent. Despite my mounting unease, I tiptoed into the hall and made my way back to Lottie. Perhaps, once I killed the hound, I could break the device holding her. Of course, I'd have to deal with the queen. And Bronwyn. *One problem at a time!* I made my way back to the doors servicing the courtyard, casting wary glances all around.

Where is the beast?!

Whispers floated from the courtyard, and I peeked around the stone frame. Outside, the queen and Bronwyn gathered near Lottie. Queen Aenor held Bronwyn's wounded arm, consoling her. Lottie seemed fine. The queen said something to Bronwyn, prompting Lottie to roll her eye and stick out her tongue in disgust.

Just inside the door, two stone lions guarded the castle entrance. I passed them and grabbed a bronze pot from a side table. My reddish-brown reflection appeared in the shiny metal. Burnt and dirty, a wild animal stared back at me. I looked no different than any other feral creature that called the Hollow home. Before I lost my nerve, I tossed the pot. It bounced down the hall, clanging as it went. I knelt, concealing myself behind a proud lion. I wiped sweat from my palms and gripped the spear. This time, it *wasn't* my father's voice that came to me, crouched in wait.

'*Land a killing blow.*'

I hoped Rook was somewhere safe.

The soft *click-clack-click-clack* of claws stalled my thoughts. Summoned from the belly of the castle, the hound approached. The steps halted, replaced by an inhale of air, drawn out and thorough. Though the hound could not speak, it may as well have said, '*I know you're here.*'

My panicked mind screamed, '*This isn't going to work!*' My muscles tensed, begging me to run. If I didn't go now, it would be too late. The hound would snatch me, rip and tear my flesh. It would drag me, half-alive, back to the queen, back to make that impossible choice—No! I had no choice; I had a task. One last chance to show my strength, to finally do what I set out to do so many nights ago. Kill the hound.

Kill the hound or die!

If the hound discovered me hiding, I wouldn't be taken alive. I would stab it, blind it—do anything I could to escape. If the beast killed me, at least my mother, Lysander, and Rook would be safe. Lottie had a knack for lockpicking, she might even manage to break out on her own.

The clicking of nails resumed.

Like the sudden chiming of a bell, the brass pot tumbled back down the hall. It bounced onto its rim and rolled in a wide circle before coming to rest at my boot. My confused face stared back in the polished metal.

Two beacons of light disappeared. And reappeared. A reflection of the hound's eyes.

It saw me; it knew I was here!

And yet... The hound approached. No time for questions; the hound was nearly beside me.

Close.

Closer.

A large paw settled next to me. Perfectly in reach, so deliberately placed that my good fortune temporarily distracted me from what I needed to do. I leapt out and drove the spear up into the beast's underarm. Such agonized snarls left the hound's throat as it recoiled. Attempting to escape the pain, the hound fled into the courtyard, where it fell into a heap of bloody fur. Without hesitating, I chased, prepared to slit the hound's throat.

Excruciating, wet wheezes filled the night as the hound shrank. Fur and snout receded, and a human nose and face formed. Familiarity faltered my steps. My hands, which only moments ago were prepared to kill, fell upon the very wound I'd inflicted. Because the beast I'd been so intent on slaying...

Was my father.

I was transported back—back to that night seven years ago. When my father shambled in, covered in blood and reeking of terror. While he had the same fair hair, I wondered, had my memories deceived me? Were his cheeks always so gaunt?

His eyes so haunted?

"We buried you!" I choked.

My father's gaze darted behind me.

"You buried someone; it was not him," Queen Aenor said, approaching. Bronwyn remained across the courtyard, guarding Lottie. I was barely aware they existed, could only feel the slippery blood rushing against my palms.

All those times alone, he could have given me a message, a whisper. "Why didn't you tell me?!" Even now, my father couldn't manage to speak. "Why?" I whispered, tears blossoming along my lashes. My father opened his mouth.

His tongue had been taken.

Avoiding the growing pool of blood, Queen Aenor crouched. She looked at the encroaching puddle with indifference, like it was simply spilled wine, and not my father's life slipping away.

"During my reign, I've gone to great lengths to bring people with magic together. To preserve it—"

"To *ensure* your reign, you mean?" All respect was gone when I spat, "And keep an eye on us, so we might not rise up, or aid those who might speak against you?"

"My reasons for protecting those with magic can be numerous." The queen placed Bronwyn's cloak over my father. "For years, Bronwyn and I have been studying her family history—well, *your* family history, I suppose. To learn, to understand patterns, to try to predict when children might be born with abilities and talents. We researched all the way back to Countess Alifaire, the legends and the castle. Naturally, we wondered, is it still out there?"

A gargled choke came from my father's throat.

Queen Aenor offered a piteous look. "We ventured into the Hollow to see if all the stories were true. To ensure secrecy, we took with us only a few guards. Our late captain, Marek, was amongst them. We trekked through the Hollow, and all the while, Bronwyn kept the creatures at bay. Sure enough, we found the castle, and we found *your* Hound. We didn't enter, not immediately. We were aware of Alifaire's curse, that the castle was her cage. So, we watched from a distance, studying the Hound's behaviour, its comings and goings. At the time, it was a relatively peaceful creature."

Queen Aenor scooched back, avoiding the blood.

"When our impatience got the better of us, we waited for the Hound to leave and slipped through the veil. We explored the castle, including the courtyard with a very peculiar tree. We knew better than to consume the fruit but—"

"It didn't keep you from stealing some?" I snapped.

"You're one to talk," she said, wearing such a smug grin I wanted to change and bite it off. "The attacks started then. I figured we'd somehow angered the beast. But that night in your hovel, I realized that while we were studying the Hound, Marek must have slipped away unnoticed, used this opportunity to ensnare the beast."

"Everard."

"Ensnare *Everard*," the queen corrected. "For his own gain."

"With the fruit in our possession, we simply had to wait for someone desperate enough to taste it. Willingly of course; we're not monsters." The queen waved at my father. "We gave him a *choice*. He could have chosen death."

The night my father died, well, the night I believed he died, the coroner had come early, almost in anticipation. They'd gone in to see my father, only to return and inform us of his passing. It wasn't sadness that rocked me, but relief. A twisted comfort in knowing my father's pained cries couldn't torment my mother any longer.

After all these years, the shame of those thoughts still taunted me.

'It's not safe to be around the body,' the coroner told us. *'We know nothing of this illness; it could spread.'* It took all of us to hold my grieving mother back, lest she beat the coroner to death for taking her husband away.

"We brought him to the castle," Queen Aenor said, breaking my recollection. "He remained in the dungeon for years. Bronwyn visited him every day, training him. Until the day he emerged in disguise." Queen Aenor looked at my father, who was gasping for breath. "So much time and effort, wasted." She leaned a fist against her chin and sighed. "Fortunately, a replacement walked straight into our arms." Queen Aenor's lavender eyes set on me.

"I won't—"

Clattering wood and metal cut me off. The device holding Lottie burst open, hitting the cobblestones with a loud *BANG!* Lottie pounced on Bronwyn, choking her. Queen Aenor jumped up, and Lottie hid behind Bronwyn. The blade Lottie used on the lock lay at Bronwyn's throat. As a queen, Aenor was practiced in governing her face, though her throat constricted when she looked at the knife, so close to Bronwyn.

Bronwyn started, "I'll—"

Lottie smothered Bronwyn's mouth and dug the knife in. "Bitch! One more word and you'll eat this blade!"

"Cut her, and it'll be the last thing you do," Queen Aenor growled. "I promise."

Lottie drew the blade along Bronwyn, prompting a muted gasp from her hostage. As a fine line of blood trickled down Bronwyn's neck, Lottie shouted, "Make a deal!"

I bunched the cloak against Father's injury and stood. "You will let us leave, and you will not pursue us." I eased my father up. He was so weak, all his weight bore down on me. Backing away, I dragged him toward the castle.

Doing the same with Bronwyn, Lottie said. "Pursue us, and I'll gut your little rat."

Queen Aenor smiled at Bronwyn, the same way I sometimes smiled at Rook. The softness of her features whispered, *'It'll be okay.'* Tenderness melted to malice as Queen Aenor's attention shifted to Lottie, and I feared my sister might freeze to death where she stood.

"You have five minutes before I send my guards." Queen Aenor pointed at Lottie. "You have ten minutes until *I* chase you."

Wasting no time, I dragged my father away. Never turning her back on the queen, Lottie did the same with Bronwyn.

"I will find you," the queen called. "If I need to."

A frozen quill etched the warning onto my heart.

We rushed through the castle with as much haste as we could muster, given we were slowed by a hostage and a half-dead man. When the great hall came into view, I said, "We'll go through there and out the passage—Lottie?" I'd been so focused on keeping my father upright, I hadn't been listening for Lottie and Bronwyn's shuffling steps. "Lottie where are you?!"

Lottie reappeared from a side room. "Hey! I'm here. It's fine." She grabbed my father's arm, easing some of the weight from my back. "It's fine—it's fine." When someone says a situation is 'fine' no one thinks anything of it. However, there are a certain amount of times a person might say 'fine' before those listening realize there's definitely a cause for concern.

And Lottie had used it *thrice*.

"Where's Bronwyn?" I whisper-shouted. Lottie only gave me a sidelong glance. "What did you do to her?!" Lottie laughed, pulling my father and me along. Dread settled in me. "Lottie, I'm serious. What did you do?"

"I took care of her."

"Lottie!" I stopped, yanking my father back. "What does that mean?"

"Relax." Lottie started toward the passage. "She was slowing us down, so I put her somewhere the guards will find her."

"Was she *alive* when you put her there?!"

Lottie threw her head back and laughed.

To this day, I don't know the answer.

Father groaned and his legs buckled. He lurched forward, tugging me with him. "Get his legs," I huffed. "We'll carry him out."

"You get his legs," Lottie argued. "I'm stronger; give me his shoulders."

"Why must you argue with everything—" But Lottie was already shoving me aside, a task she performed easily, because she was stronger. As she heaved my father up, I swallowed my sisterly contempt and grabbed his legs. We made it through the passage and into the moonlight without interruption and only minimal bumping. My heart leapt at the sight of stars, of freedom.

Could we make it?

"Agh!" Lottie's boot caught a stone. She floundered, yanking my father's ankles from my grasp. He struck the ground and cried out.

"We don't have time for this!" I scrambled to lift him, but my father's hand rested on mine. Shaking his head, the message was painfully obvious.

'I can go no farther.'

Haggard, wet breathing broke the night. Lottie and I crouched with our father, the shadow of the man from our childhood. He caressed my face, and then Lottie's. He'd given us everything we needed to get here, to escape, to be free and happy as a family. The pride that his lessons, his tools, had not been forgotten was unmistakable. Father's trembling hand located a chain around his neck, hidden beneath layers of fabric. His dirty fingers curled around the ring dangling from it. Our mother gave him that ring when she'd asked him to be hers.

He kissed it and tapped his heart.

'I wish she was here.'

My father's hands settled on his chest, as if he were preparing for burial.

'This is the end for me.'

Lottie looked to me. At the set of my jaw, she grimaced. I nodded, confirming her silent question. He's not going to make it. For the second time in our life, death was here for our father. The tingle that travelled along my fingertips as I brushed his chest was so faint. There was nothing we could do.

Nothing I could do.

A shout ruptured the cool air. As promised, the first of the guards appeared. High up on the hill, they searched in the night. Father pushed us away, pointing down the path. He waved frantically, encouraging us to abandon him. Lottie's features were stone as she climbed to her feet. She didn't take the path that led away from the castle, rather, she stalked back, toward the guards who would find us soon.

"Where are you going?" I hissed.

Lottie rounded, her cheeks splotchy and wet. "Fix him!"

"It's too late! I have nothing to sew him up with—no fabric! I *can't* do it!"

"It's not about the stupid *fabric*!" Lottie dragged an arm across her face. "I'm tired of pretending, of coddling you! You could have fixed him then, and you can fix him now!"

Guilt punctuated my words when I shrieked, "I can't!" back at Lottie. Fear rocked me. The worst night of my life was repeating itself, and I was helpless to stop it.

"You have a *gift*! Embrace it! Trust your hands! Trust yourself!" Lottie screamed. "You use whatever you have and you fix him!" Lottie's eye yellowed. "Mother will see him again, even if it—" Lottie's words died as she changed. Snarling, the one-eyed hound set down the path toward the guards. She needn't finish the sentence.

Even if it kills me.

Lottie ran headfirst toward danger, and I turned back to my father. Even if she could buy us time, what would that achieve? Despair settled on me like a blanket. What could I do?

You can't do anything!

You wanted to slay him quickly, so there wasn't any suffering, and you couldn't even do that. Look at him—just look!

If it weren't for the agonized grimace, I wouldn't have known Father was still alive. He was so near death, he could slip away any moment. A hiccup bubbled in my throat. I'd always been weak. Too soft to do what needed to be done.

Father caught my hand.

Even in his torment, he reassured me. Through all the hardships of the last seven years, his touch was delicate, still soft. Despite that tenderness, I thought the world of him. To me, he was one of the *strongest* people. Perhaps...I was strong too?

All this time, I'd been trying to prove my strength in killing a foe, to measure myself against Mother, or Lottie. I'd tried so desperately to fight who I was, who I was raised to be. Shouts rose as Lottie reached our pursuers; I pushed them aside. With no small amount of effort, I shushed the thoughts that sought to drown me, to suffocate me with doubt. An encouraging voice spoke up, one I was so unfamiliar with.

You can do this.

A violent howl, followed by mewling whimpers, carried to us. I didn't look. I focused and embraced the strength I'd always had. I pulled the cloak away from Father's wound.

And I did what I did best.

Chapter Twenty-Three

Rook

Birdsong floated from the borders of the Hollow. The first rays of dawn broke over the knoll. Beside me, Evette had fallen asleep against Lysander.

Liliwen and Lottie had not come.

As the sun climbed above the hill, I glanced at Lysander. His gaze remained on the top of the hill. My chest ached. The voice inside me, beaten by years of hopelessness, said, *'They aren't coming.'* Looking at Lysander and Evette, I wondered how I could possibly ease the passing of their family members, while I was suffering a broken heart?

Could Lili really be gone?

Heaviness clung to me, dragged me toward the dirt. I couldn't... I couldn't picture this world without her. Loneliness had been my companion for such a long time, but this was so different, so consuming. I'd tasted love. To have it ripped away... I couldn't bear it. In desperation, my mind spun.

Had they killed her?

Watching the sun rise, my agonizing thoughts turned from despair. A clawing rage screamed at the pain, frightening it off. Later, I would visit the hurt. This day, I only wanted to punish. I eased from Evette and began walking over the knoll.

"Where are you going?" Lysander called, jostling Evette awake.

I turned and continued walking backward. "I'm going to slaughter every one of them." A shadow crossed Lysander's face as someone breached the knoll behind me.

I couldn't look.

If I didn't look, there was *always* a chance it was Lili. What if it was Lottie? Liliwen would have given her life for her younger sister—every part of me knew it. Against my will, I scanned Lysander's face. I searched for a hint, or a warning, anything that might prepare me for who was behind me. A tear breached Lysander's lashes; it cast a reflective sheen down his cheek. Anticipation and terror spun me. Up on the hill, a tangle of blonde hair carried in the breeze. It was—

"Liliwen!" Evette cried.

Lili, beautiful and...alive. It was such a strange contrast, as if when I'd met her, she'd simply existed, but now she was *alive*. Her face, still smattered with soot, glistened with sweat, a trophy she'd earned fighting to survive—clawing tooth and nail to *live*. On that hill, chin held high, Liliwen smiled down upon me. It was such a proud gesture that wrinkled her eyes—eyes that shone with an unusual wildness that sent my blood rushing.

It ruined me.

Her smile was an axe, and my legs were but small trees. It took everything I had not to crumble and weep at her feet. Then and there, I understood.

I'd do it again.

An eternity of suffering—of unending loneliness and exile. I would bear twice the burden if it meant I could share this with her. Seeing Liliwen, standing alone, I could bear it no longer. I tore up the grassy incline, tripping and sliding.

Distantly, Evette whimpered, "Is she alone?"

Lili ran, reaching for my outstretched arms. Our bodies rocked together; we might have fallen apart had we not clutched one another so tight.

Never again. Never again would we part.

I brushed messy hair from her face, and she kissed me. How could someone impart such hope, such vitality onto another? Lili's sweet smile pressed my lips, and her fingers curled around my neck, pulling me closer. If she never spoke of it, those actions would suffice. From them, I knew everything I needed of Lili's feelings. She was with me, and she was *happy*.

It was magic.

Through gasps, Lili managed to say, "I ran ahead to make sure you were still here."

Shaking my head, I kissed her again. "I would have waited a lifetime." Holding my hand, Lili descended the knoll to her family.

Evette asked the question Lysander could not. "Your sister?"

Lili slipped from my arms and went to her mother. "I have something to show you." She pulled Evette up the hill.

"What of Lottie?" Evette snapped. "If my child is dead, tell me quickly." Evette's breath caught as two people crested the knoll.

Lottie...and a ghost.

Evette stopped walking—could walk no farther. She reached out before covering her mouth and turning to Lili. Though no sound came out, Evette's lips formed the name, *Jean?'*

No. It couldn't be...

The man I'd killed so long ago, Lili's father, stumbled forward. Bits of a bloodied cloak wrapped his side, and he looked as if he might faint. Evette remained frozen, choking her emotions. She scrutinized the man. If this was some trickery, she would not let herself be harmed so easily.

"It's him," Lili said. "They took his tongue; he can't speak." She encouraged her mother forward. Lottie did the same to her father. Evette advanced on her own. A cry left her throat, and she collapsed. Seeing his wife fall, a guttural sound echoed from Jean. Leaving Lottie's supporting arms, Jean shuffled forward and knelt before Evette. She let out a wail, filled with the anguish only a broken heart could muster.

Evette's cry was silenced when Jean grabbed her face and kissed her.

Not an insect dared to chirp, dared to threaten the embrace we bore witness to. In Jean's arms, Evette's chest heaved. Jean pulled away, his cheeks glistening from Evette's tears, and what looked like a great deal of his own. "It—it—" Evette chugged. "It cannot be!" Jean lifted Evette's hand, bringing it to rest against his cheek. Relaxing into Evette's palm, there was a lifetime of adoration in Jean's eyes.

Such devotion was not hindered by things as trivial as death.

Evette kissed Jean again, and when she pulled back, she remained with her forehead touching his, as if she could bear to be no farther away. "I died that night," Evette whispered. Jean shook his head. He patted his chest, his heart, and then Evette's.

'We're alive. We're together.'

On their knees, two lovers reunited.

A sniffle broke the silence. Beside me, Lysander hid his face. I looked past him, to Lottie, and to Lili. To a family, reunited.

Evette stood, bringing her husband with her. Pride tinged her cheeks pink as she introduced him to me. "This is Jean."

"The Hound—" I gulped, staring at Jean. "*I* killed you." Jean shook his head, and held his fingers up, nearly touching.

'Almost.'

Lili took my arm and said, "I told him everything." Holding me, she introduced me to her father. "This is Rook."

Breathless from shock, I corrected, "Everard."

Jean made an apologetic face and mimed punching, as if to say, *'Sorry about the beating, eh?'*

If he could forgive me, I could certainly forgive him.

"I told him of Marek," Lili said, glancing at her mother.

"I broke his leg and let the wolves eat him," Evette said. "He was alive when they tore his throat out."

Jean stroked Evette's chin, his eyes twinkling with pride. *'That's my girl.'* He made to kiss her, and Evette seemed to catch herself leaning away, as if that were her very nature. A furious set of tears glistened along her lashes, and she bent to Jean, obliging his request. Clutching his arm like a bride might hold a groom, Evette led Jean to Lysander. Jean patted his own head, remarking at Lysander's height.

"Yes." Evette beamed. "He'll make a fine companion."

Jean released his wife and clung to his son. He sobbed and beckoned his family over. They joined Jean, and every few seconds, his arms switched shoulders, as if he wanted to embrace them all at once, but his arms simply weren't long enough. Jean looked skyward, thanking the stars above. His mouth formed a shocked 'O', and he pointed to Evette's scarf, high in the tree.

"Yes," Evette remarked. "I was tempted to climb up, but"—she laughed and then whispered to Jean—"my knees are *not* what they once were." Enjoying all the perks of becoming a hound, in particular the hearing buff, Lottie looked at her mother with terrified disgust.

Jean examined the lower branches. Fearing what he might do, I walked steadfastly toward the tree. Lili grabbed for my shirt, and said, "Not this again!" But I was hasty and utterly determined. Despite my aching body, I climbed. Carefully and deliberately, I didn't stop until I grasped the delicate silk. Retrieving the scarf was emboldening, though it was nothing compared to the way my chest ached when I looked at Jean.

Elbowing Lili, he pointed to me.

'Eh? Look at him!'

In that moment, I couldn't decide which was more satisfying. Lili rolling her eyes because I'd proved her wrong and could, in fact, climb a tree to save my life...or Jean, clapping and nodding his approval.

Leaping down, I handed the scarf to Jean. Wearing a grin that squeezed my heart, he patted my arm. Then, he turned to Evette and tied the scarf around her neck. Lili tugged my sleeve, pulling me away. Her family didn't follow, allowing us privacy. We walked a little way. Under the canopy of shuffling leaves, we watched the sun rising over the knoll.

Well, Lili watched the sunrise.

When I first met Lili in the meadow, we were so intent upon destroying one another. We were both ruined by pain. When she spoke, doubt and grief dripped from every syllable. Standing beside me, she was light, as if the very breeze could carry her away. Turning, she caught me staring and smiled. In her eyes, I could almost see her frolicking in the same meadow that was nearly our end. I could see her outside her *own* cottage, knelt at the peonies, with dirt beneath her nails, and the warmest smile. I saw our future. Us, existing together for as long as we wished.

"You're cursed now," I said. "You did this all for me?"

"No." Lili shook her head. "I did this for *me*." Closing her eyes, Lili lifted her face to the sky. A silent howl to freedom.

"You'll have me as I am?" I whispered.

Tracing a sharp canine with her tongue, Lili said, "I'll do more than that."

I wrapped an arm around her, drawing her to me, and buried myself in her hair. Lost in the smokiness, I wondered, do people ever stop and think, 'I'll do anything for this person'? Do people think to themselves, 'I will give up *everything*. I will slay, burn, and die if it means this person in my arms might never know suffering'? I always thought the ones who really meant it, simply did it. Time passed, and they'd been doing it all along, and there was never an occasion when they acknowledged how far they'd go to keep their person from harm.

But when you've grown to loathe the thing you've become, and someone stands before you and says, I will love you—and I will love you *because* of all those things you hate...

I cleared my throat, trying to dispel the lump.

Lili looked up, curious. She traced my scar, and I let myself—and the weight of everything I'd become—relax into her palm. If she wanted somewhere to lay her head, I'd build her a home. If she was sad, I'd make a fool of myself so she might smile. If she were cold, I'd burn for her. Anything.

For her.

At the edge of the Hollow, Jean beckoned us back over. Looking at her father, standing before the trees in which he raised her, Lili bit back a sob. Such emotions threatened to fell her; she gripped my hand so tight.

I held her tighter.

When she looked back at me, her eyes shone. I couldn't begin to explain the joy I found there. Gripping me like a vice, Lili dragged me toward her family. Standing before the Hollow, the Valets were an intimidating sight. Reunited, they were as strong as the great yew at their backs. Momentarily, I resisted Lili's efforts to pull me forward.

Was I prepared for this?

Parents. A new brother. Lottie. People to trust—to share the burdens of life. I glanced at Lili, at her encouraging smile.

A partner.

After a lifetime of isolation...perhaps it was time. I relaxed, allowing Lili to bring me to her family. Jean gave my back a hearty pat. Standing on her toes, Evette leaned to my ear and whispered, "Only the best of men could have captured my daughter's heart." She squeezed my shoulder and pulled away. "We're fortunate it was you."

A family.

The tension in my shoulders eased, and I permitted myself a moment to feel cherished—to know that I belonged to something.

I was ready.

Lysander glanced back toward the hill. "What of Queen Aenor?"

Lottie puffed her chest. "She hasn't come for us yet."

"I have a feeling she won't follow us where we're going," Lili said.

Jean's furrowed brow asked, *'Where?'*

"I know a place," Lili replied. "A castle. A cursed place for cursed people, where we'll never be bothered again."

"There are monsters," I cautioned.

"None more frightening than us," Lottie said. She bared her new canines, with no small amount of delight. We broke our embrace and Lottie continued, "How will we choose rooms?" Lysander and Lili exchanged a glance and an irritated head shake.

Lili tugged me, pulling me toward the Hollow.

Lottie's voice chased after us. "I just think I should get the first choice, seeing as how I risked the most tonight."

And so, we abandoned the town. We walked through the trees, and the Hollow welcomed us. In the end, you get to decide whether you're cursed or free.

From then on,
Fathers warned their daughters to beware
The *Hounds* of Scrying Hollow

What's this?

My dearest reader, thank you for staying with me until the end.

I have a gift for you.

Turn the page.

I'd like you to meet some very old friends.

PROCEED WITH CAUTION: **EXTREME SPOILER WARN-ING** FOR *THE FOREST WHERE THE PHOENIX SLEEPS*!

SPOILERS AHEAD!
LAST CHANCE TO TURN BACK!

Very Old Friends...

Nell

The sun was setting as I climbed up the stairs to *the Bramble*, the café I co-owned. Pushing inside, gentle chatter greeted me. Through the glass wall, white-tipped mountains painted the ever-darkening sky. I shrugged out of my coat and hung it next to the wood burning stove. The stove crackled and kicked out a subtle—but comforting—smokiness. My business partner, Anahera glanced at the clock. Her chin, tattooed with a moko kauae, dropped.

"Is it that time already?!" Ana looked frantically for her purse. "I have to pick up Mia!"

"Tonight's my last shift before the trip," I reminded and sidestepped Ana. She hurried around, snatching items as she went. "I'll make a closing list for you." I grabbed a black apron from below the counter.

"Are you still going with—"

"I am," I cut her off and smiled at the customer approaching the counter.

Ana mouthed, *'Have a good night!'* while I took the customers dishes. I gave Ana's back a wave as she fled out and away.

311

I started a fresh pot of coffee, more for myself than anyone else. Once it brewed, I leaned against the front counter, sipping coffee and writing notes for Ana.

1. Just chuck the money in the safe, I'll deal with it when I get back.

2. Don't store gluten free items WITH gluten containing items. I had to throw out like 12 muffins last time you closed.

3. PUT THE FIRE OUT! IF YOU ONLY DO ONE THING, PUT THE FIRE OUT!

What else was I missing? I stared through the windows, absently fidgeting with my necklace—a carved nightingale. The last rays of sun disappeared behind the mountains, and gradually the café quieted. Throughout the evening, a few regulars trickled in, content to read by the fire. I passed the time sneaking glances at my phone, playing word games with (REDACTED). A message popped up on my screen.

'Morning bitch.'

I returned Sasha's text with a *'Night bitch.'*

Had our relationship taken a hit after I'd moved halfway around the world? Of course. Had our friendship disintegrated entirely? Never. We texted and had video calls, and most of Sasha's drag shows were live-streamed. When I watched, I always pretended I was in the audience and Sasha was singing just to me. One day, Sasha would visit me.

One day, it would be like we never parted.

As closing time approached, I flicked off the machines and wiped the counters while the regulars trickled out. I said, "Take care," to a pretty woman with pink hair and locked the door behind her. After I took out the trash, I grabbed a stack of cups from the stock room. I stooped and started putting the cups in neat stacks below the front counter.

Whoosh!

The front door opened, letting in the hum of traffic and bustling nightlife.

Didn't I lock the door?

The brief breeze carried wafting smoke.

Wait, did I already put the fire out? Usually, I doused the fire on my way *out* of the café. I called, "Hey!" from below the counter, with no small amount of irritation.

"Time for one more latte?"

Climbing to my feet, I said, "We're actually clos—" Two men stood in my café. At least, I think there were two.

I only *saw* one.

Through a mess of tangled brown hair, *his* keen olive eyes devoured me.

Losing awareness of my surroundings, I braced myself with the counter. It kept me standing and served as a solid object I could hold—to prove this was real—and not some delirious caffeine-induced hallucination. For the first time in my new life, I said *his* name.

"Darragh?"

Hearing my voice, Darragh's eyes closed—as someone might do when rediscovering a beloved scent, which dragged them back into a precious memory. He scarcely had time to enjoy it before the second, giant of a man cried, "Well?" Wearing a fur-trimmed jacket clearly meant for someone a quarter of his size, the second man beamed and threw his arms out. Both underarm seams ruptured, earning them a disgruntled scowl and a muttered, "That woman said this was the finest quality!"

Bowyn.

Two people I'd known so intimately in another life.

"Wha-what're," I stuttered, not making any sense at all. Words seemed to have escaped Darragh as well. He looked as if he meant to speak, but didn't trust himself. A hopeful smile tugged his cheek while he drifted closer to the counter...

Closer to me.

"Look at you two!" Bowyn said. "Reunited once more!" Batting aside a ceiling light, Bowyn reached over the counter and took my hands. "You look positively radiant, my love." Flowing mane of raven hair gone; the sides of Bowyn's hair were shaved short. The top was longer, pulled into a ponytail, but it looked brittle and dry—the shine and life gone from it. His beard was shortened too, only an inch or so long, tapered into a neat point. Most alarmingly though, his considerable bulk had disappeared.

He was thin.

Well, thin for *Bowyn*.

Darragh was too, now that I searched for it. His cheeks were gaunt, more sunken than I remembered. Looking between the two, I couldn't believe it. They were ghosts compared to the memories I so often revisited.

"You guys don't," I blurted.

"That's nice." Bowyn released me and crossed his arms. "After I came all this way?" His stern irritation faded. "Oh, I'll forgive your ill-manners. You look rather distressed—"

"You look incredible." The words tumbled out of Darragh so fast he couldn't stop them. His voice struck me—cracking and seeping through every wall I'd put up since I'd heard it. Rough, exactly how I remembered it at night laying in bed, part of me wanting to forget...but never forget at the same time.

Now that he'd managed to speak, Darragh didn't really know what to do, and he shifted awkwardly. Coming to his friend's aid, Bowyn plopped a sparkling handbag on the counter. Crossing his arms, he cast an exaggerated look at Darragh and said, "*He* says I can't take it back."

"You can't take it back," Darragh muttered. He rested a hand near mine, nearly touching it. Bowyn made a face that said, *'Yeah, sure I can't,'* while slipping the bag back inside his jacket.

"I just," I started, "how long has it been?"

"Five hundred and forty-seven days," Darragh replied.

His fingers brushed mine.

It was a silly thing, such a small touch. Why did I feel it in the depths of my stomach? Darragh met my eyes and lingered there.

A flame exists in us all.

Lately, I'd kept mine hidden. Protected from anyone who might awaken it, only to douse the fire when they'd had their fill. Looking at Darragh now, he may as well have blown into the glowing embers of my heart—stoked them until my desires erupted in an inferno that threatened to consume me. It took everything, *everything* I had not to leap over the counter and—

I hope you enjoyed that short, unedited preview from Book Two in the Forest series. Important note: This snippet has been altered from the original draft to remove certain content and spoilers. When it comes time to meet our old friends again, it will look a little different. The boss reserves all rights to change said content on a whim.

It's me, I'm the boss.

Take care and talk soon,

Brooke

P.S. If you disobeyed the spoiler warning (I respect that you cheeky devil) and have no idea who these characters are, but want to know them better, check out ***THE FOREST WHERE THE PHOENIX SLEEPS***:

Walking home late one night, burned-out barista Nell accidentally incinerates someone.

Whoopsie!

Now, if this tale began in a fantastic, far-away land, or Nell were, perhaps, a wizard, such a mishap might make some kind of sense. But this is not a wondrous, fantasy world. This is real life, and Nell just wanted to go home and eat macaroni. As Nell stares upon the smoldering corpse, she realizes something with horrifying certainty: She's magic.

And not the cute, pulling-a-rabbit-from-a-hat kind of magic.

Unfortunately, during Nell's little outburst, she suffers a mortal injury. Fortunately, Darragh, a rugged and magical outcast, witnessed the entire incident. To save Nell's life, Darragh whisks her away to a world where magic reigns. However, as is so often the case with magic, it comes at a price. In this harsh world, the entities that lurk in the darkest corners of Nell's nightmares await her in hungry anticipation.

As Nell and Darragh vanquish monsters and ghouls, their affections for one another take root. Just when this treacherous tale is beginning to look like a love story, Darragh is captured by a wretched, cadaverous queen.

Now, it's up to Nell to save him.

The Forest Where the Phoenix Sleeps *boasts portal magic reminiscent of **A Darker Shade of Magic**, the romance of **A Court of Thorns and Roses**, the action-packed adventure of **Daughter of the Moon Goddess**, and the humour of **Tress of the Emerald Sea**.*

Acknowledgements

Matt, who I couldn't possibly write love without. Casey, who shares the brain. My squad of insane women—I mean, beta and proofreaders. Emily, who makes sure I say nice things to myself. Ella, who won't rest until the world sees me. Annie, who's ready to throw down and make sure I'm educated on rabies. Kerry, my sister, who stole my fucking going out shirt and I never forgot. Courtney, who is basically me (if I understood punctuation). Randi, who's audacity I admire. Meagan, who designed my first ever graphic. Callie, who asks the questions I never consider. Sara, who posts a video every day with my book on her shoulder like a wee guardian angel. Wren, who keeps my stories alive long after they've been printed. And Sharon, who saved my butt in the home stretch.

Eeva, our enchantress, who I'm pretty sure is magic. Like, actual magic.

Kate at Paper Poppy Editorial, who tells me how good I am (but more importantly, how I can be better).

Zura, who listens so my characters can speak.

Melissa and C.G., who put me in front of important people, and did it so beautifully. Vanessa, who makes me look good (like, in a scary way). Trisha and Rebecca, who know (and love) me better than I do myself. Terri and Noemi, who tell me stories about the world.

To all the wonderful admins and mods in my book groups, and the indie bookstores who took a chance on me.

Thank you.

BROOKE MARLEY JONES writes fairy tales and nightmares filled with tenderness and terror. Her stories take place in wild woods and gothic buildings, overgrown by roses and forgotten to the world. In this lifetime, Brooke resides in Niagara with her beautiful husband and two fluffy cats.

Image by Vanessa Quinn at VQ Visuals.